BLUDD BROTHERS

JUDGE, DURIE
and the EXECUTIONERS

This is my investigation

Samael Eldritch

Published by

MELROSE BOOKS

An Imprint of Melrose Press Limited
St Thomas Place, Ely
Cambridgeshire
CB7 4GG, UK
www.melrosebooks.co.uk

FIRST EDITION

Cover by Melrose Books

ISBN **978-1-912026-65-4**
     978-1-912026-66-1 epub
     978-1-912026-67-8 Mobi

Printed and bound in Great Britain by:
TJ International Ltd, Padstow, Cornwall

To Big John. Thank you.

Contents

1

Sin

The little Thai girl closed her eyes again; a tear squeezed out from the outside of each of them and trickled down her cheek. In her mind, she saw her daddy ushering her away, into the car of the stranger. She had not heard his name, but he spoke in Thai. He had given her father a package and he had stuffed it inside his shirt and pushed them, her and her brother, forward.

The man had brought them to the city. They had been there before, a few times, shopping with their parents. This time they had come with the stranger, and then they had met the new man. The fat man, who wasn't from Thailand. He had shaken the Thai man's hand and then shooed him away with the back of his hand. He had turned to the two of them and smiled. It was not a nice smile, she had thought.

He had taken them into a small, grubby, grey building that was similar to their own home; through the front door and up the staircase that was right behind it. They had entered a small room at the back of the building. It was quite bare: a sofa, covered in a large white sheet; a table and chair; a bag on the chair. On top of the table was a mobile phone. Her daddy had one, not as good. His was old and small. This one was larger and had a big screen but no buttons to press. The man had touched the screen with his forefinger a few times. There was a folded white sheet on the back left corner of the table. He had fiddled with the phone and set it back on the table on a stand, screen facing the open room and the sofa.

The man had spoken to them. They did not understand. He had shouted at them. It did not help them understand. He had grabbed them both by the shoulder and turned them to face each other. He had pushed their faces together and had said the word "kiss". They did not understand. He had pushed their faces together and held them there. He had shouted at them, "kiss!" They did not understand. He had picked up her brother and kissed him on the lips, then he pointed at her and pointed at his lips and then to her brother. "Kiss!" he said again. They had just looked at him. They did not understand. He had picked up her brother and shook him. "Kiss your bloody sister, you little shit!" He shouted at him and pointed at his sister, at her. They did not understand. He had lifted her brother off the floor and shaken him and then he threw him across the room. Her brother's head had hit the wall and he had fallen to the ground. Blood had trickled from his ear and seeped down his neck. He had not moved since.

Now she was on her front. Her chin rested on the arm of the chair, one hand clinging to the back of the sofa, the other clenched onto the cushion below her. She opened her eyes; her brother's lifeless body lay slumped in front of her. She rocked back and forth, unable to stem the ebb and flow of the weight of the movement behind her. She could feel the sweat of the man as it oozed in between his stomach and the skin of her back that he rested upon. She closed her eyes again. The man was inside her and his movements were quickening. It was not the first time she had been here and she was just as scared as the first time. She had cursed her father the first time and he had explained that she had made him happy and that she had made sure they could eat. And she had accepted it. This time, he had given up her brother as well. She cursed him again. She would rather be hungry.

* * *

The man was sweating even more, she could feel the droplets on her back, more and more as his movements got faster. Then he stopped. He jerked. And moved again. And jerked. And then he stopped again. And then he slid off her and pushed her off the sofa.

She looked up at him. He was breathless and sweating and sat on the right-hand side of the sofa, away from her, looking up at the ceiling. At least it was over. She would be able to tend to her brother.

The man looked down at her, his eyes made smaller by his puffed-up, fatty cheeks. His hair was straggly and thin and beads of sweat ran down from its roots.

"Come here!" he said to her, beckoning with a curled finger. She did not understand the words, but she obeyed the command. She stood in front of the fat, naked man. She looked him in the eyes and saw no emotion. She did not speak. The man put his hands on her head and stroked her long, black hair down each side of her head. He wiped her tears away with the tips of his thumbs and his hands continued to slide away down the sides of her neck and they rested on her shoulders. He smiled at her. It was not a pleasant smile, more like a grimace, she thought. He shifted in the seat, shuffling in small movements towards her, clutching her shoulders and pulling on her to give himself some momentum. He was now slightly taller than her in his seated position and she felt nervous of him. His hands moved from the tips of her shoulders back to her neck. He grimaced again, short of breath. She made no movement, she did not smile back. And then his thumbs crept up the front of her neck. She gulped in some air. His thumbs

3

started to dig into her throat and he pressed hard. In her mind, she panicked and her feet kicked out at the man's shins. She kicked out as hard as she could and the man just smiled at her. It was not a smile of pity. She looked him in the eyes and saw no hint of empathy for her, they were just staring into her eyes, all feeling removed. He squeezed harder and she lashed out with her arms, flailing at his face, scratching with her nails for all she was worth. But to no avail. The heavy man just looked and squeezed, harder and harder and she felt herself slipping into a sleep. Her eyes closed and her body relaxed and she was peaceful.

Jeremy Judge scooped up the lifeless body without dropping it to the floor. He laid it onto the sofa, swathed in the white cotton sheet. He went to the table and pressed the screen of his phone and then laid it flat on the table. He went back to the sofa, pulled the material from over the back of the cushions and wrapped it around the young girl's body. He tucked the ends over her head and feet and lifted the front edge off the floor and placed it over the top of her. He rolled her forward and tucked the sheet tight under her and rolled her again, repeating until she was completely coiled up. He went to a bag in the corner and put on his underwear. He took the folded sheet from off the table and laid it out square on the grey, carpeted floor. He collected the lifeless body of the boy, settled limp against the wall and set him lengthways on the sheet. He repeated the process of wrapping the body, as he had the young girl. He stood over them, one to his left, one to his right. No remorse. He went to the bag and picked out a roll of industrial tape that he had bought in the market the day before. He rolled the tape around the feet of the girl, circling it many times for a solid fixing. He repeated it around her midriff and again around her neck. He repeated the same with the girl's brother and dragged

4

it across the carpet so that they lay side by side. He stood over them, eyes down, hands clasped in front of his swollen stomach. For a moment, he looked as though he was in prayer, but in reality, he was catching his breath.

* * *

He dressed, as quickly as he could. White cotton shirt, beige canvas pants, lightweight to help him sweat less, the weather still humid and sticky. He placed the phone in the large side pocket on his right thigh.

He moved back to the bag and took out two industrial grade plastic sacks. He pulled the bodies slightly apart and made their legs go up towards their chins, into the foetal position. He slid the bags over the bodies, small bodies that could easily fit inside the largest bags he could find on the market. He taped them up, wrapping the metallic looking adhesive-backed plastic around and around, top to bottom, end to end. He dragged them over to the door, one by one. He pulled the first bag down the stairs and stood over it, unsure which was which now. He caught his breath. He made a promise to himself to get fitter when he retired. Soon. He went back up the stairs and pushed the second bag to the edge of the top step, and pushed. The body bounced down, once, twice, three times and landed with a flat thud against the identical trash bag at the bottom of the stairs.

He collected the bag and then followed the bundles down the stairs and stepped over them. He turned the latch on the door and stuck his head out, peering out left and right. It was a busy part of town. It was Friday lunchtime in Bangkok and there was a hustle and bustle the same as any other day. It played on his mind for only a second. Outside the front door were two municipal garbage bins, rectangular steel, with flip-over orange, plastic lids. He had put them there the previous night from across the street. He flipped the lid. He had purposely put the emptier of the bins closest to his door.

He reached back inside the door and dragged the nearest bag to his feet, bent down and lifted the dead weight into his chest, resting it on his outstretched stomach. He dropped the bag into the bin. Paper and thin plastic rustled as the weight hit them. He looked around sheepishly. Nobody was taking any notice, everyone was busy. He repeated the trick with the second bag. He opened the lid of the other bin and removed a couple of thin, black plastic bags out of there and put them in the first bin, on top of the bags he had just deposited. He put his own bag on top of them. He closed both lids and had another nervous glimpse to all sides.

Confident that he had not attracted any attention, he casually turned around and pulled the door towards himself, gently turning the latch on its hub and closing it quietly. He put his hands in his pocket to check the keys were there. Too late if they weren't, he thought. He would return later for his meeting with his Thai associate, Kulapananam, who he called Kulap for short. For now, he was hungry. Lunch was around the corner. A nice quiet café, where tourists would come and the flower girls would sit astride them and smile at them and kiss them. His kind of place.

2

Nightmares

Friday October 1st, 6.45 a.m. private investigator Sebastian Bludd shrugged his collar to the cold and looked up to the miserable, dark, grey sky that was delivering the drizzle onto the Cheshire village. He paused under the wood framed porch and considered the day ahead and the night before. His worn and scuffed, slightly longer than waste-length, black, leather jacket was home to many things: keys, pen, pad and most importantly, his iPod. He patted left and right front pockets and found his keys to the right and his iPod to the left. He fiddled about with the leads and placed a miniature speaker in each ear and pressed play. As he stepped out onto the shingle driveway, an assortment of coloured reds, whites, greys, all shiny from a night of persistent fine and spitting rain, yet still dull in the darkness, he paused, feeling an inquisitive pair of eyes peering from a gap in the curtains above him. He allowed himself a half smile, knowing that his usual sleep pattern, if you could call it a pattern, would have woken Chrissie numerous times through the night, and she would be there at the window, sad to see him go, but glad that the early start would give her another hour or so to catch up on her sleep before her day would begin proper. He feigned a look back and instinctively knew that the drapes would flicker as they closed shut. He paused one more second and set off, mulching across the drive to the locked, black VW Golf parked aside the garage at the end of the property.

Behind the flickering curtain, Chrissie Morris metaphorically scratched her head. She had known Seb for two years now. Two years on, a mutual respect, a great friendship, like minds and a definite mutual attraction. She looked at him down the shale driveway, his back to her. He didn't fit the stereotypical private investigator, or detectives as they were usually depicted on television. He was no scruffy *Columbo*, or slick *Tom Selleck Magnum*. Seb's broad shoulders perfectly suited his six foot four tall body. His body was toned, not muscular, and his upper body was shaped like a V, broad shoulders and slim waist. His regular gym workouts meant that he was fit and firm. He had short, dark brown hair merged into a rough stubble that suited him and covered the blemishes of his slightly pockmarked skin, which hadn't detracted from his overall good looks. He reminded her of a little older version of the former England cricketer Freddie Flintoff. He had vivid blue eyes that seemed to pierce her brain, and it seemed like he could read her thoughts. She watched him leave most mornings and he would always seem to know that she was there, peeking at him from behind the curtains.

Yet there had been nothing physical. Not to speak of anyway. They weren't boyfriend and girlfriend, yet when asked, they would both consider the other and reply a certain "Yes, I have a partner." The night before was nothing unusual. They had gone to bed at midnight, Seb had showered first, as was his want, and they had settled into a loose spoons arrangement, him nearest the door, her nearest the wardrobes. Soon after they were deep asleep, and soon after that, she was not. In two years, he had stayed a couple of nights most weeks, once here and there to begin with, but when she had decided to start work again, he had become a regular and useful guest. In those two years, approximately 300 overnight stays, the better part of a full year, with not one decent night of full, deep or meaningful sleep. Not one sign of any physical approach, not full, not part, not deep, not shallow, not meaningful or otherwise. Nothing. It had bothered her, but she had learned not to ask, not to pry. She had broached the subject once and was met with a stern look and muttered response. She had woken him from his nightmare once as well, only to be met with a clenched fist and a look of bewilderment as Seb found his bearings and realised his surroundings. She had sat many nights, leaning on one elbow, watching his eyes twitch behind their lids, his head tossing from side to side, then stopping, almost pressing himself into the pillow, his breathing erratic. Nothing she could do except to leave him to his cold sweat until he broke the dream himself.

She had twitched the curtains back to the wall when he had seemed to look back, unsure if he had seen her. She had run back to the bedroom and dressed casually in the lounge suit that was lying on the bed and started to apply a light eye makeup, half expecting him to slip back in to the room, waiting with her perfected "no, I was not watching you!" look. Chrissie had no idea how he always seemed to have knowledge of what was happening around him. It must be instinctive, but she thought it was more than that, as if he had learned to judge situations, surroundings, reactions, atmospheres. It could well have been instinctive, may have been learned, but most definitely it was uncanny.

* * *

Five miles away to the north-east, in Maple, on the other side of the borough, Jonathon Durie tapped the digits on the security keypad and waited as the gears on the motor of the automatic sliding gate whirred. The V-grooved female engineered wheel slipped, rather than turned on the male angled iron runner. He slipped through the slowly widening opening, sideways on, saving himself half a second of waiting for a shoulder-width gap and limped across the tarmac entrance to the two steps leading to the office and reception glass frontage. His left leg, stiff and unbending, worse for the damp, cold morning, goose stepped up the paved steps and he fumbled in his jacket pocket for the enormous bunch of keys, all held together by an enormous steel ring. There were Yale keys, skeleton keys, brass, steel, long, short. Keys for doors, factories, locks. Colour coded fobs, colour coded heads, orange, blue, yellow, green. Only Durie knew which keys unlocked which locks, which location, which secrets.

He unlocked the front doors, a green fobbed Yale the chosen tool, hobbled to the base of the stairs to his right and flicked on the full bank of light switches, flooding the reception area, stairs, landing and screened off display area with yellowish artificial light. A single luminous tube buzzed and flickered, reluctant to adhere to the demands of its starter as it fizzed and stuttered, much like Durie himself, into a million rays, completing the dawn of a new industrial morning.

* * *

He stepped out of the office area, through a painted yellow, solid steel door. He ignored the signs that told him to put in his ear plugs and wear his steel-toed shoes. He stood on a steel balcony that spanned the width of the factory and was raised in the air to give a full panoramic view of the whole of the factory floor. The plant was stretched out in front of him, machinery lined up and reached into the distance. He flicked the multiple light switches that hung on the wall to his left at eye level. The factory buzzed into life, the strip lights that ran down the ceiling, eight long strobes, fizzing into the distance, one by one bringing the factory to life. He scanned the area, making sure that the night-shift had left everything in the way they were expected to. The machines were interspersed with conveyors and pallets piled high with layers of corrugated cardboard. As the lights sprung to life they shined on signs above the machines. 'Folder Gluer', 'Flat Bed 1', 'Rotary Die Cutter', Flat Bed 2'. All had their own roller conveyor running in between. Scattered brown towers of finished, flat packed packaging boxes and unconverted cardboard, all around. It was a line that spread across the full width of the floor below him, all wrapped in shrunken polythene.

* * *

The constant humming of the fluorescent tubes was replaced with an equally staccato vibration in Durie's shirt pocket. He jerked an immediate reaction and fumbled the smart phone in his right hand, seeing the pulsating spelling across the screen. "Judge" it screamed at him. He expertly tossed the phone across to his stiff, crooked left hand, the hook of the fingers a perfect mould for the rectangular shape, as he slid his right index finger across the accept icon, a lopsided smile on his face as he bellowed "Swasdi B-B-Boss".

Watching

Bludd unlocked his black VW Golf from three yards away and climbed into the driver's seat, hunched his coat from under himself and closed the door more heavily than needed, just so he could hear the gratifying clunk that you get with a car with high build quality. He checked his mirrors, not to see if they were at the optimum angles, but to check he looked OK, not that he was overly impressed with himself, but he had a certain pride.

He checked the tub of chewing gum in the centre console, finding the last single piece, solitary and needy. He used gum as a replacement for cigarettes, going through a tub of 99 pieces every couple of days. He threw the last piece from his lap and expertly caught it in his mouth, tossing the empty container into the passenger footwell, alongside the numerous others of the same brand, albeit different flavoured options, plus the empty fast food bags, sandwich packages, empty Pepsi and Red Bull cans, penalty notices, some with parking ticket information, some just vacant document wallets. Bludd didn't care to look after his car too much, it was merely a work tool to him. A way of getting from A to B, a mobile diner, an office, a stakeout vehicle, a hideout and a trash can to boot.

He drove across the sodden tarmac of the Cheshire country roads, rain still falling lightly against the windscreen, his intermittent wiper sufficient to clear the glass every three seconds. He was thinking more about Chrissie than the day ahead, there was plenty of time for the day ahead. He thought he loved her. He loved the way she looked. She was tall, at five nine, but not too tall, slim, he thought a size ten sounded about right, but maybe a size 12 on occasion. Her hair was a bottle fed flaming crimson, which suited her more than he could have believed, although he could still not decide if he preferred the ash blonde look she wore when he met her. Her skin was not entirely perfect, the odd blemish was easily covered when she was working or at a function, a family meet, or a "date" with him. What Bludd loved, more than anything about her look was her nose. It seemed a perfect nose for her face, relatively long, relative to her face that is, slightly pushed up at the end, a finger's width from her lips. The only imperfection he could see was a slightly crooked left front incisor. Even that would probably have been perfect if it was not for the client who had expected more than she was willing to offer, and more than was in her agency's terms and conditions. A quick, straight punch to the mouth had seen her smile become less frequent as a result. It was something she had threatened to have cosmetic work done on when she had some spare cash. For all that, it was her green-blue eyes that had been the first source of attraction to Bludd; alluring eyes, set back from a perfect nose in a perfectly pretty face. It was always the first thing he looked at. He could never understand why men went on about being Boob Men, or Bum Men. He often thought *What if a woman had great boobs and a nice pert bum but had the face of a pig?*

It was a full nine miles from Chrissie's home to Bludd's house and office, and on a good run it could be done, at this hour of the day, in a little under 20 minutes. At the wrong time of the day, it could be as bad as 45 minutes in the car, something nearer half an hour at worst if he was on his motorbike. Today it took a little over the 20 minutes. He was in no rush, so had adhered, pretty much, to the speed limits, which were generous on the country lanes. He had his day mapped out in his mind, an 11 o'clock meeting at a nearby Greasy Spoon, that shouldn't take more than an hour, giving him a full three hours to get around Manchester and into the Lancashire hills for his afternoon meeting with a new client.

In the hours in between he would grab a slice of toast and maybe a piece of fruit, more likely a banana, on the edge of soft. If it was, he would have it on the toast and mash it with a fork and sprinkle a good heaped spoonful of sugar across it, an energy boost and a slow energy release all in one go. He would give himself an hour to work out against the equipment in his garage and then shower, collect the evidence for his client, client A, and his client's wife, or client B.

He passed the village shop, or "Village Shoppe" as the sign proclaimed, the pub, "The White Lion", one of two White Lions in the town and one of 23 pubs within the town boundary. That was for a town that had been three villages, before merging due to a population increase, bringing a new total, at last count, to just 7,300, in an area just two miles wide and three miles long. A lot of pubs for not a lot of people in a small village-like town. The corner shop was a Post Office that had a multitude of other goods to sell in order to survive. He turned right after the Post Office and another right at the end of the row of five terraced houses, leading him into his cul-de-sac road of six terraced houses on each side. He passed his house to his right and swung around the new circular end to the road. The bulb-shaped addition that had been built to accommodate the three new semi-detached houses was a welcome one to Bludd as now he could avoid the three-point turn he would have to make to have his car pointing to the exit of the road and preferably outside his own front door. These days, most houses had more than one occupant with a car, which meant that on a road full of terraced houses, parking was at a premium. Many times he had to resort to passing his row, on the right, turning right at the end of them and then right again, leaving his car at the back of the garage, which was at the rear of his house. He never used the garage for its actual purpose, there was no room inside, what with his motorbike and gym equipment, so he left it on the grass verge that overlooked the rear gardens of the terraced houses that he had passed moments earlier that were directly linked to the Post Office corner shop.

He pulled up by the kerb directly outside his own house with its bottle green front door and locked the vehicle, pleased that it was facing the right way, just in case he needed to move quickly and save himself vital time. Not that he ever did, his days were not so full that he particularly rushed anywhere, which was more to do with being well organised than having nothing to do at all. He got out of the car and went through the gap left vacant by the discarded gate, not having to open and shut it was a small timesaver, plus he had no need to keep oiling it to prevent its incessant squeaking that had persisted over the years. He took out his keys and put the small brass one into its female counterpart. Before turning it, he leaned to his left and brushed the small brass name plate with the cuff of his leather sleeve, cleaning away the droplets of residual rain and cleaning the surface in one swift sweep to the right. "SAAB `1993 – Private Investigations" set over two lines in black text. Originally he had called it SAAB '93, but incredibly had been told to change it due to the confusion caused to potential buyers of the Swedish motor vehicle of the same name. He had argued that prospective car buyers would soon realise that the single person private investigations company, run from a two up two down terrace in Cheshire, was not really the place they should be looking for and would quickly find the correct option, if indeed they had managed to be so stupid as to confuse the two anyway! However, Trading Standards, or some such department, along with the car manufacturer, had kicked up a stink and he had made the necessary change, which he still felt was not worthwhile. He turned the key to the right and opened the door. A smattering of letters, mostly junk mail, was on his turquoise hall carpet. He collected them up and sifted through them as he went up the hall. To his left at the end of the hall there were two doors and one opposite, leading to the kitchen that was facing him, a single doorway to its right led to the stairs that led away to the right and back towards the front of the house. He opened up the first of the left-hand, green-stained doors, giving the plastic, but brass lookalike, sign a quick wipe with his thumb. "OFFICE" it read. The sparsely furnished room contained an old, second-hand Chesterfield sofa, reddish brown leather, weathered by age and poor maintenance. Opposite was a sturdy, cherry-finished wooden desk, with four drawers to each side of a plentiful gap. Not much was on the desk, just a large jotter pad and a phone, single line with a voicemail option, a light flashing. Behind the desk a comfortable high-backed office chair, with padded arms that were jaded at the ends. Under the window, there were two old-fashioned dark wood dining chairs that would be moved to the gap in between sofa and desk when necessary. Two was thought to be enough, rarely did clients visit in more than twos. Rarely did clients visit him here at all. In the corner, opposite the doorway, a walnut-look bookcase with a capacity for 100 books, but housing only 26, next to it was a grey, four-drawer filing cabinet that wasn't in keeping with the rest of the room. Bludd put the junk mail in the bin under the desk and left the two other letters on the jotter. He pressed the activate message button and listened for the two messages the machine had informed him of. The first was a sorrowful sounding lady, sad that she had to leave yet another message. "Hello dear, it's your mother. Father and I were just thinking about you and how we haven't seen you for so long. Please keep in touch. We worry." A pause. "Anyway, goodbye dear." He deleted the message and listened again. "Hi, Mr Bludd, just checking our three-thirty meeting is still on for tomorrow. Anyway, I will try your mobile. It's John Preston by the way."

Bludd had not forgotten his afternoon meet with the new client, nor had he forgotten to call his mother back on numerous occasions; he had merely chosen not to bother for the time being. He gave it little thought, but it crossed his mind that his father probably wasn't thinking about him at all. It took him all his time to remember that he had two sons, not just one, and that was before the dementia had started.

He closed the office door and went into the kitchen, put a slice of wholemeal bread in the toaster and tore a banana from the bunch in the fruit bowl. He scribbled "Go Shopping" as a reminder on a notepad, hung on the wall by the door, poured a glass of orange juice and waited for the toaster to pop.

* * *

Maxwell Johann Anderton-Bludd pulled off the road and onto a grass verge, at the side of the lane in the leafy Cheshire suburbs, having left Manchester Airport 30 minutes earlier, aiming to arrive at his parents' house by mid-afternoon. He had stuck religiously to two miles per hour below the various permitted speed limits and it had cost him another 15 minutes of non-stop driving along the 35-mile journey. He was annoyed with himself. If he had just broken the limit for once, he would have had chance to make a planned visit to his parents' house, even if it meant cutting it short. It would have meant a lot to his mother, she needed the breaks and the fresh company. It probably would have meant less to his father. Maxwell had never broken the law, never broken the speed limit, not without the blues and twos on, never done anything remotely bad. Living by the book had got him where he was today, high up in the Counter Terrorism Unit. He had trodden the path of constable, detective constable, detective sergeant, detective inspector, before making the change in roles and emphasis and started to beat a path to the top of this tree, all the time playing fair and playing by the letter of the law. He had seen things along the way that could have quickened his promotions up if he had reported them, if he had grassed on his colleagues, but he had decided against it. By the book it would be, he saw no prize in rocking any boats or ruffling the feathers of those who might serve under him in the future, not if you didn't want to be undermined at every opportunity that may present itself to them. They could do it their way and he would do it his.

He paused as he pushed the call button on his mobile phone. He wondered if his Dad would be in good shape today, if he would remember just his voice. He wondered if Mum would be coping. He pictured her awaiting his arrival, like an eagle waiting for a glimpse of its prey, desperately looking for a break in the monotony of another day. The phone rang out once. "Hi Mum!" he said in a voice slightly higher than his frame commanded. "How are you? And how is Dad? Are you coping?"

She smiled at the other end of the phone. A loving, compassionate smile that said things were not great, not decidedly worse, but when improvement was not an option, not at all great. "He's waiting for you on the veranda, are you far away?"

she murmured.

Maxwell Bludd had a rush of guilt. He chatted to his mum for a few minutes whilst he knew she was stood in the kitchen and then as she walked out to the hall and through the mahogany door into the old back sitting room he told her that he was not going to make it to see them today. He pictured her face of disappointment as she sat down in the back room. The room was not old, per se, more that it had been the sitting room for many years, many years that they had lived there since the return from Hong Kong. The décor had remained the same for all of those 20-something years and, as a result, had become more than a little dated, but still, Maxwell had felt, had a comforting feel, a homely touch that his mother had brought to all their homes, which, without her small, sometimes tiny idiosyncratic ideas, would just have been houses. He and his brother, Sebastian, had both benefitted from their mother's attitude to life, her unquestionable love, her devotion to them, but he thought that he had carried her thoughts and traditions on more than Seb would have done. He was sure, but having never been to Seb's house and having not spoken to him in many, many months, he could not be absolutely certain about anything that his elder brother had done or was doing.

He knew that his mother was still in the back room as she talked through her disappointment that he was not coming, at the same volume as she had in the kitchen mainly that she was out of earshot of his father. He knew that Dad didn't appear to take things in any more, but he also knew that his mother refused to accept that as a fact and behaved as though her husband still had all his faculties.

The back room was now a bedroom and living room combo. As his father had deteriorated, they had made the decision, between him and his mum, to move things around, to make things easier for Dad, to keep things simple. The simpler things were, the less likely he was to lose his bearings, to get confused, to get lost, agitated, angry and aggressive. His father had been an absolute stickler for gentlemanly conduct. Opening doors for ladies, offering assistance as they were seated for dinner, watching his, and his son's Ps and Qs, or Pints and Quarts, a reference to drinking too much, he had explained to his sons, and becoming loud, lairy and sweary. He certainly was not one for swearing around females, not even if there was the slightest chance that they were in listening or hearing distance, and yet his dementia had turned him into some kind of occasional sweary, aggressive lunatic. He would tell his wife to "fuck off!", call her a "bitch", demand sex from her whilst out to dinner with friends. They didn't go out for dinner, or lunch, or even drinks with friends any more. In fact, they didn't seem to have any friends at all now. The so-called chums, the former colleagues, the family, including the eldest son, never came near, never phoned. Most of them had said they would keep in touch, help out, give Mum a break. Not one of them had followed through, maybe they had not meant to lie, maybe they had every intention of being there, and maybe they were too busy still enjoying the high life, attending formal dinners, politely laughing at unfunny jokes made by foreign dignitaries. Too busy to care.

He and Sebastian had always likened their parents to the Colonel and Mrs Hathi, the elephant couple in *The Jungle Book*. It had been their favourite bedtime story as children. No matter where they had lived, whatever country, whatever city, whatever time zone, *The Jungle Book* was the first thing in the bag before leaving a previous abode, and the first thing out when they arrived at the new place. Their father (or Colonel Hathi) was a pompous, but loveable fool, stomping around, barking orders at bewildered staff, whilst mother (Mrs Hathi) had followed close behind, offering a modicum of common sense and a distinctly feminine and human touch. Father had often left people in a state of shock and confusion, mother had calmed people, made people smile, let everyone know exactly what they should be doing and allowed them to go about it calmly and to their own devices. As they had grown older, the brothers had wondered together, at just exactly how father had come to be the British Consul and mother had been just plain old Mrs Anderton-Bludd, the consul's wife.

The double bed was opposite the door, made to a military style and quality. Mother had decided that keeping things as normal as possible included her sleeping with Francis, her husband. That gesture had doubled up, without any preconceived idea, as a deterrent for Francis to want to go walkabout in the night. He would awaken and presumably look to his right and see the familiar face of Emily, his wife, and realise that all was well, all was normal, and he would turn back to face the wall and go back to sleep. Many a morning, prior to the move downstairs, Emily would wake up to an empty opposite side of the bed. She had ventured downstairs in her dressing gown, to find Frank, as she called him, looking weary and bemused, holding his coat in one hand and Charlie the dog's lead in the other. "Damn dog needs a walk," he would mutter. Mother had come to realise, mainly by the look on the dog's face, that maybe they had walked enough for one day. It had turned out that father had walked the dog, entered the hall via the front door, turned right to hang up the lead and coat and wondered why he was holding them. He had deduced that he needed to take the dog out and proceeded to do so, sometimes as many as six times before he had had enough, or the dog had simply refused to go. Charlie had long since passed away and they often thought that maybe he had literally been walked to death.

Aside from the movement of the bed and the removal of the large bookcase to the front lounge, the back room was all but the same has it had been for years. A standard lamp stayed in the corner above father's head still, but in bed now and not over his favourite chair. The same chair had been moved to the left of the patio doors, looking out of the window, and the ornate mahogany table had moved to the other side of the doors, the sofa shifting a foot to its left, nearer to the door, to accommodate the change. The patio doors opened out to the veranda, which overlooked the landscaped gardens, which were beginning to get out of hand.

"I am so sorry, Mum," Maxwell continued. "It's just that there is something big happening at work. I was on my way over and I got the call just now. Another 20 minutes and I would have been with you."

"It's nothing dangerous for you, is it dear?" Emily Bludd responded.

"Nothing for you to worry about, Mum, honest." He didn't lie, but he knew it sounded like he had. The truth was that he had no idea if it would be dangerous or not. It was reported to be something big that was going down, but there had been plenty of false alarms in the past; plenty of times where the high alert code 'critical' had been recognised, and then downgraded again soon after. But this time, he thought it was something more definite and definitely something on a larger scale. He had been on call for weeks and the whole of his department and the whole of the service were on red alert. He continued, "There is nothing dangerous about working in an office, behind a computer. You know these days most things are done by computer. It's not like I am out there literally chasing the baddies."

His mother knew better than to press him. She would not get a full and frank answer anyway, but she couldn't resist a last word, "Try telling those poor people in the twin towers that working in an office is safe. Now do you want to talk to your father?"

He thought about the pointless opportunity that had just been offered to him. Many times he had leaned over to his father and kissed his head, swivelled his father's chair round as he crouched down, placing both palms on his knees, looking straight into his father's eyes but with no response, no acknowledgement of recognition, just an empty stare, with nothing behind it. His father's head often tilted to the left and his mouth was always slightly open, slithers of drool constantly crept down his chin. Maxwell would take a handkerchief from his trouser pocket and dab the saliva away from his father's skin. His father was a shadow of his former self. The tall, huge-framed man with a straight back; the proud barrel chest that stuck out seemingly a yard from his torso; the booming voice. All gone to be replaced with a weary, frail, weak and wheelchair-bound cabbage. Maxwell hated to think of his hero as a cabbage, but there was no better word to describe him. His white hair had long been missing from the top and his mum had taken to giving him a comb-over to try and keep his old look. But his hair was lank and greasy, and the comb-over was in thick strands rather than his clean, old-style clean cut. "Go on then!" he said reluctantly, but with a sense of duty in his tone.

Emily opened the doors outwards and put a warm palm on her husband's shoulder and held the phone to his ear. "Hi, Dad!" Max said down the line, a little louder than normal.

Emily Bludd stood and looked down at her husband affectionately and tried to listen to the short conversation. Next to her husband, Frank, sat a cup of tea on a silver platter tray, next to it was a second drink, but this was poured into one of those cups with a lid and a hole as a mouthpiece, a kind of baby's plastic cup, that could not spill the contents. She wasn't sure how long it was since he could remember to drink without being reminded to, or even whether he knew what a drink was. She heard her son say, "Goodbye, Dad. Take care." Then she pulled the phone away from her husband and put it back to her own ear.

"How bad has he got, Mum? I mean it's only two months since I came last." Max asked.

His mother sighed as she moved back into the house and gently closed the veranda doors, "I can't honestly remember," she replied. "Every day seems to be a blur, for him and me. He has his moments, but they are rare now. I think it's just a matter of time."

She told Max that she would play him some music later. Putting some of his favourites on sometimes jolted his memory and she would sit with him and watch his fingers flinch and tap along. She told him that she had made a simple, but delicious tea, of steamed fish, mashed potatoes and peas. All things his father could eat and digest with minimum effort. She said she would help his father to bed and make him comfortable and then give him a quick shave and comb his hair, and make him presentable.

Max told his mother that he was sorry again, for not turning up, and that he would be over just as soon as he could be. He sat for a long while at the side of the road, longer than he could afford to with all the things happening at work. He had to get down to London and would have to arrange things back home. A home that was just as disturbing as his mother's, just as heart wrenching, just as pointless. But with uncanny similarities, his domestic issues were all for different reasons.

As he drove, he remembered the places they had lived in when he was young. Riyadh, Manila, KL, Bangkok. He remembered the places that mother and father had gone whilst he and Seb were boarders at St Augustine's, the boarding school they had attended from the ages of 11 and 10: Jakarta, Beijing and Hong Kong. His father no longer seemed to recall any of these places, or the memories he had often recited to him. He reminisced about the way he and Seb would sit on the balcony outside their embassy or consulate bedroom, the same balcony in so many different homes in cities that were hundreds of miles apart, but all the same. The same wrought iron balustrade, so many of them kinked at the bottom, stretching outwards in a curve that allowed a comfortable space for their knees as they stared out at life going on below. The same view, over the high, whitewashed, secure walls, overlooking the real life streets outside; the beggars, the paupers, the conmen, the crooks, the kids playing with rubbish taken from the better off families' trash cans; the deals, the dealers, the gangs, the gangsters, the pimps and the pimped, the mugs and the muggers. Every city different, but the same. From their daily ritual of people watching, from the age of seven and six, when they were allowed to go to the balcony, Maxwell had recited them all. But his father remembered none of them outwardly. He remembered that he had done what his mother was about to do, during his previous visit. He had put on a record, his parents still lived in the 20th century, a gramophone they still called it. Chopin had raised a small reaction, a tap of the right hand index finger against the patent arm of the wheelchair. Not in time, but a tiny acknowledgement of recognition. But then, as now, he could not get away from the fact that his father had become nothing more than a cabbage; not even a shadow of his former self. The stereotypical English stalwart, the gentleman, the hero, the only father figure he could ever want for. He knew it was a matter of time.

As he got onto the M6 and headed south, he recalled his mother's last words as he closed up the phone. "Tell Sebastian to try and come over. Just one last time."

* * *

Sebastian Bludd had collected the two envelopes from his desk drawer and set off in plenty of time to meet his clients. One at a time, and both at once. He had arrived at Joe's Café and taken a seat against the back wall and away from the window, offering a good view of the door and the passing shoppers. He would see his male client arrive from the left, or south, and his wife would follow from the right, or north. This was their pattern at previous meetings and he had counted on it being the same this time. He did not want them to meet until the moment was right.

He had chosen the café because it was more in keeping with how he viewed himself. Not great looking, but clean and acceptable, with honesty and a value for money feel about it. He could have chosen the building of the coffee shop chain 100 yards away on the opposite side of the road, but that was what his clients would have wished for, as it was more in keeping with them and their attitudes. Sanitised, false, pretentious and a watered down version of Joe's in more ways than one. Aside from that, the plastic bushes and plants might have made for a certain ambience, but it also did nothing for the view of the outside. It would hinder his ability to see his anticipated arrivals and whilst he had time to kill, it would diminish his opportunity to people watch, a pastime he had enjoyed from an early age.

He sat in the corner, left hand on coffee mug, right arm

across the seat next to him, a message that he did not want his first arrival to sit right there, but to direct him to the chairs on the opposite side of the table. He was slightly slouched, due to his being comfortable in himself and his surroundings, but not deterred from his concentration and the job in hand. This was payday, times two, and he wanted the meeting to go in exactly the right order and sequence that he intended. Maximum effect, maximum satisfaction of a job well done, times two. He checked the two envelopes again. Both were brown A4 Manila, flap tucked in rather than glued shut. Each had a pair of similar photos, the left one, marked "Mr", had three more entirely different pictures enclosed than the other, marked "Mrs". Both of them contained USB sticks, remarkably similar again.

Michael Cleary, a local small-business man of no real reputation, arrived 10 minutes late. Annoying, but expected as far as Bludd was concerned. He wandered in, wearing a long raincoat and a shifty look. *Fair enough*, Bludd thought, as it was raining, and he was shifty. He sat down opposite Bludd, as suggested by a sweeping hand gesture from the private detective. Cleary was clearly in an agitated state, eager to get his hands on the evidence that would shape his short term future. He looked at the two envelopes on the table, wondering why there was a duo. Bludd said nothing. Cleary inched a hand forwards towards the nearest Manila, but Bludd put a deterrent hand on it and a thumb across to the other, saying no, without saying no.

"Why don't you go get a brew? It's a bit rude to use the facilities, get shelter from the weather and not put your hand in your pocket. While you're there, I'll have a refill, coffee, white, two sugars, please." Bludd said. His coffee would have been a free top up due to the full breakfast he had eaten and which had been cleared away before Cleary's arrival, but Bludd didn't like him, and what was an extra £1.20 on top of the hundreds of pounds Cleary would be parting with this morning.

Cleary returned with Bludd's coffee and a tea for himself and sat back in his chair, a new confidence in himself and about the meeting.

"So, what's in the envelopes and why are there two? I am assuming one is for me and one is for you to put your cash in? No need, I have it all, already banded up and in a sealed envelope." He reached in his pocket and pulled out a thick, sealed, Jiffy-style envelope, thick through the wad of notes and the bubble padding inside the stiff, brown paper shell. He placed it on the table and again made a move towards the nearby envelope to his right.

Bludd leant forward and clasped his hands together, parting his elbows wide enough to clamp the two A4 sleeves to the table and looking directly into Cleary's eyes.

"Not yet. No disrespect, but I like to check that you have kept your end up. I know for damn sure I have mine."

As he spoke, he noticed the tall, elegant woman stride purposely from his right, the north. She, too, was wearing a long beige raincoat, '*Aw, Mr and Mrs matching coats, how romantic',* Bludd thought. Mrs Jane Cleary was quite an attractive and elegant lady of about 40, slightly younger than her husband and, in Bludd's opinion, he was punching way above his weight, but looks aside, they just about deserved each other. She was also more punctual than her husband, which endeared her more to Bludd than her husband had, and that was again what Bludd had expected, perfect timing for him to make his reveal. She wore a head scarf and sunglasses that were nothing to do with the weather, and Bludd thought she had an air of an Audrey Hepburn about her.

Now he could release the envelope close to Mr Cleary's elbow and he gave it a nudge in the man's direction. He eagerly tore at the flap, not even trying to keep it neat and tidy and so he could close it up and walk away with a sense of pride and with decorum. He tugged at the contents, pulling out a few photographs, taken from a distance and blown up enough to make out the figures and faces, even though they were slightly grainy. A memory stick dropped from the opening and skipped across the table, unnoticed, but heard by the businessman. Cleary recognised the situation in the copies immediately and was just about to remonstrate with Bludd when he felt his wife's presence next to him. He turned his head in slow motion, seeing the familiar beige of the coat. His mouth widened as it swung pendulously up to greet his wife's equally puzzled face.

"You're probably wondering what the other of you is doing here?" Bludd teased. "Well, Mrs Cleary, this is, as you know, your husband. Michael has just given me a very nice pile of cash in exchange for the envelope he has made a bit of a mess of. This is yours, I take it you have something for me?"

Mrs Cleary fumbled in her Burberry handbag, cream and blue check that contrasted her coat nicely. She returned a Jiffy bag style envelope, exactly the same make, style, size and even batch to that her husband had handed over moments earlier, the same amount of pounds Sterling inside. £900 exactly. She pulled up a chair and sat down, resting her hands on the table, fingers splayed out and outstretched, not saying a word.

Bludd continued. "Let me explain. Coincidentally, you called me within two days of each other and it was quite obvious to me straight away what was going on. You see, Mrs Cleary, Michael asked me to shadow you as he had an inkling that you were seeing somebody else, although who, when, where and how often was unclear." He pushed the envelope to his right a little further away from him until it touched Jane Cleary's fingertips. She did not take her opportunity to open it. "So, Jane, I have been watching and following you for a few weeks now, on and off, and I have to say, you made it quite easy. That's not to say you should have given it more thought that I, or some other guy like me, would be following you, but you seemed so wrapped up in your 'thing', that you didn't even consider it. So, for your information, and as you don't seem to wish to look, the envelope in front of you contains two still photographs. One is of you arriving at the house of a Mr Daniel Parkin, somebody I believe to be unknown to your husband, but somebody you visit on a regular, let's say, at least twice a week basis. The second is of you in a tight clinch, that's what they call it in movies and novels anyway. This is something you could probably talk your way out of. So, Mrs Cleary, you will also find a USB stick in there as well. This is exactly the same as the one which your husband did not seem to be too interested in." He paused and put his left index finger on the replica stick and slid it back towards her husband. "On the stick, from my time spent following you, is some altogether more interesting video clips of you and Mr Parkin, I don't think I need to embarrass you with the detail, not in public anyway. I think I would be right to think that you are actually quite a nice person, Jane, but with never seeing Michael, what with him looking after the business and then spending nights away, shall we call it 'meeting suppliers', Michael?" He glanced at a red faced Cleary, whose eyes were looking straight down at the table top. "Maybe you could be forgiven for seeking attention elsewhere. The same, I am sad to say, cannot be said for your husband, who is by anybody's standard a bit of a low life." Bludd didn't look at Michael Cleary as he continued to address his wife. "You see, Jane, almost from the first moment he called me, I didn't trust him, instinct I suppose, and you get to recognise it when you see it all the time. So, whilst I was watching your house, waiting for something to happen with you, I noticed Michael arrive home and stop, momentarily, before going off again. I thought it was a little strange, so I decided to follow him, instead of you." Cleary said nothing. "To be fair, the only thing I can say that is positive about the actions of your husband is that he takes his business elsewhere. Doesn't shit on his own doorstep, if you'll excuse the French. So, the snaps that are currently lying face down in front of Michael are of him, trawling the streets of Hucknall in Nottingham, looking for young, desperate girls. Bad enough that he is visiting red light areas, picking up hookers and so on, but I have put a few extra photographs in his envelope, don't worry, they are on your stick as well. You see, Jane, Michael seems to like to have sex with girls in his car." A pause. "When it is parked next to other cars." Another pause. "Usually, these cars have like-minded chaps in them, and to be fair, some willing participants, let's call them ladies shall we? Usually there are a few people milling about, moving from vehicle to vehicle, looking inside them all until they find what they particularly like. All in all, those USBs could be quite an interesting watch, if you are into that kind of thing. What I suggest is that you come and sit round here and have a good chat with each other. You can have my coffee, Jane. It has two sugars, so nice and sweet to help with the shock."

Neither of the two clients made any remark. Bludd slipped out of his seat and collected the two Jiffy envelopes off the table, Jane Cleary slid into the warm, vacated chair and watched as Bludd moved away. He gave her husband a tap on his head with the envelopes and whispered, "Woof! Woof! Dirty boy!" She heard him shout a cheery goodbye to the proprietor, Joe, and gave her husband a sharp kick to the left shin with her pointy-shoed right foot.

4

Bad Company

The swift success of the simple meeting in the café meant that Bludd had a couple of hours spare before setting off for his afternoon appointment in Lancashire. He had returned home and parked his car in front of his own front door, just where he liked it. It was his preferred position, facing the exit to the end of the cul-de-sac, with a quick getaway and easy exit to his next destination.

He had immediately headed upstairs and changed into his exercise clothes, a baggy tee-shirt, loose shorts and well-worn training shoes, all black and comfortable. He skipped down the stairs, two at a time, his right hand gliding over the hand rail attached to the right hand wall as he headed down, turning left at the foot of the stair, immediately right into his kitchen and straight out of the door five yards immediately opposite the kitchen entrance. He headed across the yard, through the garden gate, desperately in need of a coat of paint or creosote, or anything to protect the decaying wood. Ahead of him was the 18-inch wide stone path, separating the back yards and gardens from the row of garages. All of the garages had wooden doors to their right hand sides, handles to the left, opening inwards to the right against the side walls to maintain maximum space.

Bludd's garage was different from his neighbours. Theirs were either a home for their cars, or were dumping grounds, junk yards housing anything that didn't fit in the setting of the house, or were past their best, or surplus to requirements, or held a sentimental value, but not much. Bludd's was pristine. He valued the setting, the layout, the tranquillity. The solitude allowed him to concentrate and focus, it offered him the calm atmosphere that his tutors had insisted on to give the ultimate power to his education.

Bludd was not one for technology, but two things had grabbed his imagination. The Internet, whilst mighty useful for his work, for research, for planning, for amusement, occasionally, was his second choice, purely for its usefulness, rather than its entertainment value. He wasn't really one for amusement and entertainment, not any more anyway. He would sometimes have a reminiscent moment and go to YouTube and look for an old film clip, or download a vintage film, something from the '60s or '70s, or further back maybe. Nothing new, nothing recent, or current. As a family, they had always owned a television on their travels from place to place, but it had not been a medium of any interest to Bludd and his brother Maxwell. All the channels had been in the incumbent language, of which the family had usually learned some basics, sometimes a little more, depending on the length of stay. So, they watched films, western films, geographically western films, which occasionally included cowboy type Western films. The films were mainly in English with local subtitles. The subtitles had driven him mad. Whilst he and his brother had picked up a smattering of several languages, they were all verbal and aural, the written language, the Chinese call it Hanzi, the characters instead of words, was a mystery to them. Therefore, the symbols flickering across the screen were a nuisance, a distraction from the film itself. Bludd had roomed with a guy in a hostel in Indonesia, who had been profoundly deaf. He had not learned sign language, but had taught himself to lip read. He had told Bludd that even though he could only be certain of the dialogue if the actors were face on to the camera, he would rather pick up the gist of the plot than suffer the annoyance of subtitles, words that he didn't understand anyway, but still they drew his eyes constantly away from the main screen.

Bludd's favourite gadget and piece of modern equipment was his iPod – a modern wonder of the world in his opinion – due to the lack of televisual interest his family had, they had listened to music on a regular basis, even as a family. His parents had different tastes, tastes that stemmed from their own backgrounds. Father had come from a rich, well-to-do family and his musical tastes seemed, according with his upbringing, favouring a mainly classical interest, but with a slight diversity to stretch as far as the big bands of Glen Miller and co., or an even rarer swing, to swing. His mother had come from stock slightly, ever so slightly, down the class list and with slightly more liberal parents who had a taste for rock and roll, and then the hippy and psychedelic sounds of the late '50s and '60s. As with most children, they tended to follow their parents' lead on things like music and politics, maybe it was pure preference, but maybe there was an element of brainwashing. You hear it often enough, you grow to like it or believe in it. Bludd had observed that football supporters were probably the same. You are dressed in the shirt of your parents' team from birth and it becomes second nature and part of your identity, and you blindly continue it into your youth and adulthood and forever, rarely breaking the chain.

Bludd looked at his iPod playlist and decided to move away from the classical classics, as he liked to call them, those that everyone would know, or at least recognise without being able to put a name, or a composer's name, to them. He turned, instead, to '70s rock; the era leading out of the mod explosion, through the glam-rock and into hard and heavy rock. Rock music was his favourite to work out to. The consistency of the beat helped in his routine. If he was purely concentrating on a fighting or defensive routine, when his concentration was required to be at its highest, music was not on the agenda. Whichever of the martial arts he would practise, he would focus entirely as if he was back in the country of its origin, listening to the master giving his cue. Well-practised moves, punches, kicks repeated over and over to get them right, perfect them. Now and again, though, focus would not be required, the urge to ramp up the volume, find a bunch of suitably up-tempo, hard rockers was all that he needed to help him burn a few hundred calories. Today was a day for the likes of Motorhead, AC/DC, Rush and Iron Maiden. He couldn't work out to the calmness of '80s electro-pop and new romantics. But today was a chance for two hours of hard-rock, head-banging, adrenaline-filled, cardio madness that, rather than tire him out, would set him up for the potentially long afternoon and evening ahead.

* * *

Judge sat alone in the middle of the busy restaurant, one of many claiming to specialise in seafood. Seafood was his favourite, although sadly it did not agree with him. It could, at times, make him quite ill. Nevertheless, he returned to it time and again, sure in his mind that the lower calorific values would mean that he would be able to eat more, and yet still have less effect on his ever-expanding waistline. Not for a moment did he consider that the deep fried offerings he chose repeatedly were suffocating his arteries, especially in the volume he devoured them. Part of his enjoyment from visiting this type of establishment was the array of fish actually swimming in tanks around the restaurant. His perverse nature made him feel all powerful in his live-or-die choice for the unsuspecting creatures. Who should be spared, maybe for another day, maybe only another minute, but more importantly to him, who should die?

He had made his way through the bustling streets on foot, heading into downtown, where he mingled with a hundred thousand others, workers returning home to their city centre apartments, across to the splendour of the suburbs, or nearer, to the shabby tenements overlooking the busy market areas. All the streets of the inner city looked the same to Judge from his eye level, much on a par with many of the city's natives, although he was short and rotund, while they were mainly short and slim. High rise buildings looked down on every alleyway, minimum three-storey concrete blocks, monotone in colour, aside from the blotchy, peeling paint, the filth and grime and pollution giving many their own identity, a unique swatch of colours that would never knowingly be mixed. The pavements were overpopulated with street sellers, peddling everything he could think of, from films to fake fashion, gadgets and gizmos to griddled gizzard. Their stalls ranged from professional carts, to parasol-covered tables, to just small children or urchins with goods laid out in front of their bare feet, goods that were not worth selling, or at least not worth buying. For many, it was the only way of trying to raise any money for themselves or their families. No way that was lawful, or bearable, or worthy of consideration to any normal family.

Judge's chosen eatery was what he considered traditional. It was fairly basic with comfortable seating, comfortable enough for an hour or so anyway. There were embroidered tablecloths with traditional scenes in bright colours, with scenes of birds and trees and country styled houses and pagodas. The walls were decked with elaborate paintings, more embroideries and photographs of the owner, or manager, with famous or renowned people, local in this restaurant's case. Others Judge had seen showed a beaming owner, never just the manager, celebrating various levels of celebrity, Z listers mainly, but very occasionally, in the main areas of downtown, a major celebrity, with a hoard of happy, amazed staff and customers gathered around fussing and smiling. Judge had laughed at the almost identical pictures ordaining several walls, the celebrity clearly doing the rounds, using their status for a free meal every night, despite their enormous wealth. Judge was not interested in celebrity or fame, but he was jealous that he could not command the free food. He finished the dish of fried king prawns that were smothered in a hot and spicy sauce.

Judge's solitude was broken as he heard the rattle of the door screen's bamboo chains and, out of the corner of his eye, saw the grinning smile of Kulapananam, framed by his thick mop of black spikey hair, his right hand waving frantically above his head, his left hand preceded by a short stubby finger aimed directly at Judge's head. '*So much for a low profile,*' Judge thought.

"Mr Judge," Kulap shouted, near enough to whisper it, but wanting to show everybody that he was about to enter into an important meeting with an important client. "How are you? Are you all rested up and ready for the rest of the week I have arranged for you? It is a very full week. You will be very busy and very happy with what I have arranged. Did you enjoy this afternoon?" He winked as he finished the sentence.

"Sit down, man!" Judge responded gruffly. "I am not sure how well you know me yet, clearly not well at all, I would suggest. What I do not want is any publicity; nobody needs to know who I am, unless I tell you. Nobody needs to know what my business is, unless I have business with them, nobody, absolutely nobody should know what I am here for, what I am doing, where I have been and whom I have seen unless agreed by me. Do you understand?"

"Absolutely, Mr Judge. Can I call you Jeremy? It seems so less formal. After all, we are colleagues now, aren't we? You would be lost in Thailand without me."

Judge patted his lips with a napkin, pushed the empty plate away towards Kulap, considering his reply for a moment. He smiled. "Mr Kulapananam, Kulap, you will address me as Mr Judge. I am the customer here and you are merely a supplier, certainly not a colleague, and as such, you will show me the respect that this status deserves."

Kulap nodded, went to speak, to respond. Judge held his own stubby index finger to his lips. "I haven't finished. I have hired you for one week. When that week is over, we shall not meet again as I will have concluded all the business that requires your assistance. Of course, through your assistance you will be paid in accordance with our agreement. That is, that I get my house, I get my business, nobody, as I stated a few moments ago shall know about any of this, before, after, or ever, unless by prior agreement with me. Nobody in Thailand need know I exist for now, you can forget about me once we have concluded our week. If this is all very clear, Mr Kulap, you may speak and you may inform me of the agenda you have arranged. But may I add one reminder to you. You are not indispensable to me, nobody is. You are useful to me, but there are hundreds, if not thousands, of other people like you and you can easily be replaced. Understood?"

Kulap looked at Judge, seeking further approval to reply. No further approval came, as Judge took a large swig from his brandy glass.

"OK, Mr Judge, message received and understood. Loud and clear. No problem." He paused, again awaiting approval to proceed. Nothing again. He continued. "OK, so tonight, when you have finished eating, we can head into 'The Venice of the East' that we call downtown Bangkok. Here, I have arranged a booth in the VIP area of the Asiatique nightclub. This club, as you may know, is world famous for the special entertainment there, the Moulin Rouge of Thailand. The calypso cabaret is something to behold. Tomorrow we will go to the house, it is a villa actually. It is beautiful and the setting is like paradise, just like you asked for. The owner will have a private meeting with you over dinner, but we shall arrive in the afternoon at the time of your choosing. I suppose it depends on how late you retire tonight and how you feel tomorrow. I think we should get there early. I think you will like it. All of it. I will leave you for your meeting and I will come back for you when you are ready. I am assuming that the meeting will go well and that Mr Erichsen will provide some accommodation for you overnight if you desire." He winked at Judge again. "On Sunday afternoon, we will visit the first factory, your favoured site. I have left Monday free for the moment, because if the visit goes well, you may wish to spend Monday there as well so you can see the factory in full production, tomorrow will be just overtime crew. The proprietor is aware of this and is hopeful that by Tuesday you may be able to conclude matters. On Tuesday, we may go to see the second factory which is owned by a good friend of mine, Mr Anantasu. He is hopeful of this meeting and has indicated to me that he is very willing to discuss discounts and payment plans with you, if that helps to draw you in his direction. Wednesday is free. I thought that you may wish to visit the Erichsens again." Another wink. "On Thursday, of course you are due to return to England and you must be at the airport at 10.00 a.m. You will need to check out of the hotel at 6.30 a.m. to be sure of arriving with plenty of time for check in.

It may be a busy, busy week for you, Mr Judge, but it may also all be concluded by Tuesday. I have worked hard to secure all the appointments and meetings; I hope they will be successful for you. Just one other thing, I have to keep some time in the evenings to see my mother. She is very sick and it is important to me to be there for her in her last days."

Judge swirled a brandy glass and inhaled deeply into the bowl before taking a large mouthful. "Mr Kulap, I appreciate that you may have worked hard to arrange these things on my behalf, but after all that is what you are being paid, paid very handsomely, to do. You will of course receive the second half of the payment in acknowledgement of my being pleased with the outcome of the meetings. All of them. This final payment is very subjective, of course, so here's hoping they all go well, for both of us. As regards your personal situation, I have absolutely no reason to want to spend any more time with you than necessary, so please, go to your mother and spend all the time you need with her as many of *your* last days with her as you can."

He had intended to phrase the final comment in such a way as to see whether Kulap picked up on it. He may have taken it as a Freudian slip, or indeed seen the intimation as a purposeful threat, but as it happened, Kulap did not pick up on the accentuated language at all, he was keen to get on with the night and keen to get on with his client.

5

Plan

Bludd had picked up his voicemail and a text message from Chrissie, asking him, respectfully, not to come round tonight. She would be leaving Archie, her nine-year old son, at her mother's. It was a regular occurrence and Bludd had taken no offence. Chrissie generally got back soon after midnight, Archie stayed at his grandmother's until Saturday afternoon and Chrissie got a chance to catch up on much needed sleep. Bludd often made his excuses on a Thursday evening and let her get a full night of restful, unbroken sleep before her consecutive work nights came around, as they could occasionally go on longer than anticipated. She had asked him if he wouldn't mind watching Archie on the Saturday night and he had texted a reply of 'no problem'. Not being the owner of a television, Bludd quite liked to look after Archie, especially on a Saturday, as it gave him an insight into what all the fuss was about regarding Saturday night TV prime time viewing. He had concluded that it was really just a lot of fuss about nothing. Video clips of people hurting themselves, as far as he could see, sometimes deliberately, to claim the cash prize. Or a bunch of hopeful singers warbling through, and often murdering classic songs, the judges or mentors claiming that they were either brilliant, or that their voice didn't suit that genre of music. Bludd hated the word "genre". It seemed like a modern word, possibly invented by these TV music moguls to try and make themselves sound clever. 'This music isn't your genre,'

'I don't think tonight's theme is your genre,' they would say. Why couldn't they say style, or type or anything except genre? Occasionally there would be a half-decent film, usually old, or at least pre-1985, that he could watch again and enjoy, again. Very occasionally there would be a reasonable modern or recent film on that Bludd would have heard about and he would give it a chance and would enjoy it, begrudgingly.

He had never really bothered that Chrissie was an escort, as she had been when he met her, and he saw no reason to ask her to stop. Not that he felt that it was anything like his place to ask her anyway. It wasn't as if they were together officially, as such, so why would he? He felt closer to Chrissie than he had felt to anyone, except his brother in the early years. He and his brother were best friends in the years of moving and unrest, when the only people they knew would be around for certain, long term, would be their family. Now Chrissie was his best friend, she clearly wanted more than that, and deep down, so did he, but he was not in a position to offer anything more than he had given her for the last two years, not capable of being a proper partner, not yet. His biggest problem with the situation was that he could not see what was going to change things for him. Or when that something might occur. He knew she was attracted to him, as he had been attracted to her as soon as he had seen her. He had been working on behalf of another suspicious wife looking for evidence of an unfaithful husband, sitting quietly in the corner of the bar, waiting for the errant husband to arrive, mistress on arm. Chrissie had been there before him, first of all sat demurely at a table for two, waiting for her date to arrive. Bludd had wondered if she might be the mistress he was waiting for. She had sat, quietly, shyly, looking slightly embarrassed that she was alone, for nearly an hour. Bludd noted that she had been there on his arrival at

8.10 p.m. as he had arrived early for his expected sighting, in plenty of time to recce the area and claim his usual corner perch. He deduced that she must have been waiting for her date for an hour, an arranged 8.00 p.m. meeting, given up on an hour later, following a one-way telephone conversation that was her cancelling. She had taken her drink to the bar and ordered a fresh one. Bludd was not one for approaching women, he had no reason to, as he was not interested in a relationship, but she was different. She was tall, slim and elegant. She was resplendent in her royal blue crossover dress and high heels, long, blonde hair and sparkling green eyes, with a blue tint that the dress enhanced. He had tried to be cool, tried not to be corny, tried not to look desperate, which he wasn't anyway, but he could feel himself looking that way. He had asked her if she had been stood up, and she had looked at him and smiled, feeling like she was being hit on, badly, by somebody not good at hitting on women and definitely not practised at it. She had explained what she was doing there, that she was an escort and that her client not turning up would cost her £500 and a fiver for a Chinese takeout on her way home. He liked her honesty and openness, and he was honest with her as well. He had not been trying to pick her up, but if she would join him for dinner, it would make him look much less conspicuous than if he was alone. She had agreed without hesitation and had ordered a Chinese-style meal anyway, only on Bludd's expenses. They had had a brilliant evening, even better that his client's husband had also failed to turn up so he did not have to work. It had turned out that he was not Chrissie's client, although strangely it had later turned out that the two men did know each other. Ironically, Bludd had escorted Chrissie home, relatively early for both of them, and they had agreed to go for a drink on their next mutually convenient night off. That had been ten days later and they had been friends, close friends, but not much more than that ever since.

Bludd had reset his answerphone and had gone upstairs to get changed. It was a simple choice, for when it came to fashion, simple was really the only choice he had. He owned two wardrobes: matching pine, two-door affairs, with two small matching bedside cabinets. One wardrobe contained his dressing up clothes. Many people would think of this as his smart clothes wardrobe, but for Bludd it was more like a fancy dress shop. If he was following somebody closely, or repeatedly, he was careful to have a different appearance to avoid recognition, so he had a range of clothes and hats and wigs and coats for this purpose. He could look younger, older, scruffier, poorer, better off, posh even. His other wardrobe contained his day to day clothes. This was simplicity itself. He had black jeans, black trousers, black shirts, black jumpers, black tee shirts, black coats. Everything black. Bludd thought black, even as far as his motorcycle and car, was the most inconspicuous of colours, it faded into all kinds of backgrounds and situations. Some people wear black for its alleged slimming qualities, Bludd didn't need those, he just wanted simple, smart and acceptable. For his trip to Lancashire he had chosen black tee, black jeans and his short black leather jacket. Black, steel-toed ten holed boots finished his ensemble.

Bludd had chosen to travel north on his motorbike. He would get there at least half an hour early, have a scout around and see how this particular land was laid. His motorbike was the preference on many first visits, its off-road qualities sometimes invaluable over those of a car, even a 4x4, giving him an option to ride up embankments, sidings, fields, narrow, rough tracks and muddy roads. His choice of steed was a Yamaha WR450F Trail bike, with oversized bore, offering higher torque and top speed as well as faster acceleration. Road legal, quick and agile on road, lightweight, but sturdy and resolute off-road. He had hand painted the tank and fairings in matt black, giving it less finesse, but more incognito a finish. He had made a bespoke black back box, as standard types did not suit the style of bike, cross country bikes not having the same framed structure as road bikes have. In his black back box he had placed his binoculars, night vision lens, video camera, chocolate energy bar and energy drink, the "Freddie Kruger" brand, with the scratch marks running down the can. Plus, a tub of gum.

Travelling anti-clockwise around the city of Manchester, Bludd made his way onto the Lancashire-bound motorway and headed north a further 11 miles to his destination, Harewood, somewhere between Blackburn and Preston. He arrived at the address of his client's company, given to him over the phone by John Preston and hastily scribbled down, 'Preston Dye Supply Ltd, Valley View Road, Harewood, Lancashire', 33 minutes early for their appointment. Preston, the MD, had wanted a 3.30 p.m. meet in order to be away from the ears of his staff, who, on a Friday were apparently all keen to leave at their 3.00 p.m. early finish time. He was parked in an overspill car park of a relatively well-known home furnishings manu-facturing company opposite and noticed that he had spelled Dye incorrectly, 'Preston Die Supply Ltd' the sign showed. He knew what dye was, but struggled to think what a 'die' was, something to do with die-cast models maybe. He thought he would find out soon.

Mr Preston was right. At 3.00 p.m. precisely, a melee of vehicles raced to the exit at the company gates. Cars, vans, mopeds, bikes and pedestrians, were all fighting to be in pole position, all wanting to be the first to be on their way home for the weekend. Bludd watched the race fade to a slow conclusion, the staff at the end of the queue realising that rushing was mean-ingless. He waited five minutes and turned away to his right, followed the road a short distance until he was at the end of the nearest building and took a right turn, onto a railway bridge overlooking an east-west running track, probably running from Leeds to Liverpool, or Preston, the town. To his left was the rear of the 'Die' supply company, a long, narrow, sloping car park, with two cars remaining enclosed behind two L-shaped buildings with the long side running parallel to both the road and the train line. The building farthest away and facing Bludd was signed as Warehouse Two and another sign also indicated a reception and therefore, Bludd presumed offices. He also presumed that the building nearest to him and to his left was Warehouse One.

To his right, looking over the bridge wall was some kind of Islamic building, two in fact, one the size of a typical semi-detached house, the other looked like an office building. He thought it was maybe a mosque, maybe it was both. It was 100 feet square and set over three floors, each floor having 23 windows to the back and side elevations, the faces of the building that he could see. The rows of bricks were separated by eight vertical lines of a tan coloured brick, offset against the common red brick, the middle six windows of the second and third floor were set out to resemble the Taj Mahal, or something similar. Each corner had a spire with a spherical top, bright red and made of steel. In the middle, was a taller, wider spire with a golden-yellow spherical top.

He travelled over the bridge, turned right at the junction and checked the front of the Islamic building, virtually identical to the back, but the front door was set in an extended out section of brick, in line with the six windows at the rear in the shape of the Taj Mahal. "Islamic College of Al Jaranha" the sign above the door said, followed by a statement in Arabic text, running in reverse to the English words above. He U-turned and headed back, just past the junction of the bridge and stopped, looking over the railway to the rear of 'Preston Die Supply Ltd'. He could see the roof and top part of the pebble-dash wall, scattered with tiny stones, all whites, reds, different brown shades. Different from the front he recalled with a blink, the front was pebble dashed the same, but painted magnolia with a black border at the base where it joined the pavement. He had no view of the car park from this point and contemplated sitting on the bridge a while longer, but this offered him no real idea of scale of the place, no concept of the full layout.

He looked to his right, where there was a small gathering of around 50 houses, in three rows. The first two were set back to back, the third facing the front of the middle row, and meaning that they benefited from not being overlooked at their rear, except for the fact that the hill that rose behind them had a tiny township of sheds, each standing behind a south facing vegetable garden, each patch the same size and shape, each building in need of some care and attention, many leaning to one side or the other, probably relying on their contents to keep them upright. They were a single row of decaying wooden structures, housing a community of like-minded, mini-organic farmers.

Bludd U-turned again and took an almost immediate right turn, riding past the three rows of houses, stopping through necessity as he approached a barrier, designed to be difficult for horses to pass through, but not quite difficult enough for a motorbike. He dismounted anyway, placed the face of his helmet over the left of the handle bars, kicked out the left legged stand and walked slowly up the hill towards the allotments' entrance, looking around intensely and taking in the local landscape. The gate to the allotments was open, so presumably somebody was attending to their vegetables, or having an hour of solitude before the weekend with the wife, or husband. No need to presume that men have the monopoly on gardening, or hours of peace away from the family. He headed east, keeping behind the back of the row of sheds, stopping in between each one, deciding where he could obtain the best view of 'Preston Die Supply Ltd'. There were 13 sheds in all and left of centre gave Bludd a superb panoramic, but slightly more distant than he would have liked, view of the warehouses and office buildings. As he stood there, blinking deliberately as he turned his head from left to right, or west to east, a voice interrupted his concentration. "Can I help you lad?" A deep, rough voice with a thick Lancastrian accent asked.

Bludd had to think quickly. An off the cuff response, the best he could come up with. "Er, no not really. I guess I am being a bit cheeky, but I live in those houses down there and… to be honest, I think my Mrs is up to no good if you know what I mean. I just thought this might give me a good view of the house where I might see what's going on, you know, comings and goings and so on."

The man just tutted and puffed his cheeks out, eventually responding, "No problem lad, same thing happened to me. Fucking women, can't trust the bastards. I come here and look after me veggies now, rather than chase women. Veggies don't answer back, don't give you any grief. They don't scream when you stick a fucking big blade into their middle either!" He burst into a self-indulgent belly laugh. Bludd was surprised at the hostility, but guessed and hoped that it really was only a joke.

"So, am I OK to come up here and keep an eye on things?" he asked, knowing full well what the reply would be.

The man held out his right hand. "Course you can lad, anything to oblige. Bill, by the way. Do you fancy a beer?"

"Cheers, Bill, but I am driving shortly, in fact I am off in a moment, but I could do with coming back later I think. Seb, by the way, and a beer would be great, later." Bludd shook Bill's outstretched hand and bade him goodbye, for now.

He trotted back behind the sheds and back down the hill to his bike, fired it up with the kick-start and made his way back along the road, a left and a right over the bridge and parked up again, back in the small overspill car park to the east of 'Preston Die Supply Ltd' and south of the Al Jaranha Islamic College and the railway track.

He slipped his helmet over his left wrist and stepped across the slim ridge of grass dividing pavement and car park and noticed an articulated lorry to his right, straddling the entrance to his destination. Late delivery he thought, unwelcome over-time for somebody. As he approached the entrance a fork lift truck slotted its forks into the open canvas sides of the lorry and under a pallet, laden with approximately 30 boxes, each one approximately a foot and a half square and approximately an inch deep. The driver, a blond-haired man of about 50, sporting a thick, blond, moustache, his face lined with age and hard work, stopped and looked Bludd up and down.

"Mr Preston in?" Bludd inquired.

"Yes, cock. Go left to reception and give the bell a buzz. He's around somewhere," the blond man replied.

Bludd looked at his watch, it was 3.30 p.m. precisely. As he turned left he almost bumped straight into a tall, slim man, balding, his brown hair receding to a fringe on the very top of his head, a deep, v-shaped dimple in his chin. Bludd took a step back, "John?"

"Mr Bludd? Pleased to meet you. Please come with me to

my office, there's been a slight hiccup. Come on I'll explain everything upstairs."

They went up five steps and left through the reception door, across a short width of laminate floor and through a door secured by a keypad lock, across more laminate floor and up another flight of seven stairs, turning left into an office fronted by a door marked with a small, shiny gold sign with black writing, "John Preston – Managing Director", it stated.

The office was furnished with a new, large modern desk to the left of the door, with a longer rectangular version running at right angles to it, attached to its partners centre, forming a T shape. To the right, two filing cabinets, listed as 'Suppliers A-F', 'Suppliers G-P', 'Suppliers Q-Z' from top down in the left hand cabinet, 'First Aid' occupying the bottom drawer. The right hand cabinet had no labels. A coffee table stood shallow in the centre of the room bridging the gap between the filing cabinets and a tall cupboard opposite them with a pair of locked grey sliding concertina doors. A dark brown leather sofa, not dissimilar to Bludd's own office sofa, leant against the back wall, adjacent to the coffee table. John Preston motioned for Bludd to sit on the sofa and pushed a less comfortable office chair on wheels to the nearside.

"Shall we have a brew?" the MD asked.

"Coffee, milk, two sugars, please. So, tell me what's going on Mr Preston? But while you're telling me, tell me also what you do and what the heck is a Die, spelled D.I.E?"

The MD smiled. "A die is a wooden based cutting forme, used to cut anything from boxes and envelopes, to gaskets, carpet tiles, and medical products. Many, many things that you use on a daily basis get press cut and we supply all the component parts of the forme, or 'die', that cuts them. As well as this, we supply machine, or press parts, parts to strip away the waste created in the cutting process and even products that make a box fold more easily. There is an awful lot that goes into a box that the general public don't realise when they throw the cardboard in the bin. Anyway, I will show you round the warehouse shortly and explain a bit more, it might make a bit more sense, although I am not sure just how relevant it will all be."

He handed Bludd a coffee in a 'PDS' mug. "My father started the company over 30 years ago and back then it was based on the leather and, in particular, the shoe industry. As you can probably imagine, that has more or less all gone; migrated to the Far East along with many other industries. However, we have managed to diversify and prosper and we now have over 30 staff. Many of them have been with us for a long time, some over 20 of those 30 odd years, many others into double figures. We have had a very small staff turnover for a long time now, but just recently a few people seem to be a little unhappy with their lot. The recession has meant that, even though we have grown and appear to be doing well, margins have shrunk, really profitable products are less in demand and products with really low margins are taking their place. This means that the staff see lots more products going out of the door, but in fact the company makes less money, less profit, than it did 10 years ago when we turned over half what we do now. Aside from one or two people, the staff have not had a pay rise for three years and I think there is a little resentment floating around. Just recently, over the last five or six months, we seem to be losing stock here and there, only more recently there seems to be more and more going astray. We have introduced random stock checks throughout the month and on random product groups, or sections of warehouse, anything to keep things varied. Many times we have done a random search and the stock comes back as correct to what the computer level tells us, but days later, with no apparent stock movement in between, we can receive an order and find there is no stock, or insufficient stock, to fulfil the order. That means that either stock has gone out without documentation, which we will eventually realise, or the stock has been pinched or it has been counted incorrectly during the stock count, possible deliberately, or in other words stock figures have been fudged. This means that the individual doing the count is in on any scam that might go on, as well as somebody who is doing the physical act of removing it. There could be any number of people involved."

"OK, thanks for that. So do you have anybody in mind, any finger of suspicion pointing in any particular direction?"

"Well, obviously the lads in the warehouse, or at least one of them, must be involved. The other train of thought is the salesmen, the reps. They often come in and do deliveries, so they have ample opportunity and it has become a bit of a standing joke that any stock discrepancies get blamed on the reps. Other than that, no idea."

"OK. So what do you expect from me? What kind of evidence, how should that be presented and do you have a time frame?"

"No preconceived idea about any of this really, it's not something I am familiar with. Whatever you can get that just shows me who is responsible and then let's see if they can add anything, you know, maybe they will incriminate others, who knows? Regarding the time frame, the only pattern that seems to have emerged is that when we get a big delivery, which is weekly and usually on a Thursday, the stock gets signed off and put into the warehouse bays, but we have done a couple of immediate stock takes of the bays the day after, unbeknown to the warehouse chaps, and a few major issues have been thrown up, so we think it must be immediately following a delivery of our steel products. Funnily enough, that was the hiccup I was talking about. This week's delivery didn't come in on time, something to do with the French port workers being out in strike, again, holding the delivery vehicle on the wrong side of the Channel. You will have just seen the warehouse manager unloading it, ready to be put away first thing Monday."

"Great, could be just the break you need. Let's go and have a look around and see if you can't teach me something about dies, or formes that I might actually understand."

* * *

The warehouse manager, with the blond hair and moustache pressed the green phone icon on his mobile and got an immediate answer. "Bob, don't come to the warehouse just yet. He has a visitor so I'm not sure how long he will be here. Bloody typical isn't it, the one Friday we get chance to make a killing and he stays later than he usually does, I mean he normally pisses off at lunchtime and doesn't bother coming back. But, I'm going to butt in and make out I'm off home. I'll wait around the corner and once he's gone I'll give you a buzz and by the time you get here, a nice stack of stuff will be ready for you. Bring the cash as normal, yeah?"

A pause, while Bob spoke on the other end.

"OK, see you later."

John Preston and Bludd crossed the car park, towards Warehouse One and Bludd noticed the warehouse manager pressing his mobile and slipping it into his pocket. He noted that he looked a bit edgy. A bit guilty maybe?

"I'm done now, John. Just off, unless there's anything else?" The warehouse manager nodded towards Bludd, hoping for an introduction that explained his presence.

"OK, have a good weekend. And no, that's fine, I can see Mr Bludd out after we have finished. He is here to quote on the traffic light system we talked about, you know for the fork lift and pedestrian access to the factory," the MD replied.

Another waste of money, the warehouse manager thought as he nodded a silent goodbye to his boss and the guest.

6

Betrayal

In Bangkok, it was almost 11 o'clock. Judge left the tire-some Kulap in the nightclub, the Moulin Rouge of Thailand, laughing and joking, flirting, it seemed, with a succession of lady-boys, or at least that was what Judge thought they were. It was hard to decipher, they were certainly pretty enough to be girls, but some of them had a discernible Adam's apple, some not so obvious, some not appearing to have any lump in their throat, but an all too obvious lump in their groin giving the game away.

Judge had thought, again, that Kulap didn't really get him, not quite understanding what his desires were, although Judge knew that Kulap knew really, otherwise he would not have employed him. Maybe others like Judge liked a little sideline, a little titivation from something not normal, but not extreme, something to whet the appetite, or make them laugh, or just to give them something different to think about that didn't make Kulap feel quite so bad about himself and his involvement. Less guilt, less disgust.

He made his way through the busy streets, hunger pangs starting in his swollen stomach. He had not eaten for three hours and to Judge that was a long time. He stopped at a busy looking stall. Busy suggested that the fare was good, so he ordered a Thai green curry, chicken option. It came in a small white, disposable bowl and Judge opted for a plastic fork, still unable to operate chopsticks and his stomach too impatient to put some practise in now.

He finished the hot, flavoursome dish quickly, so much nicer in Bangkok than in England, and threw the bowl and sticks on the ground, not concerned with adding to the growing mounds of rubbish littering the roadside. His contribution wouldn't make that much difference, he thought.

He got his bearings and set off northbound along the busy street. He crossed over a small, low bridge. The road below formerly a canal, had been filled in to create more opportunities for housing. He took his fourth turn to the right and continued in a straight line until he came to the edge of a stretch of canal. He had visited the Khlong canal network before and his knowledge of the surroundings was unknown to Kulap, who believed that his client was new in town and a rookie tourist. Judge turned to his right and looked at the neon sign above the doorway of the first building. He nodded at two men stood astride an open door, both dressed smartly in black suits, white shirts, black ties and mirror-finished polish on their shoes. They parted on his approach and waved him in, no emotion, just a stern look on their faces, professional doormen, diligent guards, knowing that the short, rotund visitor was here by prearranged appointment, an appointment made some weeks ago when he last visited them.

7

Suspicion

Bludd was not too surprised by the volume of stock that the warehouse contained, but was quite amazed at the variety of product that was there. He looked around, the company MD explaining, as well as he could, what each product line did in the course of producing mainly boxes and products associated with all manner of packaging. He grinned to himself as in one section of the racking there were signs, with complex references under a descriptive name, "Mushrooms", "Carrots", two of them read. He might as well have been sat a few hundred yards away with Bill, at his allotment, sipping a beer and chastising the fairer sex. John Preston could not explain what job mushrooms and carrots performed in the whole box-making process, but he went on to explain that the main products they stocked and sold were called steel rules, a huge range of products that were purely for cutting and creasing, as well as perforating, cardboard; solid board cardboard and corrugated cardboard. He explained that most of the products came from Austria and Germany, but some of the other products, the rubbers and plastic parts came from Denmark, Poland, France, Spain, the USA and China. 'Basically, from all over the world.' Some were manufactured in the UK, some were from Europe and then adapted in the UK to perform specific tasks in the box-making process. The MD explained a particular product that was invented in Yorkshire and was now gaining worldwide acclaim, and for which his company had been partly responsible. He wasn't actually that certain how the product worked, it had been developed by their supplier and taken to market in conjunction with his sales people, but he could definitely confirm that the big supermarket chains were now specifically requesting the 'Eazi-Rip' products for their 'SRP' and 'RRP' requirements. Bludd had looked puzzled at the abbreviations and the MD had explained that they were 'Shelf Ready' and 'Retail Ready Packaging'. Boxes that could be torn open on supermarket shop floors, leaving a tray type base to house the product and allow easy, or 'Eazi', access to the consumer.

The MD's mobile had rung and he left Bludd to wander around Warehouse One alone for a short time. Bludd had tried to take in and understand the function of the different products as they had been explained to him. He was not unintelligent, far from it, he was incredibly clever, not least because of his Advanced Eidetic Memory, but he was struggling to understand all the code numbers, references and colour coded boxes representing different groups of products. *How could one product contain such a massive variety of products?* He looked at the boxes, silver-grey coloured with individual colour representative labels. He noted that 'crease rules' were all blue labels and that the references only changed by the fact that numbers went up in increments of five hundredths of a millimetre. He also noted that a product called 'Uniflex' was housed in the two areas of the racking under the banners of 'Rotary' and 'Flat Bed'. On his return, the MD had explained that Rotary was a way of cutting cardboard, mainly corrugated cardboard, he thought, in an obviously rotary motion, with a die made on a semi-circular piece of plywood called a shell, and that Flat Bed was again quite self-explanatory, in that the die worked in an up and down motion on a flat steel plate that the 'rules' cut onto. It hadn't really helped Bludd. The MD had also explained that the steels came in a number of different thicknesses called points, and their customers would decide which point to use depending on the thickness of materials his customer's customers were cutting. Bludd had seen somewhere, in some literature, somewhere in his past, that 'points' were fractions of an inch, one point being one 72nd of an inch, or in metric 0.37 of a millimetre. His memory, useful for so many things in his line of work, and partly the reason he had chosen this vocation, also brought back innumerable topics of absolutely useless information, or not as the case may be. Bludd had seen a number of boxes with '2pt', '3pt' and '4pt' in Warehouse One and the concept had begun to make a modicum of sense to him.

He asked the MD to leave him alone for a further few minutes, allowing him to traverse the many rows of racking one last time and blinking deliberately at each bay, capturing a snapshot of each one in his mind.

Some people have a standard photographic memory, allow-ing them to recall mainly visual information. Eidetic memory allows the person to recall information from all the senses. How something looks, or what is written, a visual caption. How something smells or tastes, what it sounds like or what is spoken, how it feels to the touch. Bludd's highly unusual condition of Advanced Eidetic Memory meant that he could recall all manner of things, not just in the short term, but since his memory had begun to work, and until it decided to stop working. He hoped that his father's condition did not prove to be hereditary. His mind took a snapshot of the world in front of him every single time he blinked, an image that would be imprinted in his memory until he died, possibly, or until his memory did. Not only that, but all the virtues of the other senses were retained from the surroundings. A human blinks, on average, between 22 and 25 times a minute, but this drops to four blinks a minute when reading. This meant that Bludd would take, on average, 22 to 25 mind-recorded portraits a minute. If he was reading text, or wanted a specific memory, he could deliberately blink and provide an everlasting capture of chapter and verse, available for recall at a moment's concentrated notice. If he was focused on anything specific, his mind had a built-in intelligence to allow the vision in his mind, the recollection, to expand into the peripheral vision, to take the blurred extremities and bring them into a clear and unclouded focus. It was his own little super-power, which had helped him on countless occasions in this profession.

* * *

Bludd wasn't sure how capturing the layout of the warehouse and the various stacks of boxes, all shapes, sizes, colours, with different labels and a multitude of different references, on the boxes and the warehouse racking, could have helped him. Nonetheless he diligently went round each bay, A to F sections and one to 10 rows, and momentarily captured their contents. He found John Preston leaning on the balustrade at the bottom of a set of stairs.

"I think I've got all I need for now," Bludd said.

John Preston looked surprised. "But you've only seen this warehouse, there's another one to see yet." He nodded a westerly glance towards the stairs, behind them and beyond the offices was Warehouse Two.

"No need. You have already told me that the core products are the steel rules, which seem to me to be mainly or wholly situated in this warehouse. If you are correct, and there is some stealing going on, I think it is 100 per cent certain to be coming out of this building. A thief will steal what is the easiest thing to sell. In this case it has to be the core product, the steel rules. Nobody will want to be hanging on to this stuff. It takes up a lot of room and by the nature of its name, steel rule, I am guessing it is also heavy. This stuff will need to be moved quickly and easily into the marketplace and whoever is selling it will, presumably, be making a nice little earner."

The MD pondered, stroking his dimpled chin. "You're right. I like the logic. So what now?"

"We both leave. You lock up and go home and I hang around a bit, see what happens. If anything does happen, I will be in touch. If it does not, you let me know when your next drop is due and I will put some time aside to make a return trip. Worst case scenario, you put up some CCTV cameras and do the job yourself, but I think you are conscious of the way this would look to the rest of the team. They would think you don't trust them; Big Brother is watching and all that. Morale would go even further in the wrong direction and you don't want that, do you?"

The MD pondered again, still stroking his chin. "No, you're right. Again. OK, I will look forward to hearing from you."

Bludd left the MD in the warehouse, presumably check-ing each door was secure, all windows closed and that only a member of staff would be able to get in, one with a key, which would be one of three people.

The motorbike growled as the kick-start was kicked and as the private investigator turned out of the car park he noticed a light blue Ford Fiesta at the far end, a blond-haired man sat in the driver's seat, phone pressed to his ear. He went over the railway bridge and continued to the two grey railings, there to stop horses, but not able to stop a small agile motorbike, which could negotiate the narrow gap with a delicate rider on board. Bludd sped up the grassy path and turned left on the worn track running behind the allotment sheds. He killed the engine and strolled down between the sixth and seventh sheds to find Bill waiting there with a chilled bottled of beer. He sat down in the prearranged deck chair, looked at Bill with a smile and chinked his bottle against the base of the identical container in his new friend's hand, noting the discarded half dozen bottles of the same, empty and laying at their feet.

* * *

At 5.45 p.m. as the sky was beginning to turn darker than it was light, the grey gates opened and the blond, tired-looking man walked in and shut them behind him, not locking them together. He turned northwards and then east, or right and struggling with his keys in the fading light and with fading eyesight, he searched through them before the correct one was placed into the door lock and he entered Warehouse One.

To the north, 500 yards away, Bludd thanked Bill for the two bottles of beer and his company over the last hour and a half and retrieved his bike from the back of the allotment shed and kicked it back to life. He sped down the grassy track, slowly traversed the awkward junction of the two steel barriers and passed the three rows of terraced houses, slowly over the railway bridge and turned left and then left again, into the quiet car park, south of the Islamic College and the rail track. The unoccupied Ford Fiesta sat in the far corner. He took off his helmet, turned off the engine and walked casually across the road and sat silently against the wall of a building that belonged to the home furnishing manufacturer, a fire exit and small path out to the road to his left hand side, a foot high wall either side of the path, with a concrete centre ridged stone on top making a comfortable resting point.

Some 50, patient, minutes later, with the darkness now almost fully descended, a dark blue estate car, that Bludd recognised to be a Saab 95, navy blue but probably described as Midnight Blue or Moonlight Blue by the manufacturer, passed slowly from his right and slowed to a stop, headlights facing the vertical strips of the iron gates, casting long thin shadow lines into the car park of the die supply company. A bulky, round shouldered figure emerged from the driver's door and opened the grey gates inwards and hooked them into hasps attached to the sides of both the buildings. He returned to his car and entered the company car park. Bludd was already on the move back to his bike, wrestling the keys from his pocket and taking the smallest of the bunch, so that he arrived ready to open the black back box. He pulled out his video camera. No need for the night vision, he guessed. He closed the box and ran up the three flags that formed a slope up the grass verge and onto the bridge, crossing the pavement, road and pavement again. He walked past the rear wall of Warehouse One, which backed onto the road hosting the bridge and took a quick left hand jump onto the stone wall that formed the boundary of the bridge and which was attached, at its south side, to the pebble dash of the warehouse. He had briefly noticed earlier on that the car park of the company had a four foot high, dry stone wall running down the length of its car park and over the other side was the steep embankment that led to the rail track. The bridge wall was somewhat higher than the dry stoned version 30 yards to the west, but a drop of around seven or eight feet would see Bludd able to wander along, unseen and unheard and take his place under an area in the wall of the company car park that had been damaged and rebuilt but without the vertical stones that ran along the top. This meant that Bludd could gain a view from the side elevated wall of the warehouse, leaning his viewfinder on the damaged, but not rebuilt, section of wall. The small screen popped out of the side of the camera's body to allow him to see what the lens was seeing, Bludd leaning with his legs at an angle created by the embankment. Completely unseen, except for the viewfinder, a black circular protrusion about one and a half inches in diameter, leaning on a black stone, would not be easy to see. He had already decided that the blond man had poor eyesight from the way he had squinted an inquisitive look at him three hours earlier and then struggled to recognise a key he used five days a week, without close study. Bludd had also reckoned on the blond man's associate being in too much of a hurry to worry about the surroundings having changed minutely. He would be in a rush to leave, to get out before any chance that he was caught in the act. Too late, Bludd thought, already caught, though not yet incriminated on camera, a few more minutes for the evidence to be captured.

The dark estate car had pulled into the car park and faced downhill to the west and reversed backwards, so that the rear tailgate was as near to the Goods Inwards door as the driver could achieve, triggering the large halogen security light that was centrally positioned over the "Warehouse One" sign, illuminating the entire car park in a bright white light. No need for night vision lenses.

The driver got out, his bulky frame housing a tanned face and arms, a spikey black haircut, his face stern. He was there for one reason and he wanted to get that reason over with as soon as possible. The man rolled up the sleeves on his blue on white chequered shirt and banged a fist against the corrugated green metal door. The door began to open immediately, creaking into life as the electronic motor struggled to life on the inside of the warehouse. He opened his tailgate and offside passenger door, then skipped around the front of the vehicle and opened the nearside passenger door, his every move watched and caught through the tiny black lens. The door was open sufficiently high for the bulky man to step in with a slight stoop and Bludd listened hard for the conversation, confident that business would be done, at worst, just inside the building and in a short enough distance for the camera to audibly record the words being uttered. Bludd moved forward slightly, taking a step down the grassy embankment and pivoting the camera to face inside the building. The bulky man emerged, pushing a blue steel-framed trolley, piled high with boxes. Not the boxes Bludd had seen being unloaded from the truck at 3.30 p.m. that afternoon, but with boxes that were a plain brown, a foot square by two and half feet long, he could not see the labels. He loaded them onto the rear seat, directly in front of Bludd's camera lens. The blond man was at the rear of the car, leaning on a trolley piled high with boxes of the type that Bludd had seen being unloaded. Loaded with steel rules. Bludd pressed his thumb on the zoom pad on his camera and saw that the first trolley, the only one of the three at the back of the car that he could see labels on, was laden with 'Uniflex' of the rotary variety, the types with 'tpi' or 'teeth per inch' on their labels, boxes plain brown. The expensive and therefore high profit type, Bludd guessed. The other two piled high with the silver-grey cardboard boxes. Another trolley was behind them, it was loaded with a further stash of the same load that the bulky man was hastily loading into his vehicle.

"Sorry about this, cock," said the blond man said as he straightened up and lit a cigarette. "Like I said on the phone, he had a visitor. Anyway, I've put the stuff you asked for on here, with a few extra coils of Uniflex. All three point, easier to sell you said. I couldn't give you as much as normal in case they stock check it tomorrow, without me there to change it if need be, so I've topped you up with rubber, all grey blocks, easier to sell you said."

The bulky man said nothing. He was round the other side of the car, loading the plain boxes onto his rear seat. He said nothing. The blond man took a breath of his cigarette, not moving, not helping his associate, Bob, to load the car. Bob looked at the blond man as he threw the boxes of steel rule into his load space, annoyance in his eyes that no help was forthcoming. Sweat was beginning to show on his shirt, by virtue of the fact that the content of each box was heavy, steel coils of maybe 100 metres of steel rule. Bludd noted the car suspension becoming increasingly lower, the car displaying a sit up and beg pose as the last boxes went in. The bulky man, Bob, still said nothing. He pushed down the tailgate and got in the driver's seat, closing the door with a slam of a man out of breath and in a rush. The blond man flicked his cigarette end over the wall, narrowly missing the camera lens and flicking off the left shoulder of Bludd's jacket.

"Don't forget the cash, mate," the blond man said, a little panic in his voice.

The whirr of the car window sounded louder than it should have in the darkness. Bludd could not see the transaction of money changing hands (he guessed it was in a brown envelope), and nor could the camera lens. The window whirred back up, the bulky man said nothing, and the blue estate car sped off, a slight squeaky wheel spin acknowledging the haste.

The blond man turned slightly towards the blinking of the red brake lights as the blue estate car paused slightly. Another squeak of impatience as the engine roared a speedy departure. He waved a brown envelope in the air with his right hand.

"Cheers, Bob!" he shouted as he turned back towards the open Goods Inwards door. "You fucking prick," he whispered quietly, so Bob couldn't hear him, 100 yards down the road.

Bludd clicked back the small screen into the body of the camera and made his way back to the eight-foot wall. The stones in the wall of the bridge were all pointed with mortar, no footholes to be found. The pebble-dashed walls of the warehouse would offer no assistance in his retreat to his bike. He was stuck on the embankment. The only thing he had not fully considered whilst surveying the area a few hours earlier, was how to get out again. He went to the bottom of the embankment and under the bridge, its width only that of a road and two pavements. On the other side, the embankment was a whole lot steeper. The dry stone wall at its crest would be easy to scale over, because it had plenty of hand and footholes. Getting to it was another matter. He looked across the rail track to the north, the embankment on the other side much more manageable. Taking a quick look right and left, east and west, he quickly moved to the other side of the track and up the grassy hill. Another dry stone wall and plenty of opportune holes allowed for an easy climb over.

He was on a similar grassy mound on the other side. A row of saplings, surrounded by a mesh protection and aided in its bid to grow straight by a supportive square stick, had been planted along the full length of the wall. Leylandii, Bludd guessed. They could grow to six metres or about 20 feet, maybe higher, offering a permanent screen, keeping out prying eyes. They were about three feet tall at that moment and Bludd sidestepped in between two and jogged down to the concrete of the car park. He found himself at the corner of the smaller building, the size of a semi-detached house, which was adjacent to the road running from the bridge, diagonally opposite Preston Dies Supplies Ltd. He wandered round to the front, keeping his right hand against the wall as a guide in the darkness, which was growing blacker by the minute. The front of the building was well lit and he moved across past the front door and into the main car parking area, just short of the main building. A black people carrier vehicle pulled up sharply in front of the extended brick façade and a man with a long, full black beard and wearing a white tunic got out of the driver's door, leaving it open as he moved quickly round the rear of the vehicle, reappearing on the nearside, right outside the building's reception door. He slid back the side door of the vehicle, Bludd recognised it as a Renault, the Espace model he thought, and leaned inside. Bludd moved forwards, a little closer, sensing that something erroneous was about to take place. The man leant backwards and pulled back with a mighty jerk, pulling with him a girl, a woman, in a full black traditional outfit. All black, with a slit in the head dress, only her eyes showing, the whites of them bright, and their pupils enlarged with fear. Bludd thought the outfit was called a niqab. He had seen it written somewhere. It looked like a jet black letter box. The man held the woman in the niqab by her right shoulder as he slid the side door shut angrily. He threw her forward, towards the door and then stepped to her left hand side, pushing the door open with his left hand, his right placed firmly in the middle of her back and a stern shove moved her forward in through the open door. The man shouted instructions at her in a language that Bludd did not understand, maybe Punjabi or Urdu, he thought. There was a definite anger in his voice and he was waving and pointing, his finger a threat to any non-compliance.

Bludd casually walked over the concrete car park towards the main gate, situated about 40 yards north of the centre of building, all the time staring at the bearded man, hoping he would force him to have that being watched feeling, and turn in his direction. The man did not turn to Bludd, but he moved to his left and round the back of the vehicle, jumping into the driver's seat and slamming the door behind him. He had left the engine running and now floored the accelerator and turned a quick right turn towards the gate. Bludd, rather than panicking at the oncoming vehicle, stepped to his left and blocked the exit for the people carrier. The vehicle came to an abrupt halt a yard from Bludd's statuesque figure. His six foot four frame square on, was clad all in black. His 230 pounds of toned flesh and strong bones was enough to stop a people carrier in its tracks. Bludd stood, arms folded across his chest, his eyes looking straight forward, staring at the driver's side of the screen, unable to see the bearded man through the tinted security glass, blacked out to match the bodywork. The engine revved and the vehicle jerked forwards a few inches, Bludd did not move. The engine revved again, the driver stepping on and off the gas, sounding more threatening, becoming more angry. He jerked forward again. Bludd did not move. The horn sounded and the engine revved again. Bludd did not move. The engine idled. No movement from within, no movement from Bludd. He continued to stare at the blank black window, feeling the unease of the driver. He pointed at his right eye and then with the same index finger, to the position of the driver, a promise that he would be watching. He stepped to the side, his left arm sweeping out and offering an opportunity for the car to leave, an opportunity that was taken immediately and at speed, driving straight out onto the road, without a pause, sweeping to the left and straightening up wildly, the engine screaming at the gearbox to keep up with it. The people carrier headed off straight past the front row of terraced houses and disappeared into the distance, no brake lights showing until it hit a junction a half mile further on. It turned right without indication.

Bludd turned and looked at the college, checking it from left to right and top to bottom, blinking quickly and keeping a mental image of the whole of its frontage. Nothing seemed to be going on inside. Only the reception had a light glowing inside and that seemed dim in the vastness of the building. He turned and exited the car park, turning left, then left again and over the bridge. As he walked over the rail track, he looked left and could see that the third floor of the building on its west side was lit from the middle to the back. No other lights were on to the whole of that side, just a row spanning six windows, one classroom worth, Bludd pondered. He could see three veiled heads at three of the windows and then a gap and then two without veils, but with a different kind of head adornment, the type that Asian males sometimes wore. He couldn't remember the name.

He passed over the bridge putting the camera back into the black box, and mounted his bike, sitting astride the black leather seat and placed the helmet on the top of his head, and as he pushed it down into place, he noticed a blond, very tired-looking, man pass him by, a quizzical look on his face as he stared at the black-clad man on the motorbike.

* * *

In Maple, Cheshire, Jonathon Durie had waved off the last of the day shift an hour earlier, right on time, as usual on a Friday and wished the staff a good weekend. Nothing unusual, nothing out of the ordinary.

He was responsible for the factory, and so when the workers went home, they thought that Durie would check the doors were secure, turn out the lights and lock the front door, before returning the short walk home. Difficult as it was for Durie with his bad leg, it was still a very short walk home across the road and bridle path.

What the day shift thought would happen, every night, did not happen, on any night. Durie stayed in the factory for another half an hour, waiting for the arrival of the two foremen. The two brothers would look after the factories and ensure production ran smoothly overnight, just as they had for the last five years. Durie waited for them so he could hand over the production sheets showing the jobs for that night and their order of priority and then he would retire to his house, across the way just 60 yards. He allowed the brothers to decide which one ran which factory, to fight over the nicer of the two jobs and sometimes they would literally do that. Fighting was in their nature, their culture.

Durie walked across the front of the building, the reception area still lit up brightly by the strip lights inside. He whistled a tune made up entirely in his own mind, happy with his lot as walked the 40 yards to the end corner of the factory. Happy with his job, his little sideline earner that his boss had complete knowledge of, his house, a lovely little cottage in tranquil countryside surroundings. He was especially happy with the opportunities that his friendship with Judge had presented over the years. Without Judge he would not have the job, the sideline, the house. Without Judge he could not fulfil his urges, his desires. Without Judge he would not be the man he was, he would be a stammering cripple, struggling with his confidence, struggling to get a job, to hold it down, struggling to survive.

He carried on past the end of the building and across the small car park in the north east corner of the estate, where all the cars were gone from the day shift. He wandered into the far right hand corner and up the vehicle ramp to the large wooden gate, spanning across the 12-foot wide entrance. The gate was manually operated, secured with a padlock attached to the wall to the left, the gate opening to the right and resting against the right hand wall running westerly, in line with the long side of the smaller of the two main buildings within the compound. He unlocked the padlock and opened the gate and attached it to a hook hasp on the brick wall. Durie walked awkwardly the short distance, just a little more than the length of a seven tonne truck, to the building's main door and pulled at the handle, easing the unlocked concertina entrance to his right until it could go no further. It was unlocked because there was nothing in this building that was worth anything to anybody. Nothing, except sentimental, best friends. The smell from inside the building made Durie wretch, he covered his face with his right hand and flicked the light switch on the wall, by the open door, with his crooked left. He turned and fled the macabre scene behind him. The night shift, the unlucky night shift, would be busy tonight, he thought.

Durie unhooked the gate from the hasp and shut the wooden gate back into its closed position. He took three steps to his left and unbolted the small pedestrian gate to allow the night shift crew access, leaving it open and stepping outside, turning right and locking the gate back up with the padlock. No deliveries tonight.

The padlock rattled against wood and wall as Durie dropped it out of his crooked hand and he whistled his way back down the yard to the right hand, long side of the main building, security lights flooding the concrete in front of him as he broke their radar. There were two pedestrian access doors on this long side and a large roller shutter door that sat in between them, goods inwards and goods outwards, all through the same opening. The other door was purely an emergency access door, a fire exit, and escape route. Durie jangled his keys in an effort to enhance his melodic whistling with the sound. He stopped whistling and jangling as he approached the door, focussing on the set of keys, choosing the correct mortice lock option and gliding it straight into the hole, turning it to the left in one swift movement and opening the door outwards into the yard. He entered the building and tapped the 12 light switches on the wall to his right, one at a time, a downward movement. The factory lit up, section by section, a dozen long strip lights, choosing their own order of arousal, not content with the order of Durie's choice. Durie surveyed the factory, which was quiet and cool. The lights were bright against the darkness beyond the glass roof above them. He was confident that the factory had been left in good order by the day shift management. They were a good set of workers, diligent, conscientious and loyal. A loyalty that would not be repaid in the coming days. He smiled to himself, no trace of sympathy to the families that would be affected, just a smile of achievement. His life was happy and full, but within days he hoped the next chapter would begin. A new, improved, tropical version would begin, where he and Judge would be like kings and he would have his choice of any number of willing, or not so willing slaves. He turned and headed back out into the yard and made his way back to his office, to wait for the night shift foremen to arrive. The Lupescu brothers, Andrei and Marius could take it from here.

* * *

Bludd decided he would return home after another look at the Islamic college, after another look at the room he had seen lit up earlier. There was something not quite right about the place; he could feel it, his instinct tapping him on the head and telling him to check it out.

He left his bike in the car park and headed back for the bridge, standing atop of its stone wall sides to gain a better view and perhaps a better perspective.

The building was illuminated from each corner, lights pointed to the centre, where a large red dome spanned a large area of the roof, to its right the large spire with the golden-yellow orb top. He hadn't seen the red dome at first glance, earlier that night from the view from the rear of the building. The elevated view and the proud illumination made it stand out like a beacon.

The room on the third floor was still being used, still alight. The three veiled heads to the front, the two male heads to the back. There were more heads there now, more veils and more males. Bludd could see them swaying back and forth, giving him a momentary glimpse. He wondered if the girl, or woman, he had seen being forced through the front door was there. He guessed she must be. He looked to the front of the room, the classroom? A big Muslim man stood there, resplendent in white tunic and headgear. His beard was long and bushy, black with badger like grey streaks running its entire length. He looked dominant as he stood over the figures in their chairs, round faced and powerful. He looked to be shouting orders, his hands waving manically, fists clenched and beating downwards. He pointed a single finger and one of the veiled female heads rose from its low position below him, a tiny figure, even when she stood she looked a foot and a half smaller than the pointing man. She moved slowly to the front of the room. It was hard to tell, but Bludd thought the other veiled heads seemed to be looking downwards, while the males at the back of the class did not move. They stared intently and Bludd sensed eagerness in their distant smiles.

Bludd shuffled to his left, trying to get a straight-on view into the first window. The big man stood arms folded, his left hand momentarily raised as he ran his fingers down through his beard, contemplating the situation. The veiled head was still just that to Bludd, the rest of the diminutive figure tiny below the frame of the window. The woman, or girl, stood directly in front of the huge man, head down. This time, it was clear. The man moved his arms, hanging them on his hips and then without warning hit out hard with his right fist, straight into the chest, Bludd presumed, of the female in front of him. Her head disappeared in an instant, Bludd losing sight of her behind the wall separating the windows. The big man leant forwards and Bludd saw him pull the limp, veiled female to her feet by the material covering her chest, her feet dangling above the floor. He threw her to his left, towards a door Bludd could now see in the far corner. Bludd lost sight of her again as she fell to the floor. The huge man in the white tunic turned towards the door, his arm punching the air back and forth, like a piston. The other veiled heads in the room still looked downwards, the males at the back of the room standing now and laughing, cheering, arms piston-like as well.

Bludd had seen enough. If the big man in the white tunic wanted to pick on someone, he could pick on someone his own size. He jumped off the wall and headed north over the bridge, a rage building in him as he started to sprint towards the gated entrance. He looked to his right as he sped along the road and saw the black Renault Espace as it screeched to a halt in front of the reception door. The front passenger door opened, not the side door this time and a black-veiled head and gowned body staggered from door to door and got in the vehicle, closing the door slowly behind as the Espace started away before it was shut.

Bludd sprinted back to his bike, jumping into the saddle, turning the key and kick starting the engine almost in one movement, slamming the helmet onto his head with more force than it needed and neglecting the strap under his chin. He had no idea which way the Renault would be heading, but the obvious thing in Bludd's mind was to chase in the direction he had seen it head earlier, past the houses on the right and right at the junction ahead. He was wrong. As he turned out of the car park and went right, the Espace was turning left and passed him as he approached the building of Preston Die Supplies Ltd.

Bludd skidded to a halt, dug his right heel into the tarmac surface and twisted the handlebars to their extreme right, spinning the throttle as far as his wrist could allow, his front wheel leaving the ground and he narrowly missed the kerb as it found the road surface again, his left leg leaving the bike as he struggled to steady his balance. The Renault people carrier headed straight down the hill that Bludd had made his journey into that point four hours earlier and took the sharp right turn at the foot of the hill, Bludd following 100 yards behind, struggling to keep up with the speed of the Espace. He screwed the throttle forwards and pulled the clutch back, more quickly than he would normally, and kicked the gear pedal upwards, flicking the throttle back down in a millisecond movement, full speed in pursuit. The Espace was still speeding away in the distance, rising up a hill as the road bridged the canal, Bludd still tracking behind, trying to recall the road ahead of him, but in reverse in his memory. A junction was up ahead, maybe 200 yards, he thought, hopefully traffic running across it would slow the Renault down.

Bludd sprinted the bridge and both wheels left the ground.

He hoped, momentarily, that there wasn't too much traffic at the junction as he would be running straight into the back of it, but luckily, 100 yards ahead, the people carrier was being held up by a long, slow stream of traffic. It was Bludd's chance to make up the ground on it. As he approached, a kindly driver allowed the Espace to move out and Bludd kept his speed up, longer than he should have done, and took the same advantage and having to skid to a halt, he narrowly missed the back of his target. The people carrier lurched forwards in the slow traffic and took a tentative turn to the right, and then the driver floored the accelerator and sped off down the wrong side of the road, past the stationary traffic for 150 yards, before taking the first right turn into a housing estate. Bludd followed without hesitation, praying that the driver had a clear view of what might be coming and not taking any unnecessary risk. He wasn't. Bludd turned the right turn, kicking the gears down low, in case he needed to pick up speed quickly. He didn't. The Espace was taking an immediate left turn into a road full of semi-detached houses, the brake lights glowing bright red as it pulled to a halt at the kerbside. The passenger door opened slowly as Bludd pulled up a short, 15 yards distance behind, lights off, an invisible black silhouette to the Renault driver.

The veiled woman got out and looked back through the open door, taking a moment's abuse from the driver, his voice loud enough for Bludd to hear through his padded helmet. She closed the door politely, waiting obediently at the kerbside as the window wound down and more harsh sounding words of instruction were bellowed at her. The Espace window closed up and the driver indicated right, Bludd noted it as the first time he had used the indicator on this short journey, and it pulled away, slowly and calmly. Job done.

The girl turned 180 degrees and headed up the drive, a

combination of grass and two lines of flags, not concreted in place, uneven and out of square. The front garden was overgrown with grass and weeds. A small two-foot picket fence of slatted wood, mostly rotten through neglect, surrounded it. She went straight into the unlocked panelled front door and closed it quickly behind her, right arm clenched across her chest.

Bludd sat and watched from a short distance, astride his bike, his helmet now sat on the petrol tank of the Yamaha. A small light came on above the front door and another at the window to the side of the house to the first floor, where he saw a shadowy figure pass under the lower light and a new illumination appeared in the window above the front door. Bludd guessed that the woman had gone straight upstairs and into a bedroom, which was probably the box room as they are usually found above the door front and opposite the landing at the top of the stairs. All the windows were adorned with their own individual net curtains, all of the same floral bordered design, stopping those outside from seeing inside, allowing those inside to see outside. A roller blind came down behind the net, definitely no outsiders would look in now, total blackout. A few minutes went by and the dimmed light of the bedroom, behind the net and blind went out. Bludd watched the light alter at the foot of the stairs, behind the front door, as a figure went by. A new flicker of light in the front room, same nets across a wide bay window, a dull silhouette behind them was all that could be seen of a figure that walked across. Bludd made out bright-coloured clothes, a yellow top and blue pants. The main curtains were drawn left to right and then right to left, no gap in the middle. Total blackout again.

Bludd was calm now, and intrigued. It seemed that only one person was in and that was the veiled girl, alone and possibly hurt, definitely in some discomfort from the way she held herself. It was not in his nature to walk away, so he dismounted the bike and walked slowly up to the front door. It was wooden and weathered, in need of a lick of paint, or varnish, or replacement. There was no knocker or bell, so Bludd rattled the letter box. No answer. He rattled it again. Still no answer. He thought about leaving, but he had seen her go in and go upstairs, and come down, pull the curtains together, but not leave. She had definitely not left. He rattled the brass letterbox again, determined to get a response. The dim light above the window got a little brighter as it was joined by the extra light from the front room, as the internal door was opened in between. The front door opened slowly and on a chain, ajar about four inches. A young girl was behind the gap, pretty with long curly hair, naturally black but with reddy brown streaks. Her top was an off the shoulder tee-shirt and she wore dark navy jeans, skin tight against the left leg that could be seen. There was a stern, but not hostile, look on her face. Bludd asked if the owner of the house was in. No response was all he got back.

"Are you alone?" he continued. "Only, I was just up at the college and saw a girl, maybe a woman, being pushed around. She was dropped off here and I just wanted to make sure she is OK." He said this with some confidence that this was the same girl he had seen.

No response.

"Look. I didn't like what I saw, that's all. No matter who you are, how old you are, whatever your religion is, you should not be pushed around like that or forced into things you don't want to do." He spoke directly to her, but as if she was in the third person.

"I'm OK," the girl responded mildly with a glimmer of a smile, a smile that said thanks. Bludd noted how white her teeth looked as a contrast against her dark and smooth skin. He estimated that she was about 19. She was very pretty.

"What's your name?" he asked.

"Yasmeena. Yasmeena Khan. Why, who are you? What does it matter to you?"

"Just somebody that doesn't like wrongs being done, that's all. If you are in some kind of trouble, maybe I can help you. Who are those men that were shoving you around? You looked hurt."

She paused and took in a deep breath. Bludd noticed her face wince and she held her left side.

"They've hurt you, haven't they?" He carried on.

"No. It's no problem. Honestly. I just need to rest."

"Who owns the black Renault?" Bludd continued.

"It's my uncle. It's fine; he just has my best interests at heart."

"Funny way of showing it, if you ask me. Do your parents know how he treats you?" Bludd continued the inquisition.

Another pause, no smile, no wince.

"I don't have any parents here. They are in Pakistan, they went back there. Left me in the house. My uncle looks out for me, makes sure I go to the mosque and to college. Now if you don't mind, I have probably said too much. I don't even know who you are."

It was not a question and she started to close the door as she said it. Bludd shoved his foot in the gap before it could close.

"Look, my name is Sebastian Bludd. I am an investigator. I was working up near the college and saw stuff I didn't like. It's really no skin off my nose how you are being treated, if you are happy to take it, that is up to you.. You seem like a nice girl, switched on and all that. Why would you want to be pushed around, forced to do things, hit in the stomach and probably have a broken rib or two?"

The comment was loaded and given with a nod of the head aimed at the girl's left side.

No response.

Bludd continued, "Please, take my card. If you need any help, with anything. Just call me if you need help. No strings attached." He put his right hand to his back pocket, pulled out his wallet and flicked to the middle section and pulled out a white business card, which was a little dog-eared.

The girl lowered her right hand from her left-hand side and bent her wrist back around the door, taking the card off Bludd in between her middle fingers. She smiled another smile that said thanks and closed the door.

8

Temptation

Judge had been fortunate, in his own mind, that he had been able to have breakfast and lunch alone, with a full morning to relax in between, alone in his hotel.

Kulap had arrived, on time as far as Judge was concerned, but later than Kulap had wanted. Kulap had wanted to get Judge to the villa as early as possible, to get there before the others and to have a tour around the place before anybody else arrived. He could have a private meeting with the Erichsons, hopefully conclude some of his business and then enjoy the day. Maybe choose to stay over and sample the atmosphere, hopefully if his offer was accepted, it could be an atmosphere he could get used to over many years to come.

They had been on the road for almost two hours, almost half of that was due to traffic in Bangkok. They had travelled west, around a city and through a few large towns, over a major river and headed south, following the coast road. Kulap had been his usual self, babbling inanely most of the way, most of it unheard by Judge as he had learned to switch off and think about other things. Things that were happening back home, that he had no control over while he was in Thailand. He was trusting his deputy to cover those bases and keep the ships steady. Once he was back there, hopefully, he could close all the loopholes, tie up all the loose ends and leave it all behind. The only thing he could not be certain of, if everything went to plan, was how his wife, Annabelle, would take it. It was going to be one hell of a shock. He resolved to ring Durie as soon as he knew how today had gone.

The coast road offered breathtaking views and the surroundings were beautiful green countryside, just like he and his wife enjoyed at home. Judge was sure he could persuade his wife that this was some kind of paradise and that the children would find it amazing, especially in this particular villa, if it was as good as it looked in the photographs and whether he could believe anything Kulap told him. The only fly in the ointment he could perceive was the fact that he had told Durie that he was welcome to join them, to live with them. That was going to take some understanding from his wife.

The asphalt road came to an end and Judge looked at Kulap with an apprehensive eye as they continued onto a single lane dirt track. The greenery around them was suddenly getting thicker and the road was dusty. Judge felt claustrophobic for a half mile or so. Suddenly, the thick foliage around them disappeared to their left and opened out to a fantastic view over the Gulf of Thailand. Judge smiled and Kulap looked at him, beaming with pride at a good start to this part of his contract. "It gets better," he proclaimed.

The road and the coastline swung around to the right and the view became totally out to sea, the city over the other side of the estuary now behind them over their left shoulders. Another mile of dirt track and then Kulap allowed himself another smile as they approached the high walls and the elaborate iron gates. Judge was equally pleased, but restrained himself from a smile; keeping Kulap on his toes the aim.

Kulap slowed the car ten yards short of the gate. An intercom was mounted on a steel stand and hidden by a bush that had wrapped itself around it. Kulap pushed the button, ignoring the keypad below it. He said nothing, just looked straight ahead and gave his usual over-the-top wave, an exaggerated statement of his arrival. The gates opened, parting at their centre and retreating backwards. Kulap drove on gently, crossing the line of dirt track and then onto tiled concrete, imprinted with a mottled effect and coloured terracotta, with subtle hints of ochre yellow in uneven shapes scattered across the surface. The driveway rose up, a curved right hand sweep, lined by whitewashed concrete walls to each side, above the walls planted slopes, full of lotus flowers and wild orchids, many specific to Thailand. Bright fuchsia, lime green, violet, white and black, all mingling together, to provide a tropical mass of colour. A large pink shower tree at the top of the slope almost masked the villa beyond.

Kulap swung his convertible BMW, white to reflect the sun, around a sharp right turn as the driveway straightened out and parked in the only space available in a small car park directly behind the pink-flowered tree and 30 yards from the white wall of the villa.

Judge and Kulap got out of the BMW and Kulap led the way around a flagged path that arched around the car park and around the other cars parked there. All of them were prestige marques: Mercedes, Lexus, Porsche and Jaguar. The path ran to the end of the white wall of the villa and to another ornate gate, six feet high, pedestrian width, this time with a sliding bolt that was fixed into an equally high wall, whitewashed and disappearing gradually down a long, easy slope heading for the ocean.

Kulap unfastened the bolt and opened the gate in towards the side wall of the white villa. A short paved path, 12 yards long led to the first of 30 steps that turned right at the 20th, the villa going from a single-storey building in the car park, to two storeys to the rear. As he turned the corner at the twentieth step, Judge stopped. He could see why Kulap had been so excited about the place. It was perfect, just as he had instructed Kulap to find. The angle of the stairs followed the natural slope of the landscape and the tropical flowers continued to bloom along the border, vivid green lawns on their far side cascading down the slope and down to a path, extending out of the patio area at the bottom of the steps, around a swimming pool, trapezium-shaped, a diving board at the end nearest the house, steps to the other end, the shallow end. Another path branched out behind the steps to the pool, a small separate building, the same size as a double garage, the same as Judge had at home. Some kind of shed, Judge thought. It was a holding room for the loungers and parasols that were littered around the pool and on the patio. Behind the building, high Cassia fistula trees ran the whole perimeter of the gardens, save for a small gap, which had another path running to it and through it, in a southerly direction, running away from the pool.

In his excitement at the surroundings and his pleasure at the thought of bringing his family here, Judge had almost not seen the people milling around the pool and patio area. Kulap had continued down the steps and was shaking hands with a tall, blond, well-tanned man in white Speedo swimming trunks, his dark brown skin a stark contrast to the white material. Judge took another sweeping look at the garden. There were groups of people. At the side of the building near the shallow end of the pool, a small group of children were playing in a small area, with a play sandpit, toys littered around, the group growing in number as two more appeared from behind the building. On the far side of the pool, four men, all oriental looking, maybe Thai, maybe not. Judge sometimes couldn't tell one nationality from the other. The nearside had two people under a parasol, though Judge could only see the back of one of them and the legs of the other, the one farthest away hidden by the nearer man and their parasol. A third man was sleeping on a lounger nearer to the poolside with no parasol to cover him. Judge realised that he was naked.

Judge heard Kulap beckon him down the steps and he duly followed the annoying voice downwards, but unable to take his eyes off the naked man. "This is Mr Erichson. Mr Erichson, this is Mr Jeremy Judge." Kulap announced.

Judge turned to face the tall, blond man, red faced and embarrassed at his lingering stare to the left. "No need to be embarrassed Mr Judge. Our good friend over there, Mr Jansen, likes to, as you say, let it all hang out. Pleased to meet you by the way. Would you like a drink?"

Judge nodded, still too embarrassed to speak. Erichson handed him a beer from a refrigerator next to him on his left, outside the patio doors leading into the villa.

"Please, Mr Judge, feel free to have a wander around our beautiful home. We hope you like it. It has served us well, but sadly, it is now time to move on. Perhaps, if you do like it, we can talk business later and come to some agreement?"

Judge just nodded. He was mesmerised by the place. He turned away from Erichson and Kulap, still not having uttered a word. Kulap took advantage and, holding the elbow of Erichson, he leaned over and helped himself to a beer and pointed inside. "Perhaps I can start Mr Judge's negotiations for him?" he suggested. Judge heard him, but could not be bothered to interrupt and stop Kulap from overstepping his brief. He had done a good job so far and Judge wanted a look around. Kulap had said that there was more to the place than met the eye and Judge didn't doubt it. But he wanted to look around alone, to settle his own intrigue as much as possible, and besides, whatever deal Kulap struck, he was sure to be able to knock the value down some.

He took a few steps forward, leaving the patio area and stopping on the path at the poolside. The pool looked cool and inviting. Judge was relieved that today's weather was warm and dry. At this time of the year it could be so different, the wet season having started weeks earlier. Today could be dry and warm, tomorrow wet. Very wet. But still humid. He hoped that when Annabelle and the children arrived, that the weather was with him, helping him convince them all that the move was the right thing for all of them.

Judge moved around the pool, trying not to look at the naked man but intrigued by his size, jealous at the comparison with himself. The naked man, Jansen, did not move, although Judge felt sure he must have been aware of his gaze. The two other men were watching Judge and he gave them a slight nod of acknowledgement, ashamed, again, that he had been caught looking at the naked man.

Judge continued around the pool and headed towards the separate building near the play area. There were five children in all. Judge tried to work out their ages. It was difficult to calculate with Thai children as 10-year-olds could look like they were seven or eight, seven or eight-year-olds could, in turn, be passed off for five or six-year-olds. He guessed they were between eight and 10, a mixture of boys and girls, again sometimes difficult to work out who was what. He moved up the shallow steps to the building. A wooden door to its right-hand side, nearest the play area, was ajar. Some of the children looked at him, wary, nervous. The others ignored him, or pretended they hadn't seen him. They carried on playing in the sand.

Judge opened the door wide, allowing light into the building. He was right and wrong. There were a number of loungers, chairs and parasols propped against the wall opposite the door. Counting those he had already seen outside, he estimated enough seating for at least 30 people. Today's gathering was small compared to the possibilities. At the far end of the building there was a more adult play area. Three sofas were set out in a U-shape, one with the back to Judge, one on each side wall. A pool table sat in the centre of the sofas. A large flat screen television was on the wall at the far end of the building; to each side of it were two fruit machines and other arcade games; four in all. The two ends of the room were separated by a small bar, three, high, bar stools in front, the wall behind mirrored, and above the mirror, a variety of optics, all imported, expensive brands. Judge entered the building and wandered around slowly. The room was dimly lit by two windows to the front of the building, the sun not quite at the right angle to light the room fully, but enough to show dust particles floating around the space. Judge rolled a ball across the pool table and walked across to the arcade games. They were both switched off, but the artwork on the surround suggested that both dated from the early 1980s. This told Judge that they were to entertain people of a certain age, people who would have been in their early teens when these games were brought out. People of his age.

He left the building. Two of the children were being led to the main building by a woman. She was wearing a red bikini top and white canvas shorts and sandals. Judge guessed it was Mrs Erichson. The other three children continued to play, paying no attention to Judge, or that two of their group had left the area. Judge turned left and went to look behind the building. There was an extension to the play area. Two swings, a see-saw, a wooden horse on a heavy duty spring, capable of rocking in all directions, all backed by the line of Cassia fistula trees. Judge followed the line of trees around the back of the building, walking along the top of the landscaped lawn that they fringed, looking for the gap that he had seen earlier, where the path had run up from the poolside. The paved path ended as it arrived at the trees. A narrow gap of about four feet had been manufactured into the branches and at seven feet high the branches started to meet again. The path to the other side was not paved, it was just a dusty, foot-beaten line through the shrubs, no steps, just following the slope of the hillside.

Judge stopped at the top to get his bearings. The road into the villa had swept round to the right, a long arc following the plantation, sea to the left and sloping gardens to the right, heavy with small trees and bushes, the orchids and bright colours of the lotus flowers contrasting against the green shades of the shrubbery. Judge had not seen any such path on his way in, nor, therefore, had he seen any landmark that one could lead to. He followed the sloping, dusty path, down the slope, curving to the right, heading for the sea, or so it appeared. It was a 100-yards walk, quite a lot for a man of Judge's size in this heat and on this terrain, and then he could see what the path led to. Another smile formed as he realised that Kulap really had found a gem of a place, exactly to what he had asked for, even better than he had expected. He stopped, took a handkerchief from his trouser pocket and mopped his brow, the humidity of the day and the unusual exercise making him start to sweat. His shirt showed droplets under his arms and down the centre of his chest. He took a deep breath and continued, the slope now falling away to his left a little more steeply, but the path running along flat. Judge reached a small, single-storey building and stopped again for breath. The dusty path had stopped and a paved area sat to the front of a small, white building, a single chair pushed underneath a table, parasol folded away and under a plastic cover in its centre. To the left of the table was a small swimming pool, approximately 10 feet wide by 20 feet long, no path around, just a single line of small tiles, the same terracotta colour as the patio, and the road up from the main gate. There had been no evidence of the pool or the building on the way up the road to the villa, but it was a welcome surprise. *This could be ideal for Durie*, he thought. Away from the main house, away from Annabelle and the kids, his own little miniature villa in paradise. Judge crouched down at the pool's edge; he could just see that if you were in the pool, resting against the far edge, where the single tiles surrounded it, you would be level with the horizon, looking out to sea, but with nothing to see as far as the eye could take you. He turned around to the building. A large window fronted it, allowing maximum light to break into the rooms beyond. Judge tried the door, almost central in the front wall. It was locked. He moved a step to his left and cupped his hands over his eyes to form a barrier from the light and allow him to see inside. A small living area was to the fore, two sofas, one to the left hand wall, the other sat in front of a white wall, not brick and about three to four feet high, above it cabinets attached to the ceiling. There was a kitchenette, a door to its left-hand side, in the far corner of the building, the back door and fire exit. The right side of the room had a single door to the centre. Judge guessed that this was a bedroom and en-suite. He felt the heat from the sun cool on the back of his neck and looked up at the sky. A dark, black cloud was drifting in swiftly from the south, laden with heavy rain and speeding towards him. Judge had already seen enough to satisfy him and turned and headed back towards the main house, jogging as fast as his short, stocky legs could run.

He reached the gap in the trees, out of breath again, leaning forward, hands on knees, as the shadow of the cloud overtook him and he felt the beat of the raindrops flicking the back of his neck and the top of his head. He stood under the trees, contemplating staying there, seeing out the storm under the cover of leaves, his heart racing. The rain in front of him, between him and the house, was hammering down onto the grass and the patio, into the pool like a hail of bullets. The children and the group of men, the two men, and Jansen, were nowhere to be seen. The sky was blacker than before, the sun had given way to the cloud, only a few stray beams flickering through and offering any defence to the darkness. The rain soaked through the trees' leaves and Judge's cotton shirt had changed to a new and darker shade, hiding the patches of sweat that had formed all over it. He made a run for it and took a few slippery strides to the bottom of the path, meeting the patio and stumbling as he found the tiles slippier than those of the path, no run off, just a flat surface harbouring small pools of water. He looked over to the patio doors. They were closed. Kulap and Erichson stood behind, peering out at the soaking wet, fat man struggling in their direction. Judge wasn't sure they weren't laughing, pointing and jeering at his misfortune, or his flabby frame clear to see under his clothes that were pressed hard against his skin. The doors opened, right-hand sliding to its left, Judge waded in. Nobody was laughing.

"Sorry for the change in the weather, Mr Judge," Erichson remarked. "This season is open to such turnaround. It can be beautiful one moment and like this the next. It can last ten minutes, or it could last a week. My prediction is that this will be a short one. You get used to it, become able to forecast without the need to look on the web, or watch TV. I hope it doesn't put you off. Come, let me find you a towel, you can have a look round the inside. I hope the outside met with your liking."

Erichson crossed an area of tiled floor, shiny black tiles with no furniture on it and around 10 feet square, leading to the kitchen. He reached around the workbench and slid open a drawer, pulling a small towel upwards and closing the drawer with his free hand. He strolled back to Judge and handed him the towel. Judge thanked him and dried his face and the back of his neck of the rain and sweat. He motioned to hand it back to his host, but Erichson chose to ignore him and turned away.

"As you can see, Mr Judge, the villa is not huge, but there are three bedrooms, all double sized, two bathrooms, one en-suite, the other in between the two other bedrooms. Do you have children, Mr Judge?"

"Yes, I have two, one of each. Twins actually," Judge replied.

"Really?" Erichson replied, surprised. "They will love it here."

Judge chose not to reply. He wanted to keep his cards close to his chest and not seem too interested. He scanned the area of the ground floor. The kitchen was to his left. It was very modern, unlike the farmhouse style he had at home. It was full of bright white doors and drawers, pristine clean and shiny. The worktops he could see on the far wall were black marble or granite and had a sparkly blue effect glistening in the down lights. There was an electric hob, an upright wall oven, a bit high for him, but probably perfect for Annabelle he noted. There was an abundance of drawers and cupboards, again ideal for Annabelle, and the modern bright-red handles matched the tiles above the worktop and below the cupboards. In front of him was the living area, furniture facing away from him and towards the far wall. The theme ran through from the kitchen, white walls all around, set over a black, shiny tiled floor, white leather sofas forming a U-shape and surrounding a fake chimney breast that housed a huge television attached to the wall and above what Judge presumed to be some kind of electric convector fire. The glowing flames were fake and televisual.

Judge's eyes drifted right. There were two identical sideboards, white again, and almost certainly made bespoke to match the kitchen cupboards. They were white and shiny and hovering above the floor, with no legs supporting them. Judge couldn't help but think that this was all a bit too clinical for him, but especially for Annabelle. The red theme of the kitchen was continued through the lounge with accessories in the form of a red rug in front of the fake hearth, red vases and glassware on the sideboards and the occasional tables that were in between the sofas. Pictures adorning the walls were modern, canvas with no frames and made up of vertical and horizontal lines and different sized square or rectangular shapes, all crimson, scarlet and pinks.

Judge had almost failed to see that Mr Jansen was in the living room, sat with his back in to the centre of the middle sofa, the one facing the television, only his curly sandy hair and tanned shoulders visible. Judge doubled back his look and realised that Jansen had a child to either side of him, a third sat alone on the right hand sofa, all of them staring at the television. Judge made the assumption that Jansen was still naked and another pang of envy jolted his thoughts. Whilst he and Jansen may have had some similarities in their sexual deviations, Judge was never going to be in a position where he would have the confidence of Jansen. His body was a source of embarrassment to him. He was short and overweight, obese even. Jansen was tall and slender, muscular even. Jansen had a penis that Judge suspected was larger when flaccid than most men were when they were erect. Judge had a penis that was the size and look of an acorn. It had been a constant worry to him when he was younger and the teasing he received at school from the other boarders had made him angry and shy and ashamed. He was certainly never going to sit naked in public, like Jansen. In fact, he only undertook any sexual acts in complete privacy, whether it was at home with his wife, which was rare and some long time ago, or if he was acting out one of his deviant fantasies, usually whilst away from home on business. If anybody else was to see him, they would have to be very close and like-minded friends, or it would be on film and he would edit out any evidence of his problem.

Judge noted that the children all seemed happy as they laughed out loud and Jansen was joining them, his laugh a deep baritone against the high pitch of the children. Judge looked at the television, a cartoon mouse pursued by a cartoon cat, in turn pursued by a cartoon bulldog. *Tom and Jerry* was universal slapstick comedy. Judge smiled. His kids, Alfie and Molly, loved *Tom and Jerry*.

Judge turned his thoughts back to the rest of the villa. The sideboards were set on the wall, above the floor and with a modern art picture above each of them. Above the pictures a balcony ran almost the whole length of the long wall and Judge guessed that ran parallel to, and level with, the car park and the top of the outside steps. To the left-hand end of the balcony, a door faced the walkway, with a further three doors facing Judge. The balcony was reached by a set of stairs to Judge's right. Kulap and Erichson were engaged in discussion at the bottom of them. Erichson, his back to the foot of the stairs, caught Judge's eye and beckoned him over with his right hand, his left hand resting at arm's length against the frame of a door situated a foot away from the bottom of the steps. Judge ambled over and Kulap, standing opposite Erichson, opened the door, right to left. Erichson made a sweep with his right hand as if to usher Judge into the room. Judge stood at the door. The room was small with plain white walls, again. Mrs Erichson sat in a large and comfortable looking leather chair in front of a simple desk, housing a laptop and mouse. To Judge's right, and facing Mrs Erichson, was a wall of television screens; security monitors with black and white, silent pictures. There was a bank of nine screens, three by three. The bottom line of three had nothing on them, just blank, black screens. Top left showed a still of the car park, a row of high end cars parked beside a pink, but black and white, shower tree. Top middle showed a deserted patio and pool area, the rain still beating down and visible as the pool rippled with the volume and force of the drops. Top right showed the also deserted building at the top of the garden, inside as Judge had seen it, with switched-off arcade games and pool table with dark and grey balls, not red and yellow.

Middle left showed a frontal picture of what Judge had just been scrutinising: the living area, but looking from above the television, in the direction of the room where he now stood. The shot on screen showed a naked and laughing Mr Jansen and three children, all laughing wildly, accompanied by a sound that was not from the screen, but from behind him. Middle and centre screen showed a more than slightly bemusing sight and Judge squinted at it to make sure he was not seeing things. The two men who had been sat together at the pool were sat next to each other on a black leather sofa. There was no other furniture in the room, but in its centre was what Judge thought was a young boy, but he was dressed in a ballet dancer's tutu and leggings and was trying to perform pirouettes and the like, but failing terribly. His poor attempts didn't seem to matter much to the two men as they watched him intently whilst performing a manual sex act on each other. The boy did not seem at all disturbed by this as he continued to jump and arc his arms above his head to his audience.

Judge looked at Erichson, his eyes wide and his mouth turned down, a look on his face as if to say "Am I seeing things?" Erichson smiled and replied to the look with, "Whatever turns you on, I suppose." He gestured for Judge to look back at the screens and Judge did so, focussing quickly back on the centre screen to convince himself again. The scene had not changed. Judge moved his eyes one screen to the right to the final picture. There was the other child, a girl this time he thought. She was kneeling in front of the four Oriental men he had seen earlier by the pool. The men formed a small semi-circle around the kneeling girl, whose hands were clasped together in a prayer. Praying for her ordeal to be over? Or giving thanks to God for the chance to earn some money for her family, no matter what hell she had to go through? The men, all backs to the camera were agitated by the flickering motion of the CCTV.

Judge turned away, not because he had seen enough, but he did not want to show that he had become aroused at the final two screens, subconsciously at first, but then through a realisation that he had a movement in his groin. He put his hands to his pockets on both sides, trying to repel the feelings, not that he needed to for the Erichsons' sake, nor his own for that matter.

"I am sorry, Mr Judge. I hope you are not offended. We thought that this was part of the reason you wanted to come here and buy the villa." Erichson addressed Judge, but looked at Kulap as if to question whether he had indeed misunderstood.

"No offence taken, Mr Erichson," Judge responded, "But I do not need to see anymore to know that I am very interested in the property. I am sure it will be acceptable to my wife and the twins. Have you had any thoughts about the price after your discussions with Mr Kulap?"

Erichson nodded, Kulap smiled a smug and hideous grin. "Mr Kulap thought that a 10 per cent discount might be mutually acceptable?"

"Did he now?" Judge removed his right hand from his trouser pocket and stroked his chin. He offered Kulap a wary glare and then turned his back to the two men, still stroking his chin. He paused, theatrically, knowing that the reduction was in actual monetary terms quite sizeable and he was more than happy to accept, but he wanted to have the last word. He turned back to the two men. "If you are willing to sell at the reduced price, and be out of the property by the end of the month, we have a deal."

Erichson paused. He stroked his own chin for a short moment. "What will you give me for the furnishings?" he asked.

"Not interested." Judge replied without hesitation. "They will not be to my wife's tastes, I am sure. However, if you wish to leave them as part of the deal in order not to have any moving costs, then that would be fine. We could use them as a stop gap until my wife finds things to her own tastes."

Erichson paused again and turned to his wife for advice. Mrs Erichson just shrugged her shoulders. "OK, Mr Judge, it's a deal, and you can keep the furniture, but we will take the artwork. It was quite expensive."

Judge smiled. "Whatever turns you on, Mr Erichson." He offered his hand to Erichson and it was accepted. "I will have my people draw up the contract and look forward to receiving the paperwork from this end." He turned to Kulap. "Mr Kulap, shall we go?"

Kulap nodded and turned to Erichson and shook his hand

vigorously, his commission payment value rolling round his head. He bowed to the tall man as an expression of thanks and gratitude and turned to Judge. Judge stood a yard from the sliding door and waited for Kulap to open it, sliding it from left to right. The rain had subsided to a drizzle and without a further look back at Erichson, Judge walked out onto the patio. Kulap gave a final bow to the tall European and slid the door shut again.

"Well, Mr Judge, I think we did a great deal."

Judge did not acknowledge the comment, or question, he was saving his breath for the walk back up the steps and to the car. He turned at the corner of the house, at the top of the first flight of steps and looked back, surveyed the garden area again and smiled to himself, *A great deal indeed*, he thought to himself.

As they walked across the car park, Judge thought about what was happening on the other side of the long white wall. He stopped. "Mr Kulap, it appears that I now have a day free tomorrow. If you would be kind enough to drop me back at my hotel tonight, I will meet you at the same address as we met at on Friday. I would very much like you to bring something for me."

"OK, Mr Judge, whatever you want. You know me, I can make anything happen." Kulap nodded.

"I enjoyed myself there on Friday. I want you to try and see if it can be bettered. I want you to bring me some more children. This time they have to be the same sex, preferably girls, aged about nine. Tell their parents I will take care of them. Just like the last time. You sort out the payment and I will reimburse you later."

Kulap looked at Judge, questionably. "Serious?" he asked.

"Deadly," Judge replied. No pun was intended.

9

Nemesis

Seb Bludd had woken at 7.30 a.m., as usual on a Saturday, with a clear head and no plans for the day ahead. He had lain in bed, with his alarm clock tuned into the second national radio station. His alarm was programmed to wake him up with the usual song, designed to get him in a good frame of mind for the day, in spite of what type of night's sleep he had had, which was usually not good. Having turned off The Boo Radleys' 'Wake up it's a beautiful morning', it automatically went to the radio station that had played a variety of music which spread across the four decades that he had been listening to music. On a day with not much planned, he could listen for a while and bring himself round at a nice slow pace. No need to rush to get up, no need to come round too quickly. Saturday morning radio was different to the weekday schedule in that the weekday breakfast show started at 6.30 a.m. and ran through to 9.30 a.m. and the Saturday version started and finished an hour later. Bludd had often thought that DJs mostly had a nice, easy job. Three hours a day and five days a week constituted part time in his eyes and even his job, which was as part or full time as he wanted or allowed it to be, was always more than 15 hours, and whilst his pay was generally good, no doubt it did not compare to the jocks in charge of British Broadcasting's premier slots. The weekday breakfast show was hosted by a witty ginger bloke, with an enviable ability always to be happy and, to Bludd's mind, funny. The ginger-haired DJ had a brain that was not unlike his own for memories of the last 30 years and an uncannily similar sense of humour to his own. What was so strange was that they appeared to have had completely different upbringings and backgrounds. Bludd promised himself that he would, at some point, sit down and read the redhead's autobiographies, just to see if there was any crossover in their characters and any hints at a reason why they seemed so similar.

As usual, the first sign of a run of songs that did not appeal to him, generally two songs in a row was enough. Bludd would shut down the alarm radio, exit his bed and engage in a short stretching session, only lasting a couple of minutes and generally consisting of three or four moves that were designed to flex the important muscles and get the heart beating at a slightly higher rate than the rest period beat it had pounded at for the last eight or nine broken hours.

After a breakfast of a round of wholemeal toast and a banana, honey and yoghurt smoothie, he undertook an attacking martial arts workout that also encompassed a weights routine that was more about the anaerobic properties than the muscle building that it also enhanced.

He returned to the house from the garage gym, showered and dressed and reluctantly began a quick attack on the polishing and vacuuming that he had neglected for the past number of weeks. His theory was quite the opposite of his mother's, in that, whilst she would have had a team of cleaners to provide the service whilst they were growing up abroad, and had kept the standard up herself in their English abode, she had maintained a daily routine, whereas he had a mentality of when you can write your name in the dust, it was maybe time to address the situation.

He had finished his half-hearted attempt at an autumn/ spring clean at 10.45 a.m. He tended not to worry too much about his front office as so little real time was spent in there, that there was less of a likelihood of an accumulation of dust and so it needed attention less often. However, in the interests of offering due diligence to any possible client visits, he showed his head round the door to the room and offered a quick scan around as sufficient interest as to the state of the room's cleanliness. His eyes were averted, easily, as in reality he was not too concerned for the state of the room, to the flashing red light of his telephone's voicemail alert.

He hadn't heard the phone ring, so assumed that it must have been whilst he was vacuuming, or earlier in the gym. He moved to the rear of the desk, keeping his eyes fixed on the little red light, as if to check it really was flashing. A significant proportion of his work was lined up during the week, that being that a significant proportion of it related to cheating spouses and the cheated partner would call during the week whilst the cheater was working, making a Saturday morning work call quite unusual.

He pressed the button to listen to the message,

"Hello... Mr Bludd, my name is Annab ... Anna Bell."

The woman paused. Bludd immediately recognised the change of course. Clearly she was called Annabelle "Something", but didn't want to reveal her real surname and had not decided this until that very moment.

She carried on. "I think I would like to meet with you to discuss the possibility of you carrying out some work on my behalf."

She continued with her number and asked Bludd to call her back at his earliest convenience. Bludd wrote the number down and pondered over ringing her back too quickly. He didn't want to look too keen as to seem desperate for work as, in truth, he was not, but likewise, he did not want to miss out on the work. He was also intrigued at the pause and the name change. He decided to give the office his intended once over before he called her back.

The number she had given was a mobile, not unusual as landlines were dangerous to the client as they were generally trying to hide the fact that they had contacted a private detective.

The shrill tone rang in his ear as he lounged back into his office chair, pen and paper at the ready to note down a name, a real one perhaps, address, case details, if given, and meeting information.

She answered.

"Mrs … Bell?" he asked, a deliberate pause a pointer to her that he had recognised her own deliberation.

"Speaking," she replied sheepishly. The line was poor, a crackle muting her echoed reply.

"Sebastian Bludd," he continued. "You called me earlier with a view to me possibly helping you in some way? You mentioned possibly meeting me."

"Yes, but it's difficult to talk here, the line is poor, as you can tell. Could I come to your office? I have the address." She sounded as though she was whispering and Bludd could not decide if it was the poor reception, or the woman was hiding something. "It is quite urgent. Could I come round this morning?"

Bludd checked his watch. Five past 11, not much of the morning left and 'come round' meant, to him, that she was not too far away. "Sure," he replied, "come straight away." He wanted her to set off immediately so that he could gauge how far she had travelled. His semi-rural location meant that the roads were similar all around the surrounding area and he would be able to at least put a radius to her distance.

"What was the name again?" the question pointed to check if there was a pause again.

There was.

"… Bell. Anna Bell, Mrs."

"OK, Mrs … Bell. I'll see you in what, half an hour?" Bludd left a pause again, signalling he had noticed hers.

"Fine, see you shortly," the woman replied.

Bludd reckoned the half hour estimate he had offered was about right, which meant that he had 30 minutes to do a proper clean in the front room office and put a black long-sleeved shirt over his black tee. It was more formal for a first meeting, he thought.

* * *

The woman, "Mrs Bell" arrived 28 minutes later and Bludd made a swift mental calculation and guessed that she had come from one of the rural options he had kept in mind since his conversation with her earlier. The 4 x 4 she was exiting only convincing him that she had come from Buxton, or its outskirts.

From his front bedroom window, Bludd watched the woman exit the car and approach the front door. The car was a Black Range Rover, big and powerful, often used by business-people as a show of wealth, or drug dealers as a show of power and authority. She looked tall and slim, with long dark hair, parted at the centre. From that distance, she looked pretty; he guessed that she was about 35.

She rang the doorbell, which did not work, but Bludd was already on his way down the stairs, slowly so as not to arrive at the door too quickly and appear eager. He gave himself a quick dust down, subconsciously, but in light of the fact that she was attractive and slightly younger than him. He opened the door and swung it right back in a confident manner.

"Mrs Bell?" No pause. "Please come in, pleased to meet you," Bludd opened.

He didn't give her chance to reply. He just stepped back and swept his arm left to right in a theatrical manner, motioning her in. "First on the left."

The woman gave a slightly coy smile and ushered past him, turning as she did so, keeping a distance between them. She walked down the hall and Bludd, for all his lack of interest, could not help an instinctive look from her ankles to her bottom. She was easily 5 feet 11, with a medium heel and about 10 stone. She was elegant and alluring. She turned left as instructed and Bludd almost followed, but stopped inside the doorway.

"Please take a seat. Tea or coffee?" he asked, interested to see if she sat at the desk chair, or in the comfort of the sofa. The answer would give him an inkling if she was relaxed or not, or if she would be completely formal and therefore business-like only.

The woman paused. "No thanks, I am fine."

Formal and business-like, Bludd thought.

She sat at the desk chair and crossed her legs at the knee, hitching both her knee-length, olive-coloured dress and her beige overcoat down a little so that it just covered the apex of the joint, wiping imaginary creases away as an excuse to stretch the fabric a touch further.

Bludd was unusually mesmerised by the woman. Her hair was shiny and black, just past shoulder length and it had a natural kink. Her eyes were green and large and round and seemed to emanate shyness. Bludd had become distracted, but his instincts kicked in. The woman had clearly lied about her name and whilst she appeared shy, her mannerisms, on the whole, were of a confident person. Her vehicle was also a pointer to the fact that she was no mug.

"So, Annabelle ..." Bludd resisted the urge to challenge her about her name. "Tell me how I can help."

The woman paused and took a deep breath. "Well, it's difficult to know where to start really. Basically, the problem is my husband."

You don't say, Bludd thought. "Go on," he said.

"Like I said, it's difficult to know where to start. He is a good husband and a good dad too. He provides a very nice living for us all. We have two children, Alfie and Molly, who are twins. When he is home, he is great with them. Part of the problem is that he is away an awful lot, abroad working, looking for new markets for his business, setting up new ventures."

"Doing what?" Bludd interrupted.

"He is in both the packaging and waste industries," she continued. "He has a trio of businesses. The main one was his first, which was handed down by his father, which is a packaging company. The others are in the waste sectors, but completely unrelated. One is incineration, where they dispose of animals, mainly dogs. They have a long-standing contract with a number of councils. The last one is a bit of a front really. They purport to be recyclers. Basically, they have contracts with some of the major supermarkets and other businesses to collect their packaging waste and recycle with a view to reusing it again in the packaging factory."

"Why do you say it's a front?" Bludd cut in.

"Well, it did used to be a recycling company. They have a big factory not far, as the crow flies anyway, from the other estate. The packaging factory and the incinerator are situated together. They did away with all the recycling machinery when they realised that recycling was becoming a lucrative business, without actually having to do the recycling, as well as the fact that the property they had was such a valuable asset as well. So, they continue to collect the waste, charging a nice fee, but take it to others to provide the recycling service, then they buy it back as recycled board, you know like corrugated sheeting."

"So what's the problem? It all sounds OK to me. I mean burning dogs is probably not a pleasant thing, but it's not illegal."

"No, that's just it. Nothing seems illegal, but something isn't right. I mean, there might be nothing going on, but something just does not add up. I used to do the books, full time, before I had Alfie and Molly. Then I gave up for a while whilst they were babies and then went back to part time. But by then, he had already got somebody else in, full time, and I was like a spare part. In the end, I kind of just stopped going in, but I felt more like I had been pushed into it. The thing was, nothing was ever said. It was four years ago. At first he would still keep me up-to-date with things, you know, new contracts, day-to-day stuff, and gossip even. But then, it just kind of drifted away to nothing. But throughout it all, he never commented on me not going in. I am still on the payroll, I still get a monthly salary, and yet I never even visit the place any more."

"Still not sure what your issue is. Sounds like a cushy number to me."

"Well, that's just it. My lifestyle has improved no end. The company seems to go from strength to strength. Jeremy flashes the cash like there's no tomorrow, like he's making up for the time he spends away, which is a lot recently. The thing is, I still look at the books now and again, I can access them remotely, and all the passwords are still the same."

"And?" Bludd questioned.

"The books don't seem to add up. I mean, the packaging

company has doubled its turnover in the last two years, yet it hasn't doubled its staff. In fact, there are less people there than when I was there. There has been investment in machinery, but that was supposedly paid for by the sale of the recycling factory."

"But you said they still owned the factory. 'It's not far, as the crow flies', you said."

"That's right. He said it was sold, surplus to requirements and worth a fortune. The thing is, the building is still registered as theirs, but I've been there and it has been turned into flats, or studios, as Jeremy calls them. Lots of them, by the look of it."

"And?" Bludd questioned again.

"They don't appear to earn any money from it. I thought maybe they still owned it and rented out the apartments, or even that they had shared ownership with some kind of housing association or a property developer. But nothing, it's still listed as collateral, but doesn't earn anything for them. And that's just not Jeremy."

"Maybe they aren't occupied, maybe no tenants means no income."

"No, that's not it. Like I said, I went there. There are definitely tenants. Well, at least there seems to be lots of coming and going."

"Which means? Maybe he set up another company? Maybe he just doesn't want to tell you about it. Maybe he's keeping something up his sleeve. You know, women are quite well known for taking their husbands to the cleaners if something goes wrong in their marriage. Maybe this is something for him in the event you start to try and fleece him. It's probably in somebody else's name, or another company name, one that you have absolutely no access to."

"Either way, it means that Jeremy is lying to me. He said they had sold it and used the money to invest in plant. They have not sold it, so how does a company find the money to invest millions of pounds in machinery and double its turnover with less staff to run more machines. It does not stack up, and I want to get to the bottom of it."

"How many trucks do they have and where do they keep them? If they still own the trucks and shift the recycling materials around to the recyclers, where do they keep them?"

"I don't know, they had seven or eight articulated vehicles. The other site is huge, so they must house them there. I have not been there for a long time, certainly not at night, which is when I expect them to be parked up, and be out on the road during the day."

"Maybe they don't own the trucks any more? Maybe they were sold and that was the investment money? Where else do you think they could have got the money?"

"No, the trucks are still on the books, they definitely still own them. The only thing I do know is that the board of directors have changed somewhat. One of his managers has been made up to operations director. There are two foreign names on the board, who I had never heard of and one of his old board has disappeared off the books, but he was never an employee as such anyway. I know that Jon Durie's parents left him a lot of money, he's the one made up from employee to operations director. Maybe he and these foreigners put the money up."

"Jon, Durie? Not as in Jonathon Durie?"

"Yes, do you know him? He has a stutter and a limp."

Bludd felt the hairs on his arms and neck stand up, goose bumps shooting up all over his body. For a moment he felt dizzy and sick. He sensed the colour draining from his face. "Yes, I know him," he murmured. "He was a friend of my brother at school. I am guessing, therefore, that Jeremy is another of his friends, Jeremy Judge, another of my brother's school friends."

The woman waited before replying. "Yes," she paused. "I know you know him. I am pretty sure you have some bad history between you. I have heard him talk about you and from what I have heard, you don't have a lot of time for each other. That's part of the reason why I contacted you instead of the other options I had. I guess I thought you might be more inclined to help if it turns out that he is doing something wrong. Did I guess wrong?"

Bludd did not answer straight away and the woman saw a distinct change in his body language. He had been quite confident, inquisitive and interested. Suddenly, he looked hollow and lost in his thoughts. Bludd closed his eyes and his mind flashed back over 25 years to a picture of his nemesis. To the man that was responsible for most of the upheaval in his adult life. The reason he could not have a normal relationship, the reason he had travelled the world, learnt skills he had never intended to, such as languages and martial arts. He had also learnt self-respect, self-discipline, patience, calmness and a love of music. All because of an act committed by Jeremy Judge. His mind had brought back a vivid picture of Judge, then replaced it with another, then another and another. Bludd had begun to shake, subconsciously. A bead of sweat ran down his forehead and nose, dripping from the end and landing, with what felt like a splash, on his forearm. Bludd's eyes sprang open, a look of alarm in them, like he had forgotten where he was. He pinched his forefinger and thumb to the outside of his eyes and drew them in towards his nose, squeezing tightly and pinching hard against the bridge.

"Are you OK? You look awful," Annabelle Judge asked.

Bludd kept his finger and thumb on his nose and in his eyes, allowing time to compose himself.

"So Anna Bell is really Annabelle Judge? You hid your name from me. You knew that if you gave your real surname, I wouldn't be interested in you or your case. So my question to you, Mrs Judge, is what do you know? What do you know about me, and more specifically, what do you know about my problems with your husband?"

Annabelle Judge looked down at the floor, spanned her thumb and forefinger across her forehead, shielding her eyes from Bludd's gaze. She could feel his eyes burning into her, trying to read her thoughts. She moved her hand away and looked up at him.

"The truth is, I don't really know anything. I just know that there is a deep hatred, which looks like it is mutual now I have met you. I don't know what you did to him, but he really loathes you. He has never said it to me, but I have heard conversations over the years, seen his face contort when somebody has talked about you. Yet he has never explained it, won't talk about you when I have asked him. It's almost like he blames you for all the bad things that have happened to him, like you have made him like he is."

"All the bad things that have happened to him?" Bludd's voice was loud and angry. "Seems to me like he has it made. Loads of money, beautiful wife, two point four kids, no doubt a big house and a successful company. What is there to hold against me? And just for your information, I have never done anything whatsoever to your husband, not that he didn't deserve anyway. In point of fact, you are right, the feeling is mutual, and I do hate him. But with reason. Reason I am not willing to discuss, before you ask."

Annabelle Judge looked deep into Bludd's eyes. They were clouded over, misty and yet disturbed and angry. Whatever the reason for his hatred of her husband, she felt it was deserved.

The man opposite her had changed in an instant of saying his name. He had gone from bold and confident, to a shivering wreck at the blink of an eye. She needed to know why.

"What did he do to you? He won't tell me why he hates you. Please tell me why you hate him."

Bludd just stared at the woman. She was sitting in his office, just three feet from him. She was elegant and pretty. Her long, shiny, dark hair was reflecting the light coming in through the front window. Thick, but well maintained eyebrows, lashes longer than he had ever seen and wishing-well deep, dark, green eyes. She was tall, slender, dressed demurely and was almost spellbinding. He was struggling to understand how Judge had managed to end up with a woman like this. Obviously he had money, that would help, but surely money doesn't matter as much as personality, charisma, even looks. Judge, as far as he could remember, had none of these and Bludd's memory was second to none.

"Sorry," he replied, "no dice. Go ask your husband again. In fact, don't waste your breath. He will never tell you and neither will I. Now please leave. I don't want your case, I don't need your case and I certainly don't need your money, especially as it is really his."

Bludd got up and walked to the office door, held it open and ushered Annabelle Judge out less theatrically than he had ushered her in. She got up and looked at him in the eyes. He looked away and motioned the exit with a gentle hand movement. The woman offered no argument. She looked down at the floor and left the room, turned right and went and stood a foot away from the front door. Bludd reached over her left shoulder and undid the latch, opening the door as far as he could without hitting her in the face. She moved back a step and turned to face him. Bludd ignored her, he made no eye contact, didn't turn his head towards her. The light of the early afternoon flooded into the hall and lit up Annabelle Judge's face. She looked into Bludd's eyes again. They were no longer misty or cloudy, not even angry. Just staring and empty. He made no move to look at her; he just stood looking out of the door at nothing at all. Annabelle Judge moved out onto the step. She took a deep breath and turned to Bludd. "Please?" she pleaded. "Surely you, more than anyone, would want to find out if Jeremy is doing something wrong?"

Bludd did not respond. He closed the door slowly without looking at the woman. He clicked the latch and turned into the dim hall, pressing his back to the wood and slumped down. He closed his eyes, clasped his hands around his ankles, leant his forehead onto his knees and screamed angrily.

* * *

Jonathon Durie stood at his front gate waiting for his two o'clock appointment to arrive. His sideline in animal, mainly dog, cremation was a regular weekend earner for him. He didn't really need the money, but if people were stupid enough to pay for the service, he would gladly take it off them. His house was a stone's throw from the packaging company and was part of the company's estate. He enjoyed the luxury of living there rent free as part of his package, on the proviso that he was the key holder with responsibility for keeping an eye on the place and answering any alarm situations, which were few and far between in their semi-rural location.

The house itself was a detached cottage with a long drive-way to the left side as you looked at it face on. To the front were gardens which swept around the right-hand side and into the rear. In the garden to the right was a garage. Originally, it had been a workshop and attached were the old outside lava-tories; two single wooden doors were still there, but not used. The main garage doors were symmetrical rectangles with a half dozen nine inch square windows in the upper half of both, windows frosted like those in the two smaller doors. Both sets of doors were painted a light sky-blue, like the sash windows and the doors of the main house. The garage had a chimney stack to the right and a circular metal chimney to the centre of the flat roof. A gravel path had a paved centre leading from the centre of the two main doors right to where Durie was standing at the wrought iron front gates. A trolley was standing idly on the paved path to his right.

Durie turned and leant against the stone gatepost and admired his lot. The cottage was picture postcard stuff. Pleasant surrounding gardens, well maintained, old-fashioned style woodwork, red Cheshire brick to all sides, but the left-hand elevation was three quarters covered in the Welsh slate that the roof was made from. He was happy there, but couldn't help looking forward to the next adventure that his boss and friend, Jeremy Judge, was planning.

His thoughts were interrupted by the sound of a car approaching. He straightened his black tie and thumbed the lapel of his black, suit jacket and gave his shoulders a swift wipe. Whilst the operation was really a scam, Durie made every effort to make the grieving family feel like they were getting value for money. The car came out of the trees and into sight and the driver motioned to Durie. The car was a Volvo 240 estate model and Durie guessed that the deceased dog would be in the boot space, so he motioned back to the driver and made a suggestive move to turn the car around and reverse to the gates. The driver understood the rotating hand gesture and swung the car around and reversed up to the gate that Durie was opening in towards the house. He pulled the trolley forward and beckoned the driver backwards until the tailgate door was almost on top of him and held his hand up to signal to stop. The driver got out. He was about 40, Durie guessed. From the other side, a woman got out of the front passenger door and a child, a boy of about 11 exited the rear passenger-side door.

"G-g-good afternoon. S-sorry for your loss." Durie said as he held out his hand to the man.

The man opened the boot lid and revealed a black bag that looked like a suit holder. He moved it round so that it was facing long ways away from them and Durie pushed the trolley right up to the car's rear bumper. He stepped to the side and he and the man took two corners each and gently lifted the bag onto the trolley. Durie moved to the trolley's rear and moved it slowly away from the car, very slowly, very carefully and showing great respect for the deceased animal. The man shut the car boot and Durie moved the trolley a further three feet before going to the other end and gently, slowly, pushing it down the paved path towards the garage, his limp less obvious during the slow walk with something to lean on. The three family members followed solemnly as it if was a human funeral procession. Durie stopped at the garage doors.

"Would you like to say a prayer, or have you any w-words to say? Perhaps you would just like a mer-moment's thought." Durie offered the opportunity for the family to speak by clasping his hands together at the front and lowering his head as if in prayer himself. The family took his lead and copied him. Nobody said anything. Durie counted to 30 in his head and then looked up.

"I will see to things from here," he managed to say without faltering. He motioned the family back towards the gate and they turned. The boy turned his head back and muttered with a trembling voice, "Goodbye, Jess." His mother put a comforting arm around his shoulders and they walked slowly back to the car. The boy and his mother got straight in. The man offered Durie his hand and said, "Thanks." His right hand was poised to go to the back right pocket of his trousers, but Durie interrupted. "The ashes will be ready to collect at fer-four o'clock. You can per-pay me then."

The man smiled and got in his car. Durie repeated the clasped hands stance and waited, unmoving until the car was nearly out of sight, offering a pleasantry wave as they disappeared. He limped back to the trolley stood outside the garage and smiled. It had been an easy £150 for very little work. He opened the door on the left with a Yale key and entered into the darkness, pulling a cord to his left as he entered. A strip light buzzed above him and, after a few flickers, came to life. The light flashed around as it reflected off the dozens of porcelain urns stacked five high and three deep on a metal shelving rack that ran the full length of the left-hand wall. Durie lumbered along its lengths sideways, thumbing the rack until he got to a sticker marked "25–30kg". He picked up the first one and unscrewed the lid, tilting it forward slightly, not breathing. The urn was three-quarters full, suggesting that the ashes inside may belong to a dog that was around the 25 kg mark, about the size of the Labrador that he believed 'Jess' to be. He screwed the lid back down and gave it a quick wipe with the cuff of his jacket. He pulled the light cord again and plunged the garage back into darkness. He closed the door and the latch clicked as it locked. He moved over to the trolley and found that the bag was indeed a suit holder. He pinched the centre between finger and thumb and unzipped it about 12 inches, peering inside. The owners had left the collar on the dog, a tag with 'Jess' and a telephone number on it that shimmered slightly as the light peered in. Durie reached inside and undid the collar. He thought it came across as a nice touch to attach the collar to the urn, to give the ashes some ownership, even if they were not the true ashes of the deceased animal. He leant the urn against the black, shiny plastic cover that was encasing the dog, zipped up the suit holder and pushed the trolley back towards the gate, stopping at the top of the driveway and turning right, back towards the front door of his home. He picked up the urn and hobbled to the front door, opened it slightly and placed the urn carefully on top of the oak cabinet that was inside his porch.

He shuffled back up the driveway, opened the iron gate and pushed the trolley over the rough ground. Small gravel stones underneath the solid hard wheels made the short journey harder as they impeded the rotation. He shoved the trolley over to the sliding gate at the front of the estate and fingered the digit password into the fob. The motor kicked in and the gate started to open wearily. Durie leant on the trolley in front of him and rubbed his left leg. It was stiff and sore. It was like that most days, but got worse as the year drew on and started to get colder. He massaged his thigh down to his knee, easing the pain with his thumb and forefinger and the heel of his hand. The gate opened wide enough to fit the trolley through and he moved into the estate, leaving the trolley for a moment to stop at the gate and set it back to close, pushing the red button and the lower green one marked 'close'.

He paused for a moment, bending his knee and readying his leg for more work. He gave the trolley a quick shove to get the get the inertia moving forward again and pushed it along towards the long wooden-gated entrance of the smaller building in the far corner. He passed the front wall of the packaging plant, the drab, weathered, grey paint not enhanced by the drab afternoon. A slight breeze struggled to blow the cool afternoon into life. The short walk to the concrete ramp hurt Durie; the pain in his upper leg would start suddenly and last from one sharp spasm to multiple stabbing pains followed by a period of numbness that made it all the more difficult to walk. Massaging the area constantly helped, but the constant twinges and cramps made him miserable and angry and his mood could change at a moment's notice. He moved awkwardly up the ramp and unlocked the padlock, hanging the lock in the hole of the hasp. He gave the gate a solid heave and turned back to the ramp and the trolley. A sharp jarring pain hit his thigh and he grabbed the area and squeezed it to ease the discomfort. He paused until his leg felt normal again. He stepped back down to the trolley and swung it round a half circle. He grabbed the handle and dragged the trolley towards the ramp. The shallow slope caused him a problem and he struggled to get the energy to move the trolley. He went round to the other side and eased his back against the steel frame and gave it all the energy he could muster, trying not to put too much pressure on his left leg. It took five shoves to get the trolley back on level ground, but it took a lot of Durie's energy. He stopped to get his breath and calm his mood; he could feel the anger building up. He raised his right hand in the air, clenched his fist and slammed it down hard into the black plastic suit cover and into the torso of the deceased dog inside. The motion caused his left leg to jolt again and he repeated the punch, hoping that the action that had caused him pain would be relieved by repeating it. It didn't, and the pain worsened. He pushed the trolley slightly away from himself and put his head down between his outstretched arms, taking a deep breath. He stood back up and moved himself and the trolley to the concertina door in front of him. He pulled the door open from left to right, just enough to squeeze the trolley through. He flicked the light switch and the room became dimly lit, rather than flooded with light. The normal procedure would be to open the door as far as it would go and allow the natural light to illuminate the building. But he was not staying long enough to worry about a lack of light.

The high pile of bodies that had been there the previous night had all but gone. The night shift had indeed been busy and at first glance, it looked like they had done their usual thorough job and clean up.

The now small piles of canine bodies were in small, similar sized piles set across the width of the building. In front of the piles of bodies were two huge machines. They were identical: a brick base, with a steel upper, arch shaped from the front, about seven feet high by the same wide. The machines were incinerators that went back about 12 feet overall. Their steel frontage housed large, black, steel doors that both opened outwards from left to right on heavy hinges. The doors were pristine clean. Durie peered between the two tunnel shapes and noted that the outside shells, also blackened with a matt paint finish, were also clean, not shiny clean, but dust free and efficient looking. He opened the door of the right hand furnace and looked inside through squinted eyes, trying to get a feel for the state the internal surfaces were in. He found them to be acceptable. The inside was layered brick all around its surface, from bed to rounded ceiling, the bricks following the contours of the arc. The high temperature brick skin was broken twice to each side with a small steel inlet, the funnels from the burners housed on the outside steel covering, two to each side, four in all, capable of bringing a temperature inside of 1000 degrees.

The two incinerators had originally been built during the panic of Mad Cow Disease in the 1990s. The company had bought one then to cash in on the public panic surrounding CJD

(Creutzfeldt – Jakob disease) cases and the company had got planning permission passed quickly due to there being numerous local cases and the council being eager to be seen to be helping speed up the disposal of suspected cases. The second machine had been added when the Foot and Mouth outbreak had occurred a few years later. Identical to the first, they were both capable of disposing of dozens of hoofed animals in a day. When the need to burn so many carcasses had died away, Durie had hit upon the idea of utilising the incineration capacity for other uses, namely domestic animal and, more lucratively, pet cremations. The high temperatures required for burning cattle and the like in such numbers were not necessarily needed to burn dogs in much smaller numbers, but domestic pets having a higher muscle content, and therefore less fat content, would still need high temperature and the load capacity that the two machines offered meant that they could still burn dozens of animals in a day. In turn, this meant that several councils, veterinary surgeries, and even animal charities, would use their services. The councils would turn up with lorry loads of deceased dogs, vets would bring one or two at time and the charities would usually only bring one at a time. Each one of them had different levels of care and sincerity in the way they handled their cargo. The council would literally reverse their vehicles in as far as possible and launch the bagged bodies into an indiscreet pile. The veterinary van would pull up at the gate and await the staff on duty to arrive with a suitable vehicle to take the deceased into the compound. The charities would drive up very slowly to the gate and expect the staff member to collect one end of the solitary bag and slowly and respectfully place on a trolley for one.

In reality, the end result was the same. If the council opera-tives showed little respect for their dead cargo, then the staff in the incineration plant showed a complete lack of interest in the contents of the bags. Large or small, the body bags would be unloaded inside the building, but rather than being carefully placed directly into the incineration equipment, generally they were thrown in the corner, into a pile. When there were sufficient to warrant firing up the burners, they would throw the dead dogs in with scant regard to their breed, size or life gone before them. The incinerators were originally made to burn two cows per burn, but they could easily manage 20 dogs, depending on the breed and, therefore, the size.

Durie opened the door to the left-hand machine and found it to be in similar clean condition. He brought the trolley carrying 'Jess' right up to the brick floor of the incinerator and lifted it in, placing it on the brick and then giving it as almighty a shove as he could manage. He picked up a tool with a long handle and flat faced end to it, like a brush without bristles, and pushed the animal back as far as it would go. Momentarily, he thought about putting a few extra bodies in from the small pile to his left, but decided against it. There was probably around 40 dog carcasses left in the piles, enough for two burns. That would not take the upcoming nightshift too long to dispose of and they were unlikely to question a solitary bag already put into the machine. They rarely questioned anything.

His only concern now was that he had plans for the following day that would require the dead bodies of the 40 dogs piled in the corner to be left to rot another night. He would need them to fill the incinerators the following night. Tonight was no good. The Lupescu brothers were on a rare night off, or at least they were away from the factory. They were working, but it in the city centre, recruiting a replacement for somebody who hadn't yet left their employ, somebody who wasn't even aware that they were leaving. The nightshift would have an even rarer night off. For one of them it would be their last.

10

Haunting

Bludd ignored the vibrating mobile phone jumping around the bench near the door. He had turned it to silent after Chrissie had made her fifth attempt to ring him. He wasn't in the mood to talk to her, or anybody else for that matter. He wished he had turned it off completely.

His knuckles were sore, red raw, but just short of opening and bleeding. He had punched the Muay Thai bag hanging from the garage's centre joist until his hands couldn't take any more. He had pumped his 15 pound weights until his biceps had burned and could not lift any more. He had thrown the smaller weights across the garage in anger, leaving them strewn in all corners of the floor. Now he was attacking the Wing Chun wooden training dummy. His wrists were smarting from the downward smashes to its false arms and the skin on his shins was open and blood had started to trickle down them. He altered his stance and began to kick out with the top of his foot, kicking as hard as he could and ignoring the pain. His feet were beginning to get smattered with deep red blotches as the residue from his shin transferred to his insteps. Kicking too hard could easily result in broken bones; the metatarsal bones a sure weak spot. Bludd ignored the possibility of the damage and ignored the pain. His whole body was aching, his muscles were burning in every limb, and his heart was pounding like it felt it would burst out of his chest, pulses matching every straining heartbeat. His face was purple, with rage and anger, aggression and pumping blood vessels. His head was pounding like the worst hangover. Yet he carried on, venting his anger onto the inanimate objects in his gym, ignoring the repeated buzz of the phone, not wanting to speak to anybody, but especially Chrissie whilst he was in this state. He didn't want to say something he might regret, or want to lash out at anyone, not least someone special.

The skin at the feet and ankle joint began to tear, the pain growing with every blow, and yet he continued through it. His leg muscles strained at every sinew until he couldn't lift them. He collapsed on his knees, legs tucked underneath him, the soles of his feet looking up to the ceiling, stretching the broken skin at his ankles. He rolled to his side, turning his toes upwards towards his knees, the pain lessening as he closed the broken skin back together. The floor was cold, but felt refreshing against his raging hot body as he rolled onto his back. His chest was heaving up and down like a bellow stoking a fire, his knees bent, heels to the floor and toes in the air. He didn't move for an age. His body calmed, his heart retreated to a normal rate, pulses slowed, sweat rolled down the curvature of his body, gathering in the cleft of his back and soaking his two-tone shirt. Two tone where wet met dry.

He closed his eyes. Jeremy Judge's face seemed to be tattooed on the back of his lids. Each time he closed them he saw him, the image different every time, the young Judge, the teenage Judge, the angry, vengeful Judge. He stared at the ceiling. He was tired, mentally drained and physically exhausted. He decided that he needed help. And Jack Daniels was the man for the job.

* * *

Maxwell Bludd had arrived home earlier than he had expected, but still later than he should have been. He stood at the top of the concrete ramp leading up to the front door of his bungalow and waved off the carer, watching as she drove away, smiling even though she had worked extra hours that inevitably would not be paid to her by the agency she worked for.

He took in a deep breath of cold Nottinghamshire air and turned back into his home, ready for another night on his own, mentally speaking at least. He closed the door and leant his back against it, taking another deep breath. He cupped his hands to his face and rubbed his forehead with the full length of his fingers, stretching them back down to the skin under his chin and pressing his palms together, like a child in prayer before bedtime. He paused for a moment, eyes closed, gathering his thoughts. He was not sure how much longer he could carry on. Speaking to his mother about his father had made him think the whole way home. His mother was a saint. She had tendered his father for six years. The last few of them had been a living nightmare for her. She had been his sole carer the whole time; no help from the State, no help from him or Sebastian, not nearly often enough from either of them anyway. He had done as much as he could, but with promotion at work and his own domestic situation to contend with, he could not do more than he had already done. The same could not be said for his brother, Seb. He had tried to call him during the journey home, but had no response. He had an instinct that Seb was just ignoring him. He felt that most of the time. He had left dozens of unanswered voicemails over the years. His latest was at the request of their mother and he had hoped that by really spelling out the severity of their father's decline, that Seb would at least give their mum a call, even if he could not be bothered to ring his brother back.

He understood why they had drifted apart. He had no doubt as to why Seb had changed, but had never sought to offer a shoulder to cry on, or a helping hand. He had never offered an explanation to his parents when they had asked if he had any idea of Seb's sudden and complete change of personality. He had never backed them up when they asked Seb to stay on at school and complete his studies, nor had he begged Seb not to leave the country, even though his parents had asked him to. He had done nothing to stop them from drifting apart. But how could he?

He rubbed his face up and down again, the top of his knuckles pressing into his closed eyelids, circling the ball underneath them with added pressure to spark them into some life. He wanted to at least look awake, and aware, and interested and attentive, even if the hollow glare he would get as a response did not warrant the effort.

He went into the kitchen, past the dimly lit bedroom on the left without a look inside. He called out as he passed, "Can I get you anything?" No response was expected and none was forthcoming. He pulled a mug out of the cupboard above and filled it with fresh black liquid that had fallen a drop at a time into the glass jug in the tray. He leant his head against the cupboard door and took another deep breath. Eyes closed, he stayed still for a moment. He gave the cupboard door a slight tap with his forehead and eased back, straightened up and picked up the coffee. He headed back down the hall and turned right into the bedroom. He stood for a second in the doorway. The curtains were drawn, distinct mustard-yellow near the lamp in the corner, fading into darkness as the light fell away. Another dimly lit lamp sat on a small mahogany table in the opposite diagonal corner with a comfortable, oversized, bright-red armchair placed next to it, angled so that it faced the bed that was housed in the centre of the opposite wall. An over-bed table, with a C-shaped frame, on castors with a laminate top was at the end of the bed. A jug of water, half full with an empty glass and a bottle of orange cordial drink, sat to one edge.

The bed itself looked like it had been vacated in a hurry and the covers just thrown back across. A couple of creases ran down its length. Maxwell moved across from the doorway to the side of the bed and looked down. "Hello, you!" he said purposefully and loud. "I'm back now." He leant towards the head of the bed and kissed the forehead of his partner, stroking the thin strands of hair as he stood back up straight. He looked down and stroked the back of his fingers across the prominent cheekbone and into the hollow of the skin beneath.

He got no response, except a rasping outward breath struggling to escape through dry lips. The frail and boney arms that hid underneath the top sheet struggled to hold the weight of the cover above them. Another crease line formed parallel to the two that were created along the length of the bed by bones covered in diminished muscle and wrinkled skin. Pointed knees offered no movement in response to the words.

Maxwell rounded the bed and poured cordial into the empty glass, a third full and then topped up with water from the jug. "Not long now for dad, I'm afraid," he muttered, stopping himself from saying the 'or you'. That had passed through his mind at the same time. He went to the far side of the bed and gently put the glass to the dry lips, tipping it slightly and watching most of the liquid stream down both sides of the mouth and meet at the tip of the pointed chin below. Maxwell, felt in his pocket for a tissue and gently dried the liquid away with a loving softness. *Not long now*, he thought.

Chrissie had given up trying to call Bludd. She had called the agency and cancelled her night's work. She would not get paid tonight and the agency was far from happy with the short notice, but she was more concerned about Bludd than for the money, or the agency. Sometimes he didn't answer her calls, but usually, if that was the case, he would send her a short text saying, "Can't talk now. Later." Or suchlike. She had been calling him for hours, more than a dozen times. At first it had only rung once and then gone to voicemail, as if it had been turned off. The last half dozen attempts had rung out for longer and then gone to voicemail as well. She had left a few messages, at first just asking Bludd to confirm that he was OK for looking after Archie that night. The last one had been a worried message about not hearing back from him and she had made it with an angry tone to her voice. She was not in the least bit angry, but she knew that Bludd would not want her to be worried and that angry was altogether more acceptable to him.

On getting no reply after several hours, she had decided that, for only the second time, she would go to his house and try and find him. It had been so long since her last visit that she had almost forgotten the way and was glad to see his car outside to confirm that she had got the right place, albeit if it did not confirm that he was in.

She had banged on the front door, rattled the knocker and peered through the front room window. No reply had come. She had ventured round to the back of the house and found that the garage door, the door to his gym, had been left wide open and her mind had started to worry even more. She looked in through the kitchen window and could see down the hall, but could not see Bludd. Finally, she looked in the back room window and could see him pointing away from her, lay face down on the sofa, head cocked to the side facing the back of the furniture, right arm hanging by his side and a bottle of Jack Daniels all but finished on the floor, but with no glass.

She banged on the window with the fleshy part of her closed hand, the sound muffled by the padding. She clenched her fist and used the sharp knuckles to rap hard against the window, a hard, loud but dull thud sounded back at her. Bludd didn't move. Apart from breaking the window, she wondered what else to do. Then it struck her. If Bludd was in some kind of mood that meant he could not be bothered to shut his garage door, the chances were that he would not have locked his back door. She moved back across the back wall of the house, passing the kitchen window and raising an expectant hand to the door handle, twisting it downwards sternly. The door opened and she moved in quickly, not closing it behind her, but going straight into the back room and crouching down next to Bludd. She tilted her head to the right and heard him breathe, hard and deep, breathing her own sigh of relief as she did so. She moved the nearly empty bottle to the side of the sofa and settled on her knees adjacent to Bludd's head. She prodded his shoulder. No response. She gripped the top of his arm and squeezed her fingers into it, pressing hard to penetrate the hard muscle. No response. She leant into his ear and whispered, "Seb. It's Chrissie, can you hear me?" Again, no reply. She stood up and thought, her hand pinching the underside of her chin. She leant over and picked up the bottle of spirits; about an inch worth was left in the bottom. She unscrewed the top and sniffed it hard and took a little swig. Just enough to wet her lips and let her tongue feel the warmth of the taste. Then she tipped the dregs onto Bludd's head. There was not enough to spark a jerk reaction, but it did enough to raise a groan and Bludd slowly turned his head, lifting it slowly off the cushion it was resting on and turning to face Chrissie, her knees level with his face. The effort needed to turn his head had been immense and flopped it back down on the cushion, turning his eyes upwards for a squinted blurry view of a none-too-happy Chrissie.

"Why the fuck have you not called me?" She dug her knee into his upper arm and threw the empty bottle in between Bludd's left side and the back of the sofa. "Stupid question!" she continued. "You've obviously been busy getting yourself in a state." She gave him no time to comment, a light groan came from the side of his mouth, three-quarters of it seemingly unable to open. "Whats up? What's happened? You're no drinker."

She went back through to the kitchen and set the cold tap running. She opened the left-hand cupboard above the main kitchen worktop and pulled out a pint glass, put it into her left hand and shut the cupboard, running the water over her fingers to check it was running as cold as possible and then filling the glass to three-quarters. "You got any paracetamol?" she shouted through to the back room.

No words were coming from Bludd and Chrissie went back into the room and held the water in front of Bludd's head. He was now sat up, head in hands and fingers running through the hair on his temple.

"Do you want to drink this or wear it?" Chrissie threatened.

Bludd looked up, a sharp pain making him squint as if he had got a stiff neck. He took the drink from her. First he sipped at it and then when the cold hit his tongue, he took a gulp and swallowed quickly, the cool water soothing the back of his dry, parched throat. "We need to talk," he said.

"That would be a nice change," she replied sardonically.

11

Revelations

Bludd stretched back on the couch and took a deep breath. He held it as he looked at the ceiling, gathering his thoughts and breathing out slowly as he dropped his head towards the floor; his head in his hands clamped either side of his head, fingers digging into his scalp. "How long have we known each other?" he asked.

"Well, that's subjective," Chrissie replied. "I came across you about two years ago, just over I think. But as for knowing you. I'm still not sure that I do."

"Exactly," Bludd said. "It's about time you did. You'd better sit down, this could take a while."

Chrissie sat in the armchair sliding her hands down from her buttocks to the back of her knees. "If this is some kind of watershed moment, I'd better be comfortable I suppose. Are you going to put the kettle on, or am I doing it?"

Bludd didn't answer, he just got up slowly and went into the kitchen, flicked the switch on the kettle and sat back down again, his hands on his knees and he took another deep breath. "What I am about to tell you is more than just a watershed moment. It's a lifetime of shame and embarrassment, and anger and resentment."

"Why not throw regret into the mix and go for a full house?" Chrissie interceded.

"Because regret, like most of the others, is a wasted emotion. I just can't help feeling the others. I don't actually regret much.

Anyway, if you can just shut up and listen for a while. This is actually quite important!"

"Sorry!" Chrissie, put her head down, a trace of guilt. She had waited a long time for this moment. "Go on."

Bludd continued. "You know I travelled quite a lot with my parents when I was young. My dad was with the Foreign Office, actually he was an ambassador to a number of countries in the southern Orient. You know, like Thailand and Malaysia, Singapore. So I picked up a little of the language of quite a few places, although we were taught, Max and I, privately and in line with English curriculums. Anyway, when we were 10 and 11, we got shipped off back to England, to a boarding school. My mum wasn't very happy about it, but my dad insisted and he generally got his own way. Mum always backed down because of his position and not wanting to be seen to undermine him in countries where the woman's view was not always really valued. So he got his way. They went off to Hong Kong, as my dad had been appointed assistant to the Governor. We went off to Blighty."

He paused and went back into the kitchen, continuing from the other room. "It was weird, because I was always the more confident one out of me and Max. Me being the older one meant that he kind of looked up to me, copied me a lot, let me lead things. But then when we got to boarding school, it all kind of changed."

He came back into the room with two coffees. He handed Chrissie hers and sat back down. They both put their mugs on the floor.

"Max fitted in really well at the school. He made loads of friends. I, on the other hand, hated it. I had one good mate, Steve Martin, who was a bit of a lad, not that interested in studying, funny and always pulling pranks. He got me in trouble a few times. Max had four or five really close mates that were never apart. It meant we didn't see so much of each other and was the beginning of us starting to drift apart. I suppose it was a shame after being so close for all the years of it being just me and him surrounded by foreigners. Anyway, we pretty much went our separate ways, but I wasn't happy with the company he kept. The group were all hoity-toity, well-to-dos. I'm not saying we weren't well off and well heeled, but we were grounded, thanks to Mum, and we knew how to treat people and respect people. Max was getting involved in some stuff that kids should know better about, you know, like bullying and extorting the really young kids. I'm not saying Max was directly involved, in fact I am sure he wasn't. He's always been little goody two shoes. But the others, and especially the ringleader, a lad called Jeremy Judge, was definitely up to no good. I confronted Max about it and he said there was nothing to worry about and that if things got out of hand, he would sort it."

"And did they? And did he?" Chrissie asked.

"I think he buried his head. Maybe the top dog had a hold on him in some way. It was a bit strange, really, like I could see things but he couldn't, and he was closer to it all than me."

"And did you step in?"

"More than once. We were there for five years and I would have had a set-to with Judge on a good half dozen occasions until the main one."

"The main one?"

"Yes, the main one. The one that changed everything." Bludd cupped his hands together and massaged his fingers, like he was drying his hands under a warm air drier, pushing some pain, or guilt, out of their tips.

"Go on!" Chrissie shuffled forward, sat on the edge of the chair.

"Well, Judge always seemed to have some kind of hold over the younger kids. Don't forget, he was a year younger than me, but he had been at the school longer and it seemed clear to me that from day one of us being there, he was some kind of top man, like an unofficial head boy. Like I say, he had rubbed me up the wrong way a number of times and I had got to the point where I had him by the shirt collars against a wall and warned him that I knew what his games were and if he carried on, I would put a stop to them. In fact, I had no idea what he was up to and I suppose this is where my detective skills started. I kept a close eye on him over a few months. He would often disappear with a young kid and then they would reappear, sometimes together, sometimes a moment apart. Sometimes the younger kid wouldn't appear for quite a while. Usually, Judge had a smug look on his face, like he had got his own way and the young kid would be upset, or at least embarrassed. Or both. Then, one day, I got up early and showered, not necessarily with any preconceived ideas about following Judge that day, but just because I wanted to. Anyway, the shower blocks were all sort of centralised and as I came out of our block, I heard something next door, in the block that was for the year below. I crept in and found Judge peeking through a hole in the wall where a tile had been removed. He was jerking off. Now, ordinarily, you might think that this was OK. We all tried to have a look in the girls' showers now and again. I failed miserably by the way. But the girls' block was away from the boys, which meant that Judge was jerking off in the boys' showers and the way the block was set out meant that these were boys of about 12, i.e. two or three years younger than Judge. Sometimes, depending on the timetable, some kids started before the others. He must have known it."

"What did you do?" Chrissie's voice had an unexpected

excitement to it.

"Well, straight away it hit me what he had been doing with the younger boys on his little disappearing moments. He wasn't extorting them, or bribing them, he was abusing them. My blood went to boiling in an instant. I ran over to him and grabbed his shoulder, spinning him round before he had time to react. It meant that his pants were around his ankles and his face was red with shock. A moment later it was red with the smack I gave him. I threw him to the ground and started to give him a kicking. Now don't get me wrong, at this point in my life I was no tough guy, or troublemaker, but I knew that Judge had been up to no good and he had a good kicking well overdue."

"So you gave him a good kicking? Wasn't that the end of it?"

Bludd paused a second. "Nah, it was just the start, but things started out on my terms."

"What do you mean?"

"Well, the best thing about catching him at it was that his pants were well and truly, literally, round his ankles."

"And?"

"His penis. His penis was like an acorn. There he was, on his back, this ruddy faced, chubby kid with a shitty attitude and an erect penis that was no bigger than my thumb. I stopped kicking him and just stood and laughed and pointed at him. And mocked him and mocked him some more. He was no longer chubby, or red faced, or slightly spotty, or anything else I wanted to take the piss out of. Now he was an acorn dick. And I was going to get a bit of something back for all the kids he had abused, by letting everyone know just how much of a man he wasn't."

"Wouldn't it have been better to have just given him a beating?" Chrissie questioned.

"Probably. Certainly with hindsight."

"Why, what did you do?"

"Like I always did, I took it too far. Took the piss once too often and that little bit too publicly."

"How?"

"Well, we had those rotating blackboards in some of the classrooms. One day we had a lesson in the room that the year below, Max's year, Judge's year, was about to follow into. I drew a vagina and then I drew an acorn in an obvious penis shape and named it "Judge's Genitals". Ultimate humiliation."

"A bit immature."

"Maybe, but it became a kind of quiet war. We never spoke, never had any verbal confrontation, just random acts of piss-taking. The difference was that nothing could hurt me. He had nothing on me that mattered. Not until he got his gang to back him up one night."

"But wasn't your Max in his gang?"

"He was, but not on this night. It was a fortnight after the blackboard incident, a week before the start of my final exams. I was in my room, alone. Steve Martin had been called out and I had dropped off after studying hard. Four of them came into my room and put a pillow case over my head. While they kept me pinned down, they hit me hard in the face, maybe six or seven hard shots and no way of avoiding them. I could feel the blood soaking into the cotton from out of my nose and mouth."

"Did they leave you unconscious?"

"No. They hadn't even started. They dragged me out of my room. Never said a word between them. I tried to memorise the route they took me down, but I am only good with visual memory, and the only memory that was in front of my eyes was a thin veil of blood-soaked white cotton. It became apparent later that they had taken me into the main library."

"Don't tell me they read you a story?" Chrissie asked trying to be ironic.

Bludd gave her a wry smile. "Not funny, but good try. More like taught me a lesson, or tried to. Basically, in the most straight forward terms, they held me face down, debagged me, as we called it back then, and Judge raped me from behind over a table in the library." Bludd clasped his hands together, as if in prayer and pulled his bottom lip down towards his chin, a pensive look all over his face, eyes wide open.

"My God!" was all Chrissie could say, before she mustered, "You poor sod." She got up, went and sat next to him and put an arm around his shoulder, hugging him tightly to her side.

Bludd said nothing, just stared in front, eyes not even blinking.

"What did you do?" Chrissie asked eventually. "Some kind of revenge?"

Bludd took a moment to reply. "You would like to think, wouldn't you? But no. I was beaten. In the short term, I took the pillow case off my head and went back to my room. The physical pain I had been given was nothing compared to the emotional effect it was to have on me. I went to bed and never moved all night. Steve had come back in and had gone to sleep. I got up the next morning at five, well before lights on and showered. And then I left. Went AWOL. Absconded. Did one. Fucked off."

"Where to? Surely not to Hong Kong?"

"No, I didn't want my parents to know anything. I just left the school and laid low. It was my 16th birthday a week later and I had to just survive to that day. If I had been found, by the authorities, or the school, I would have had to go back and there was no way that was happening."

"But what did your parents say?"

"Nothing. I didn't contact them until my birthday. By then they couldn't do anything. You see, my grandparents were very well off. They left a lot of money in their wills. But the best part was that they had left some for Max and I in trust funds. The first came to fruition on my 16th birthday for £10,000. I phoned my mum on my birthday and told her that I was taking my grandparents' money and going to America."

"America? Why America? And what did she say?"

"America, because it was something new. Something they couldn't try and influence, somewhere none of us had been. Somewhere they couldn't find me. My mum was as good as gold; she sorted out the paperwork for me, unbeknown to Dad. My dad was a nightmare. He tried to put a block on the money; it was from his parents' side. He forbade me to go. You can imagine how that went down with me."

"What about Max? What did he say?"

"Nothing. Not a word. I didn't speak to him, or hear from him until I saw him again in Hong Kong two years later, but even then, neither of us said anything. It was like nothing had happened."

"Wasn't that a bit strange given what had gone on?"

"Maybe. But a lot had happened, to me anyway. I had changed massively. A lot had happened since I had last seen him, none of which I wanted to go into with my family."

"So you went to Hong Kong after America?"

"In a roundabout way via Bangkok, Kuala Lumpur and Jakarta."

"Why the long way round?"

"Well, that's what drove me to be the way I am."

"What? Quiet, moody, sulky?" Chrissie said with a smile, although there was more than an element of truth to her irony.

"Funny," Bludd replied. "But actually, yes. I mean from an

137

attitude, persona, outlook point of view, very much so. I don't trust people, not easily anyway. You are an exception to the rule really. I pretty much trusted you as soon as you opened your mouth. Very, very unusual."

Chrissie sat back a little and held her hands out, palms upwards. "What's not to trust?"

Bludd looked at her, his head slightly leaning to the right, eyebrows raised, eyes rolling left to right.

"Anyway, right now I am trying to make a massive point, one that I have never made to anyone. So if you would like to hear it, I will carry on. If not, no problem, we can just carry on as before."

Chrissie looked apologetic. She sat up straight and mimicked a zipper across her mouth.

"OK. I went to America with no plan. No destination in mind, just following my nose really. Then it turned into a kind of musical journey. I went to Kentucky and Tennessee, to the home of country music, the Deep South to hear the blues, I searched for the home of rock 'n' roll, which took me to Gracelands in Memphis, I went to Detroit for Motown and New Orleans for jazz. Basically, I was a young lad that had been wronged and I was looking for a way out of the misery I had found myself in. Music is a great leveller. Music brings people together. I made friends, something I was not good at. I learned to trust people again. I started to get my life back. Then it all came crashing down again, it went full circle, well 350 degrees at least. Instead of giving somebody a beating … I killed a man."

12

Revelations Part 2

"What do you mean?" Chrissie interjected.

"The reason I had gone to America was to get away from it all. Family, England, being raped." He said it in a matter-of-fact manner. "What's the chance of that happening again?"

Chrissie put her hand over her mouth. "No!" She elongated the word in her expression of shock.

"Not quite, thankfully. I was in Florida, no real reason, not following any musical paths, just the way the journey had taken me. I was getting a little low on cash and had started to bum lifts, hitch-hiking, staying with people if I got a chance, cheap digs and youth hostels if I didn't. This particular day, I had hitched with a guy from Macon in Georgia and headed south. My destination was Orlando. This guy, Ged he was called, lived near a place called Gainsville. He offered me a place to stay, as long as I wanted, he said. Gainsville is only a day, two at the most, of good hitching, to get to Orlando, so it was ideal really. I had been there a few days, and to be fair, it was all OK. He went to work and left me to it. Then I said I was going to leave the next day and he went a bit sulky. He said he enjoyed me being there and was going to miss having me around. Then he seemed to buck up, kind of over the top happy. He said he would give me a ride the following day, all the way if I wanted. I declined, I already felt an obligation to him for letting me stay there, and I didn't want to owe him any more than I already did. He went sulky again and said that the least I could do was to have a few beers with him that night, watch a film or something. Of course, I felt that I had to agree. So we had a few beers and watched Ged's favourite film *Zardoz*, which starred Sean Connery, you know, James Bond?"

Chrissie nodded.

"Well, it was OK, nothing special in my mind, but I am not a big film person, as you know, but especially sci-fi. I told him I was going to bed and he begged me to stay with him, which I did. He seemed quite drunk, which I thought was strange, as I wasn't and he had drunk the same as me. Then he got out his hash pipe, which he called a hookah, which I had never heard of at the time. It's like something you would see in Morocco or Tunisia; a glass bowl bottom, with a steel stem and a pipe coming out about halfway up. He stoked it up and started to smoke it. It relaxed him at least, but then he wanted me to have a go. I was only 16 nearly 17, and I had never tried any kind of drugs. I had only started drinking in the few months prior to this and even that was sporadic, mainly because I had been in and out of dry states and I was too young to drink in America. I refused, but then he started to get angry and aggressive, so I caved in and tried it."

"Did you like it?" Chrissie quizzed him, with a tone of self-interest.

"No! It was bloody awful. But worse than the taste and the smell and the fact that I was not a smoker, was the immediate effect it had on my body. My head was blown away straight away. I just lost all my senses. I don't know what he had in there, but it was stronger than I had expected, although I didn't really know what I was expecting. I remember starting to laugh, and Ged started to laugh hysterically. I had another go and just laughed more. Then I remember not being able to feel my legs and everything got a bit hazy, my peripheral vision was all blurred and I had tunnel vision. Then Ged stopped laughing and stood in front of me. He dropped his pants and started to play with himself in front of me. I remember feeling mortified, and yet still laughing. He sat next to me and put his hand on my knee, squeezing it hard. Then he moved his hand up my leg. I was wearing shorts and his hand was creeping slowly up, like slow motion. I wasn't sure if it was the drugs or whether he was just taking his time, knowing that I would be in a state of disablement. I remember my laughing slowing down and his voice sounded like it was in slow motion and I looked down, in slow motion, at this hand up my shorts, picking at the edges of my underpants."

Chrissie's hands clasped around her nose, her thumbs under her chin.

Bludd continued, "I had a flash back to the library at school, strangely in real time, and then I don't know where it came from, but he touched me, touched my penis and it was the catalyst for me to do something. He gave me some kind of strength by touching me. I had the hookah in my left hand and he was sitting to my right. My legs wouldn't do what I wanted them to, but my arms reacted, thankfully. At the time I remember thinking it was because they were closer to my brain. Anyway, I smashed him in the face as hard as I could muster. He rolled over, holding his face. Blood was oozing from a gash across his right cheek and his eyes were shocked and angry. He didn't move. I guess he wasn't expecting it. Then my legs answered the call and I stood up, a bit uneasily, but my mind was focussing. I hit him again, harder than the last time, my muscles reacting properly to my brain's commands. I smashed the glass bowl over his head. His head split open and blood spilled into his hair. I couldn't stop. I hit him again, with the steel part, the top came off and rolled away. Ged was just sat on the floor begging me to stop. But I couldn't. I took the steel stem in my hand and turned it over. I took a jittery step backwards, grabbed his hair and pulled his head up to look at me, and he was scared and crying. He was sobbing, apologising, and begging me to leave him alone. I rammed the sharp broken edge of the glass into his throat. Blood jetted out, all over my feet. He grabbed his neck, blood running through his fingers. He gripped his throat harder and harder, but the blood kept rushing through the gaps. I saw the colour drain from his face and his eyes started to close and his head dropped and he just sat there on his backside, legs all over the place, lifeless. I just sat back on the chair opposite him. I waited for the drugs to wear off. All the time my vision was coming back, my senses repairing themselves. I had no thoughts for what seemed an age. I don't know if it took a long time for him to finally die, but it seemed like it. Maybe it was the drugs. I thought the drugs had stopped my remorse, but when they had worn off, I just sat there and looked at Ged's lifeless body and the remorse never came. I was quite removed from the situation, all very matter-of-fact about it. I left him where he had died, got myself cleaned up and went to bed. I slept like it had never happened."

"What did you do then?"

"The next day I got up and went to the airport, booked a flight and went to KL. I left Ged where I had left him the night before."

"Why didn't you go to meet your family?"

"I did, after another couple of years. I went back to Malaysia and Thailand, then Indonesia. I spoke to my mum and she made some arrangements for me. I went and stayed with families of the servants we'd had when my father was in office."

"And you stayed for two years?"

"I had decided, after the Ged episode, and, of course, the

library episode, that there was no way I was going to get myself into any more situations that I couldn't get myself out of. So I went back to those countries to learn how to defend myself. The families I stayed with were brilliant to me. I hadn't seen them in six or seven years, more in some cases, and I had changed massively, both physically and mentally. I wasn't the happy-go-lucky little kid they knew before. I was sulky and moody compared to the old me. And compared to most of them, I was huge. I was six-four and 13 stone, which is slim, but to them I was like a giant. Anyway, they never questioned me as to why I was there, nor why I wanted to learn how to fight. They just put me up and sent me off to the best martial arts tutors I could have wished for. I learned Wing Chun, Muay Thai, that's kick boxing, and Silat, that's like an Indian fighting style. I haven't had a situation since that I haven't been able to handle."

"Well, that all kind of makes sense of things now. But why are you telling me all of a sudden?"

"Because Jeremy Judge is back in my life, reappeared, like the worst proverbial bad penny."

"How? When?"

"This morning, his wife came here to see me. She thinks he's up to no good and she's probably right. She wants me to look into it for her."

"And will you?"

"I more or less kicked her out. Which is the same as a 'no'?"

"It's a big coincidence isn't it that she came to you out of all the private eyes available?"

"It was deliberate. She's aware of the feud, although she doesn't know the background to it. She came to me because she thought I would definitely take the job."

"You should. It might sort out a few of your demons. You

said regret was a wasted emotion, but it seems to me that you do regret it."

"Wishing something hadn't happened isn't the same as regret. What's done can't be turned around. I live with my demons and I'm OK with them now. Getting involved would just stir things up."

"You're joking, right? You are clearly not OK. You don't sleep properly. I don't sleep properly! Some kind of nightmare about the library, or Ged is my guess. Or both?"

"Always the library. But I can get by without sleeping well."

"Well, that's all right then! But what about the other problem? No doubt that's because of the library as well."

"Other problem?"

"You need me to spell it out for you? In the time that we have known each other, you have never touched me. We have never made love. That's not normal, surely. I mean, I'm not the most beautiful woman, but I'm not bad, even if I do say so myself."

Bludd said nothing. Chrissie was right. He had plenty of demons and they weren't going away. They had not gone away in 20-odd years, so why would they now? Annabelle Judge's appearance had almost certainly made things worse. He picked up his coffee and took a swig, it was warm and sweet, just what he needed. He looked over at Chrissie, who was sipping her coffee. Dust particles were floating around in the dimming light. He thought his cleaning had done nothing more than stir the dust rather than clean it. They both sat on the edge of their seats, thinking about the last few minutes' conversation. Chrissie broke the silence, "You have to take the job. What does she think he's up to anyway?"

"Some kind of fraud thing. But you can put a pound to a penny it will go deeper than that if Judge is involved."

"What do think it might be?"

"Who knows? He's a very controlling person, least he was. He was also someone who preyed on kids. This could be leading down all kinds of avenues."

"Avenues that you don't want to go down? Surely if this bloke was capable of doing what he did to you all those years ago, he could still be doing it to others, maybe worse. You want to live with that thought to go with your nightmares?"

Bludd sipped his coffee again, a long slurp. He swished it round in his mouth and took a swallow. "You know what? I don't think I can, can I? I'll give Mrs Judge a call in the morning."

"No time like the present," Chrissie said. "You might change your mind in the morning."

"My God!" Bludd replied with a sigh, "Anyone would think we were married! OK, I'll do it now."

13

Prey

Andrei and Marius Lupescu had been driving around the streets of Manchester for nearly an hour. They had seen plenty of homeless people, people sat begging, others in small groups, sat around metal cage bonfires, keeping warm. They had not seen what they were looking for. They wanted somebody young, mid-teens at the oldest, male, nice looking was an advantage. But most of all they needed to be hungry and desperate.

Andrei, who was driving, had insisted that they start in Salford. They had found a few strays there in the past and he thought that their type would always be found in similar locations. Not this night. Marius had become angry. He had wanted to head straight for the gay area near the city centre and now, after a wasted hour, he began to shout at his brother in his native tongue, his hands slapping the dash aggressively.

Andrei had to admit defeat and they headed east towards the city. The problem with the gay area was that it was partly pedestrianised and so they would have to be more persuasive about getting their prey into the van, rather than his preferred method of throwing them into the back. Parking was not easy. The van was too high to use any of the car parks and multi-storeys close to their preferred location, so they would have to walk a half mile or so.

The brothers were not twins, but they could easily have been taken as such. They were both six-two and both in the region of 240 lbs. Both had shaved heads, although Marius had slightly longer hair. Neither had enough to hide the ripples of skin that came up from the back of their necks to the base of their skulls. Their foreheads both had that elongated bone above their eyebrows, like Neanderthals, which served to make their eyes seem dark and sullen. The brothers had been in many fights over the years and many of those were with each other. As a result, their faces had been broken and scarred and had taken on a misshapen appearance as their bones and skin had recovered and reset. Their broken noses, both broke on several occasions, were, from the side, flattened. From the front, they were wide and crooked. All in all, they were not a particularly pleasant sight. Their skin was dark and rough and they had an unwashed look about them, even though they were meticulously clean.

They had chosen to wear similar clothes, a bit like twins seem to do: quilted tartan shirts, Andrei's blue, Marius' red, a plain white tee as a vest underneath, tucked into dark blue denim jeans and heavy-duty work shoes, polished to improve their look. They parked the van outside some industrial arches, home to garages, workshops and warehouses. Both of them splashed a palm full of aftershave across their unshaven faces and they headed off into the city's gay zone.

* * *

Bludd put the phone down to Annabelle Judge and turned to Chrissie.

"Well?" Chrissie asked.

"I meet her at ten in the morning, at their house."

"Where's that?"

"Somewhere over near Kirkholme. It's not a street name, so I guess it's probably big and isolated, somewhere on the

Connulton road."

"I reckon I should leave you to it. Try and get some sleep, clear your head and go with an open mind."

"OK, thanks. And thanks for listening. I've never told anybody else what I've told you, don't suppose I ever would have done, so thanks."

Chrissie got up, collected her mug off the floor, did the same with Seb's and took them both into the kitchen. She came back into the room and hugged him, her arms round the middle of his back and her head in his chest. Bludd didn't hug her back, but he pulled her head up and looked her straight in the eyes and kissed her lips. He closed his eyes and lingered. Chrissie kissed him back; she closed her lips around his lower lip and pulled away, scraping with her teeth as their lips parted. She looked him in his eyes, stroking his face with her left hand gently. "Good luck! Keep in touch."

As she left, Bludd was already thinking ahead. Check out the address, check out Jeremy Judge, and call your brother.

* * *

Marius Lupesku was travelling in the passenger side seat of the van with one of the two young men he and his brother had picked up in the gay district next to him, in the middle. The first had been easy. He had been sat in a doorway. He had a thick bubble jacket with a fake fur-surrounded hood, denim jeans and fake Caterpillar worker's boots. On his head he wore a patterned woolly hat with wool string ties, the kind that's made for a baby, or toddler, but had become a teenage trend. His face was fresh and plump and clean. His teeth were clean, and so were his clothes and his rucksack that lay next to him with his belongings. Andrei had taken the lead and left Marius in the van. He knew that the boy had not been on the streets long and his appearance was immaculate compared to long term runaways. He was a perfect target for the brothers. Andrei had established, after a little coaxing from the shy youngster, that he had been in the city two nights and this would be his third. His name was Ben. He had run away from home in Liverpool and come to Manchester as he thought his parents would look locally first and he would have a chance to get himself sorted in this city before anyone came to look. He was 15, but admitted that people thought he was younger. His skin was blemish free, no spots or blackheads, like many 15-year-olds have. Under his woolly hat, long blond wavy hair crept out all round. It gave him a more youthful and slightly feminine appearance. Just what the brothers were looking for.

Andrei had promised him a place to stay. A bed, food, friends with similar stories, who would look out for him: Somewhere that his parents had no chance of finding him. He could stay there as long as he wanted. All he had to do was work a little for them in exchange. As long as he was a good worker, he could stay. He was promised that he would be learning a trade. He could leave them and go and get a job anywhere, and never have to go back to Liverpool.

The boy had almost jumped at the offer. He went back to the van and got into the loadspace without any thoughts or fears, just happy that his stay on the streets had been a short one. He had been locked in for a while before he heard the engine start and the van move. They had travelled for about 20 minutes, although it was not a comfortable ride, so it felt like more. Then they had stopped. He had heard conversation, muffled, but it sounded like it was between two or three people. They were laughing and joking.

Marius had found the second passenger, another teenager,

in the heart of the gay district. He was tall, but very slim and wiry. He was 17, but looked a little older. He had a black tee-shirt, black denim jeans, and polished black shoes with a heel. His arms were not covered with clothing, but had numerous tattoos of names, boys and girls, Mum and Dad. A heart on each arm, a patterned band on each, at the end of his shirt sleeve. He had cropped, jet black hair, but with a fringe that flicked across his forehead and heavy eye make-up, mascaraed lashes and slightly browned lids. He was called Stephan, but preferred Stef.

Marius had noticed him standing alone, leaning back to a wall that overlooked the canal. He sipped delicately at some kind of dark mixer drink, one foot on the floor, the other flat against the wall. It was still relatively early, although darkness had fallen, and the crowds were still made up of small groups. Groups were no good to Marius, he did not want to have to integrate with them. It was also sometimes difficult to work out whether a group was made up of homosexuals, or maybe straights who were just in town to look at the circus. Maybe the odd one was not sure of himself and would be there to try and wrestle his feelings. Either way, Marius had a target, and that was a lone, skinny, obviously gay, young man. That target was Stef.

He had casually and confidently approached and offered a drink. A Black Russian was requested and Marius had duly obliged, handing it across with the line, "A Black Russian from a white Romanian."

Stef was confident in himself as well. He flirted with the big Romanian, touching his lower arm gently and then squeezing the triceps and biceps.

Beauty is in the eye of the beholder. One man's meat is another man's poison. Whilst Marius was, to most people, a big, ugly brute of a man, to others, many in this area it seemed, he was a rough, butch-looking, big, strong man. He had a charm about him and his accent made him that bit more individual.

It had taken one drink and Stef had agreed to go with Marius. He had welcomed the chance to meet his brother, given that he was apparently very similar to Marius, and he had headed off excitedly with his new Romanian friend.

Andrei had been waiting at the van, leaning on its white bonnet, arms folded across his chest. He greeted his brother and their new friend 'Stef' with a big smile, teeth either crooked or missing, but still with a friendly warmth to it. They had kissed on each cheek, like foreigners do, or like acquaintances do at a dinner party. They had sat Stef in the middle of the three of them and had set off and headed out of town and had talked and laughed. The brothers had told him they were going to a party and that he would be made very welcome. Within minutes, Marius had leaned over and kissed Stef hard. He had put Stef's hand onto his crotch and Stef had responded positively. He had performed fellatio on Marius and then winked at Andrei when he had finished. Andrei had taken that as a sign that he would get the same later on.

They had stopped after a 20-minute drive out of the city and had come to a stop on a large industrial estate. Stef had not questioned why they had stopped; he had anticipated that the party would come later. They had got out of the van and gone behind a large, yellow, steel rubbish skip. He had performed fellatio on the other brother, Andrei, and Marius had satisfied his own, and Stef's, needs.

Now he stood up and smiled at the brothers, doing up his belt buckle. "Party time?" he asked as he turned to face them. His back was to the van as he took a couple of small steps backwards. Andrei appeared from the back of the skip and stepped up close to Stef. He put a comforting left hand on Stef's shoulder as Marius came into view, fastening up his trouser and belt.

"There is no party, my friend." He took his left hand off Stef's shoulder and slapped him hard across the side of the head, the heel of his hand smacking into the young man's cheekbone. The force of the strike knocked Stef off his feet and his shoulder hit the wire mesh fence surrounding the car park and he fell onto his side.

Marius approached him and his right hand grabbed the material of his tee-shirt, pulling him back to his feet. "Such a nice boy," he said, slowly and deliberately. "So eager to please us." He let go of the shirt and slammed his open hand into the left hand side of Stef's face, replicating his brother's blow and sending him sprawling into his brother's arms.

Andrei gripped the young man around his neck with his huge left hand and raised his index finger to his lips. "Sshhh!" he whispered, wary that too much noise may be heard by the younger man in the back of the van. He released his grip on Stef's throat and rested both his hands on his shoulders, then raised them and gave a light slap to both cheeks. "Good boy," he said.

Marius took a step closer. He stared straight into his young victim's eyes. Eyes that were full of fear, staring wide and filling with tears. Marius cupped his left hand round the back of Stef's neck and he launched a massive right-handed punch into his midriff. Stef doubled over with the weight of the punch and the pain as his breath was taken from his lungs. He felt rough hands grab both of his ears and a flash of denim came up past his eyes. He felt the knee smash into his face and the crack that followed seemed like an age later, but sound filled his head. It seemed to enter through his eyes rather than his ears.

He felt a hand grab his hair at the back of his head and, dazed, his head was lifted up, blood streaming from his nostrils. He felt it running into his mouth, and he closed his lips tight, not wanting the taste of blood to confirm what he already knew.

Marius grabbed Stef tightly by his shoulders and turned him in the direction of Andrei. Stef tried to speak, but no words would come out. The blood trickled across his lips and down his chin at each side. He felt Andrei's hands grip him round the neck and his feet were lifted off the floor, thumbs closing tightly against his windpipe. No words could come out. Stef tried, but he could feel the air trapped in his throat. He looked down at the big Romanian, pleading with his eyes. No pity could be seen in Andrei's in response as he moved to his left, still keeping Stef's body aloft. Stef's feet started to kick at the Romanian's shins. "Stop kicking, pretty one!" he said. He shuffled close to the steel skip. Pleading turned to panic in Stef's face, his body started to feel limp, deprived of air, his muscles were failing, his heart pounding faster as adrenaline kicked in, his organs were confused, his brain started to shut down and his eyes started to close.

Andrei let go of Stef's throat with his right thumb. It was a moment of brief respite as the young man's eyes flickered, opened, just as his head was slammed onto the corner of the metal skip. The skull smashed open, the brain inside pierced and burst, blood squirting out in a single line of discharge. The body fell limp and Andrei dropped it to the ground, blood seeping out of the side of the skull, the blood from the nose slowing to a stop.

Marius strolled to the back of the van and opened the rear doors. The young boy, Ben, looked up out of the darkness. "What's happening?" he asked with a worried tone. The big Romanian didn't answer the question. He smiled down at the boy. "In 20 minutes, you be in new home," he replied, as he leant over and gathered together a pile of blankets that were stashed by the doors.

He slammed the doors shut and returned to his brother, who was standing over the lifeless body. Andrei took the sheets from his brother and wiped the blood from the corner and side of the skip, from the floor, rubbing hard to remove the solitary jet. He threw the bloodstained sheets over the body strewn on the floor. The brothers worked together to wrap the body up, winding the material round tight. Marius opened the back doors of the skip one at a time, hinges creaking as unoiled metal turned on unoiled metal. The skip was half empty, half full of black bags, broken wooden pallets and paper. Marius leaned in and moved some of the garbage to the side and Andrei effortlessly lifted and then threw Stef's corpse into the void that his brother had made. Marius quickly covered the blanket-wrapped body with various bags, paper and wood until they were satisfied that it would not be uncovered as the skip became full.

They went back to the van, Andrei was to drive again and he looked in on their other passenger first. "OK. We go," was all he said. The young man, Ben, gave no response, not even to question why a different man had spoken to him. He had not seen Andrei to that point and had not recognised the difference between the two Romanians, not even that the shirt was a different colour. He was too busy wondering what lay ahead, excited that a new life lay ahead, with friends and food and warmth; some of the things he didn't always get at home.

The van moved away and he settled his back into the corner to stay steady and closed his eyes, thinking of the future, and only briefly of the past.

* * *

Sebastian Bludd pressed the phone's screen and the image of his brother Max appeared in front of him. It was not a recent picture, he had not seen him for nearly two years, but he doubted the image would have changed much anyway. Max had their father's genes and his thick, grey hair could only have gone whiter and his slim face already had a few worry lines. The crow's feet at the corner of his eyes had been there for years and could not possibly have changed. *Maybe his hair might have thinned a little*, Seb thought.

"Hi, Max, it's Seb."

"I know, your name comes up on my phone. It's called technology, you should try it."

The dry tone and harsh greeting was intended and Seb knew that there was no malice attached. For a long time they had been straight to the point with each other, no niceties, no love shown. Even when they had been inseparable as youngsters, they had always been sarcastic with each other, always sending the other one up, playing tricks so that the other would get the blame from their parents.

"Yeah, maybe I will one day," Seb responded.

"So what do I owe the pleasure? It's not often you bother these days."

"I know, but I suppose I've been really busy, you know, work and all that."

"Oh yeah, like the rest of us, putting the world right I guess?"

"Something like that. Anyway, that's the reason for the call really. Sorry, it's not a social."

"It's fine. What's going on?"

"Just some stuff that you might be able to help me with."

"Go on."

"Your school chums. What happened to them?"

"What St. Stephen's?"

"It's the only one we went to."

"Well, let's see." There was a protracted pause. "Well, there were six of us. I'm doing OK. I haven't seen the others for a long time."

"Do you keep in touch?"

"Not really, bit difficult in some cases. There was a car crash 10 years ago. The chaps were on their way over to see me, when I lived in Cambridge. David Fothergill was driving, Jeremy Judge was in the front passenger and the others were in the back. You remember David, don't you?"

"Oh, I remember them all, don't worry about that. What happened?"

"Well, seems like they were going too fast over the tops of Derbyshire. The roads can be straight one moment and tight bends the next. They crashed near Cromford, over near Matlock. David died immediately. Jonathon … Jonathan Durie suffered some horrible injuries that I believe are ongoing. Richard Cartland also died, but not straight away, he was sent through the windscreen from the middle of the back seat, severed a major artery and died of blood loss before help came."

"What about Diego and Judge?"

"Jeremy got away without so much as a scratch, unbelievable if you saw the wrecked car."

"Typical. What about Diego? You called him Jimmy, didn't you?"

There was an even more protracted pause. Seb felt an uneasiness transmit down the line.

"Max, what happened to Diego?"

"Jimmy Del Campo suffered massive injuries. He hit the seat in front of him. Brain damage and a broken back. He was pretty much dead when they got to him."

"So he died?"

The pause was more prolonged than before. Seb had a hunch that a lie was about to be told, but felt he would be unable to question it directly.

"Yes," Max whispered. "He died that night."

"So three of them died?" The statement was loaded and not at all sympathetic. "What of the other two, Durie and Judge?" he asked in that order purposely.

"Well, Jeremy was already heading up his father's business and I believe he has total control now. I think his parents both passed away. Jonathon works with him, some kind of managerial role, but I think maybe a director as well."

"Do you know where?"

"Somewhere over in Cheshire, it's called Forster Packaging, I think. Not a million miles from you, I would say. That's assuming you haven't moved?"

"No, still in the same place. Anything else that you know?"

"Sorry. I haven't spoken to them in about five years, bit of a fall-out to be honest."

"Go on."

"Nothing that would help you, I don't think. It was about broken promises, that's all. Sorry, it's a long story and of no consequence to whatever you might be looking into, I'm sure."

Seb knew that there was more to this than was being divulged, but he had no time to quiz his brother any further that night.

"OK, Max. Thanks anyway, you've given me something to start on. How are Mum and Dad, by the way?"

"Well, you know Mum, she's a trooper, strong as an ox that woman. Dad, well he is not good. Not good at all. You know, you really should go and see him. You might regret it if you don't."

"I've no time for regrets. But I will go and see them, soon as I get done with this. I promise."

* * *

Susan Kerby looked in the mirror as she combed her long, blonde hair into a pony tail and wrapped it into a ball atop her head. She held it deftly in place while her other hand reached across the bed and picked up the pale-blue hair net and stretched it over her head, front to back, encompassing the ball of hair and keeping it in place. She picked up the navy-blue cap and placed that over the netted hair.

She looked at herself in the mirror. She was 18, 19 in a month, or at least by her reckoning she was. She had lost count of the days and weeks, the months and years were even more difficult to remember. She noted that she looked that little bit more like her mum these days. In her early teens, she had seemed to resemble her dad more. People had commented, she was a bit of a tomboy, not at all womanly they had said, quite matter-of-fact they were sometimes. But she had changed since she had left, she thought. It is difficult to see when you look in the mirror every day. Minor changes don't happen daily, but over time they add together and become more obvious. Now she looked in the mirror and saw a young lady. No tomboy. Her mum was a good-looking woman, and the fact that she thought she was beginning to resemble her pleased Susan. She had a figure as well. When she was 13, she was easily and quite often mistaken for a boy. She was flat-chested and skinny. At 15, she was no different. At 16, she looked at her reflection and saw a difference; a stark difference. She had shape. She had breasts. And she was five feet nine.

Quite often she had thought that they had brought her here

thinking she was a boy. The work was more a man's work. She and Theresa, her friend across in the opposite bed, whom she called Teri, as everybody did, were the only two females that had ever stayed there. Men and boys had come and gone, some stayed for years, some only stayed a few weeks. One or two had only stayed for days before they moved on, or were moved on. She and Teri had been there five and three years, but they had never been close to the escape that others had achieved. Not that she wanted to escape, she was quite happy with her camp friends, and food, and warmth. But the promises of her own flat, the continued employment and the freedom to have a normal life, had not yet materialised. She had wondered why many times. She had seen male friends go on to get their freedom, although she often wondered where they worked. She had assumed that they would still work the night shift in the factory. Still be part of her team. Maybe they were part of the day shift. She wouldn't know, the two shifts never saw each other. No job handovers, no messages. It was like her friends had disappeared. She had asked after them, but only ever got the response that they were happy and in a better place.

She stood up off the bed, slipping her navy-blue, waist-length, work jacket over her shoulders and stretching her arms up the sleeves. "Come on you lot, best get a move on. We don't want to make the brothers angry. Let's go."

She clapped her hands in a bid to hurry her colleagues along. They didn't need to be told; they shuffled out of the hut one by one and stood in a straight line of nine. Susan Kerby joined the back of the queue to make the squad of 10 complete. She checked her watch: 9.50 p.m. Perfect, the gate would open any second.

* * *

Sebastian Bludd had opened up his laptop and clicked on the web browser. He entered Forster Packaging and Jeremy Judge. Max had been right in his estimations of the locality to his older brother. The packaging factory was less than 15 miles from Bludd's house and approximately 25 minutes' drive. He had Googled the address and put up an aerial view of the factory and its surroundings on screen. It was in an unusual place, at the junction of a road, a canal and overhead to both of these ran a railway line. The address of the factory was Junction Industrial Estate. The canal ran over an aqueduct that ended almost at the factory gate and ran 100 yards long across a 100 foot deep valley with a river running along in a southerly direction. It curved around and almost met an offshoot of the railway line that encircled the industrial estate. To every side there were trees; in the valley with the river, in the circle created by river and train line, on the other side of the river, the other side of the viaduct, everywhere trees, like a sea of broccoli florets in the photograph. It was Maple forest, which Bludd thought was ironic as there was not a maple tree to be seen.

Aerial views are good for some things, but getting an accurate idea of scale, even though there is a scale to the map, can be difficult. Bludd had looked at a feature on the aqueduct whilst he was searching for the actual industrial site. It was classed as an ancient monument, built in 1800, was Grade I listed and was indeed 100 yards long. The railway viaduct that ran 30 degrees from parallel to it, had 12 arches to the aqueduct's three, and ran approximately 125 yards across the dip of the valley. By Bludd's judgement and using these distances as a guide, the industrial estate was around 100 yards wide by 200 yards long, the length running south away from the three-way transport junction. It appeared that there were just two main buildings and several smaller buildings to the rear of the larger building. Bludd guessed that they may have been prefabricated huts, or storage containers, judging by their estimated size.

The main building, which had to be the packaging factory, was about 50 yards wide and maybe 100 yards long, so a quarter of the estate. To its left, as Bludd looked at the aerial view, in reality to the east, was a smaller building with its own enclosed yard. Bludd guessed this was the incinerator building. That left over half of the yard space for staff parking and for the overnight parking of numerous garbage or recycling trucks.

Bludd took a long, hard look at the screen, blinking purposefully a few times as a permanent snapshot and filed it to memory.

He took a look at Companies House, the UK's directory of business. He looked at Forster Packaging, their last posted accounts showed £6M of turnover and a net profit of £1.2M. Staff numbers were in the category of between 10 and 30, which did not really help Bludd in his attempt to assess what kind of resistance he might meet if he were to get inside, but it didn't concern him too much anyway.

He decided to look at the breakdown of directors' details. There it was, in black and white, managing director, Mr Jeremy Judge. Address details as already noted during the conversation with Mrs Judge. Then came the operations director, Jonathon Durie, address Junction House, followed by the postcode that matched the industrial estate. Bludd made a mental note to check that out. Then two non-executive directors, Mr Andrei Lupesku and Mr Marius Lupesku; both having a nominal shareholding of two per cent each. Durie had got 25 per cent, leaving 71 per cent for Judge.

Then Bludd decided to look back five years. His brother, Max, had mentioned a fall-out. He had not mentioned any reason why. Nor had he mentioned any link that he had business wise with Judge. Bludd had noted the pauses in Max's answers to some of his questions and he had a niggling suspicion that something was not stacking up. He opened the page relating to five years previous, and his hunch proved to be right. There, listed as a director, with a paid dividend, was Diego Del Campo, or Jimmy Del Campo as his brother referred to him. Max had said that he had died on the night of the car crash, alongside two others, although later, with brain damage or something. The crash had been 10 years ago, and yet here was a dead man, so-called, collecting dividends just five years ago. Bludd made another mental note to go back to that point the very next time he spoke to Max.

Bludd went back to the aerial photograph. He zoomed in on the industrial estate and looked slightly to its right. There it was, or at least he thought it must have been; Durie's house. More likely a cottage, from this view. It was situated about 50 yards from the gate to the estate, at the end of the road, a small bridge elevated over a narrowing in the canal almost at his front driveway. *Quaint*, Bludd thought.

He switched off the laptop and got himself a glass of water. An early night was in order. An aerial view photograph is one thing, up close and personal was another. He would pay the site a visit before he made the trip to meet Annabelle Judge. Meticulous preparation could be the winning of any case. In this one, he had too much of a vested interest to leave any stone unturned.

* * *

Suasan Kerby checked her watch again. The brothers were late, which was very unusual. It had gone ten o'clock. The shift should have started. They would not be happy, even though it would be their fault. Lost production time was unacceptable.

Then she, with her nine colleagues, heard the metallic clunk of the thick hasp on the steel gate and gate post, the shrill screech as metal is dragged over metal, then the squeal of the hinges, the hefty gate resting on vertical steel pins. The camp was dimly lit, low wattage lights facing directly down to the ground, providing intermittent pools of light on the forest floor.

The brothers appeared from the darkness of the trees. They had stern looks on their faces and Andrei, out front, looked at his watch. "Come on, let's go! You are late to start." Nobody answered back. They inched forward and stopped again. Marius pushed forward, in front of him, a small, blond boy, fresh faced with rosy cheeks.

Marius held his fist in the air, his thumb outstretched, pointing backwards, to and fro, like he was thumbing a lift. "Go now!" he said sternly, the thumb movement an obvious direction for the workers to go through the gate and into the trees then on through to the factory at the other side.

Susan Kerby, being the last in line, was the last to start moving off. But she was halted by a hand to her chest. It was Andrei's hand and she resented him putting it there, even though there was no hint that he had done it for any other purpose than to stop her. "Susan. You sort new boy out. His name is Ben. Sort clothing, show him round. Get him settle in. No work him tonight. Then you go, quickly, to factory." Marius had already left the camp. He would be issuing the night-shift orders and she would make sure they were carried out and that the shift would end with the factory looking untouched as if they had never been there.

She looked at the boy. She remembered her first night. A bit frightened, but quite excited at the same time. Lots of promises for the future, so far unfulfilled. Still, a new arrival usually meant that somebody was leaving, or had left. She still had her team of nine. Now it was 10. Somebody would be drawing the Golden Ticket soon and going on to fulfil their dreams. Maybe this would be her turn. "Come on, Ben, let's show you around. I'll get you a uniform sorted tomorrow. You can have a shower and settle in tonight. We'll show you the ropes tomorrow. You'll like it here. You'll make friends and be happy. I'll make sure of it."

The boy gave her a shy smile. It meant a new home, new friends, a new life. The smile turned wider and brighter. "Thanks, Susan. Thanks a lot."

14

Location

Sebastian Bludd switched off the ignition on his motorbike and freewheeled in the darkness. It was 4.15 a.m. and he was earlier than he had expected to be. He had woken an hour earlier than his alarm had been programmed. The nightmare had returned, as it always did, but with a much more vivid clarity than it usually had. Normally, he would just see darkness, his head shrouded in his pillow case. Voices muffled, not saying much, keeping their identity secret. Hands weighing down on his wrists and arms. Fingers clawing into his head, keeping it still, despite his efforts. The humiliation behind, the last thing to register. This time, he had not been inside his pillow. This time, he was watching from above. He could see the culprits, the accessories to the breach of his dignity. Durie was the one holding his head, David Fothergill had hold of his left arm, Richard Cartland on his right. Diego Del Campo had removed his pants and then secured his leg, stopping it moving. Just. Meanwhile, at the back, Judge was exacting his revenge. In his dream, his nightmare, he could see all their faces. Durie and Judge laughing like mad men, heads swaying back and forth, hysterical. Fothergill and Cartland both stern, concentrating on the job they had been given. Del Campo, eyes closed, no expression, a flicker of a grimace. Maybe regret.

He had woken in a cold sweat. He looked at the time and decided it was not worth trying to get back to sleep. It was only an hour lost and he doubted he could close his eyes and not re-enter the nightmare in the library at St. Stephen's.

The tyres hissed against the tarmac, no engine noise to drown the vague noise. Bludd hit a pothole and the bike jolted and he had to adjust quickly. A bike with no power is more difficult to control than one where a squeeze on the throttle can assist the control. He had mentally calculated the road to be a mile from the main road to the entrance to the industrial estate and to Durie's cottage. He guessed he was about three-quarters of the way down it and jumped off the bike, running alongside it while it still had some momentum. It was pitch dark. The early hour and the surrounding trees blacked out any moonlight. Bludd wanted to ditch the bike and go the rest of the way on foot, but he needed to hide it, in the likelihood that he would not return to it before light. He also needed to leave it somewhere that he would be able to find in the dark. He knew that the canal ran parallel to the road, but the aerial view he had in his mind did not give any clues as to what was in between. He stopped, squeezing the bike's right hand lever, the brakes bringing it to a halt assisted by Bludd's calf and hamstring muscles. He squinted to his right. There was a faint outline of picnic tables, a stone bridge crossing the canal, a lock gate, but nowhere to hide a bike. He looked hard to his left, just bushes and trees. A slight breeze rustled the leaves that were still clinging to branches, a trickle of water as a series of tiny streams met and fell away together at the side of the road. Bludd decided he would have to leave it hidden in foliage. It was Sunday morning, so the chances of anybody passing were slim. The factory would likely be closed, so no workers, too early for dog walkers, unlikely that serious fishermen would try and catch anything in a canal. Only Durie lived down here, although there was another cottage further up the canal, but any inhabitants were unlikely to be awake.

Bludd pushed the Yamaha into the bushes and tried to pull leaves around it. He made a mental note of the blurred surroundings and another to remember the distance he was about to walk. He wore his customary black outfit: Unseen black tee, thick black jumper with a polo neck right up to his jawline, black leather, waist-length jacket, black jeans and black boots. His helmet, black, with shiny black visor, was kept on his head for the moment; visor up to give him some kind of visibility.

The aerial view photograph had offered a one-dimensional aspect to the area and Bludd had tried to imagine how the canal and railway line had sat with each other and what view he might get of the factory and estate. He walked at a medium pace, eyes flicking side to side, keeping all his wits about him. He began to get accustomed to the darkness. He could see that the trees were creating a square tunnel over the road, their branches twisted and bent, growth stunted by continuous passing of high rectangular lorries. The road swayed to the right and Bludd saw moonlight at the end of the tunnel of vegetation. He crept up to the right-hand side of the road, trees and bushes beginning to thin out. The road turned from tarmac to gravel. He stopped behind the last tree. To his right, the road was a bridge, Durie's cottage was at the end of it, a slight shimmer of light twinkled off the roof slate. Ahead, the beginning of the aqueduct and to its left a high, green, metal fence. At the end nearest, Bludd noticed that it chamfered off at an angle, gated. Above it, the dark metal of a railway bridge, higher than a lorry's trailer, running in the direction of the gate, attached at the far right to the stone of the viaduct. A capped wall ran down from the left-hand end of the metal bridge to the road right in front of Bludd.

He slipped across the road and up the slope, right hand clutching the wall as his feet dug into the ground and he levered himself up the slope. The rail line was a single track, raised on a gravel bed. Then to the left it ran off, disappearing quickly in the darkness, arching around to the right in the distance. To the right it ran over the viaduct. Bludd closed his eyes and visualised the scene from above. He reckoned the viaduct would give him an ideal view into the industrial estate and down the canal, even possibly into some part of Durie's place perhaps. He dumped his helmet by the end of the metal bridge and moved down the track slowly, hunched so that his silhouette would be under the bridge and viaduct walls.

He stopped about 100 yards in, to the left-hand side of the track. He poked his head above the stone wall of the viaduct. He could make out the outline of the buildings and block shapes in the distance. He reached inside his jacket and pulled out the night vision lens and put it to his right eye. He scanned the area, left to right. From the gate to his left, he could see the front of the larger building, a large window at what Bludd guessed would be the reception. It had brick frontage, with large glass-panelled office windows to the upper storey. From this angle the length of the building looked like a saw blade, the roof mainly glass panels, set at angles for the rain to run off and the sunlight to get in. The building to the right had a large gate across the front of its yard and some kind of large concertina door across the width of the building itself. The block shapes in the distance were the articulated trucks, two facing front on to Bludd, two, maybe three more sideways on. 'FORSTER PACKAGING LTD' was set out in large, probably white lettering, across the top and running the length of the trailer Bludd could see. 'Specialists in SRP and RRP Containers' underneath and in lower case. Bludd thought back to his meeting on the Friday afternoon and closed his eyes. What had John Preston said? SRP and RRP, 'Shelf Ready

Packaging and Retail Ready Packaging'. Bludd still wasn't much the wiser.

He reached inside his jacket with his left hand and unzipped the inside pocket on his right side. He pulled out his iPod, switched it on and scrolled the dial round on the menu until he found 'Easy Listening'. A list came up and he rolled his finger round until The Eagles came into the bar. He pressed to play and slipped the iPod back into his pocket and pushed the earphones loosely into his ears. The Eagles were nice enough to listen to, not too loud as to deflect his concentration, not too slow to let him fall asleep. Fast enough to tap his feet to and keeps the blood flowing.

He raised the night vision lens again and scanned across the landscape in front of him again. No change. He took it away from his eye again and ran his naked eye along the same path, trying to get them to focus and adapt. He squinted and strained. He would wait for daylight. It was unlikely that any trains would run until after he was gone, after all it was a Sunday and he would get a better look at the yard in the light. It was unlikely that anything would happen until then.

15

Stakeout

Bludd had listened to his iPod Eagles collection and had switched on to Dire Straits, similar 'easy listening' but from different sides of the Atlantic, background music really, not too boring to fall asleep to, not too upbeat to distract.

It was 5.50 a.m. and nothing had happened. Nothing of any consequence anyway except a dog walker out very early, passing by on the canal path. Bludd had got accustomed to the darkness and used his night vision lens intermittently if he thought he had seen some movement. He hadn't.

He raised his lens to his eye, more out of something to do than anything else. Boredom was setting in and it was cold. He scanned the area, left to right, east to west. There was movement. A figure entered the yard, out of a side door of the main building. It headed across the yard and to the smaller building to the right, where Bludd had guessed the incinerators were housed. It was a man, definitely, too big to be otherwise. He opened the large gate enough to squeeze by and then marched across to the concertina door on the front of the building. He left it open slightly.

Then nothing.

Bludd checked his watch: 5.53 a.m. Seven more minutes went by and then he saw the concertina door open wider, slightly. He raised the lens again and he saw the man exit the building, followed by two other blurry figures. The big guy shut the door tight and appeared to lock it. He was fiddling with what looked like a set of keys and a padlock. The three figures all came out into the main yard, squeezing through a gap in the big gate. The last man through was the big guy and he had to open the gate a little wider to get his bulk through. The other two were much smaller than him and they all seemed to have a similar uniform on, all dark clothes anyway. The smaller people both wore hats, the big guy didn't.

As they walked across the yard, the same door that the big guy had exited seven minutes or so earlier opened again and a line of people came into his view. They walked in a neat line, curving round an imaginary cone at a marching pace. The other two from the smaller building joined them at the rear. Bludd counted them. Nine smallish people and one big guy, who was now stood still and watching them march away from him towards the far end of the yard. *Maybe it was brew time*, Bludd thought, and they were heading for one of the mobile units at the far end that he thought he had identified earlier from the overhead photograph. The side door of the main building opened again and another big guy came into view and stood next to the first big guy. They looked like bookends in the blurred vision of the night lens, same size, and same shape. It was uncanny. Another figure appeared. Another small figure, tiny looking as it walked past the two big guys, who stood shoulder to shoulder. The smaller person put on a short jog and caught the group, still marching towards the far end of the yard. The two big guys followed, slowly and with a kind of a swagger. The line of smaller people stopped, in a straight line heading directly away from the two guys and from Bludd on his distant perch.

Then something happened that surprised Bludd. One of the big guys stopped. The other carried on to the end of the line, and carried on some. He went into the trees that lined the back of the yard. Tall trees, Bludd guessed about 50 feet high. A second later, he reappeared and his left hand motioned for the line to move off. One by one, the line moved into the trees and disappeared. Bludd counted them down. From 10 down to one. Just as the last one moved out of sight, the hat came off and a mass of hair dropped down the back. It was difficult to say for sure, but Bludd thought it was blonde.

The big guy by the gate walked back to his twin and they high-fived and then continued to walk back down the yard in Bludd's direction. They re-entered the larger building by the side door. Bludd waited a half hour and saw nothing more. Sunlight would be up in another half hour and he wanted to be away by then. He placed his night vision lens back inside his jacket, zipped it back up high and moved off to go and search for his bike.

* * *

Jonathon Durie closed the gate behind him and looked at the sky, it would be light soon enough, although the weather prospects he had just seen on the television meant that it might not be a particularly bright morning. The forecast was rain, all day: heavy in the morning, intermittent showers in the afternoon. He had woken early, as he usually did, with the pain in his leg stabbing at his knee to start moving, and stabbing at his brain to get some pain relief. He made himself a coffee and took the pills and watched the news for 10 minutes, followed by the weather bulletin. The news showed no good news and the weather didn't get any better.

As he stared at the sky, a single raindrop fell on his forehead and trickled down his brow and onto the bridge of his nose, rolling away at the bump, down his ruddy left cheek. He wiped it away and as he did so, he looked across the canal bridge and saw a silhouette moving against the dark backdrop of the trees and railway sidings wall. The figure glided down the hill and came to a stop as it met the tarmac surface at the bottom. It disappeared for a moment and then almost immediately came back into view. It was carrying something, something oval, or round, he couldn't tell what in that light and his eyes weren't brilliant anyway. The figure moved off at speed and then, just for an instant, he forgot himself and considered giving chase. Anybody up on the rail track at this time in the morning was probably up to no good. His brain told his body to move and his leg told his brain there was no chance.

He put it out of his mind and hobbled across the gravelly road. He would catch the brothers before they headed off to their apartment, and see that the nightshift had been trouble-free. It usually was. He knew that they had been out the evening before and he wanted to know if they had come back with anything that may be of interest to him: whether any fresh meat was on the menu; whether they had fed themselves first, or whether he had been in their minds and whether they had put his preferences first. It had been a few weeks since they had rotated the staff and a hole needed filling. Maybe it would need filling again before too long.

16

Truth Hurts

Sebastian Bludd had taken the motorbike home and warmed himself with a coffee and a slice of toast. He had arrived back at just after seven and he had plenty of time to kill.

He sat back on the sofa and closed his eyes. He focused on the last few hours. Not much to remember at all really. His mind flashed with images, playing out on the back of his eyelids. The dog walker. That was around 5.30 a.m. Then he fast forwarded to the two big guys, first one going to the smaller building, coming back with two smaller people. Then the other big guy joined them and then the others came out in line, almost marching up the yard. He focused hard and zoomed in. The two big guys were not just big, they were huge. The darkness made any chance of putting a face to the body unlikely, but they had distinctive shapes. They had not been wearing hats, the rest of the people had. The two guys' heads were massive and of a shape all of their own. Almost Neanderthal at the front, a long forehead, like an overhang over their eyes. The back seemed rippled, like a Shar Pei dog's fur. The shape of their skull seemed misshapen, like the chocolates you get in the bargain bucket, not fit for the box it was intended for, but still tasty enough for someone to buy. Bludd didn't know if his mind was playing tricks, or the poor light had distorted them in the distance, but he was sure that this pair, whoever they were, were probably not the nicest folk you could meet. And then his mind flashed back to his meeting with Annabelle Judge the previous morning in his front room. What had she said? "There were two foreign names on the books." She had not known who they were. Bludd bet himself a pound to a penny that these men he had seen were the two foreigners.

And then she had mentioned Durie. And he had seen Durie that morning. And Durie had seen him, he was sure he had. There was no mistaking it from Bludd's point of view. The sandy hair, fringe cut straight across with no style, just like a basin cut that kids all had at some point when they were little in the 1970s, irrespective of wealth. Durie still had it, except now it continued down into a sandy-coloured beard. He still wore the glasses, possibly the same pair, presumably with different, stronger lenses. Durie's eyesight had been appalling at school and he had worn thick lenses. This was the first source of torment for Durie, all the kids who had glasses were all "Speccy four eyes", but his glasses, like jam jar bottoms, had singled him out for extra ridicule. Then, when they had tired of that and the teenager teasing had kicked in, the other kids were ruthless. Durie was always the quiet one, too shy to speak due to his stammer. But at times, he was forced to, like reading out loud in class. The others kids would just do it, read out loud. It was easy. Not for Durie. He would sit there, sweating, waiting for his name to be called out for his turn to read. The longer the wait, the worse his speech would become. He would stutter his way through line after line, his breathing getting faster, his ability to get through a whole sentence without stopping or stuttering almost completely gone. He had ruined many a chapter of *Far From The Madding Crowd* and was lucky that the teacher had taken pity on him when it came to doing play readings. He had only ever had small parts, generally no part in any of Shakespeare's works. As far as anyone knew, none of the Capulets or the Montagues had a speech impediment.

Oberon definitely did not. Bludd had only seen Durie fleetingly that morning, but had noted that the swagger that he had walked with at school when he had his group of friends around him had gone, and had been replaced with a pronounced limp. He flashed back to school. In his mind he watched Durie and his gang, led by Judge, with only his brother, Max, missing from the scene. They were walking away from him, swaggering, laughing. He swore he heard Durie mutter, "Yer, you showed him, Jeremy."

Bludd opened his eyes, the image of Durie enough to jolt him into action. He checked his watch. He had maybe an hour to kill. He would get up to the Judge house in plenty of time to have a look around before he met with Annabelle Judge. He put on his headphones and pushed the play button on the remote. A bit of rousing *Rachmaninov* and some stirring *Strauss* would keep him motivated and Bludd felt that they were appropriate for a Sunday morning. *Brahms* and *Liszt* were on hold until this case was closed.

* * *

Durie met the Lupescu brothers at the motorised gate. It was just creaking to a shut position as they came out of the reception door. "Good ner-night, last ner-night?" he quizzed them.

The brothers looked at each other and smiled. "Yes, was good. Good for you too," they said in perfect synchronicity.

Durie smiled back and his hands instinctively rubbed together. "Really? Tell me more."

Andrei answered, "Nice young boy. He's 15. Blond. You will like, I think."

Durie's good hand stroked his beard. "Bring him to me later, I want to meet him. Maybe ber-bring the other ber-blond lad,

Karl. He is coming up to 16 soon. I want to give him an early present. You can take the young lad and show him the apartments and let him see what a ger-good life he can make for himself." He said it with a slanted smile and a raised eyebrow.

The Romanian brothers looked at each other again and gave a crooked, bad-toothed smile. "OK. See you about four?" they said, synchronised again.

"Fer-four will be fer-fine," Durie replied. He tapped Andrei on his shoulder as he shuffled past him. He would work for a few hours in the morning and have the schedules for the coming week put together. Dayshift and nightshift would both be prioritised. He would have a spot of lunch; maybe go to local pub for a short while. Then he would have a look on the Internet and see what he could find. He would trawl through his history and find his favourite sites, get himself in the mood to meet a newcomer and maybe get to know Karl better than Karl would ever imagine.

* * *

Bludd decided to go on the motorbike again. He had looked again at Google maps. Firstly, he had called up the overhead view of the factory at Maple Forest. At the top of the yard the trees met the fence. The mass of tree tops carried right through to the railway track and river that encircled the forest. Or at least that's how it looked. Bludd zoomed in and focused. He squinted as he scrolled left and right and back again. Then he saw it, a tiny clearing, with small paths shooting off like spokes on a wheel. The broccoli effect that the tree tops offered was there, but it was very uniformed and had straight edges to it along the spoke paths. It was almost impossible to see, certainly if you were not looking hard for something. The straight edges could only be one thing in Bludd's mind. Buildings. Or huts at least. He focused hard and the spokes numbered six, which meant that there were six huts in between them. Nothing else could be deciphered from the image. There was no option to zoom down and take a frontal or rear look at the area, no roads around meant no photographs at ground level. Bludd knew that whatever was in the camp was key to what Judge was up to and he would have to get beyond the fence and into the forest.

He tapped into the maps page again, briefly searched for, and found, the Judge property. It was quite isolated, set away from the main road by a driveway that must have been 100 yards long. It meant that he only got an aerial view, the photographic vehicle not able to get close enough to take pictures of the buildings. There were two structures, the main one about half as big again as the smaller one. The main road ran north to south and the main house was nearest to it. The way the driveway looped around made Bludd think that the back of the house was nearest the road. The front would then be facing the other house. Or maybe it was a garage, or an office. Perhaps both. The rear of the larger, main building was shrouded by more broccoli florets and they ran all around the north side to the side of the smaller building. The whole place looked like it had been a farm. A dirt track led from the smaller building to one that made the house look tiny. A barn, Bludd thought. The place looked like it was, or had been, a working farm, but there were no machines on the scene and so it was odds-on to be the latter. It had been working farm.

He had recognised the plan view of the local area as it was home to a well-known attraction for climbers. The rocks at Whaley Ridge were only a few hundred yards from the Judge home and Bludd knew that he could skirt round the back, climb the hill and have a decent view of the premises from the south and be a good 80 feet above them. It was a good enough view to recce the area, but one that he could only get to on the bike. Using the car would have meant quite a long walk and then he would have to walk back to retrieve it. Using the bike meant that he could ride right up to the point where he got the best view, and then when he had seen enough, he could ride right on down to the front door.

He pulled up on the footpath looking down on the property. The larger building was L-shaped, not like he had seen on the photograph. The legged extension to the far side had been recently added and stretched out from the main structure towards the smaller building. In the centre of the buildings was a circular gravel-topped car park. There stood three cars. The black Range Rover that Annabelle Judge had visited Bludd's house in, a sports car, but not a standard one, it was a four-door version, clearly, by its shape, it was a Porsche. Bludd closed his eyes and focused. It was a Porsche Panamera, not that it was important. The last car was a Mini, except in Bludd's mind it wasn't. Cars did not excite him; they were a tool to get from A to B. But some cars annoyed him, or rather the manufacturers did. The Mini Countryman, which he thought this was, was a Mini that had just been enlarged to make it a four door and it was a four-wheel drive, but it was no longer a Mini. It was much larger than many of its category rivals and therefore did not suit the name or the brand. In Bludd's mind, it was a cynical move by the manufacturer to stretch out the sales opportunities.

He looked over the dry stone wall, high over the Judge home. The smaller building was actually a double garage, but it seemed to be two-storey as there were two single window dormers that both had a central apex that was tiled the same as the roof. From above, as Bludd had already seen, the dormer would not be visible; the tiles would just mingle into each other.

The main house had a central door to the original building, a sash window to each side of the door and an identical one to the first floor, directly above them. In the centre, over the front door was a round porthole style window. Bludd was guessing at the floor plan and had a visual in his mind of how the building was set out. The right-angled extension that was a new addition to the existing building had been built in keeping with the original brick and without the prior knowledge from above, a viewer may well think it was original. Bludd had his floor plan mapped out as: hall, family living room to the left, kitchen to the right, dining room attached, the extended section would be some kind of cinema room, maybe with a gym attached. The latter would be for Mrs Judge to use, because she was in fine trim. He did not think that Jeremy Judge would have changed so much to be a fitness fanatic.

There was not a lot more that could be gained from the view he had against what he had seen on the computer screen earlier that morning, so Bludd kickstarted the bike and twisted the throttle and made his way slowly back the way he had arrived. He joined the main road, a link from Macclesfield to Buxton, and slowly approached the Judges' abode. He blinked his way along the driveway and approached what he had thought would be the rear of the main building, taking a visual picture of the building as he approached, then passed. He circled the bike round into the parking area to the front and kicked out the bike's stand from under the engine, leaning it over and dismounted. He removed his black helmet and rested it on the seat.

It was 9.50 a.m. Ten minutes early, but he wanted to start as soon as possible and then he could get back to the packaging factory in plenty of time to have a proper look around in daylight. He was desperate to get back behind the fence, especially the one at the far end. He wanted to see what and whom the camp was home to and find out what went on there.

Annabelle Judge opened the large, overly wide oak door. She had clearly been waiting for Bludd's arrival and she herself was keen to get on. Her husband was not due back until much later in the week, but he had a habit of cutting trips short when his business was done, and the way he worked was ruthless. She had seen it many times. He always got what he wanted and more often than not, he got it ahead of schedule.

Bludd ruffled his hair and patted it down as straight as he could, not wanting to look too dishevelled. He looked at Annabelle Judge. She was dressed down compared to last time, but she still looked stunning in a pair of dark blue, denim jeans and a check patterned blouse, white with a navy print. Simple, but on her, amazing. Her long legs were emphasised even more by the heeled, brown boots that came to just below her knees. Bludd noticed that the blouse was quite tight fitting and one thing he had not noticed at the first meeting was Annabelle Judge's breasts. Or rather the lack of any. At the first meeting she had worn an overcoat and it would have been impossible to notice, even if Bludd had been looking. Now, in the coldness of the October morning, a slight breeze was forcing the material against her body and her nipples protruded out sharply. Bludd looked up, aware that he had begun to stare and clearly Annabelle Judge had noticed as she blushed at him. He blushed back. He looked her in the eyes and remembered how beautiful she was. Her shiny, black hair had been freshly washed and was loose and flowing, Strands flicked across her face in the wind. Her green eyes sparkled, but were looking down and away from him with her embarrassment and shyness.

She moved the hair from her face and ran her fingers behind her ears to try and set it in place. She smiled a little. "Please, Mr Bludd, do come in."

She moved back into the house, leaving Bludd on the doorstep and went into the room to the right. Bludd couldn't help having another sneaky look at her long legs, accentuated in tight denim. He was slightly annoyed that she wore her blouse out of her pants and it was just long enough to cover her bottom, although Bludd was sure that it was in keeping with the rest of her and would be perfectly round and yet slim at the same time. He closed his eyes for a mental picture; he could leave the rest to his imagination.

The room to the right was the kitchen, as Bludd had guessed when he was sat on the hill overlooking the property. It was a large, old-fashioned, farm-like affair, with a deep white enamel sink and a steel cooking stove, finished in bottle green, as close a shade as could be found to the drawer and door fronts around the kitchen. There were worktops to three sides and a large oak, or beech, table in the centre. He stood in the doorway, another door directly in front of him. He had guessed that this would be the dining room and he was sure that he was right, no sense in it being anywhere else but next to the kitchen.

"I was just about to brew up. Do you want one?" Annabelle Judge asked, disturbing Bludd's thoughts.

"Great!" he replied. "Coffee, milk and two sugars, please."

She grabbed a glass jug from the base of the black, glossy machine and filled two mugs, already set out on the black marble worktop. She moved to a fridge to her left that Bludd thought was nearly as big as his entire kitchen. She poured milk into the mugs and returned it to the fridge, its silver door not in keeping with the country feel of the rest of the room.

"Two sugars?" she confirmed by question. Not waiting for

an answer, she put them in his coffee and passed him the mug, her fingers clamped around the top, like those machines you see in fairs where the grab hand hardly ever keeps hold of the prize. She offered it to him handle first. "I'm glad you decided to come," she said.

"It took a bit of persuasion from my girlfriend to be honest, but I will let you know if I'm glad I came later in the week, maybe sooner. I'm not giving you any guarantees here, let's just see where things take us."

Bludd thought he saw a faint look of disappointment in her eyes when he mentioned that he had a girlfriend, but then he thought he might be getting mixed messages, and carried on.

"How many shifts run at the factory?"

Annabelle looked to the ceiling, thinking. "As far as I know there is just the one. When I was there it started at eight and finished at five. I'm not aware of any changes, but I don't think I would be told something like that anyway. The only thing that used to change, or at least was flexible, was the truck drivers' hours, which depended on how busy they were and, of course, where they were going. Why do you ask?"

"I was there this morning. Don't forget, it's Sunday. There was nothing going on until about six o'clock. There had been lights on all the time I was there, but no sign of life until just before six. I saw 12 people. Two came out of the smaller unit and they met up in the yard with the rest, including two enormous men."

"The smaller unit is where the incinerators are housed. I think I told you that they burn dogs for the council and others. You think they are running some kind of night shift?"

"They are definitely up to something. It looked like they were doing a shift. They all had a kind of uniform on, dark and plain, and hats, except the two big guys. They looked like they were in charge. But here's the weird thing. They all disappeared to the back of the estate and into the trees. Only the big guys came out."

"What? I don't understand. At the end of the estate is Maple Forest, it more or less surrounds the estate and goes on for miles uninterrupted except for the canal and the railway line. And the river."

"You would think so, even if you were looking from above. But there is some kind of a camp there, some way beyond the fence, probably out of earshot distance. I reckon there is a night shift, but it is some kind of illicit thing by the looks of things. You mentioned two foreigners who had become directors. When was this?"

"About five years ago. More or less the time that I took a back seat. Do you think they have something to do with the camp?"

"I'm not sure about anything as yet." Bludd took a slurp of his coffee. It was strong and sweet. Perfect. "What I do know is that there are a lot of bad people around. I am making the assumption that the foreigners are the two guys I saw earlier and let me tell you, they don't look like they are sent from heaven or anything. The first thing that crossed my mind was that maybe they had easy access to illegal immigrants and these workers are there on the hush-hush. They probably pay them in food and clothes and lodgings and not much more. That would mean that they could run a whole shift on not a lot of outlay, not compared to what they would be paying the day shift anyway. That would certainly help towards expanding your profits and not having to employ anyone through the books and all the costs that go with it. This is all speculation, obviously, but there is something illegal going on, I am sure of it. I just need to find out what."

"What can I do to help? I mean, I don't know anything that goes on up there. All I can do is access the sales system and ledger remotely, but I don't think that will tell you much and I can't do that without getting into Jeremy's office, which is in the other building over there, I need to be plugged into his modem. Mr Bludd, does any of this have any link to your feud with Jeremy?"

"I don't think so. Let's just say that, to my mind, your husband is a very bad man. Well, he was anyway, and I haven't seen anything yet to make me change my mind. Quite the opposite, in fact. I need to get into the estate. Do you have keys?"

"Yes, to the offices, but there is a digital lock on the gate and the fence is high, you can't just climb in. It's a very secure site; you can only get in on business."

That gave Bludd an idea. He could get in on business. Not his own, but if Preston Die Supplies dealt with Forster Packaging, he might be able to hitch a lift right through the gates. He took his mobile phone from his pocket and closed his eyes. His memory flashed back to the note he had made on his desk a couple of days earlier, John Preston's number. He dialled it.

"Hello, Mr Bludd." John Preston answered in a flash. "Do you have news?"

"All sorted, John. Piece of cake. I just need to run you a copy of the disc and drop it in."

"Great, come over when you are ready. Sooner the better for me. How much do I owe you?"

"Well, I might be able to waive my fee, but I need a favour in return, which I am not sure you can help me with."

"OK," Preston responded, "Sounds interesting? How can I help?"

"Do you, as a company, have any dealings with a packaging company called Forster Packaging?"

"Doesn't ring any bells, but I am not in touch with the customers and even less so with the converter or packaging customers. Hang on though; I am in the system, just doing a bit of work from home. Forster Packaging you say?"

"That's right; they are in a place called Maple."

Bludd heard the tapping of the keys at the other end of the phone, then a momentary pause. He imagined the egg-timer spinning around as the server searched for the name.

"Got it!" Preston exclaimed. "Yes, we do deal with them, just bear with me." The keys tapped again. A few seconds passed. "OK, so they buy a few bits and pieces from us. I guess they have a die-shop or forme room there. It looks like they buy cutting rule from us, flat bed and rotary. The volumes aren't big, though, so it may just be for repairs to the dies. The last thing they purchased was what we call a Perforating Pizza Wheel, it's like a pizza wheel that you can use to cut samples of shelf-ready boxes. In fact, they have an order on with us at the moment, which is due for delivery on our van on Tuesday."

"Any chance it could be delivered tomorrow? First thing?" Bludd asked.

"I can't promise first thing, it depends on whether the order has been picked. Probably that would get done tomorrow. I can get the lads to do it first and stick it on the van; it would get there about mid-morning. That any good to you?"

Bludd paused and gave it a moment's thought. He would get there early again, see if anything was going on and see if the night before was a one-off or a regular thing. He could meet the van, jump in the passenger seat, or the back. "Could I borrow one of the warehouse jackets, with your logo on it?" he asked.

"Sure." Preston replied, "I will get the driver to bring it over. So what's the deal? You give my driver a copy of the disc and he gets you into the customer?"

"That's about the size of it. There will be a bit of playing by ear going on once we get in, but I will not keep your man any longer than necessary."

"It's a deal, then, Mr Bludd. Does the disc give me anything conclusive?"

"More than enough. Can you get your man to call me as he approaches the factory, I'll be waiting on the lane. Thanks."

He didn't give Preston time to respond and he pushed his phone to end the call. He thought for a second about the timing. Could he gain anything by going back up there this afternoon? He wanted to have a look at Judge's office, in the other smaller building across from where they stood. He thought that he could possibly spare a few hours later to go and have a look at how he might get into the camp at the back of the factory. Probably better to do that when it was dark.

"Well, looks like I'm in," he said to Annabelle Judge. He took a swig of his coffee. "I want to have a look at your husband's office, please."

"Sorry, but he locks the door. I only have access to the garage and storage below," she replied with a glum look and with a tone to match.

"Show me!" Bludd replied.

He put his coffee on the table and set off out of the room and out of the front door. Annabelle Judge did the same and picked a set of keys off a hook on the wall and followed Bludd. They crunched across the car park in unison. Bludd stopped halfway across and looked up at the dormer outcrops jutting out of the roof. On the front, there were double garage doors, flip-over style. To their right was a single door, presumably the door that would lead to the office, via some stairs. He walked to his right and looked at the side elevation of the building. At the end of the building, to the second floor, was a small window. Bludd guessed it was probably the same at both ends, to allow as much light in as possible.

"Got any ladders?" he asked Mrs Judge.

"I think so, in the garage." She searched through the bunch of keys and bent down low to the handle at the bottom and centre of the wooden door. Bludd could not help but notice that her blouse rose as she crouched and his suspicions about her shape were confirmed; she was truly awesome in all areas. To his disappointment, she turned the handle and yanked the door upwards and over, her blouse dropping back to cover her again. She looked through the keys again and found a small padlock key. On the wall was a set of ladders, hung high on two struts 10 feet apart. She fiddled the key into the padlock at the near end and the chain it was holding chinked as it fell against the wall. Bludd stepped in and behind her and removed the ladder from its holder and went outside.

"What are you going to do?" Annabelle asked.

"I think some burglars have paid you a visit." He leaned the ladders against the wall and pushed the internal section upwards so that the tip was just shy of the window.

"That's not a good idea. Jeremy will go mad."

"Let him," Bludd replied. "I need to have a look in here to see if there is anything that will give us a clue as to what he gets up to." He steadied the ladder against the wall and pulled down to push the base into the gravel. He turned around and saw a decent sized stone across the way and wandered over to it. He collected it in his right hand, giving it a manual weighing, sizing it up to see if it was man enough for the job. "Don't worry, when did you say he was back, Thursday? It will all be done and dusted by then, I promise."

"I don't think I said when he would be back. And I hope it is all over by then. That's if there is anything to be finished." Her tone had changed to a worried one and she put an outstretched hand across her forehead.

Bludd hit the window with the stone. It didn't break. He tried again, a little harder. It didn't break. He looked down at the nervous Annabelle. "Sorry, looks like I am going to make a mess." He threw the stone with all his strength and smashed the window into a hundred pieces. He took his elbow and knocked out the larger pieces that had stayed in the frame, picking at the smaller ones with his fingers and throwing them to the floor inside. "Looks like we are in," he shouted down.

"Looks like you are," she replied. "I can't have anything to do with this." She turned away and headed back to the house.

Bludd got rid of the last shards of glass from the bottom edge of the window frame and hitched himself up so that his stomach lay across the wood of the frame. He pushed his arms up straight and locked them out, brought his foot up and over and into the building and sat astride the window. He turned around and brought his right knee up to his face and twisted it in to join his left leg. He jumped down and dusted off the tiny fragments of glass that were on his shirt. There was a door to his left, at the top of the stairs he guessed, and a short hallway in front of him leading to another door. The carpet below him was a coarse weave, almost industrial, and it was covered in glass. The door was of an internal standard, quite lightweight, but it was locked. He tried the handle a second time just to check. He thought it was likely to be locked. If Judge had something to hide, he would hardly make it easy to access.

He stepped back and kicked at the door with the sole of his boot. It didn't budge. They rarely did at the first attempt, no matter what the quality. This one was heavy duty compared to his at home, but it would not stop him from getting into the office beyond. He kicked again, right footed and aimed at the lock and handle to the right of the door. He kicked again, and again, not feeling as though there was any movement happening to the door or its frame. He kicked out seven more times and then he heard the shallow crack of timber. The door frame had splintered on the other side. He gave it another kick, then another. Then he gave it a barge with his left shoulder, turned around and used his right. No difference in impact, but he felt more comfortable using his stronger side. The door frame cracked some more and he could see the different emphasis of the light inside the office, peeking through the split. One more kick was all that was required and he summoned all his energy and straight kicked the lock. The door flung open with a snap of wood and a whoosh of air.

He stepped inside. There was a large desk to the left-hand window and a long, dark wood bookshelf, lower than the window and running into the corner. There was a metal cabinet on the opposite wall and an identical one behind him. To his right, the ceiling sloped away and a three-seater leather sofa was set towards the far corner. A television was above the far arm of the sofa, hanging from the wall.

Bludd pulled out the leather office chair from under the desk and pulled at the drawers to either side. They were all locked. He looked out of the window and from the dormer he could see Annabelle Judge pottering around the kitchen, her denim-clad legs moving in and out of Bludd's vision. It crossed his mind that she might be making lunch. He hoped she was making enough for two.

He stood and stepped back, taking a panoramic look at the long, low bookcase. It looked like it was full of trade magazines and instruction manuals. There was a bunch that were called 'Corrugated Box News'. Next to them were 'What's New in Packaging?' Then there was a row of smaller, A5-sized books that were a set of training manuals all from the same publisher. 'Negotiation Skills', 'Effective Marketing', 'Managing People', 'Lean Manufacturing'. There were ten in all, but they all looked as boring as each other to Bludd. There were four cardboard file boxes. Two were labelled 'Bobst', the others 'Martin' and 'Ward'. He ignored them.

He stepped over to his right and tried the handle of the metal cabinet. It was no shock that it was locked. He took his phone out from his pocket and dialled the Judge house number. Annabelle answered it quickly. "What is it? Have you found something already?" she asked with an air of anxiety.

"Nothing yet, everything is locked up. Can you throw me a hammer up, or a crowbar, or something."

She put the phone down and Bludd checked that the other metal cabinet was, in fact, locked as well. He saw Annabelle leave the house and head across to the garage. She looked fantastic as the wind gusted and blew her hair back off her face. He sensed her looking upwards and she took a quick step or two, so that she was out of view. Clearly she was a little uncomfortable with him. She needn't have been. He might always have a look, but he would never touch. There was no point. Even if he wasn't with Chrissie, he wouldn't bother trying to get to first base with anyone else, as there was nothing past that for him. It didn't stop him from flirting though. Perhaps he would try a little harder with her later. Perhaps over lunch.

He heard a call from outside the broken window and went back down the hall, peeping his head through the opening. "Look out!" Annabelle shouted as she tossed a claw hammer up to him. Bludd instinctively stuck out a hand and caught the tool in mid-air.

"Is that all you could find?" he shouted at her.

"No, there is an iron bar, but I don't think I can throw it up."

"Well, bring it up the ladder then, I can hold the top from here."

She looked at him and puffed her cheeks out, then let out a big sigh. She disappeared for a moment and then came back into view. She tucked the bar through a loop on her right hip and mounted the ladder, checking it for steadiness as she did.

Bludd leaned out of the top and held the ladder at its top. Annabelle reached the top rung and was a foot below where Bludd's face was looking down.

"We must stop meeting like this," he greeted her.

She smiled sarcastically. "I'll make you a sandwich shortly and get some fresh coffee on. Let me know if you need me."

"Will do," Bludd said, as he disappeared from her view. She was slightly taken aback that he had not stayed to hold the ladder for her return to the floor.

Bludd went back to the office. He had no idea what he was looking for. Maybe a set of accounts, maybe a computer, a laptop. Instinctively, he went to the metal cabinet on the far wall. He switched the hammer from his left hand to his right and crossed over with the bar. The bar was two foot long and had flat ends. He smashed the hammer head down on the handle. It broke off, but the door remained closed, but a bit twisted at the lock. He slipped the end of the bar into the slither of a gap and wrenched it forward, pulling back on the bar and twisting at the same time. The gap got wider. He slid the bar in more and got the full inch of its diameter inside. He pulled back and pushed forward. The metal squealed as the torque of his leverage stretched the steel against the internal lock mechanism. He jammed the bar down against the lock and wrenched at it again. It squealed and scraped and then all of a sudden it broke. The right hand door flew back open. Bludd put the tools down at his feet and opened the left hand door outwards with his left hand.

There didn't seem to be much of any interest. A full three shelves of concertina folders on thin steel racks, labelled A-Z, 'Customers', 'Suppliers', 'Manuals'. There seemed to be a mass of box or cardboard samples on the floor of the cabinet. On the first shelf a green cardboard box folder was labelled 'Flutes'. Bludd was slightly intrigued and pulled it out. He opened it and inside were hundreds of small pieces of corrugated card. All the same size, but slightly different in thickness and the size of the corrugations were all ever so slightly different. He did not realise there was so much to a cardboard box. He went to slip the folder back in its slot, but something took his eye. A slight flash of metal which dulled as he closed the light from the gap he had made. He put the folder on the floor and pulled out the next one to it and laid that on the floor as well. At the back of the cabinet was a laptop computer and another cardboard box file. This time it was a dull black colour.

He pulled out the laptop and the black box and took them over to the desk. He laid the computer down and opened the box, pressing the small black button on the side. Inside was a mass of discs, unclear if they were CD or DVD types. Each one had a title, written in thick, black lettering.

He opened the laptop and pushed the power button. The laptop was not a new one, by any means. It was an ancient looking DELL and it was quite battered in appearance, the shiny silver top chipped at the side to reveal black scratches and gouges. The computer powered up and then came a silver rectangle, the marker flashing and asking for a password. *Shit!* Bludd thought. Passwords were usually a word associated with the owner's past, or a hobby, or a family member, or a pet. Bludd thought about Judge. He did not think he was the sentimental type, so kids' names probably didn't come into it, nor would his parents. He tapped in Annabelle. A red circle with a white cross jumped out at him. He tapped in Forster. Same response. Bludd closed his eyes and focused on the past, something he did not normally do when he was thinking about Judge, quite the opposite. *What was Judge into?* he asked himself. *Kids and Rugby* was the answer that shouted back. He thought about where Judge was from. He was born in Middlesex. Bludd closed his eyes, he saw a picture of a 13-year-old Judge, the school blazer on, jade green. Around his neck was a multi-coloured scarf, wrapped around, one end at the front, one draped over his back. The scarf was red, green and white, light blue and maroon. It was of Harlequins Rugby Club. He opened his eyes and tapped in Quins. The instruction came back that it was incorrect. Passwords are usually six letters or numbers, or a mix, apparently that is preferred. He tapped in the full name. "Harlequins". Incorrect again.

He thought hard. His own passwords were all anagrams of his family's names. *Too sentimental for Judge*, he thought. Then it struck him and he tapped in the name Rembrandt.

Bingo. He was in.

The screen lit up a second later. Rembrandt had been the dorm in which Judge had been in during his stay at St Stephen's. Each year had a different group of famous people that stayed with them through their school journey. Bludd was in the year above Judge and his year group stayed in dorms named after famous engineers. Bludd had stayed in Arrol, named after the man who built the Forth rail bridge. Max had stayed in Constable Dorm, his and Judge's year being named after artists.

Bludd clicked on the e-mail icon and up came another silver box. Password and log in required. *Shit!* Bludd thought again. He clicked on the password and up came Judge's email address. That was simple enough. He clicked on the log in box. He tapped in Harlequins.

Eureka. He was into Judge's e-mails.

Then he turned his attention back to the box of discs. He pulled one out at random. 'Be Prepared' it was called. He pulled another out. 'Lucky Teacher'. The third one said 'Phil 05'. He pushed the button on the side of the laptop and the disc player tray popped out. He looked at the three options in front of him and picked out 'Be Prepared'. He slid it from its transparent plastic sleeve and pushed it into the tray, pressing the centre so it clicked into place. He shut the tray and the whir of a motor started. The whirring gathered pace and the screen went blank, a white circle with a triangle pointing to the right appeared in the centre of the screen. The whirring slowed and then sped up again as he clicked the mouse on the triangle.

All sorts of flags and foreign language came up in front of him. German, Danish, Swedish and then English. 'This film is for adults only' it said, and then it flashed on the Spanish flag and presumably the same words.

Bludd sat back in the chair and leant back into its soft leather back.

The screen lit up. Two cub scouts were climbing some steps. The title came up and overlaid the film. 'Be Prepared'. Bludd remembered it was the Scout movement motto. The two young boys knocked on a door and held out some kind of tickets in their hands. A man opened the door. He was bearded and wore a brown Paisley dressing gown that was thigh length. He looked at the boys and they pointed at the tickets. He smiled and patted the pockets of his gown. He cocked his head to the side and waved the boys into the apartment and closed the door. Bludd smiled as he looked at the décor in the man's living room: brown and orange wallpaper and wooden cladding. *This was definitely from the 1970s,* he thought. The two boy scouts stood in front of the man as he reached over and picked his wallet from a sideboard. As he opened it, coins fell out and ran across the floor in all directions. The boys immediately dropped to their knees and scrabbled around collecting the coins as quickly and diligently as they could. The man stood over them. He moved his gown to one side and revealed his erect penis. He started to stroke it. One of the boys looked up and looked away embarrassed. The man held out his left hand and the boy emptied the coins into it. The man put them into his pocket, but held the boy's wrist with his right hand. He put the boy's hand on his penis and made him stroke it. The other boy looked up and stared at the man's genitals. The man ushered his hand upwards and the boy slowly obliged and took over from his friend. Then the man pointed the first boy and pushed his penis towards his mouth. The boy turned to his friend and they giggled at each other.

Bludd clicked the mouse over the stop button. He had seen enough and knew what would follow. He did not need to see it.

He removed the disc and picked up 'Phil 05'. He entered it into the tray and closed it. The motor kicked into life again and the circle and triangle came up. He clicked on it. This one was no 1970 professional porn film. This one showed the grainy shots of a beach, a crowded beach somewhere he recognised. There were people all around, mainly white, but plenty of Oriental Asians there as well. He clicked on fast forward. Then he stopped. The beach was white and long. It stretched as long as the eye, or the camera, could see. Palm trees and parasols faded away into the perspective distance. Bludd recognised

Palaui Island from when he had visited it on a family holiday in 1976. They had not lived in the Philippines, but they had once visited for a holiday. It was a beautiful place.

The camera panned around towards the sea and focused on two little children playing at the water's edge, jumping over the tiny wavelets and splashing each other.

Then it stopped and a new scene started. It was by a swimming pool and there were three men sat at a table. One had the camera, and then there was Jeremy Judge and an Oriental man. Probably a local. The cameraman spoke. He stuttered. It was Jonathon Durie. Absolutely no doubt in Bludd's mind. The camera panned right, away from the other two men and towards the pool. On the other side a man, another local, walked towards them, holding a child's hand to each side. Bludd took a gulp, certain that he did not want to go on with the viewing. The man and the children came to the table where the three men were. Judge and the Oriental man patted their heads and Durie said "Her…hello ler…little ones."

Bludd switched off the film. He knew what was coming.

He looked over to the open cabinet and pulled out a box file. Inside was lots of paper. Letterhead paper from all different sources. Quotes perhaps, in to Forster Packaging. He flicked through bottom to top, running the paper under his middle finger. Nothing of real interest. He studied the box files. They were labelled with numbers, 00 to 17. Bludd thought that they may have represented dates, or years at least. He grabbed the box that he guessed would be from five years ago, if he was correct. He took it back to the desk and moved the laptop back a little and picked out the paperwork inside.

His phone rang. The laptop chimed. He pushed the paperwork to one side and looked at the screen of his phone and then the screen of the computer. He answered the phone to

Annabelle Judge. He clicked the flashing 'envelope' icon.

"Did you find anything?" she asked.

Bludd didn't answer straight away. He clicked on the inbox's latest entrant. It was an e-mail from Jeremy Judge to himself. It was titled 'Enjoy'. He had copied in Durie and A Lupescu and M Lupescu. Underneath, he had copied several more names that Bludd was unfamiliar with.

"Yes," was all he replied.

The e-mail had an attachment. Bludd clicked on it; it was a wmv attachment. A film or video.

"What?" Annabelle Judge questioned. "What have you found?"

Bludd did not reply. On his screen was the headless body of a man. His stomach was huge and swollen and it rested on the back of a young girl. They were both swaying back and forth.

"You'd better come up," Bludd said. He put the phone down. He saw Annabelle leave her front door and start across the gravel. He pushed back his chair and left the room and walked slowly down the hall. He looked out of the window and Annabelle had already started to climb the ladder.

"What did you find?" she shouted up.

He didn't answer. She got to the top and he dropped his hands down in front of her. She grabbed him one hand at a time and pushed her feet up onto the last rung. Bludd pulled her up and she got her feet onto the window sill. She jumped in, but stumbled and Bludd caught her in his arms, her face wrapped in his chest. She looked up, embarrassed, but at the same time happy to be there. Bludd let her down; she was an inch or two off the floor. He said nothing. She was a little disappointed. He turned and led her along the hall, entered the room and stood to the right of the black leather chair. "You'd better sit down." He commanded her.

"Sounds ominous," she replied.

"I should perhaps explain why your husband and I don't get on," he started.

"Please do."

"Short version is this. At school, I found him masturbating whilst looking at the younger boys whilst they showered. I tried to out him, but nobody would believe me over him. I resorted to a bit of physical violence and a lot of piss-taking over his lack of luck in the trouser department."

Annabelle Judge did not reply to that, although Bludd knew from her look that things had not improved for her husband in that department. "What have you found?" she asked.

Bludd continued. "That was in 1984. I have just found something from, I guess, 2005 and have just seen something from, I guess, today. Which do you want to see? Neither of them is pleasant."

Annabelle Judge gulped. "You're scaring me now." She cleared her throat. "Today I guess."

Bludd clicked on the envelope again and the list came up. He clicked on the top e-mail and on the attachment. The screen filled with the vision he had seen a few minutes earlier. He clicked on the volume button and slid it up the scale. There were heavy grunts and muffled sobs.

Annabelle Judge sat wide mouthed and red faced. She looked at Bludd. "That's Jeremy," she said, with a shocked tone. "I would recognise him anywhere."

"Even without seeing his face?" Bludd asked. "How old do you think the girl is? About eight or nine would be my guess," he continued.

Annabelle Judge did not need to answer. She blurted out a cry and put her hands to her face, covering her eyes that were screwed tightly shut behind. "Turn it off!" she cried out.

"We need to see the rest of it," Bludd said, as a matter of fact.

Annabelle turned the chair to her left, back to Judge. "Turn it off!" she shouted again.

Bludd did not turn it off. He turned the volume down again. He watched it. He saw the man pull away from the girl and sit down, breathless and sweating. He saw her stand up and go to him under instruction and he saw her body droop, lifeless through strangulation. He was about to switch it off completely when Jeremy Judge had wrapped her up, but to his surprise, another body was dragged across into view and the wrapping up was repeated.

"We have just witnessed, well I have, the rape of a child and the murder of said child. We can also say that a second child was also murdered. I told you he was a bad man. It seems he is a whole lot worse than I could ever have imagined."

He closed the lid of the laptop and swung the chair around anti-clockwise so that she didn't have to see it, even though it was closed. He picked her up from the chair and put her in his arms. It was exactly the position they had been in minutes earlier. This time, she just wanted to be comforted. No flirting. Just to be held, by a man that wasn't a murderous paedophile, like the one she had held and had loved and had children with. She looked up, startled. "My kids?" she whispered.

"I doubt it. You would know." He pushed her head back into his chest. "Come on, let's go and get that fresh coffee."

* * *

Susan Kerby sat on the bed next to the newcomer, Ben. He told her that he had left home and gone to Manchester to get away from an abusive stepfather; abusive in a mental and physical way, not sexual. She could understand him; she had been there herself and done exactly the same thing. She had been hit once too often and without the back-up she craved from her mum, she had taken matters into her own hands and run away.

She explained to him that she had been away only a couple of weeks. She had run out of money and had been eating at a shelter and sleeping under some arches with a group of other homeless people. They had looked out for her and shown her the ropes. How to survive.

Now she would do the same for him. The people in the camp were all teenagers. At 15, he would be one of the youngest. She had arrived there at 13, just before her 14th birthday, so it was almost five years since she had been picked up. She reassured him that he would be safe. In the time she had been there, people had come and gone. They had never been mistreated and many had met their goal of a new life, by getting their heads down, working hard and waiting for their chance. She told him that he would probably start work that night and that in between he would probably meet the boss, Jonathon. In the meantime, she advised he should get some sleep and try and get his body into the routine of being asleep in the day and awake to work hard at night.

She had walked him around the camp and shown him the different huts. There was the shower and wash hut, the canteen hut, the laundry hut, the rest hut and the bedroom. They all shared every hut and were well catered for. They got grocery deliveries every Sunday afternoon. They had a routine of washing their uniforms on a Sunday morning before they went to bed. She had given him two sets of navy blue pants and jacket, with a navy tee shirt to go underneath. He was given two hats and a pair of size nine boots with steel toes caps. These would be all the clothes he would have apart from what he came in wearing. He could wear them in his down time, which generally involved sitting in the rest room and watching television and chatting. There was not much else to do, but they were all happy to be part of the group and be safe.

The boy, stripped off to his underwear, shyly. Susan told him to forget about any inhibitions. Nobody would take advantage of him, nobody would hassle him, nobody would put him under any pressure to do anything. The boy had smiled and slid under the quilt. He lay there and smiled at Susan, then turned over and tucked his knees up near his stomach. She rested a comforting hand on his hip for a moment. She felt like his mum for a moment. She smiled. She would look after him.

* * *

Bludd and Annabelle Judge sat at the kitchen table. She had not spoken since they had returned to the house. Bludd had made the fresh coffee and she had sat there, head in hands, mind in bewilderment.

"I can't believe it," she muttered.

"Believe it. Shit happens. It happens all over the world. It's just that people don't like to think that it does."

Annabelle pondered, holding her mug to her lips. She lowered it to the table. "He is in Thailand. He goes there every few months. He says it's on business, but he must be going to satisfy his sick needs. The dirty, lying bastard." She paused a moment. "No wonder he doesn't come near me any more. I feel sick."

"Like I say, this stuff goes on. There are thousands that go out there, not just to Thailand either. It's sick, never mind feeling sick. I lived there for a while. I've seen it and I've done nothing about it. I wish I had. I could have stopped some of it, but it's more than a one-man job. But I can tell you something, I am glad I came. I'm not glad to have seen what we both just saw. But it has made me determined to do something about this particular situation. I want you to phone him and tell him there has been a break-in. Get him to come home early. Tell him that his office has been ransacked. He will shit himself. He'll be back in 24 hours. When are the kids due back?"

"Tomorrow, after school. I'll keep them at my mum's; they can stay off school for as long as it takes. They won't see their father again, that's for sure."

"I guarantee it." Bludd's tone of voice was serious.

Annabelle knew what he meant, and at that precise moment, she wasn't bothered if she never saw her husband again. Bludd grabbed an apple from the bowl of fruit in the centre of the table.

"How long have you been with your girlfriend?" she asked sheepishly.

"A couple of years or so. I say girlfriend, it's kind of a strange relationship really. My fault. Mentally, we are made for each other. Physically. Let's just say I have issues and she is very patient. She's a good woman."

"Would you do something for me?"

"I thought I already was."

She paused. "I think what you are doing, what you are going to do, is as much for you now as it is for me. It will probably be for a lot of people. Some you will be avenging, some you will be saving. At least from Jeremy."

"Can we call him something else? Let's not use his name again."

Annabelle pushed her half empty mug to one side and reached across the table. She wrapped her fingers around each of his wrists, his hands still wrapped around his mug.

"Would you make love to me?"

Bludd didn't react. He looked into her deep, green eyes that were saying 'Take me, I'm yours', like the line from The Squeeze song. Any right-minded bloke would have taken her there and then, on the table. She needed it. He really needed it. But it would not be fair to Chrissie, even if he could do it, he would not.

He chuckled out loud. "Sorry. I really am. And I'm flattered. Honestly. You are beautiful. But I really can't. It would be wrong for so many reasons. I want my first time to be special, not some crude thing over a kitchen table with a woman I hardly know."

Annabelle still held his wrists and the revelation she had just heard, whilst surprising in one way, had not knocked her sideways like it could have done. Bludd was clearly a complex character, but a virgin was not something she had him down to be. She squeezed his wrists. "No, I'm sorry. I should not have asked. It's just that knowing what I know now and having not been touched, you know, for a good while. I need to be wanted. By a real man."

"Don't worry about that. The men will be queuing over the hills and far away when this is all over. A gorgeous woman, own house, own business. Maybe. Just choose well next time. But let's get this over with first. What happens in the future will happen. Que sera sera and all that."

Bludd pulled his hands away and Annabelle reluctantly let him.

"I want to have a proper look at those business folders. You can help me with it. You know his business; you know how to read accounts. Let's find out what the hell goes on at Forster Packaging."

17

Calculating

His wife's face came up on his phone. "Annabelle, what's up? I am just about to head into a meeting."

The voice at the other end seemed to quiver. "There's been a break-in. You need to come home."

"What? When was this?"

"Last night, I think."

"What do you mean you think? Weren't you there? What's been taken?"

"I don't know. It was your office, not the house."

"You mean the garage?"

"No, I mean your office. They broke in through the window at the side, got up on a ladder. I've had a look. It's a mess up there. Papers everywhere, but I don't know whether they took anything."

"Shit!" He ran his fingers through his thinning hair, front to back. He took a deep breath. "I'll get a flight home as soon as I can. It will be tomorrow, I have things here to attend to tonight. I'll let you know the details. Can you make sure it's secure? Get the window boarded up or fixed."

"OK, sorry." She paused. "I love you," she lied.

Judge had not listened to the last part of the conversation. His mind was in overdrive. He needed to get this meeting out of the way. He had come to the factory with a view to a takeover. To buy it, lock, stock and barrel. If he could buy the villa and the factory today, it would be an impressive weekend's work.

But now getting home was more important. He was concerned about the break-in. There were items in there that he did not want anybody to see, although the real bad stuff would be protected by security and passwords. Nothing could be seen that would get him in trouble. He stood deep in thought, assuring himself that it was true.

A voice interrupted his thoughts. "Mr Judge, we need to go in now, Mr Nirattpattana was expecting us at four o'clock, and we are already late. Come."

"All right, Kulap. Perhaps I have some more important things to think about right now. Listen, I want this deal wrapped up as much as you do. If we can do a deal today, I will get contracts sorted out via e-mail and I will transfer your fee as soon as I am satisfied. So let's get in there and do the deal."

Kulap looked like a scalded child. "But, Mr Judge, I was hoping to be paid before you leave. At least for my time and services this last few days. I have made many arrangements and provided good service. No?"

Judge stood and gave the statement some thought. Kulap had indeed been useful. He had arranged the visits to the villa and the factory, and another factory tomorrow, perhaps unnecessarily now. He had found the children. But if all went well in the next hour or so, he would be surplus to requirements. Judge could make all the arrangements for the purchases himself. He smiled at Kulap. "You know, Mr Kulap, you are right. Let's go in here and strike a deal. Then I need to go and get a flight home, there is a problem that I urgently need to attend to. I will sort that and then we can have dinner and settle what I owe you."

Kulap smiled. "Thank you, Mr Judge. Thank you very much."

Bludd had retrieved the folders from Judge's office, covering the last five years. He and Annabelle Judge were sifting through them trying to understand how the company had found money to invest. They looked for anything to do with bank loans, hire purchase agreements, cash injections. They had found when Durie had put money into the business and they had found the arrival of the two foreign names on the board. Lupescu. Bludd imagined they would be Romanian. Names that ended in 'oo' usually were.

Then Bludd had found confirmation of what he had seen earlier. Up until five years ago, Diego Del Campo was listed as a director of the company. He flashed back to the conversation with his brother Max. He had told him that Diego Del Campo had died in the car wreck alongside two of his other school-mates. Durie and Judge had survived, Judge unscathed. But Del Campo had died that night. That had been ten years ago.

"Do you recognise this name?" He showed Annabelle Judge the sheet.

"Del Campo? Yes, he was a director for about four or five years that I was involved with the company. I never saw him though, nor spoke to him for that matter. He was like a silent partner. He took a wage and any dividend that was due, but it was usually nominal, according to his share. Why, is it significant?"

"Don't know. My brother told me he died."

"Maybe he did. Maybe that's why he's no longer on the board."

"Wouldn't his estate have got a pay-out, or still be getting the wage, or the dividend?"

"If he had a will, I guess. What's troubling you about it?"

"My brother told me that he died 10 years ago, not five."

"Maybe he didn't have a will and it went to probate?"

"Maybe. Or maybe he didn't die five years ago. Maybe he didn't get a pay-out and that's why my brother fell out with your husband? One thing is certain, he did not die 10 years ago as my brother said. Something doesn't stack up. Again."

Annabelle carried on sifting through the papers. "What I can't find is the evidence of any investment that allowed them to buy machinery that costs millions. There is no documentation regarding the sale of the recycling plant buildings, no big money transfers, or agreements, not even any evidence that they bought the machines. Yet it was one of the only things that Jeremy has filled me in about in the recent history. It was such a big thing and I was overhearing conversations so often that he could not really keep it from me."

"Maybe he paid cash?"

"What £1M? It would still have to be from somewhere. A bank statement would show it. Withdrawal '£1M'. That's not something you see every day. It would jump out and slap me in the face."

"What if he was paid cash for something and just did the same along the chain. He gets cash, he pays cash. For the machinery, maybe?"

They continued to look through the piles of paperwork. Bludd blinked at every sheet, taking a mental picture, not necessarily comprehending any of them.

"When did the machines get installed?" he asked.

"About four, four and a half years ago. We already went through that file; there was nothing in that year."

"Perhaps he doesn't keep all the paperwork here. Perhaps he's hiding something. Let's face it, there is no 'perhaps' about it. He is hiding all sorts of shit here."

"You got any conspiracy theory worked out yet?"

"I think I am getting there."

"Go on."

"Well, let's look at the facts. Workers who disappear into the night forest. They don't exist. A night shift, that doesn't exist. Cash injections, that don't exist. A director, who apparently does not exist. There are all sorts of unanswered questions here."

"So what's the theory?"

"Human trafficking, people smuggling, something of that nature. I reckon there is big money in it. Maybe these two foreigners are at the heart of it all. Maybe they are bigger than your husband in all of this, but he is the figurehead. What if … what if they have made a pile of money smuggling people? Workers, prostitutes, kids. Kids would fit. Right? What if it is so dodgy that they have wads of cash and no way of banking it? It's not legitimate. So they find a friend. Maybe a friend that they have had dealings with in some of the things I just mentioned. Maybe someone who has bought kids, or hired them, from them. God knows how that works. Maybe they had some leverage over that person and decided that they would use it to buy into the company. Maybe they are just good mates, with similar sick tastes. Don't forget the e-mail. It was addressed to Durie and the two Lupescu names. So let's think about the dates. You stopped being involved about five years ago. So you are effectively out of the way. Diego Del Campo, a director of a few years, suddenly disappears off the board. Durie injects some inheritance money. Two new directors come onto the scene, seemingly without putting anything in. New machinery is bought, without trace, or at least as far as we can find. All this within about a year. Now there are at least nine or 10 unknown immigrants, or something, working in secret. Living in secret. Who knows how long they have been there?"

"Some story. Let's say it's all true. What do we do about it?"

"It's got some truth to it. I'm just not sure of the facts yet. What do we do? We smash it right open, that's what."

"How?"

"Not sure yet. I would love to ask my brother to help, but he has told me lies, or at least he hasn't told me the truth. So looks like I will have to go it alone. You can help, but I don't want you anywhere near the factory. You are going to have to meet your husband tomorrow and play dumb. Act normal. Can you do that?"

"I'll have to. But to be honest, I think it will take me all my time to stop myself throwing up."

* * *

Judge and Kulap were on their way back to Bangkok. They had spent an hour and a half at the factory. It had been like travelling back in time for Judge. The plant was not dissimilar to his own. Not as pristine. Not as new. The machines here were 20 years old or more. His company had similar machines to them many years ago, but they had been sold and updated machinery brought in. The machines were exported to India at the time. He had been impressed with the factory though, and its owner, Mr Nirrattpattana, or Nirratt, as he had introduced himself. This was as good an opportunity as he had hoped for. Although the factory itself was not working, it being Sunday, he saw enough potential to expand it. The books looked in good shape as well, a tidy profit for the last few years. He had not wanted to miss the opportunity, so he had made a decision, on the spot, to pay over the odds. That meant that he had agreed to pay what Mr Nirratt was asking, which, in theory, was not over the odds at all, but he did not like to pay anybody their asking price, not usually. Mr Nirratt had agreed to stay on and run the place for two years. That would take him to retirement age and he would go then. By that stage, Judge would have his family settled, learned the language to a degree that would allow him to conduct business and he would take over the running of the place, with Durie as his right-hand man. The Lupescu brothers would be doing whatever they were doing with the Maple factory and they would be out of his hair and a thing of the past. Things would be set in motion this week. He would arrange for the money to be transferred from the Romanians. Above board and legal this time. He would do nothing with the night shift, the brothers could take care of them, and they were their responsibility, anyway. Maybe he would let Durie decide if any of them deserved to be let go. Maybe they could earn their freedom with Durie, in his favourite way.

Right now, he needed to get home. He was not unduly worried about the break-in, nor was he worried about Annabelle or the children. Annabelle was clearly OK. The kids would be at her mother's. Again. That was going to change. The old witch was not going to be coming to Thailand with them, so she could see as much as she wanted of them for now. The break-in might even prove to be a help to him in persuading Annabelle that a move abroad was a good thing.

He had been on his mobile since the journey back to Bangkok had started and hardly muttered a word to Kulap. He had agreed that the meeting had gone well and that as soon as papers were signed and the deal was completely, legally wrapped up, that he would pay Kulap in full. Kulap had suggested an interim payment and a value. Judge had agreed it and he had seen the surprise on Kulap's face.

He pushed the 'confirm booking' box on his phone's screen. The flight would be back in Manchester the following day at midday.

He brought up his contacts list and scrolled down. He touched the screen on the long Thai name. Kulap drove on. He had been watching Judge's activity on the screen of his phone from the corner of his eye, but could not see what he had done.

Judge spoke. "Hello, I would like to make a booking please. Bangkok to Manchester." He read out a number, Kulap thought it must be a credit card. He had been told many times by Judge not to listen in to his private conversations and had tried to do as he was told. It meant that he heard some things and not others. It meant that he did not always grasp the full meaning of conversations. That was good. If he did not know about it, he could not get in trouble for it.

"Seven o'clock at the desk. Got it. I will get the paperwork there. Many thanks. Many thanks indeed." He touched the screen and shut the phone off.

Kulap looked across. "OK, Mr Judge?"

"Everything is more than OK, Mr Kulap. Everything is just falling into place." He strummed his fingers on his knees and smiled. It was a wicked smile that Kulap did not see. He was watching the road and had his own smile of satisfaction on his face.

* * *

Bludd had sat with Annabelle Judge and they had eaten an early lunch. He had watched her prepare it and thought about her earlier proposal. He had thought of Chrissie. He had wondered what it would be like to be normal. To have the ability to take it a step further than flirting with a woman, or to take it to second base with Chrissie. She had apologised several times over lunch and he had, for a moment, thought about grabbing her hand and taking her upstairs. It could have been the beginning of the revenge against Judge. But he had thought about Chrissie and how patient she had been. And he had thought about the fact that it probably wouldn't bother Judge anyway.

They had gone through the books and were no clearer as to the goings on at Forster Packaging or Forster Waste. There was no evidence of money changing hands between Judge and the two Romanians, but clearly they were on board.

Reluctantly, he had decided to leave Annabelle Judge at her house and head back to the industrial estate that was home to her husband's business premises. He was quite taken aback at the effect she had made on him. She was easy listening and easy on the eye. A non-musical version of LeAnn Rimes. He could have quite easily gone ahead and tried to do what any normal man would do, but in the end, he had settled for being very flattered at the opportunity offered by a very, very beautiful woman.

He stopped at the same place he had left his Yamaha before. He got his tiny, compact binoculars out of the back box and pushed them under his jacket, his chest bulging out like a pigeon's. He pushed the bike into the bushes, placed his helmet underneath the engine and pulled the foliage around it, covering it as best he could.

He walked along the tarmac road and decided to take a turn and head over the canal. Some ramblers were taking a mid-afternoon break at a bunch of picnic tables next to the lock and bridge over the canal. He bid them good day. They all happily waved back. "Pity about the weather," one of them shouted to him. It was drizzling. It had been all afternoon on this side of the hills. He had left Annabelle Judge in a cool but sunny area. A man was fishing in the canal. He stood, eyes fixed on his line, jogging a little on the spot to keep warm, his olive raincoat keeping him dry but not helping from a thermal perspective.

Bludd crossed the canal and headed left, down a gravelly set of steps with wooden planks forming the centre of each tread, the edges sloping away with wear. To each side of the steps was a worn away hollow that grooved the path right along as far as he could see. *Probably made by mountain bikers,* Bludd thought. He trotted down the steps along the path for 100 yards. Another canal lock and another sloping drop in the path. The pattern continued for a further 400 yards and a further four locks. A white cottage with smoke billowing from its chimney was to his right. A big, overweight man was stood in the doorway, ignoring the rain and cold in his heavy white, trawlerman-style jumper and a thick dark beard. He raised a steaming mug and winked at Bludd. Bludd smiled back, lifting his jacket collar to offer some protection from the cold and spitting rain.

Then he came across Durie's cottage. It was quaint. Like something you would see on a postcard perhaps, or a picture cut into a jigsaw. There was a silver vehicle to the far end of the driveway, some kind of jeep 4 x 4, but with only two side doors and a gate-style back door. As near to the door as it could have been. The left-hand side of the garden ran away towards the canal. There was a small harbour-like area just where the aqueduct became the canal and the viaduct swept overhead. A broken up, half sunken barge, that looked like a throwback to the industrial revolution, when it would have been a regular means of transportation, poked its nose out of the water. A pyramid of rusty, red, steel tubes were piled on the grass verge next to it. Bludd wondered what their purpose was, but thought it was maybe the last freight to have been carried on the barge, but had never completed an onward journey.

He turned his back to the cottage, not wanting to dwell there too long. Not wanting to bump into his old foe just yet. Not until Judge was back in the country. He mustn't know about Bludd's appearance on the scene until absolutely necessary. Bludd had it in mind that he would deal with Durie before he got chance to speak to Judge.

He walked across the stone-walled bridge and turned right and onto the bridleway. He headed towards the aqueduct, passing the tall, green security fence that surrounded the industrial estate. It was much bigger than he had previously thought. In the dark of the previous night, it had not registered as anything out of the ordinary, just a fence surrounding a yard. But it was high. Annabelle had said it was. It must have been 20 feet high, with three pronged spikes cut and twisted into the tip. He carried on walking, watching through the gaps in the green spires as he went. Looking to see any kind of movement on the other side. There was nothing. The large gate that was the entrance to the incinerator building was shut and padlocked. The whole estate was quiet and inert. Bludd could hear the patter of the rain hitting the glass and iron of the factory roof in the distance.

He walked for a moment, crossing the threshold of the aqueduct. It had a number of parapets jutting out at regular intervals across the span of the structure. Bludd took a moment in the first one and looked down. It was easily 100 feet to the floor below. Right below him, tips of trees were struggling upwards in an attempt to touch the brickwork. To their right a gap, the river below offering a natural breaks in the mass of trunks and branches. He looked straight ahead. The 20-foot green fence continued right along the side of the industrial yard, past the incinerator building and beyond, disappearing into the trees in the distance. The trees themselves were climbing the slope that led from the river up to the industrial area. Up to the end of the incinerator building the drop to the floor 100 feet below was almost sheer; nothing but a few bushes poking from the stony side of the precipice. Further along the trees had found enough ground under their bases for roots to get a hold, the sharp incline not enough to quell their determination to grow. Bludd was no tree expert, but some of these trees were 80 feet tall. There was probably a mix of oak, elm, silver birch, amongst others. They went as far as the eye could see. Maple Forest was vast. He turned around. To the other side of the canal and the viaduct, the trees dwindled to nothing but a few small thickets dotted around a landscape of fields, dividing walls and a couple of smallholdings and cottages. One had a small horse jumping ring, with tiny fences of crossed planks of wood attached to old plastic barrels.

Bludd wanted to go down to the river and see if there was a way across to the other side and then to see if there was a way up the steep incline and most importantly a way into the camp that lay somewhere in the middle of the forest. He also wanted to go and check out the old recycling buildings. He checked his watch, smearing the raindrops from across its face. Twenty past two. He decided to check out the river first.

He turned to his right and put his earphones into his ears. On his iPod was an old rock ballad by Foreigner, 'Waiting for a Girl like You'. He thought about Annabelle for a moment. He turned his jacket collar up and, with his head down, he headed across the aqueduct.

Just past the far end of the aqueduct, away from the industrial estate, heading towards the industrial yard were the two Romanian brothers. They were talking, but Bludd could not hear them above his music.

Bludd glanced upwards as he approached them. The logical thing to do would have been to look back to the ground and make no eye contact, but Bludd had already decided that these two were the bad guys and he made eye contact with both of them, staring at each of them in turn and then fixing his gaze onto the nearest of the two, Marius. He deliberately took a step to the right so that he was walking straight down the middle of the two brothers. He continued to fix his eyes on the brother now to his left and walked straight at them. The two brothers glanced at each other and then back at Bludd. He was not going to change his path, so they had to change theirs. They split from each other and moved a step each way, making them two steps apart. There was plenty of room for Bludd to saunter through. He kept his eyes firmly fixed on the eyes of the brother to his left and went through the gap. The Romanian also fixed his gaze and followed Bludd after he had gone through them and had his back to them. His right hand clenched into a fist. His brother stepped forward and placed his right hand on Marius' left hip. He did not speak, just motioned to the left with his head and gave him a shove in the same direction against his hip. They moved off to go across the aqueduct and Bludd carried on towards the path that led down towards the river. He stopped at the break in the wall that was the start of the path. He turned and looked back towards the brothers. He was surprised at the sheer size of them, close up. He smiled to himself. His mum would have called them bookends. *Ugly ones,* Bludd thought. Marius Lupescu turned round. He instinctively felt Bludd's eyes continuing to glare at him. He caught Bludd's eye. Bludd stopped, one foot on the stone step that indicated the start of the path down to the river. He saw the Romanian and winked at him. The Romanian, confused, winked back.

Bludd turned left as he went through the gateway. He stopped momentarily and thought about Chrissie. He hadn't spoken to her since yesterday and she might be wondering what he was up to. She rarely rang him when he was working as often the phone call would be at an inappropriate time and he would either not answer, or not be pleased to be interrupted. He called her. It came up on his screen as a 'call failure', there was no signal. He slipped the phone back into his pocket and set off down to the river.

The trail was a sandy, gravelly path that was covered at its edges with fallen leaves. The path meandered along, swinging left to right and back again, every few yards a step down, fronted by a wooden plinth with a nailed-on peg at each end that was probably buried a foot deep to keep the step and the ground in place. He stopped for a moment again. He made a mental picture of the aqueduct above to his left, with the river below running between two large concrete base blocks at the bottom of the legs of the arch. Another two sat either side of these, but sunk into solid ground on the banks of the river. A further one was probably the same distance again away on the other side of the river, but the arch disappeared into the trees and was lost to sight. He carried on. The path took a sharp turn to the left and a couple of steps later it hooked back again and the steps became steeper and closer together. The trail got slimmer as overgrown weeds, fallen leaves, bushes and stinging nettles encroached into the space from both sides. Bludd counted 30 steps and the path flattened out and he found himself level with the river, running about 10 feet to his left, a few smaller trees thinning out between him and the water, the thick band of trees now to his right or over the water on the other side. The thin line of trees faded to nothing but bushes and fern, and the path widened a little before heading right to avoid a small sandy area that was like a small deserted beach. He continued along the path to find that it widened significantly and bushes faded away into a grassy area. A wooden hut, some kind of clubhouse, was to his right, old and in need of attention, but nothing that a lick of paint or creosote wouldn't sort out. Over the door was a shabby sign, 'Maple Canoe Club' it said in faded red letters. From the wooden veranda, a path led away to his left and ran down to a planked wooden jetty that jutted out into the water a little and became a T-shape. Bludd walked down to the water's edge and stood on the jetty part that ran with the direction of the water. The opposite river bank was about 12 yards away from him and looking right and left, he could see that this was most likely the narrowest part, for a stretch at least. The thick crowd of trees across the water hid the industrial estate high above him, but he knew he must have been adjacent to the incinerator building, or slightly further along, maybe level with the parked trucks.

He needed to get across the river somehow, so he could try and get up the hill and into the trees, and then hopefully find a way through the trees and into the camp, somewhere in the middle of the forest.

He walked back towards the clubhouse and noticed a trailer to the left. There were a stack of canoes resting on the trailer, four high by three wide. Bludd strode over to the trailer. It was in as bad a state as the clubhouse was and the canoes were all covered in a mossy grime that told Bludd that they had not been used for some time. He moved to the clubhouse and tried the door. It was locked, but the wood was rotten and splitting. Bludd took a step back and gave the door a kick. The wood crunched and the door and its frame bellowed backwards and then eased back into place. He kicked it again and he heard the wood splinter and the frame cracked away from the face of the building. Another kick and more splintering. The wood below the lock had broken away from the steel block that held the lock and Bludd knew that another few kicks and he would have a way in. He kicked again and again. The wooden panels broke apart and a hole appeared, two planks wide and not enough for Bludd to squeeze through. He kicked again to the side of the lock and angled his foot so that he was attacking at least three planks. They cracked and he kicked again and again. They split and pointed to inside the clubhouse. Bludd gave them a kick with an upwards swing and, one by one, they broke away and were sent scampering along the floor inside. Bludd could get in. He got his torch from his pocket, crouched down and crawled through the hole. He flicked the button on the torch and the light beamed across the room. On the far side was a small bar area, another faded Maple Canoe Club sign was on the back wall and three empty optics hung off the wall. There were two tables, each surrounded by three wooden chairs, all resting on their front legs and tipped forward to lean against the tables. Cobwebs spread across the chairs and onto the table's legs. The bar, too, was enveloped with lacy patterns and strands of dust-covered webs hung from the ceiling joists. In the left hand corner was a door. No lock. Bludd walked carefully across the dusty room, the only light from his torch aided by a short stream of daylight that came through the hole he had made in the door. There were two windows to the front of the hut and one to each side, but they were encrusted with dust and a slimy moss on the outside blacked them out.

He opened the door and shone his torch in. There were hooks on the left-hand wall that were housing canoe oars. Two stacks of them elevated into mid-air, 10 in total. On the floor beneath were two blue barrels. Bludd entered through the doorway into the store cupboard. He shone the torch into the drums and saw that inside were a bundle of red and white striped sticks all topped with a steel ring. The back wall was covered with plastic helmets that looked a bit like bicycle helmets and on the floor underneath them was a pile of yellow life jackets.

He flicked the torch to the right-hand wall and found what he was looking for. A dozen hoops of thick rope were hanging off long nails. Three rows of four rings. Bludd guessed that each one would span the width of the river and that they would probably be hooked around tree trunks and have the striped red and white poles hanging off them to map out a course for the canoeists to traverse and race through. He grabbed the nearest hoop of rope and a paddle and stepped out of the cupboard. As he did so, he struck upon an idea and stopped. As things stood, he had no way in and no way back out of the camp or the industrial estate. That meant that it was likely that the people in the camp had no means of getting out either. If they had, then why would they still be there? Maybe he could help them get away before he dealt with Durie and Judge, and the two Romanians. And anybody else that got in his way, or was part of whatever sordid shit that was going on. Maybe the ropes and the canoes would come in handy at some point, he wondered.

He squeezed back through the hole in the door and back out onto the wooden veranda and the daylight, squinting his eyes to help them adapt. He breathed in fresh air. The hut had been dank and muggy.

He put the rope over his shoulder and pulled one of the canoes from the middle of the trailer. He laid it in on the floor and picked it up by a wooden toggle on a string hoop at the front end. He assumed it was the front end as, in truth, he did not know one end from the other. He picked the paddle up in his left hand and dragged the canoe down to the water's edge. He had never canoed before, but it looked pretty easy, he thought. He pushed the front end into the water and edged it in so that the seat was just over the lip of the water's edge and the back half was still on gravelly, dry land. He placed the oars across the front of the hole and eased himself into the seat, legs first. He pushed his hands into the gravel and tried to push himself into the water, bumping his body forward, but hardly moving. He grabbed the paddle and stuck it into the ground behind him and heaved all his weight against it and pushed hard. The canoe moved sideways into the water and Bludd dug the blade into the gravel again and gave it another push. The canoe moved right into the water and Bludd pulled the paddle into his body. There was a slight current running right to left, as Bludd looked across the 12 yards of water and he figured that he had done the easy part, as he drifted with the current. Getting back might be a different story altogether.

* * *

Durie thanked the supermarket delivery driver and tipped him a £5 note. It was not in his nature to be generous, but the driver, who was the same one most weeks, had never asked why Durie always had the delivery put into the back of his jeep rather than into his house, even though he had clearly thought it by the look on his face the first time he had delivered. Durie wanted it kept that way and thought that a £5 note slipped into his hand each week would allay the need for any inquest.

As the delivery vehicle disappeared from view, Durie closed the door on the mountain of blue and white striped bags and got in the jeep. He reversed out of his drive and carried on across the bridge in a backwards direction until he could swing it around on the other side and find himself facing the gate to the estate. The motor-driven gate was already in motion and the brothers stood to the open left-hand side and they playfully pushed each other from side to side. *Like teenagers,* Durie thought. He pulled up next to them and Marius got in the passenger side whilst Andrei set the gate to close again. Andrei opened the back door and stood on the rear bumper, slapped the roof twice with his hand and shouted, "Go!" Durie drove down the yard and stopped at the far end, stopping the vehicle in the middle of the yard, adjacent to the fence and trees beyond. Andrei jumped off and Marius got out and headed to the back door. Andrei dialled the digits on the keypad and he opened the gate.

On the other side, a line of navy-blue-clad people stood awaiting their arrival, and as the gate opened in front of them, they filed out in a line and waited by the silver door. Marius handed them three bags in each hand and they, one by one, moved silently back through the green gate in the fence and disappeared back into the trees. Susan Kerby was the last in line and she gave Marius a happy smile and turned away from him to return with the others. Marius leant on the jeep and eyed her up and down from behind. She was not his type of thing, but he knew she was a pretty little thing, and that maybe he would break with tradition and use her at some point soon. "Tell Carl to take shower for later," he shouted to Susan and she gave him a quick look backwards over her shoulder and replied, "OK."

Andrei closed the gate and gave it a tug to make sure it was secure. He watched for a moment until Susan Kerby had completely disappeared from view and then went back to the silver jeep, climbed onto the rear bumper again, hit the roof twice and hung on as Durie hit the gas and returned them to the front gate. Andrei jumped off and slammed the silver gated door on the vehicle shut and set the motor on the gate running to let Durie out of the compound. Marius got out of the passenger side and waited patiently with Andrei until Durie had headed off. The gate ground along its runner and thudded to a stop. As Durie closed his front door across the way in the distance, the two brothers turned to each other and mimicked a boxing match, arms up to their chests as a guard and mock jabs stabbing out at the other's face, both of them ducking and weaving. Andrei swung a looping right punch and caught Marius clean on the chin. Marius stopped and stepped back, stunned. This was how all their fights started. He looked at Andrei sternly and Andrei stepped back and held his hands up by way of apology, but Marius had already launched his retaliation and hit his brother with both clenched fists full in the face. Andrei scrambled backwards and Marius grabbed at his brother's jacket collar and pulled him towards him, anger in his face and ready for more. Then he noticed a trickle of blood run from Andrei's nose and he stopped, let go of his brother and laughed. Andrei put his finger to his nostril and dabbed at the red liquid, looking at his crimson-tipped index finger and then at his brother. And then he laughed out loud as well. He wiped the blood against his trousers at his hip and flung his right arm around Marius' shoulders and they both laughed together and headed up the steps and into the reception area of the factory.

18

Treachery

Jeremy Judge sat at the desk in the room that he had used to make his film two days earlier. On the desk was a black shoe box, lid on. Inside the box was cash. Thai baht to the value of £10,000. Judge looked at the box and then at his phone that sat between him and the box. He strummed his fingers on the table and then slid his index finger across the screen, left to right. The screen opened up on the text that he had sent as soon as he had been dropped at his hotel by Kulap. He had already made the arrangements with his associate and the text was confirmation of the conversation of that morning. He had arranged with Kulap to return to the room that he had dropped the twins off at on the previous Friday. Kulap was to be there at 8.00 p.m. sharp. And he was waiting. He sat back in the chair and clasped his hands together, a confident smile wide across his face, fingers fidgeting together in anticipation.

He heard the door at the bottom of the stairs creak on its hinges as it opened slowly. The stairs groaned and squeaked. He hadn't noticed the noise the other day, or when he had used them earlier. Both times he had been focused on other things and he was unaware of his surroundings. Now, he had sat waiting, his senses became accustomed to the surroundings and he was aware of the dampness of the walls, the dust circling in the air, the squeaky hinges and the creaky stairs. He counted them, all the way up. 13 clumps of feet against 13 creaking stairs.

Kulap stuck his head round the door sheepishly. His eyes flicked from left to right as he assessed the room. "Come in, Mr Kulap! Don't be shy. Nothing to be afraid of." Judge lied.

Kulap entered the room, shuffling slowly along, and a nervous grin on his face. He ran the fingers of his right hand through his hair and stood next to the sofa that was positioned in front of the desk that Judge sat behind.

"Please, sit down!" Judge asked, but as an order. Kulap did as he was told and placed himself in the middle of the sofa, looking up at Judge.

Judge stood up and pushed the chair backwards with the back of his legs. He felt strong and in control as he walked to the front of the desk. He stopped in front of Kulap and leant backwards against the desk. "So, Mr Kulap. I would like to thank you for the effort you have put into my trip. I think you will agree that it has been quite interesting and worthwhile?"

"I hope so, Mr Judge. I really tried to make it so," Kulap replied, a little more relaxed than a moment earlier.

"So, to recap. I have had an offer accepted on the villa and, given that all goes to plan, I should be the rightful owner by the end of the month. The factory purchase is sure to go ahead and I will set the paperwork in motion as soon as I get back to England. Hopefully, we can finalise things with Mr Nirratt and I will own the factory while he still runs it. Of course, I appreciate the other elements of my time here that you have facilitated."

"Thank you, Mr Judge," Kulap responded.

"So, Mr Kulap, it would seem that I owe you some thanks and remuneration." Judge reached round his back and slid the shoe box to his left-hand side. "Can you trust me?" he asked Kulap, but didn't give him time to answer. "I think, for the moment, you have to. This box contains a payment, but it isn't the full amount you were hoping for. The balance, plus a little extra for your patience, will be paid in full on completion of the purchases of the villa and factory. Is that OK with you, Mr Kulap?"

Kulap thought for a moment. "That will be fine, Mr Judge. Can I ask how much is in the box?"

Judge pondered for a moment. "Mr Kulap, I said you have to be able to trust me. You know too much about me for me to double cross you, or short change you. I think you will be really quite pleased when you see. Of course, I will need a ride to the airport tomorrow morning, so your work is not quite finished for this trip just yet."

"Of course, Mr Judge. You just give me the time and I will be at your hotel ready and waiting. Ready and willing."

"Good. And thank you again, Mr Kulap, you have proved to be a very useful partner. I will leave you now. I will text you later with my pick-up time."

Kulap smiled at the word 'partner'. He didn't respond to Judge and didn't move until he had heard the bottom stair creak and the door to the building click shut. He stood at the desk and flipped the lid off the box. Sure enough, Judge had been true to his word. The amount was more than he had expected. He picked each wad from the box and counted them out in a straight line at the front of the desk. Each had 100 separate 1,000 baht notes per bundle. He counted 45 bundles, 450,000 baht in total. Kulap had imagined the moment he received his payment many times and was thankful that the notes were not loose, as he had imagined throwing them up in the air, as if he had won the Lottery. As it was, he placed the money back into the box and put the lid back on. He sat back down on the sofa and smiled to himself. He nodded without realising he was doing it. This was his time now. All of his financial problems would be solved. Maybe he could afford to get some treatment for his mother, make her more comfortable, if not better.

Outside, Jeremy Judge had crossed the street and made a left turn at the end of the terrace of shops. He found the two men in the darkness of the first alley on his left, as they had arranged and confirmed by text. He took the men, dressed in black, as he had only ever seen them, to the corner opposite the building that he had left Kulap in and pointed his finger in the direction of the building. They nodded agreement silently, having had instruction from their boss earlier. Judge stepped back from them and saw the man to the right hitch up the back of his long dark coat and pull out a sheathed Meed Mor dagger that hung from his belt. He heard him slide the dagger out of the sheath and, as his right hand dropped to his side, Judge saw a glint of streetlight reflected across the wavy steel blade.

He looked at the other black-clad man. He too slipped something from the back of his coat. It was a gun, and as he turned and nodded to his colleague, Judge saw him clip and screw a silencer to the end of the barrel. The two men crossed the road and Judge turned away as he saw the men enter the building and headed back to his hotel. He would have to book a taxi for the journey to the airport.

Kulap heard the door open with a whine of the hinges. "Mr Judge?" he called inquisitively. He got no response and he jumped from his momentary daydream. He listened carefully. There were two sets of footsteps, out of synchronicity, hitting the stairs at different intervals, moving quickly and stealthily. Kulap made a loud gulp in his throat, his stomach sank to his knees and his knees buckled. He realised that he did, indeed, know too much about Judge and that whilst he had trusted the

Englishman, it was already clear that the same trust had not been returned to him. It was clear to him what his fate was.

The two men entered the room and stood side by side. Kulap did not know them, but their black coats, with black shirts and ties gave him all the clues he needed to guess who they were. It was at that moment that he realised that the money in the black box was not for him. This was blood money for the two men stood in front of him. They had been sent to put him to death because he knew too much. The money was theirs and the blood was his; no financial stability for his family; no treatment or comfort for his mother. His poor family and mother; poor in more ways than one.

Kulap picked up the box and dropped the lid on the floor. He had no idea why, but he ran at the men, their arms behind their backs, stood side by side in the doorway. Was it an element of surprise that he thought he had? The two men stepped forward into the room, their right hands emerging from behind them in a simultaneous fluid movement. Kulap threw the box at the men and lunged towards them, letting out a desperate, wretched scream from the bowels of his stomach. The man on the left lunged forward and plunged the Meed Mor into Kulap's side, the curved blade slicing into his spleen. Kulap did not feel the pain. The man to his left had swiftly brought his silenced revolver level with Kulap's head and pulled the trigger without a moment's thought or delay.

The men stood over Kulap's dead body, his forehead smoking from the entry hole, the back of his head disintegrated into a million tiny fragments and strewn across the floor with the globules of brain and a spray of blood. The man with the dagger retrieved his weapon from the side of the still body and wiped the blood against the corpse's clothing. He stood and stepped around the body and collected the bundles of money that were scattered around the floor. Some of them were stained with Kulap's blood and would now have to be laundered, in more ways than one. They turned the body over and collected the one missing wad of baht, then left Kulap where he was, closing the door behind them. The clean-up operation was somebody else's job. Their deal was done. They returned their weapons back to their sheaths and tucked them back under their coats, strutted down the stairs, opened and shut the front door with a click and set off into the darkness with no thought for what they had just left behind.

19

Discovery

Bludd had managed to get across the river in the canoe and he had got out and dragged it onto dry land and across into the trees. Now he clambered up the steep slope, grabbing at the branches of the trees to pull against and give him some leverage. It was 100 feet to the top, he had estimated when stood on the aqueduct. The drop down from the industrial estate was a sheer one and he had to walk along the river for a few hundred yards to get to a point where the slope was climbable. He hoped that this would be an advantage anyway, as it should have taken him past the end of the yard and somewhere near level with the camp beyond it and in the middle of the forest. He had tried to bring up the aerial picture in his mind, but even with his superior memory and ability to focus on a memory, it was hard to distinguish the distance the camp was from the end of the industrial site. In his mind, he zoomed in and out, like he had done when he used Google Earth to identify the camp, but on 'zoom out' the picture was just like a sea of broccoli tops, 'zoom in' did not allow him to see the camp and the industrial estate in one picture. There was only so much even his mind could do.

As he pulled himself up the slope, digging his toes into leaf-covered soil and hauling himself along with all the strength his arms could muster, he ran his mind over the last two days and what might lay in the coming two. He realised how little sleep he had had since the phone call from Annabelle Judge. Not that it really bothered him; he hardly slept well at the best of times, so living on just a few hours in two nights was nothing new. Ordinarily he would grab a few hours here and there to catch up when he got too tired, but now he was so focused on what was going on around him, that he had not even considered sleep until now. He knew there was something bad going on and he knew that all the answers would be found soon. What he was going to do about it all remained to be seen, and he felt sure that some decisions would have to be made on the spur of the moment that would be likely be life changing. Definitely for him, probably for others.

He thought about what he would find in the camp, about who he would find in the camp. How many were there? He had seen ten in the line that morning at six o'clock. Were there more? How old were they? They hadn't looked very old, but that was hard to judge, he was going off size and from a distance that was no way to guess. Were they all men? Were they all women? He was sure the last one in line had been a female, with long, blonde hair, but that was nothing to be certain of these days.

He got to the top of the slope, the ground flattening out as the number of trees grew and the thickness of the forest became apparent. That was good. The industrial estate had the fence running around its perimeter and in the corner that he was closest to, there were only a smattering of trees in a thin line, the sheer drop not allowing roots to take a hold. He looked back down at where he had climbed up from, sure it was going to be much easier going the other way if that was the route he ended up taking.

He got to thinking about those in the camp again. What if they weren't prisoners? What if they were happy there and didn't want to leave? Surely they would if they knew who they worked for and what they were up to. What if they were complicit? There were lots of 'what ifs'.

He tried to set a compass in his mind. For all the power of his memory and his photographic mind, he would find it difficult to map out his path in and out. For one thing, he didn't know where he was going, and for another the trees looked so dense from here that once he got into them, it would all look pretty much the same. It was one of those moments when planning has to take a back seat to best guessing and fingers crossed.

He looked up at the sky, trying to find the sun and get a handle on its location against time, two o'clock in the afternoon, giving him a clue to the direction he wanted to head in. His memory had been a brilliant abetment to him in his life, especially during school, but it did not solve everything for him. As in mathematical equations, he could memorise a page from a text book that would show some kind of calculation, but when it came to an equation he had never seen before, it would take him an age to look into his mind and see the calculation and how it worked, and then correlate that to the one in front of him. Now, as he tried to calculate the location of the sun, against the time on his watch and the direction he wanted to go in, he had to admit to himself that he had no idea.

Best guess scenario. He moved forward, feet kicking through fallen golden leaves, eyes focused and blinking, hoping that the pictures he could conjure would mean something later. He guessed that if he took as straight a path as was possible, given the lay of the trees, that he would eventually arrive at the camp, or at least, more likely, the fence that surrounded it. He was of course assuming that there was a fence.

He strode on, zig-zagging between the trees, leaves rustling under his heavy footsteps. He picked his feet up higher than he would normally, aware that he could not see any roots under the autumn carpet of gold and brown. He was aware that his walk might look a bit silly, if anybody could see him, it was a bit like a child who runs into the sea and steps over each little wave as it reaches the beach.

Five past two. He thought he would have reached something distinguishable by now. Maybe his straight line was not as straight as he thought.

Then suddenly he was upon it. The fence was still 20 feet high. He looked up. The three-pronged spiked tip had continued as it was around the industrial site, but now the steel lengths were painted a mix of brown and green, mottled in places to look like trees with leaves, except the trees had no leaves and the fence had played a trick with his mind. When you are focused on something, you don't consider what season it is and what state the surroundings are because of the time of year. He was looking for a circle of huts, or a green fence, and he was so focused on the picture in his mind that he had almost run into the camouflaged balustrades in front of him.

He peered through a gap. The trees were just as thick on the other side as they were on this and he could see no sign of any hut in the distance, just leaves on the floor, trunks rising high and twisted branches intermingling and fusing together. Then it struck him. He looked along the fence to his right and then left. Whoever put this in must have been able to charge a fortune. It must have taken weeks to uproot a line of trees that would allow them to put their own groundwork in. There was a four foot gap on each side of the fence before the line of trees started. Bludd looked to his right along the path that had been carved out of the thicket, the brown and green fence running off into the distance. He made a decision that he would have to go in that direction, going to his left would take him nearer to the industrial estate, and he wanted to steer away from anywhere that he might bump into Durie or the Romanian brothers before he wanted to. He guessed that somewhere along here, the branches would stretch out and reach over the fence and he hoped that they would be accessible and strong enough.

He was aware that the fence represented the fact that he was getting closer to the camp. He consciously walked more carefully now, stepping on top of the carpet of leaves rather than kicking them along. The fence curved around to the left after 100 yards and continued to sweep around. Bludd thought back to the 'zoom out' picture he had in his mind. The forest was split by the river and it ended on the other side as the rail track encircled it. Bludd guessed that the fence ran around in a horseshoe shape, the open end would be at the end of the industrial estate and the round end was following the contours of the ground and route of the river. He continued around the fence, occasionally stopping to look through and see if there was any sign of life, or the huts of the camp. He had walked for a further five minutes and reckoned he must be at the south-west side of the ring. Then he found what he was looking for. It was almost like this area had been neglected. The trees seemed closer to the fence, but they weren't, it was just that the branches were lower and thicker, *stronger*, Bludd thought. He found a tree that had enough branches sticking out over the fence and that were accessible by branches lower down and that Bludd could use to get a foothold and scale it. He looked across. The tree on the opposite side had to replicate the one on this side, otherwise he would have a 20 foot drop to contend with. That was not a great problem, he could lower himself off the branch and drop the 14 foot between his feet and the floor below. The problem was that whatever route he chose to get in, he may need to use to get out again.

The tree he had found was not quite ideal. It was perfect on this side of the fence, but on the other side the tree opposite leant away slightly, which meant that the branches pointed upwards slightly. Bludd assessed the height comparison of the branches and made a decision that this might be his best option and he would make the best of it. He jumped up and grabbed the first branch, it was about eight feet off the ground and he had to stretch his arms and then dangled for a moment before swinging his legs and using the momentum to help his arms hoist his body up and he rested his stomach on the branch before reaching for the next and bringing his legs up. He continued up the ladder of branches until he was level with the top of the fence, which was now just painted green again. Clearly they doubted any approach from this direction, probably down to the proximity of the rail track. He slid his feet along and shuffled across the branch, holding the one above him for balance. He got to the end of the branch and as it got thinner, it got weaker and began to bow, the one above was, luckily, thick enough to give him enough confidence to go that far. He tentatively put his right foot onto the top of the fence, the three prongs digging into the sole of his shoe. He looked across at the tree on the inner side of the fence. It was far from ideal now he was up level with it. There was no easy step across, the branch that he wanted to grab with his hand ran away to the right and the one his feet would step to was pointing up and left. There was no going back now. He was wobbling on a piece of steel that was 10 millimetres thick and a branch that was bowed within an inch of snapping. He lurched forward and twisted sideways at the same time and lunged, arms stretched at the branch to his left. He clung to it, fingers clenched tightly around its greasy bark. The branch bowed and sprung back upwards and Bludd heard the first splinters of a crack. The branch bowed downwards again and Bludd looked at where it met the trunk and cringed. It might have taken his weight if he had just hung from it, but the force of his weight arriving from a height, with added stress from the lunge he had made, meant that the branch was inevitably going to snap. He braced himself as he heard the elongated crunch and the branch came away from the body of the tree.

A second later, Bludd hit the floor, his knees compressed up into his chest and he fell backwards and lay there, the wind knocked out of him. His chest hurt where his knees impacted and he thought about broken ribs. The thought soon went from his head. He stood up and dusted himself down, took a deep breath. No pain. Most importantly, he was in.

* * *

Susan Kerby and Carl Hampson were putting the delivery of shopping away in the stores hut. The freezers were full, the refrigerators were full and now they stacked up the tinned food and cleaning materials: bleach, kitchen cleaner, toilet rolls, soap. There were no brand names on any of the products, just the basic range of the supermarket's own logo and colour scheme. It didn't matter to Susan and her friends that there were no frills attached to their weekly delivery; they got every-thing they needed to get by. They didn't have air fresheners, or deodorants, or fancy ingredients to cook with, or even nice clothes.

"So, you have to shower this afternoon. What do you think? Maybe this is it, maybe this is your time?" Susan Kerby asked.

Carl Hampson had lived in the camp for two years. He had been picked up in Manchester in the gay village. He was not gay, but had been there with friends on a night out in the city and they had gone there to see whether it was as outrageous and funny as they had heard. He had become split from his friends and he had started to walk back to the train station alone and hoping to meet up with them before the journey home. Instead he had taken up the offer of a lift with the Romanian man, who had promised him a lift to the station, but had then taken him to the camp. He had complained on the way and the Romanian, Andrei, had stopped and pushed him into the back of the van, where he had met the other Romanian brother, Marius. He was in the back with another lad that they had picked up in the gay area. The other lad was called Martin and he was gay. It looked like they had been kissing when Andrei had slid the door back and put him in with them. Martin had been taken to the camp with them, but he had earned his release a few months earlier and they had heard nothing of him since. At the time, Carl had been baffled by Martin receiving his freedom ahead of him. He felt that he had worked as hard as anybody else, and in fact Martin had done much less than the rest of them.

"You think?" he replied. "I don't know. I'm not even sure I want to go. I mean, it would be nice to get out, especially if what they have promised is true. A flat, all paid for out of the day shift wage. It sounds too good to be true. But hey, if I can get to see my mum and dad and my mates again, why not? I just don't like the thought of leaving you and the rest behind. You're like, the best mates anyone could ask for and the thought of not seeing you for ages, until it's your turn, or maybe never, makes me feel a bit sick."

Susan laughed. "I don't think it will ever be my turn. I've been here longer than anyone, except Teri. Seems like us girls are a permanent fixture and you lads can get out and live your life again. But I'm like you. I quite like it here, and I love you all."

"Ah, well. I suppose I should go and shower and get my clean clothes on, make myself presentable and all that. I'll see you later."

Carl left the hut and headed off to get his clean clothes and his shower bag.

Susan Kerby put the last of the shopping delivery away and closed the door to the cupboard. She pulled the cord and turned the strip light off above her head. As she left the hut, she pulled the door shut, turned the key to lock it and backed down the steps.

Bludd had heard the voices as he crept through the forest and used his ears to navigate through the trees. He had seen the boy leave the hut and head across the ring of wooden buildings and disappear into the one opposite. He reckoned on the lad being in his mid to late teens, height about five-ten, taller than he had thought from a distance, and dressed in the navy blue uniform that he had seen them in from the railway bridge that morning.

The camp was quiet and empty, the others having entered various huts and not reappeared.

Now the girl had left the hut and she had her back to him as she locked the door. He leapt forward and grabbed her, one hand on her right hip the other wrapped around her face and cupping over her mouth, stopping any chance of her screaming. He pulled her in close to his body. She was small, compared to him and light enough to lift with one hand. He pulled her round the corner of the hut and swung her round so her back pressed against the wooden wall, keeping his hand over her mouth as he did so. The girl looked at him with panic and surprise in her eyes. Bludd pressed a little harder with his left hand and put his right hand index finger to his lips, signalling for her to keep quiet. She nodded eyes still wide open and nervous.

"Don't worry," Bludd prompted. "I'm here to help," he promised.

He released his left hand from over her mouth and put his finger of his right hand back to his lips, as if to remind her not to scream.

She didn't. "Help with what?" she asked, a bit dumbfounded.

"Getting you out of here. What else?" he replied a little perplexed.

"We don't need any help getting out. We can get out if we want. We just have to work hard and eventually we get out, if we want to go."

"And do you want to get out?" Bludd asked.

"Dunno. Not much for me to get out for really. All my friends are in here."

"What? You haven't got any family?"

"Well, yes, but not any that gives a shit about me. If they did, maybe I wouldn't have come here in the first place."

"What you came here of your own accord? How long ago was that?"

"Well, not really. I was brought here. But you get used to it after a while and you get settled. I came here five years ago, as far as I know. Anyway, who the hell are you? You nearly gave me a heart attack!"

"My name is Bludd, Sebastian Bludd. I'm a private investigator and the wife of the owner of the factory in there has asked me to look into some things that she isn't happy with and I have just kind of stumbled across you. What's your name?"

"Susan. My name is Susan Kerby."

The name being spoken was like a lightning bolt striking Bludd and it stopped him in his tracks. He closed his eyes and thought back five years. He saw a 'missing persons' poster pinned to a telegraph pole. It read "MISSING. Susan Kerby aged 13. Missing since 17th October. Please help. REWARD £5000 for any information leading to her safe return."

He opened his eyes and looked at the girl's face. He closed his eyes again and focused on the picture that was in the poster: a slim-faced girl, with boyish looks and short blonde hair adding to the boyishness. Big blue eyes. Not pretty, but certainly not ugly. Just not very girly.

"Are you from Macclesfield?" Bludd asked quickly.

"Yes I am. But how do you know?" The girl looked nervous again, like this was some kind of trick question.

"Susan Kerby. Age 17, nearly 18. Left home to go to school on the 17th of October 5 years ago, but has not been seen since."

The girl looked shocked. "Yes. But how do you know all that? Is this some kind of trick?"

Bludd grabbed her left hand and pulled her away from the hut and into the trees. The girl was resistant and she dug her heels in and pulled back. But she was slight and Bludd was at least twice her weight and seven inches taller than her. He picked her up by her hips and ran with her into the trees. The girl started to scream and Bludd dropped her quickly and smothered her mouth again.

"Please don't make a noise," he urged. "I promise you this is no trick. Just let me explain how I know. OK?"

The girl nodded.

"You left home because your stepfather had been abusing you. You had confided in your mum, but she hadn't believed you and you decided to run away from home. Am I right?"

"Yes, 100 per cent. But how?"

"I know your mum. She kicked your stepfather out. Partly because she didn't believe his side of the story and partly because he stopped looking for you, although I am not entirely sure he looked too hard in the first place. I know all this because she gave up on the police and contacted a friend of mine, another private investigator called Mick Dylon. Mick worked really hard to try and find you and he recruited me and a few other local investigators to help to try and find you as well. We all put our time in for free because your mum had put up a reward for you and she could not afford to pay for that, if anybody found you, as well as investigator fees."

Susan Kerby started to sob. Her shoulders were pushing up and down and her body was shaking. "So my mum did care?"

"Oh, yes. Cared enough to put up her life savings to get you back. More importantly, she believed you. But she nearly went out of her mind with worry. I haven't seen her for a couple of years, but it really did affect her, you know, mentally."

"Is she OK now?" She wiped her eyes on the sleeve of her jacket.

"As I say, I haven't seen her recently. What I can tell you is that my mate, Mick, spent so much time with her that he fell in love with her and last I knew he had moved in. Listen, I think it would be really great to give them a call and at least let them know you are OK. More importantly, I think we need to get you back to your mum. I think we should also figure out a way of getting all your friends back to their families as well. Something doesn't stack up here and I think that the sooner we get you out of here the better."

"There's nothing bad going on here you know. We get fed and watered and looked after. All we have to do is work hard on the night shift and keep our heads down. Carl might be getting his freedom today. That means he gets a flat and a job on the day shift. He's going to contact his friends and family as soon as he gets chance. But I think I would like to speak to my mum, maybe going back home would be nice after all."

Bludd took his mobile phone from his pocket and slid his finger across the screen. The words in the top corner were disappointing. 'No service'. "Sorry Susan, I can't get a reception on this phone around here. It will have to wait. You stay here. Don't mention me to your friends and I will be back for you as soon as I have figured out what is going on and how to get you away. OK?"

"OK. But how are you going to get out. I mean, I can get you into the main compound, but there is no way out of here either on this side or in the main compound, except through the front gate."

"How? You got a key or something?"

"No, I just know the code to get into the main area. I don't know if it's the same one to get out of the front gate. I've never tried."

"Just get me in there, please, it will have to do. But listen, like I said, keep this to yourself. I think there is some serious stuff going on here and I need some time to get to the bottom of it. All I ask is that you trust me and believe me that I want to help you all. How many of you are there by the way?"

"There are 11 now, we just had a new lad come in. But Carl looks like he might be leaving, so 10 again by tonight with a bit of luck."

"OK, I will try and find a way of getting all of you out at once. Hopefully I'll be back before tomorrow."

She led him around the back of the ring of huts and through the trees. There was a slight path cleared through persistent walking over the same ground, leaves kicked to both sides. They reached the gate and Bludd watched her tap in 'CY1560'. He memorised it in case it might come in useful later.

Susan Kerby opened the gate and Bludd went through, a line of trees, three or four deep covered the camp fence to the industrial yard. He looked back at the girl. "Trust me," he urged.

The gate locked and Bludd dived away to his left. He figured that he could make his way to the corner of the yard and have a look round, assess the situation and make a plan from there. He stayed close to the tall green fence and found himself in the corner of the yard, the fence darting off at right angles towards the north end of the industrial estate. Bludd crept along the fence until he came to the end of the thin cover that the trees had offered him.

He crouched down on one knee. To his right was the main factory. At the end of the building nearest to him, there were two mobile units that looked like they were used as some kind of extra office space. They were grey, prefabricated buildings with a flat roof and a single door at the middle of the front wall, three steps leading up to the door, both buildings identical. Beyond them, the green fence continued to that side of the yard. Bludd could not tell if it ran all the way to the front of the building, or if it was attached to the factory and would stop. If that was the case, he might be able to get onto the roof of the factory by using the mobile units as a step up. He looked again at the units. They were about 12 feet high and the roof of the main factory was about 30 feet from the floor. That was a problem. Even if he could get up there, maybe there was no easy way off the roof at the other side. A 30 foot drop was 50 per cent worse than the 20 foot drop from the fence and tree he had made earlier when he hurt his chest. He remembered that he had hurt his chest and rubbed his sternum with the knuckle of his thumb. The pain had gone, but it didn't make the thought of jumping from a higher point any more appealing.

He looked straight ahead. The trucks were parked in a line in front of him, facing the main factory, backs to the fence that was above the sheer drop down to the river. The trucks were in a row that seemed to lead all the way to the back wall of the incinerator building. Bludd could not see the building from here, but he closed his eyes and pictured what he had seen from the railway bridge that morning before sunlight. The building had a flat roof right across, left to right and front to back. It was slightly lower than the top of the trucks. He tried to focus on the west wall of the building and what might lie behind it. Was it a sheer drop, or was there a way he could use this roof to lower himself to a route out of here?

He had to choose between two options, neither of which was offering him anything certain. The roof of the factory was glass, it meant he could at least get a look inside the packaging factory, but that wasn't important to him at the present moment. He decided that the incinerator building offered him the best chance of a route out. The trucks were about 20 yards from the edge of the trees that were offering him cover.

He bolted for the nearest trailer. It took him a few seconds to dive behind the back of the trailer. He read the side of the vehicle as he ran. 'Forster Packaging – Specialists in SRP and RRP' it said. *Shelf Ready and Retail Ready Packaging,* he thought.

He stayed crouched low. He had no idea of the whereabouts of Durie and the Romanians and he did not want to alert them to his presence. Not yet. Not until he knew exactly what was going on here.

He moved along the rear of the line of trailers, staying low, shuffling from side to side, keeping his eyes alert for any movement from the factory that faced the front of the trucks. He carefully passed between each four foot gap, moving more quickly in case there were cameras or wary eyes watching the yard. He reached the last trailer. The fence was attached to the end of the incinerator building. The trailer was only a couple of feet away from the rear wall of the building. If he could get on top of the trailer, he could get on the roof, no doubt about it.

He leant back against the fence, trying to get his eyes to see what lay behind the long west wall. To see if there was a ledge, or was it a sheer drop from the wall? Surely a building of this size and height would need some hefty foundations and that would surely mean that there must be a gap between the wall and the edge of the drop down to the river.

The trailers had solid back doors and canvas sides. He could not see any way that he could climb up the canvas side walls. The back doors were shut and locked. The locking system consisted of two steel bars that had a twist and lock mechanism and ran from top to bottom. There was a one inch gap between the bar and door. Bludd tested if he could get his fingers in between the bar and the wooden panel of the door. It was a tight fit, but Bludd thought that might be an advantage. He would have to force his fingers in and then they would not be able to come back out without him forcing them out the other way. He could use the pressure to aid him in his climb, as painful or uncomfortable as it may be.

He stood on the steel rear bumper, a steel frame that held the 'Long Distance' sign and registration plate. He reached up as high as he could and shoved the fingers of his right hand in the gap and gripped the bar as well as his fingers could get a hold. He stepped up as high as his left foot would go and reached high again, shoving his left hand fingers into the gap and pulling back on the bar as he jerked his right foot up high. It was not easy as his fingers were trying to do the work of his biceps, but four repeat upward steps and he put his fingers over the top of the back door and grabbed a lip that was the join of door to roof. He clutched it with both sets of digits and hung for a moment. As soon as he was on the top, he would be clearly visible to anybody that might be watching. He swung his legs upwards and launched his body in the same direction all in one motion. He straightened his arms and pulled his legs up straight, toes dragging against the back door of the truck, swung his left leg over the lip and pushed up, straightening his knee and pulling his whole body onto the roof. He dropped down and lay flat, not moving, facing the factory opposite. The office windows were just to the left, 11 o'clock. He would have to move fast. He could see the back of a figure, one of the brothers, leaning against the office window, he thought.

He stood back up and ran a couple of feet and jumped the gap from trailer to the roof of the incinerator building and landed on both feet, dropping to his knees immediately and then onto his front in one motion. He looked right. The figure had not moved. He shuffled his feet around so that he was facing the packaging factory and he could shuffle left, on his chest , keeping a constant eye on the body, which he guessed from its size must belong to one of the Romanians.

He shuffled left, glancing across to see if there were any obstacles. The roof was flat with a felt covering and lead around the edges. There were two stainless steel chimneys sticking out about two feet from the roof, spiral lips running like a helter-skelter around the outside and a mesh cap on top to stop birds flying in. They were spaced 10 feet apart and were about 20 feet from each side of the building. Beyond them, a leaded raised area rose up to the same height. Bludd assumed that this was a roof light or window panel.

He shuffled his body across and his head was offered cover by the chimney as he faced the packaging factory opposite. He peeped around the stainless steel tubing and looked across to the windows of the factory's offices. One of the brothers was still standing with his back to the window; the other was out of Bludd's sight. He shuffled backward a yard or so and then moved left again, so that his head and body were behind the raised lead flashing around the window panel.

He peeped over the top, no movement from the Romanian. He lifted himself up on his fingers and leaned forward, like a sprinter at the start of a race, and peered down through the wire mesh reinforced glass. It was dark and gloomy inside, the dull October sky not offering enough light to allow him to clearly see inside. He put his hands to the side of his face, a shroud around his eyes, stopping the light deflection. He could see two large black boxes, probably blackened steel, and the chimneys pointing upwards out of the far end of each box: the incinerators. The floor to each side and to the front of both of them was littered with small piles of what looked like dog carcasses. He thought he could make out a German Shepherd on top of the pile nearest to him, the tan colour a clear outline of its underbelly, legs and neck. The tongue, a dash of pink, hanging limp from its mouth.

He glanced across the glass and over the yard to the office windows of the packaging factory. The Romanian he had seen with his back to the glass window had now turned around and was looking directly at him, his left hand shielding his eyes from the light, his right hand pointing and stabbing thin air, his mouth shouting as he beckoned his brother to see what he had seen.

The other brother appeared in view and just as quickly Bludd saw them both turn and disappear. He had been seen, no doubt about it. Now what? He could not afford to get trapped in the yard with them, even though he was confident of dealing with them, he would still need to get out of there. He stood up, no use trying to stay under cover now, turned and stepped across to the edge of the roof. He looked down, the drop was a big one, but he could dangle himself off the roof and lessen it by six feet four inches. Below him was a ledge, as he had thought, a few feet in from the 100 foot sheer drop down to the tree-lined river bank. The ledge narrowed to almost nothing to his left as the fence stood almost atop the cliff edge. To the right, the ledge stayed the same width and then got covered in bushes and privet. At least the fact that they had taken root meant to Bludd that there was ground underneath and he would have to head that way.

He lowered his legs over the edge of the roof, scraping his toes down the brickwork and resting his stomach on the lead flashing that hung over. He lurched backwards and grabbed the edge of the roof momentarily and then dropped down to the ledge below.

The ledge was three feet wide, so Bludd turned and faced the aqueduct that was about 70 yards away across the tree tops. He ran, keeping as close to the edge of the building as he could, not looking left and over the edge, a 100 foot drop, a mass of trees and branches and a fast running river below. He tentatively stepped through the bushes, the bricks of the building being replaced by 20 foot high, green-painted steel fence struts again. He held on to them as he moved forward, slowly wading through the intertwined twigs. The bushes stopped and the narrow ledge got a little wider as it came to meet the tan stone of the aqueduct. The wall was high, too high to jump up and get a hold, no footholds in the brickwork. To his left, two feet away from the edge of solid ground, a black, steel bolt protruded from the stonework, surrounded by a two foot square end piece that locked it into the side of the aqueduct. It must have been some kind of restraining support bolt that ran right through to the other side, underneath the man-made base of the canal. Bludd looked across and each arch of the brickwork was topped by two of the steel rods, at 1 o'clock and 11 o'clock on a clockface. He could step over and stand on top of the black steel and if he jumped at the same time as landing it, he could probably get high enough to get a grip of the top stone of the aqueduct and haul himself upwards. That said, if he missed his grip, he could easily fall 100 feet to certain death. But there was no other way to go. He had to do it, and do it quickly. The Romanians would be there soon enough and he needed to be on solid ground before they arrived.

He stepped across and jumped, grasping at the rounded top stones of the brick wall, his fingers arching and their tips digging in for all their worth, letting go with one hand and stretching up and over, desperately trying to get a hand hold. His feet pushed into the bricks, and with small steps, he stuttered up, his right hand now curved over the top of the wall and hanging on whilst his feet inched upwards. As he neared the top, he brought his knees together and bent them in up to his chest, and with all his energy, his toes and knees sprung him out and up and he vaulted the wall and landed on the other side on the concrete towpath. He leant back against the wall, breathless and relieved.

There was no chance to get his thoughts together. He looked to his right; the two big Romanians were lumbering towards him. It was like there was a mirror between them physically and facially they were almost identical. The one to the right was dressed in the same blue uniform as the people in the camp wore, the one to the left had dungarees, with braces, made from the same blue material, backed by a checked shirt, black and red. The pair of them wore hefty work boots. Bludd reckoned they were a cert to be steel toe caps, even if they weren't, he would not fancy a kick from them, by either of these boneheads.

He looked across the canal. A six foot jump would have him across the water and safely on the slim concrete path on the other side, a 100-foot drop only three feet further on from the water, a precise jump would be needed, but he would have relative safety. If either of the brothers tried it, he was sure he could grab them as they landed and give them a little helping hand to go that bit further and plunge to their death.

He looked left. The canal stretched 200 yards into the distance and then narrowed to the right, beyond that he had no idea as he had not had time to explore further. It was the next thing he had intended to do. Annabelle Judge had suggested that the old recycling plant was round there somewhere in the near vicinity.

He turned back. The brothers were almost on him, and they were slowing their pace, rolling up their sleeves, catching their breath.

Bludd stood facing them directly, feet apart, arms relaxed and by his side. He breathed deeply and blinked, a photograph of the faces of the two angry looking brothers permanently etched in his mind.

The brothers were on him, the one to the left, in his dungarees, threw a right hand haymaker punch, a split second before his brother replicated him. Bludd's arms swirled up, anti-clockwise, as a pair and batted the oncoming fists away, switching back to a clockwise direction as soon as he had deflected them. His arms stayed loose, his training kicking in, a loose and relaxed arm can generate more power than tensed up muscle, and his wrist flicked hard as he simultaneously smashed the brothers' jaws. The brothers were dazed, not pained by Bludd's hit, but with surprise at the speed of his arms and the technique he had used to defend himself. Before they could get their senses together, Bludd had rotated his right arm and smashed an uppercut into the brother to his right, a crunch sounded out as his front teeth smashed together and splintered their tips. His left arm flicked back the other way, clenched fist held backwards and lashed the left hand brother across his already flattened nose.

Both brothers were stunned but standing tall despite the swift and well-aimed hits. Bludd took a slight step back, a distance big enough between them to avoid the inevitable retaliation. The left hand brother took a short shuffled step to his right. He stood close to the edge of the concrete, inches from the canal water a foot below. They both inched forward and the brother to the right shot a momentary glance to his brother, awaiting his approval to attack. Bludd saw a slight nod from the other brother and immediately launched a flat-footed kick into the crotch of the man on his right, who let out a loud groan as he doubled up, head down towards his knees. Bludd's left foot applied the same technique to the other brother but with a higher kick, aimed at his stomach, enough to knock the wind out of his lungs and send him stepping back a foot, the ball of his foot teetering on the edge of the concrete.

Bludd ignored the right hand Romanian and turned to his left, where the man swung a slow roundhouse punch aimed at Bludd's skull, but it was too slow and too deliberate, Bludd ducked his whole body down and left, stepping to his right and rising up, body weight fully behind his ascending right fist, a change in style to maximise the power he would unleash. The fist pounded into the mouth of the Romanian, a jagged tooth flew up into the air, white and clear against a grey sky. The man's head rocked backwards and his balance tipped his head beyond his heels. Bludd gave a left forearm to his throat and his head jerked forward as his body lunged backward and his feet lost their footing and he fell into the canal below, scraping the back of his head against the canal wall on the opposite side.

Bludd swiftly spun round. The other man was still doubled over, holding his groin and watching in disbelief as his brother splashed into the slimy, green water. Bludd launched another kick, one practised so often on his Wing Chun dummy and his right foot smashed into the face of the Romanian, straightening his stance and turning him to face Bludd. He followed with a barrage of loose armed strikes to the head and face that knocked his head from side to side as he fell backwards against the wall of the aqueduct.

Bludd had done enough. One brother was too dazed to retaliate; the other was in no position to do anything other than rest his arms on the canal side and catch his breath, gasping at the air and try to gather his senses. Bludd turned towards the water and planted a pointed toe straight between the eyes of the soaked and dazed brother, not enough to knock him out, but enough to send him back across to the other wall, blood oozing from his nose.

Bludd walked away in the direction he had arrived that morning, he needed to check the recycling building out and he wanted to get there quickly. It was now three-thirty and he wanted to speak to Chrissie, and Annabelle Judge as well. He would have to get back to his bike and then go to the main road to get a signal. He would then go back over the aqueduct and pay the recycling building a visit, sure that it had something to do with the story behind what went on at the camp and the industrial estate.

20

Perversion

Jonathon Durie stepped out of the shower and wrapped a towel around his waist. He stood in front of the mirror and examined himself. His body seemed more twisted in the mirror than he felt it was in reality. He leant slightly to the left, on a tilt. It was a legacy of the car crash that he and his friends had been involved in 10 years earlier. His left leg had a kink in it at the knee that caused him to limp badly and caused him pain. His arm had been broken in several places and his hand crushed, the bones broken and ruptured, his index and middle finger, flattened and virtually severed, had been sewn back on and put back together as well as the surgeon could manage. The bones were so damaged that they had not been able to knit together without the assistance of wire inserts that kept the bones in place, even though they were fragmented. But his hand was permanently disfigured into a claw-like appearance that could not extend fully, nor completely contract either. Durie looked at it with disdain. His face had been scarred, but he had managed to cover the damage with his sandy coloured beard that covered 60 per cent of his face. He was not a bad looking man until the crash, now he felt like a cross between *The Elephant Man* and Hugh Laurie's character in the American TV series *House*. In reality, it was nowhere near as bad, but he felt like it was. He had never had a partner, probably never would. He could not fulfil their needs anyway. Another legacy of the crash was his impotence.

He had tried all kinds of things to bring back his libido. First of all he had sought help from his doctor, the conventional way of medicine. It had not worked. He had tried herbalists and alternative medicines, but neither had worked. He had visited sex workers, none of whom had been able to help. He had felt the slightest twinge of something when he had visited a sex show and had enjoyed watching the orgy take place in front of him. Then he had thought that watching that sort of thing in the privacy of his own home, with nobody around to judge him or pressure him to get involved, would help. He had watched all kinds of things, from straight to gay, masturbation to mass group orgies, from amateurs to celebrities. Some of it had excited him, but only mentally. Not physically.

Then his searches had become more focused. He wanted things that were out of the norm. He wanted something different, something that was unusual. Something that the normal sites could not provide. He had spent hours looking through the usual sites and had become bored with the tameness of even the things that most people would find to be vile. He had progressed to bestiality and then found sites that contained necrophilia. He had liked that. He felt a little guilty and knew that it was bad. A bad thing to do, a bad thing to be watching. And he had stopped himself from watching. For a while. And then he had gone back on again, starting where he had left off, watching people having sex with dead bodies. He had watched as graves were disturbed and freshly buried bodies exhumed and defiled.

Then he had progressed.

He had found snuff videos. He had found scenes where people are killed during the act of sexual intercourse. Actually killed on screen and not acted out, right before the camera.

Then he had progressed to torture and mutilation and sexual

intercourse. And death. People were killed in the most grue-some ways imaginable, and all whilst being raped or sexually mutilated. Genitals removed. Breasts removed. All while the victims watched until they passed out, never to come round again.

Then he had found the Lupescu brothers. They were from a small village in central Transylvania, almost in the dead centre of Romania. Their rural surroundings had lost their interest, but the history of the myth of their region had become a fasci-nation. Vampires. Count Dracula. The fascination had turned into an obsession.

Some people might have thought to manufacture dolls, or set up a museum, or do guided tours of fake sites and fake sightings. But the Lupescu brothers had hit upon a much more lucrative idea. Not that they had thought it would be, it just happened that there are lots of sick and perverse people around the globe, and if you can find them, or get them to find you, it can make you a lot of money. Millions, in fact.

Durie had found their website and he had watched in awe as the brothers performed deviant acts on men, women and children. At first he had been sick, feeling like his gut had been physically wrenched from his torso. Not dissimilar to the actual films themselves. And then he had become immune to it. Fascinated by the way the brothers filmed things, the angles they shot, the stories they tied in, sometimes the lack of a story and just the hideous way that they had conjured the killing and the torture and how they had combined it with sexual acts. He had wondered where they had found the people to 'star' in their films. How they had persuaded them to the studio, what lies they must have told, or promises they must have made and broken. There was no gain from any appearance in these films. Just pain. Immense pain and eventual, certain death.

The films were not available to buy. He had looked for a way to buy them, but the site was hardly an 'add to trolley' kind of site. He had registered and joined many thousands of like-minded individuals around the globe. He had paid his subscription fee and he had paid lots of times to watch the full film, enticed by a trailer that stopped short of the best bits, the pivotal moment, the end game.

Then he had clicked on the 'contact us' button and expressed his admiration at their work and their imagination. He had asked if he could be involved. The brothers had replied and after many conversations, Durie had found himself offering a perfect scenario. Come to the UK. Buy into his company, buy some of the shares, invest in a legitimate company and use it to launder their ill-gotten gains. He even had an idea how to get a constant supply of unwilling participants, which, it turned out, was exactly how they already did the same in Romania.

The brothers had visited him. They had liked his plans and they had reason to come to the UK. That was because they wanted to leave their own country. The authorities would be sure to track them down eventually. There were clues, and they had begun to get a reputation to be avoided, like they were some kind of gangsters, or even bad luck charms. They already laundered their own money through a bogus agricultural company, and to anybody that could be bothered to look, it was clearly a front. The Romanian authorities were slack, but they had had a run that they felt would have to come to an end at some point, and the timing of Durie's suggestion had made their minds up.

They had gone in with Durie in a three-way split, meaning that, as brothers that always stuck together, they would always have the final word. Actually, Durie had turned out to be quite impressive with his own ideas, and far from holding them back in just how far they could push the boundaries, he had actually added even more sinister plots to their own ideas.

They had bought into the company by buying the old recycling plant, which in recent history had also been a paper pulp and recycling factory. They had converted some of it into luxury apartments and had plans to complete the whole mill by the end of the following year. They lived in a separate building across from the recycling plant. The old Dye House had been converted into studio apartments. One for each of them, plus offices and a filming studio.

Now that Durie, and his friend, Judge, were threatening to leave the UK and pass the running of the other businesses to them, they would have full control and could churn out more films than ever before. It would mean more workers would have to be sought and more false promises made and broken. What fools they were to think that they would all be given flats or apartments eventually. No, the apartments would be sold off and they would make a legitimate fortune to add to their already healthy financial situation, made from less legitimate means, but filed through their background company and through the packaging company. Having Judge out of the way was the real bonus of him and Durie leaving. Judge had agreed to the brothers working for him and he knew what they did as a sideline, to a certain extent. But he had drawn the line at pushing the money through his company. At least until he had stopped his wife's involvement in the accounting, and then he had allowed them to funnel the moneys through the books. It inflated the value of his company, although it was all false as the money would eventually find its way back out into their pockets. And Durie's.

Durie had dressed and put on his clean clothes. He wanted to look as normal as possible when he met Carl. They had met before many times, and Durie always had to concentrate on being seen as the professional boss of a packaging company. He had to focus on keeping his thoughts clean and his mind on the job. The benefits sometimes took years to come to fruition, and today was a day that Durie had been looking forward to for some time. He looked in the mirror by the front door as he left, combing his beard with his fingers and straightening his hair one last time before he clicked the door shut and walked across the bridge to meet the brothers at the reception and run through the next few hours.

21

Freedom

Bludd had gone back the mile along the road to the factory to the main road. He had got a reception on his mobile phone and spoken to Chrissie. She had been more than a little worried and her sleeping pattern had resembled Bludd's the night before. She had learned to ignore herself and let him get on with things, but last night, and this case, felt different for her. He had told her that things had taken some twists and turns and was much bigger than he could have ever expected and he could not tell her when he would finish and be back home, or in touch again.

He had also phoned Annabelle Judge and explained about the camp and Susan Kerby and the others. She had been mortified. She had asked if there was any evidence of abuse or cruelty, reminding him of the email that they had both seen from her husband. He had told her that, in fact, it seemed quite the opposite on the face of things and that the people had appeared to be content enough, and that many of them had earned freedom and, in fact, by the sound of it, gone on to be rewarded and be offered the opportunity of a nice life. She had concluded, in the same way that Bludd had done, that it all seemed too good to be true, and that there must be something more to it, and that he should keep looking and try harder.

Bludd had put his helmet back on, fired up the Yamaha and headed back to the factory and aqueduct. It was all quiet when he arrived. He had a quick look over at Durie's house and stopped adjacent to the industrial estate and peered through the fence. Nothing was happening. He had half expected to see the brothers still lying on the concrete path of the aqueduct, but they were gone. Licking their wounds, Bludd hoped. He passed the spot that he had fought with them and saw the a few spots of blood on the path, he presumed from the one who had been in the water.

He had travelled on, over the aqueduct, past the opening that led to the path down to the river and round the curve of the canal. He had arrived at a tunnel and the path continued up a slope to the left. A wooden hand rail ran along the right-hand side of a brick, gravel and dirt path that was made up of shallow steps that were four feet apart. Bludd rode the bike up the left-hand side of the path. A shallow stone wall ran along its left-hand side, a steep drop down to the floor of the forest to the other side. The path rose around 40 feet over a distance of 70 yards. At the top, the path swung round to the left and sloped down to the canal again, the other end of the tunnel topped by a wall that circled down with the path to the water's edge. A road clipped the path and swung away to the right.

In the distance, Bludd could see the whitewashed wall of a large building. Three rows of two sash style windows were housed in the wall. Bludd rode his bike across to take a closer look. The front of the building was also whitewashed over concrete rendered brick. It was clean and bright, well maintained. The front of the building had a series of four arches to the ground level and then at the rear was a raised area that was concrete topped and backed by a brick wall. The arches were split, along the floor, into two, by a white painted line that ran from the outside of the building to the back of the bay and Bludd was sure that each was a parking space, which meant that this huge building was home to only eight apartments. Above the raised level, the wall was home to an arched window that was placed in the centre of each of the parking bays. Bludd tried to imagine how the building would have looked in its previous life. The large archways were big enough to accept a lorry, which probably would have reversed in and dumped its load onto the raised area. He reckoned that the wall that held the arched windows was probably a later addition and made an extra floor for each apartment. He parked his bike and put it on its stand. He flipped up the visor of his helmet and wandered over to the front of the building. He looked up to see that there were two rows of eight windows above the archways, all arched in the same design as those below and all in the same wood material, a dark wood which looked like mahogany. To the left side of the building there was a single door, made from the same material as the window frames, high quality wood and shiny with varnish. Bludd walked through the second of the archways and jumped onto the raised level. He peered through the left-hand window of the two. There was a large room, a door to the centre at the far end, but nothing at all in the room. It was completely empty.

He moved to the right and looked through the first window that lay at the end of the next parking bay space. It was exactly the same, a door to the centre and an empty room. He repeated it again to his right at the last room and again to the room to the left of the building next to the front door. All the rooms were empty.

He tried the front door, with little expectation of it being open. A mortice lock and a digital lock were housed to the right-hand side and the door was well and truly locked. Bludd had got no idea what was in the building. It looked like an apartment block. It looked like there were eight apartments. But it also looked like there were no inhabitants.

He decided to look around the back. It meant that he would

have to go back to the path that led down to the canal and the north end of the tunnel. As he walked back, he noticed a separate building, also whitewashed render, much smaller, but with a central door, the same wood as the apartment building next to it. Windows only ran along the first floor, four of them, equally spaced. A track, wide enough for a car, ran down to it and then swung left and stopped in front of the building. The road dropped away to the side of the building and a black Toyota pick-up was parked front facing towards the canal.

He jogged up the road and turned right and headed down to the bottom of the sloping path. To his right, the tunnel mouth was pitch black and ivy dangled down over its filthy stonework. In front of him, as he stood at the bottom of the slope, was the smaller building. It was similar to the front. Four windows were equally spaced, but on this side, they were to the top floor. Drainpipes ran from below each of the outside windows. A single pipe ran down the very end of the left-hand wall from roof to a few inches above the waterline of the canal. In the centre, a foot above the waterline was another outlet; its end was flush with the wall. Underneath it was a red stain that ran from the hole and to the waterline, narrowing as it neared the water. The rest of the wall was white, but not clean like the front of both buildings, a layer of grime covered the paint, and the render ran all the way into the water. It had not been cleaned or repainted for some time and the red stain looked a stark contrast to the sullen paintwork to the rest of the back wall.

Bludd thought about what Annabelle Judge had said about the recycling plant. She had said that it was some kind of printing works before her husband had turned it to a recycling facility. Maybe the small building was some kind of ink store, or dye store, or a colour mixing station.

He walked on a few yards. The back of the main recycling building, that was now a handful of apartments, was not rendered like the front and side of the building and the whole of the smaller building, but was just standard brick-faced. The building seemed larger from the back. There were the same two rows of mahogany-framed windows, and a series of drainpipes running down to the water line. But then there were lots of shabby areas that looked like the renovation team could not be bothered to do the rear side, or at least not finish it. At the left-hand end, there was a rusty, steel-framed bridge, some kind of fire escape, which ran from the end of the first floor and spanned the canal, over the path and stone wall and attached to an upright that dropped right down to the forest floor.

There was still no evidence of what was behind the walls of the building, and no evidence that there were any inhabitants.

Bludd headed back to his bike, flicked down his visor and kicked the engine into life again. He had decided his next move. There did not seem to be much going on at the factory, or in the estate yard, or in the incinerator building, or the recycling plant apartments. He needed to concentrate on how to free the people in the camp. Judge was due back in the morning and he wanted this thing over with by then. Then he could deal with his nemesis.

He twisted the throttle and the rear tyre spun and kicked the back end of the bike out as he headed back across the path that traversed over the tunnel, down the 70-yard slope at the other side and round the left-hand sweeping curve of the canal and its path. He stopped at the path that led down to the river and flipped the front wheel over the step, gunned the throttle and jumped onto the path, hopping down the steps and swivelling left and right, dropping the revs as he dropped down the path's wooden slats. He stood on the foot rests and dropped the bike from left to right as he avoided the foliage of ferns and nettles. He pulled the bike to a stop at the canoe club hut, switched off the ignition and leant it against the balustrade that ran along the veranda.

He dropped down and crawled through the hole in the door and sidled his way through the furniture, in the semi-darkness, to the store room in the far corner. He opened the door and grabbed three loops of rope from the right-hand wall. Then he grabbed one of the red-and-white striped poles. He didn't usually think about having a weapon, happy to rely on his skills and strength in any situation he had put himself in. But this was different. The two brothers had been no match for him earlier, but now they would be angry and probably want revenge, if the opportunity arose, which it was bound to at some point in the near future. Bludd was sure of that.

He put the rod on the seat of his bike and took the ropes to the end of the jetty. He jogged back up towards the hut and went to the front end of the trailer that was parked next to it, lifted the front that rested on a small pilot wheel and pushed, hard. He leant forward and put his left hand against the middle of the framework of the trailer, giving himself and the trailer balance and more grip to move the trailer to the water. He stopped at the near end of the jetty, rounded the trailer and pulled the middle of the canoes from the central rack. He returned to the waterside on the jetty and rested the canoe on the edge. He picked up the first hoop of rope and made a loop in the end, tying a reef knot in place to keep the loop and hook it over the round post that was at the end of the jetty. He unravelled the rope and fed the other end through the small hoop of rope and toggle at the end of the canoe and then repeated the same thing at the other end of the jetty and the other end of the canoe with the second hoop of rope. He wrapped the rope around the wooden post at each end and then dropped the canoe in the water. He stood and looked across the water and turned to the trailer and tried to calculate if the combined width of the canoes would be equal to the width of the river and whether his pontoon bridge solution would be good enough to hold the escapees as they would clamber across it.

* * *

Jonathon Durie had met the brothers in reception as planned. What was not planned was the state of their faces. Marius was not too bad; he was walking awkwardly, but only had light, early stages of bruising to his face. Andrei's face was a mess, he had already got swelling around his eyes, and the skin underneath all puffed out and reddened, making his eyes squint. There had been blood coming from his nose, which they had managed to stop and he had cleaned himself up. The brothers had gone to collect their new member of staff and Carl Hampson.

At first he thought that they'd had one of their many spats, but was troubled when they had explained about the intruder and the way that their intended attack on him had turned into a heavy beating. He wished Jeremy had been around. He put the matter to the back of his mind. They had other things to concentrate on and he had been looking forward to this particular forthcoming episode for many months.

There was a knock on his office door. The brothers entered before he had responded. They were followed by two young men. Durie recognised the older one, the thin one, to be a long-term camp member and night shift operative, Carl. The other one was unknown to him. He was a few years younger, or at least he looked it. A nice looking kid, fresh faced and nervous looking. This was the one the brothers had intimated that he would be pleased with. They were right. The new boy was just his type. He was slightly on the plump side, ruddy cheeks and wavy hair that was almost curly. There was something almost feminine about him. One for later, but not too much later, Durie decided.

"Hi, ber-boys. Have my friends her-here explained why yer-you are here?" Durie started, trying to keep his stutter to a minimum.

The boys looked at each other, and then they looked back at Durie. "We are going to the apartments that were promised us when we agreed to come here." Carl Hampson responded. "I am going to be staying there and starting on the day shift, and Ben here is going to spend the night with me and see what he can aspire to. He will return to the camp tomorrow."

Carl Hampson was well spoken and articulate. He was also keen to be moving on and getting his life back. He was especially keen to get into the real world and make contact with his family and friends that he had not seen or spoken to for the last two years. He was keen not to say or do anything that might stop his freedom from coming to fruition.

"Cerrrect," Durie said, his word elongated to stop the stammer. He stood up and moved from behind his desk and leant against the front of it, offering his hand to Carl. "You have der-done well, Carl. Yer-you have earned everything you get. The-there are a fer-few formalities to ger-go through and then we will ser-settle you in and introduce you ter-to the day shift ler-lads." He turned towards the youngster and offered his hand again. "Ner-nice to meet you yer-young man. Take ner-note of Carl here. He her-has worked hard and ker-kept his nose cer-clean and now he has his rewards wer-waiting for him. Yer-you can aspire to follow him ber-by der-doing as you are asked and wer-waiting your chance. If you are a really good boy, it mer-might come ser-sooner than you think." Durie curled his mangled fingers of his left hand into the boy's hair and stroked down his right cheek. He had already decided in his mind that Ben could very well earn his stripes quickly by performing certain favours for him. The boy flinched as Durie's claw-like hand ran under his chin. Durie became instantly disappointed. Maybe the boy Ben would not be too keen to do his kind of favour, but he would be patient and he would get his way before he let the brothers get theirs.

"Take the boys to the ap-apartments, please. I have to jer-just get the paperrrwork together and I will fer-follow you over sher-shortly," Durie instructed.

The youngsters turned and left the room and Durie could not help look down at their bottoms, and he allowed himself a smile. The two Romanians followed them out, but noticed Durie's lingering glare and they turned to each other and smiled, knowing that soon after, the smile would turn into a growl and the stuttering would be replaced by a screaming high pitch cackle as Durie urged them to carry out his tasks.

22

Monsters

Bludd had secured the canoes into a makeshift pontoon bridge and tied them, at both ends, to trees on the far side of the river. He had considered trekking back up the steep slope and using the third, and unused, rope to get himself back into the camp and use it as a means of getting the people in there out. He metaphorically scratched his head. He wondered which way to proceed. If he rescued them, what would he do with them? They could hide out in the canoe clubhouse, while he went and found some transport. He annoyed himself. What was he going to do? Book a taxi? *"Take these people somewhere and don't spare the horses."* It brought him to his senses. If and when he got these people out, he would have to have a plan. He would have to know what each of them would want individually. He did not have time to think about each one individually, or to arrange separate transport to who knows where.

There was something else that was niggling him. It was his instinct. He could not be certain of these people wanting to come with him. Susan Kerby had not shown any interest until he had proved to her that he knew, for sure, that her mother had been devastated by her disappearance and was desperate to have her home. But he had no inside information for the others that might seal the deal for them to want to escape. And yet he was certain, absolutely 100 per cent certain, that there something bad going on behind all this. His experience of Judge and Durie would not allow him to think otherwise. But what was really niggling him was that he knew, somewhere in the back of his mind, that something bad was on the cards, and that it might just have to happen for him to give the others a reason to leave.

He kicked his bike back into life and spun it round in a long 180 degree turn, spinning the throttle hard and spraying dirt out from behind as the back wheel kicked out and dug in to the ground. He used the bike's off-road characteristics to good effect, flicking the throttle back and forth as he made easy work of getting back up the twisting path and wooden, dirt-covered steps. His mind was racing. What to do? How to time it? Where to take them? Who to meet?

He arrived back at the main road and opened up his phone, relieved to see a reception bar in the top left hand corner.

A choice.

He rang Annabelle Judge. He had considered Chrissie, but aside from his involvement, it was nothing to do with her. And it could turn out to be dangerous. Why should she be involved?

"Mr Bludd," Annabelle Judge answered formally.

"Please, call me Seb. Actually, right now, call me what you like. I need you to do a number of things for me. It might not be straight forward, it being Sunday and all that, but I need you to try and arrange some stuff, for tomorrow morning, first thing. OK?"

"OK. Fire away."

"Right. Firstly, I need you here at first light, that's about half six, earlier if you can. That's the easy part. I need you here in a mini-bus, capable of carrying 10 passengers. It has to be a hired thing, not a taxi, I don't want anybody down here and involved that isn't already."

"OK, I'll see what I can do, but you've left it a bit short notice."

"Pull some strings, flash some, or splash some, cash. Just do it. Next, you need to bring somebody from one of these home-less charity things, you know like Shelter, or something. We need to keep these people together for now. I have no idea if they will all come with me anyway, but I have even less idea of what to do with them or where they will want to go. It might be an idea to have them bring some kind of assistance for people in trauma, some kind of psycho-analysts, or something. I don't really know what to tell you to tell them, I am sure you can think of something."

"Bloody hell, Bludd. You don't want much do you?" It was a rhetorical question and said with an element of humour that Bludd got, but didn't have time for.

"Finally, we need somewhere to meet. I haven't got time to go looking, I need to get back over there and keep an eye on things. I have a horrible feeling about today and I need to be watching that factory. I need you to find somewhere that I can find you with these kids. Google maps are your best bet."

Bludd closed his eyes and ran it back to when he was looking at the factory from above. Businesses were sometimes highlighted above their buildings and he could see in his mind the zoom out version of the photograph, and he could see that there were not too many options. He focused hard on the image. The canoe club was there and Durie's cottage shown as 'Junction Cottage'.

"There is a pub not too far away to the south, but it's quite public. To the west there is a church, St Simon's. Check them out. See if they are suitable and accessible for me and the others. If there is anywhere more suitable, you will have to let me know how to get there. Either way, you decide and you let me know. Send me a text, leave me a voicemail. Both. I can't get a signal near the factory, so it going to be a bit hit and miss."

Annabelle Judge let out an audible sigh. "Like I said, you don't want much do you? Don't worry, I will map it out and get back to you. Is there anything else?"

"Yes. Whatever happens, I am coming to the airport with you. I think it's about time I made friends with your husband."

* * *

The two Romanians had walked to the old recycling plant that was now plush apartments with the two young men, Carl and Ben. Ben had not said much, he was a bit disturbed by the bearded man, a man who he had only just met, stroking his face. It was strange, and had worried him greatly. Carl, on the other hand, had not shut up all the way along the walk by the canal, between the packaging factory and the apartments. He was ecstatic about getting his freedom and could not wait to see what they had done with the apartments. When he had joined the camp, the building was still a shell, having been a recycling plant, and they had only just started the work on the flats. The camp members had been given a tour, shown planning drawings and been made promises about how they could choose their own décor and would be given a small budget to furnish the rooms that would be deducted monthly from their new day shift salary. He told Ben about his friends and his family and how he had not run away, and how they would all celebrate after the passage of time that he had spent in the camp.

The Romanians had walked behind, talking in their native tongue and laughing between themselves at the conversation in front of them and how Carl's dreams were soon going to be shattered.

They arrived at the apartments and Andrei unlocked the mortice lock and keyed in a number on the digital lock. He twisted the knob under the buttons to the left and pushed the door inwards. Andrei stepped back and ushered Carl and Ben forwards to go up the stairs in front of them. Carl did not need asking twice, he waltzed past Ben and virtually ran up the steps. Ben took a little longer to start the climb, dubious that all this wasn't too good to be true: questioning himself, questioning his instinct, asking himself whether he could be wise enough at 15-years-old to be sure, or unsure, of all the things that were going on.

They all climbed the stairs. They led to a corridor that ran the length of that level of the building. Carl was almost dancing in front of the first door.

Marius opened it for him. "This one not yours. It just example, so you see how it look with furnishing. You stay here tonight, both of you. Then you get money for shops tomorrow and you go with Mr Durie to choose things. OK?"

Carl could not believe his ears, or his eyes. The apartment was fully furnished. There was a modern, dark brown leather sofa, with tan corduroy seat cushions. It was placed in front of an ivory-coloured fireplace with an electric fire that was made to look like a real log fire. A huge flat screen television was attached to the wall above the fire. A beige rug with brown and orange pattern running through it lay in front of the fire. The walls were painted burnt orange, giving the room a warm glow and feel.

At the back was a kitchen diner, all the appliances were built in and hidden by glossy black doors that matched the glossy, new black cooker and hob. White, sparkly, granite worktops housed the sink unit and all the small appliances he would need: a microwave, toaster and kettle. There was a wine rack with red and white bottles and a small beer fridge, full with cans. Stainless steel pans and cooking utensils adorned the walls on stainless steel rails.

Marius disturbed Carl's thoughts. "This door lead to bedroom, the far door to bathroom, there is door in between them, like en-suite." He pointed to the corner of the room to their left and then into the far left corner. Carl raced over to the nearest door, followed less enthusiastically by Ben.

"Oh my God!" Carl screamed as he opened the bedroom door and saw the plush bed and furnishings in front of him. A wrought iron-framed bed was adorned with a silk covered duvet and plump, fluffy pillows, with scatter cushions lined up along them. A fur throw rested on the opposite end dangled down to rest on the floor. A simple white wooden set of drawers matched two bedside cabinets and a tall wardrobe. Carl had never had anything like this before. It was so much better than his parents' house. At his age, he never dreamed that he would have his own glorious apartment, a bachelor pad like he could not have wished for. He would be the envy of his friends, his brother and sister. They would all be welcome to come around and see him, so he could revel in his success and share it with them.

Andrei dropped into the room. "Carl, it is time to go and see Mr Durie. He has papers for you to sign and make things completed. We go now. Ben, you stay here tonight. No contact anybody, just watch television, get comfortable and relax, yes."

Ben did not reply, he just smiled uncomfortably.

"See you later flatmate." Carl shouted as he skipped out of the door.

* * *

Bludd had passed the packaging factory again and had seen nothing happening, again. Then he had seen Durie pass behind him in the jeep vehicle and head towards the main road that

Bludd had been at a few minutes earlier. He rode the bike past the entry to the steps down to the river and along the canal path and up the 70-yard slope up to the road that led to the recycling plant apartments. He turned right and turned back to face the two buildings he had checked out earlier. He pulled to a stop and killed the engine, a foot to each side of the bike propping himself and the bike. He opened his visor, slightly.

He sat there for 10 minutes and waited for something to happen, sure that he was on the right track. He played the waiting game every week, but never with so much anticipation and trepidation.

Then, in the distance, they came out. The two brothers and the lad he had seen and heard talking to Susan Kerby earlier: Carl, she had called him. They left the main building that was now flats, or apartments Susan Kerby had called them. *Very American*, he had thought.

They walked across to the other building, the whitewashed building that was some kind of paint or dye house. Dye with a 'Y' Bludd remembered. Carl was laughing and Bludd could see that, even from this distance, he was almost skipping down the track that led to the front door, clapping his hands as he got to the front door. Then Bludd saw another vehicle approach. It was the silver jeep, with Durie at the wheel. It swung round and then veered left and parked in front of the building, a moment after the door had closed and the others had disappeared behind it. Durie got out and hobbled the few paces across to the door and let himself in.

Bludd gunned the engine and slapped the visor of his helmet back down. He pulled the throttle back and kicked with his left toes to shift the gears. He raced to the front of the building. He could not work out why he was so pumped up, so nervous, so scared. Scared for Carl. He knew what Durie was and had been capable of all those years ago. Not that Durie had carried out the actual attack on him, but he had definitely aided and abetted Judge. What if the same thing was happening to Carl?

He dumped his bike against the wall that ran along the length of the road and ran to the front door, pushing at the wood as he tried to turn the handle. No surprise to find it was locked. He took a step backwards and looked at the windows above, wondering how he could get a look into the building. He considered knocking on the door and knocking them all out and grabbing Carl and dragging him away to safety.

He banged the front of his helmet with a clenched fist. What if all the things that Susan Kerby had told him about were true? The flat, the job, the freedom. What if Carl was just about to get all the things he had dreamed of? What if, in 24 hours, Carl would be holding a party with his mates? Mates that he had not seen for years.

He decided to do nothing. He walked back to his bike. And left it where it was. He turned right and walked down the slope to the other side of the canal and the mouth of the tunnel. He studied the building again. There was no way in but the front door. No way out either. The other building had a fire escape that opened out to a bridge that spanned the canal. This smaller building had nothing, just the line of windows at the top. It crossed his mind that there must be some kind of health and safety issue going on. And then he put it out of his mind. There was probably no issue if this was not a dwelling. He guessed that as a paint store, or something of that ilk, that there was no need for too much by way of regulation.

He cocked his right leg over the small dry stone wall and sat astride it. He took off his helmet and placed it on the wall in front of him. Another waiting game ensued.

Carl Hampson stepped into the room and the door clicked shut behind him. The room was a strange setup. It was confusing. To his right there was an L-shaped, black leather sofa that ran into the corner and along the wall. In front of the sofa was a large, black woollen rug with a large, round, ebony coffee table. To his left was a large kidney-shaped desk backed by a black leather office chair and fronted by a smaller, cheaper, black office chair. The floor was covered in an industrial grade, coarse carpet. Half way up, the room changed, and this is what confused Carl.

The floor was coated in a grey resin, like a plastic covering that went right to the edge of the floor and up the wall about four inches and then was met by a plastic lip that ran all the way around the room. Above the lip the walls were covered right to the ceiling with a plastic cladding, the surface smooth and unbroken. On the back wall there was a wheel that resembled a ship's wheel from an old clipper or schooner. A cube of dark wood protruded out from its centre. To the left of the wheel was a tap, solitary and the pipe ran directly upwards and disappeared into the ceiling. In the far corner there was a large steel cupboard, dull grey paint, like a warship, with two doors. Carl looked up at the ceiling. In each corner of the room there was a CCTV camera and there was an extra one pointing down from directly above the ship's wheel.

Then Durie came in. He was carrying an envelope and some glasses, actually champagne flutes and a bottle of Moet & Chandon. Carl smiled. "Proper celebration, hey, Mr Durie?" he asked.

"Inder-deed, Carl. Now then, per-papers first, or a drink?"

"Sod it. Let's have a drink; I've not had one for two years.

It'll probably go straight to my head." Carl giggled.

Durie gave Carl a knowing smile. "No doubt about it," Durie said with no break in his speech.

Durie unwrapped the foil from around the neck of the bottle and unscrewed the wire that secured the cork in place. "What do you ther-think?" he asked, nodding to the room and creating a distraction.

"Very security conscious," Carl giggled again.

He failed to see Durie drop the tablet into the flute, nor did he see him swill it round to aid its dissolving quickly. The drink fizzed a little more than it should have. Durie handed it to Carl.

"So where do I sign?" the youngster asked, appearing impatient and taking his first gulp of the bubbly beverage.

"There's no rurr-rush, is there?" Durie clinked his glass against Carl's and sipped it gently.

Carl took another swig, and another, swirling the glass around and clinking Durie's flute in return. And then he started to sway. "Whoops." He giggled again, lowering himself slowly onto the sofa. The room began to spin and he felt sick. All he could think of was how not drinking for two years made you so rubbish at taking alcohol. He looked at Durie, who was laughing with him, or at him. Durie was waving the envelope in his face and laughing in a weird and hostile way, his head spinning around. Carl's thoughts went to a vision of the rock group Queen and their video to their song 'Bohemian Rhapsody'. The bit where the heads of each band member is going round in circles with Freddie Mercury stationary in the centre. Except now Mr Durie was playing the part of all the band members. Carl closed his eyes and tried to focus, but when he opened them his vision was blurred. He shut them again, but the lids were so heavy. He could not open them, it was too much effort, so he gave up and leant back against the sofa and gave up the fight.

A half hour passed and Bludd stood up to stretch his legs and give his bottom a break from the coldness of the wall. There had been nothing to see. He could not get a view into the windows along the top of the back wall. The black pickup had not moved. He wandered along a little down to the bottom of the slope and walked a few yards along the path. Durie's jeep had not moved either. It crossed his mind that maybe the apartment was in this building and that they were just showing Carl around and settling him in. He slapped his forehead with a clenched fist again. *Stupid thought*, he thought. This surely could not end happily.

Then he saw movement. It was not human movement. The dull red stain of the dye that had congealed to the exit of the hole in the wall close to the waterline brightened as a slow trickle of red liquid oozed from the hole and tapered to a narrow band as it entered the water. A small red pond settled on the grimy green water of the canal, a striking contrast.

Then there was noise and movement from the front of the building. Bludd crouched down and settled back into the wall behind him, trying to make himself invisible. The two brothers appeared pushing a trolley that looked like a linen truck that you see in a hotel or laundry, or a hotel laundry. The brother that he had kicked in the face on the aqueduct disappeared behind the pickup and Bludd heard the bottom of the tailgate drop down and then saw the lid flip up. The other brother pushed the trolley across and it disappeared behind the truck. Bludd heard the two gates slam shut and the brothers reappeared and got in the front to each side. The engine roared into life and started to reverse away from him. As the pickup swung around to face the apartment building, Bludd started to move away up the slope. He noticed that the red liquid had changed to a diluted pink colour, the flow more aqueous and the pool below had filtered away into the green of the canal water.

Bludd jogged around to the front of the building. Durie's jeep was still parked there at the front door. He was alone, Bludd was sure he had not left. All thoughts of planning what he would do and what he would say had gone out of his mind. He stomped past the front of Durie's vehicle and smashed his forearm against the wooden door, kicking at the base. His mind was in frenzy, a sudden realisation of what he had just seen. The red liquid, the linen trolley. Why had he not realised earlier? Why had he not smashed the door down? Why had he not saved Carl?

The door opened slightly and Durie peeped around the gap. Bludd smashed the door into his face and sent him sprawling into the wall on the other side of the hallway. Durie landed back flush to the wall and his legs splayed out across the width of the hall. Bludd burst through the gap, and kicked, toe upwards into Durie's jaw, his chin bucking backwards and his head banged the wall a second time. Durie looked up in fear and recognition. "You?" he muttered without stammering.

"Yes, me, you dirty, filthy piece of shit. Where's the lad?" Bludd questioned, knowing it was a waste of breath.

Durie leaked a croaky snicker of a laugh from his throat as Bludd grasped the material that covered his whole body. Durie was wearing a white, paper-like full body overall, like the type that scene of crime officers wear. Only his head wasn't covered, a hood creased into a ruff behind his neck.

"What the fuck have you done with him?" Bludd screamed.

Durie just cackled. An earthy, throaty laugh that stayed in his throat. Bludd stemmed the noise by squeezing Durie's throat. He threw his head backwards into the wall again, stood up straight and kicked his right leg out and in again, landing the full force of his foot to the parietal bone in the side of Durie's skull. Bludd judged the force to be enough to knock Durie out, but not kill him. Not quite. A quick death was more than he deserved.

Bludd kicked Durie's body over. He opened the door in front of him that was central to the corridor he stood in. And realised just what Durie and the Romanians had done.

The room was split into two sections. The front half was very office-like: desk, office chairs, hard wearing carpet and a sofa in the corner.

The other half was like a laboratory, or some kind of clean room with resin floor and plastic clad walls. The back wall had a large circle hung from it, four arms sticking out in a square. Above it was a small CCTV camera, and there were a further two on the ceiling at that end of the room, one to each corner. On the floor to the left of the black circle was a tripod housing a professional looking camera, bulky, with a long lens. Another identical camera was placed directly behind it. In front of the circle was a pressure washer, yellow body with a black hose and gun which lay on the grey floor. Foam bubbles were in small patches around the floor and a small puddle of water trickled into a square, steel mesh-covered grid near to the wall.

A battleship grey cupboard was opened in the corner. The cupboard was empty, but on top was a cardboard box, flaps to all four sides open. Next to the box was a modern, hand-held video camera. Bludd had seen its type before. It held a DVD disc and allowed the user to record straight to the disc.

Next to the camera was a tool. It looked like a pizza cutter, but had a series of teeth cut into the cutting edge. The teeth and the face of the steel disc were splattered with blood. There was a leather pouch next to it that resembled a holster for a cowboy's gun, only the type that was for a toy six-shooter.

Bludd was drawn to the hand-held camera, although in his mind he already knew what he was going to see when he ran the disc.

What he got was nothing like what he expected to see and Bludd gulped as the picture before him told him exactly how the brothers had made their money.

Do people really buy this type of stuff? Do they like it, enjoy watching it? Why? This is like porn and torture and snuff films all rolled into one.

Of course people buy it, and watch it and enjoy it. There are all sorts of sick bastards around the world. People are cruel and people are weird. All kinds of thoughts were going through Bludd's mind as he pressed play on the side of the camera.

The Romanian brothers were stood in front of the black circle that was mounted on the wall. Their faces were hidden, but it was clearly them. Huge stocky bodies, not muscular, not fat either, just huge. Their necks were wide and their shoulders rounded, chests firm, stomachs large and slightly protruding without being fat. They wore shiny black leather, or patent leather shorts, tighter than they should be, with a shiny silver zipper down the front. Their legs were wide and toned. The only visible difference was that the man on the left of the scene had a completely bald body. It was shaven and possibly waxed. It looked like it was oiled up in some way, the surface shiny and glistening. The other man was the polar opposite. He was as hairy as Bludd had ever seen a man, his whole body, from his ankles to his shoulders, and over, was like a gorilla's. Both men wore a mask made from the same kind of material as their shorts. Only eye holes were showing and the nose was wide and round and looked like a pig's snout. They stood, arms folded across their chests. Bludd thought that if this wasn't such a serious situation, then the whole thing would have just looked comical.

In between the men was Carl, the young man from the camp. Bludd recognised him in spite of his contorted face and closed eyes. He was virtually naked. His arms were stretched out and attached to the top two arms that stuck out from the black circle. Bludd looked away from the camera for a moment at the corner the scene was filmed in. It looked like an upside down table. Carl's legs were spread out the same way as his arms and attached to the two legs at the bottom of the circle. There were hooks placed into his mouth and wires came away from them and ran away from his face in a cross shape and were attached to the side of the circle. They were pulled tight so that his mouth was pulled wide open in a rectangular shape. The whole thing looked like a hideous crucifixion.

The brothers did not move and there was no sound made. Bludd pressed fast-forward on the side of the camera and watched until he saw movement. Carl was waking up. He must have been drugged as his eyes were rolling and he was blinking like he was unable to focus. Maybe he was just trying to comprehend the situation he had woken to and was blinking to see if he was still asleep and this was some kind of nightmare.

Carl's head tried to move, but the hooks in his mouth meant that he could move very little and his eyes jerked from side to side and up and down, wide open. Panic made them enlarged and suddenly they stopped blinking.

The brothers turned simultaneously and started to stroke Carl's chest and ran their hands over his arms in unison. Carl looked upwards and then closed his eyes. The two men stroked his face on either cheek and ran their index fingers from the side of each of Carl's eyes, down his neck and his chest, brushing his nipples on the way down and met at his navel. Carl was naked apart from a tiny red ribbon that was tied around the base of his penis. He was not erect, but his penis was enlarged and swollen. It looked as though the brothers, or Durie, had got the boy aroused whilst he was unconscious and tied the ribbon tight to keep the swelling of extra blood in place.

One of the brothers dropped to his knees and pushed the leather snout over Carl; the other stroked the boy's chest and seemed to be whispering in his ear. Durie was holding the camera and he moved around to his left to get a better view for what seemed to be his personal video; the two professional cameras would probably be filming the scene from their tripods.

Bludd pushed fast forward, watching, but at twice the speed. He watched as the brothers spun the black circle that Carl was attached to and his head was now at the bottom, a couple of feet off the floor. One of them pulled down his zipper and knelt in front of the boy, the other stood over his brother and leant forward. They both rocked back and forth. The boy struggled, but his head movement was stymied by the hooks in his mouth and his screams were muffled. He pulled and twisted his head and the hooks began to slice into his lips and the corners of his mouth.

Bludd pressed fast forward again and watched at four times the normal speed. He saw the brothers rotate themselves between kneeling and standing positions and they rotated the circle back round. The young man looked dazed and dizzy. He would have spent many minutes upside down, blood rushing to his head. His look of fear had changed to shock and bewilderment. Bludd slowed the camera to normal viewing speed and looked at Carl. The Romanians had gone out of view momentarily. Bludd studied the young man. His chest heaved up and down, his breathing was heavy as he must have been gulping in air the moment his mouth was free. Bludd saw Carl's eyes seem to come back into focus and they flicked from side to side still looking in disbelief. And then Bludd saw them change back to shock and fear and he heard a gurgle come from the depths of his throat. Then it was drowned out by a voice closer to the camera. "Oh yer-yes," Durie said, with an excited tone to his stuttering.

The brothers stood on either side of Carl Hampson. The brother on the left of the screen held the pizza wheel with the serrated teeth that Bludd had seen a few minutes earlier. He pressed the wheel into Carl's jugular notch at the top of his rib cage. Bludd could see from the pain etched on the young man's face that there was pressure being applied and a trickle of blood ran slowly down his chest. The Romanian used the line as a guide and followed it down with the wheel, slowly perforating the skin, puncturing and missing it in equal spaces. The boy screamed, but unable to move his face or mouth, it came out from the depths of his lungs as a painful gargle. The wheel stopped at the top of Carl's pubic bone and the brother who held it went off screen. The other brother used his left index finger and placed it where the wheel had started its impression. He pressed his finger hard into the perforated skin and created a hole that his fingertip sank into.

Carl Hampson screamed and his head tossed from side to side, the hooks in his mouth failing to clamp his head still. He fought against the pain, and the finger in his chest outweighed the tearing of his lips, his mouth and face ripping in four directions, blood pouring from each corner. He passed out.

The finger in his chest popped the perforations like a zipper as it ran down the torso and his skin burst open, the wound a finger's width and the depth of a Romanian fingernail. The man in the mask held his finger aloft, like a magician with his wand, and then pushed his hand through the hole in the snout that fronted the mask, a second later pulling it free and pointing a now bloodless digit at the camera.

The first brother, with his wheeled weapon, reappeared and they spun the black circular table around and the wheel was placed on Carl Hampson's scrotum and was swiftly drawn away, slashing at the skin. The wheel was spun round again and the other brother sank to his knees and smothered the area, which oozed with thick blood, with his mask. The wheel was placed on the jugular notch again, but this time it ran upwards and blood spurted out as the skin and vein were sliced apart. The man with the wheel forced his face against the boy's neck and Bludd heard Durie shout. "Go on, Andrei, suck it out of him!" The masked face pulled back and a spray of red liquid spewed from the nose of the mask and splashed across the unconscious boy's face. Both the Romanian men stood back away from what was surely now a dead body, blood still pumping from the neck and seeping from the torso and genitals. The man on the right held the hand that was anchored to the black circle and plunged downwards, the circle spinning and blood began to spurt out in a sickening revolution, like sparks from a Catherine wheel firework, and created a line that ran in dotted fashion along the ceiling, down the wall and across the floor, Durie's camera following its gory path.

The two masked men stood front facing, the crucifixion wheel behind them still spinning, slowing down, and their arms by their sides. And then they took a bow.

Bludd stood for a moment. His mind was blank. He had put the images out of his head as soon as he switched the camera off, knowing full well that his memory would not be able to erase what he had just seen. It was a new nightly dream to contend with. The agony that the boy had been put through, far worse than what he had been through himself; a nightmare to replace a nightmare. Bludd began to wish he hadn't watched the graphic film, but realised that had he not done so, he would not have known how barbaric the situation he had become involved in really was. He had been confused as to how to deal with what he might find, but now he was clear in his mind. There was no place for people like this on this planet. They had to be removed. Extinguished. Deleted.

Bludd looked at the corner the film was made in. The tiles were clean, hosed down, free from any evidence of what he had just witnessed. He realised then that the red liquid he had seen on the outside wall was Carl Hampson's blood. When he had looked again and seen it running into a diluted pink, it was when Durie was washing the tiles down and watering the blood down at the same time.

And then he had a flashback. In Judge's office, opposite his house, the computer had flashed up a new email. The addresses meant something to him at the time, durie@transvisionvamps. com. At the time, he had seen an image in his mind of the 1980s pop-punk-rock group, with the blonde girl lead singer. Now it meant something completely different as he realised what it actually stood for. Transylvania, famous for vampires, was their inspiration, a bloodthirsty myth that was being lived out in Maple.

23

Retribution

Bludd heard a murmuring from the other end of the room and he turned round to see Durie, pushing himself off the floor and struggling to get to his feet. Bludd ran at him, anger pouring out of him. Durie looked up, no fear on his face, a realisation that they had been found out and an acceptance of what would happen to him. He had waited for this day, knowing it was likely to happen at some time, but expecting it to be the authorities that knocked on his door. Not Sebastian Bludd.

Bludd grabbed Durie's hair and pulled him to his feet, smashing a clenched fist into his throat, middle knuckle stabbing into Adam's apple. He let Durie drop to his knees, fighting for breath, his windpipe crushed. Durie clasped his hands to his throat, trying to massage it back into shape. Bludd looked down at him, and as Durie looked up, a booted toe landed under his chin and ripped his head backwards, consciousness leaving him before he hit the ground. Bludd had wanted to stamp all over his head, but stopped, telling himself that a quick death was too good for such a vile creature. He also thought that when Durie came round, he would be able to coax information out of him that might help him rescue the others. He went to the back of the room and carefully put the pizza wheel in his pocket.

Bludd dragged Durie's limp body outside and hauled it across to his bike. He dropped Durie to the floor and stood the machine upright, leaning it on the back of his legs as he heaved him over the bike's petrol tank. He kicked the machine into life and closed his eyes, wondering how to approach the next problem of getting inside the industrial estate and tackling the two Romanians. His mind threw up the picture of the aerial view of Maple Forest and the surrounding area. He thought back to how he had found the factory, before zooming in on it. The railway line ran in an arc around the industrial area and the eastern edge of the forest, but it straightened out across the canal and the river below and Bludd searched his memory to move along the view. The rail line must pass by somewhere in this vicinity. He kicked the gear pedal down, pulled back the throttle and headed to the right, ignoring the canal paths and carrying on along the road that swung away left. The road narrowed to a single lane, hedgerows to each side forming a boundary to the fields behind them. He came across the level crossing a minute later. The rail line, a long straight track to his left and right, but in the distance to the east, he could see where it swung to the right and headed over the canal and the river. He twisted the handlebars to the right and trundled down the track, his wheels skipping over every raised sleeper and his suspension bobbing up and down to cushion the bumpy ride. Durie began to stir, the motion of the bike and the undulating ground rocking his head back into life. Bludd slung his left leg over the back of Durie's neck and pinned his face down against the engine, hoping it would warm up in time and to a sufficient temperature to cause Durie some pain.

The track ran into a long curve as it approached the bridge over the canal that led to the industrial site and where Bludd had waited on his first stakeout of the factories. He brought the bike to a halt as the estate came into view and he squinted across to it, trying to get a glimpse of the brothers. He had now realised that Carl would never be found, and in a way, he was glad. The brothers would surely be holed up in the incinerator building, igniting the burners and vaporising any evidence of the young man's existence. He could not see the brothers, nor could he see the linen trolley that must have been carrying Carl's body. What he could see was the concertina door to the incinerators was slightly open.

* * *

He flicked the throttle again and Durie tried to push himself up and off the bike. Bludd thumped him, with a closed fist, on the back of the head. They rode to the end of the bridge, and as the track rolled over onto solid ground again, Bludd pulled to a stop and threw Durie off and onto the floor. He dropped the bike to the ground and stood over Durie.

"Now then, Durie. The only way that you are going to get through this is to help me. I know all about your sick video films and your weird Romanian vampire mates, and believe me, I would like to see the lot of you suffer and die, die a slow death like you put people like young Carl through. But I need your help. One way or another, I am going to put a stop to all this and those kids will be coming out of that camp with me. You can help me do it and then face the authorities, or you can die a horrible death." He paused and looked around. "Maybe you could be run over by a train. Maybe you could drown in the canal, or fall off the aqueduct into the river below. Maybe both of them would look like suicide? What's it to be?"

Durie rubbed his throat and thought about the two stints of unconsciousness he had been through in the last hour. He thought about how much he was hated by the man who had put him in these states. He thought about how there was little evidence of anything apart from the disc he had just made, which was damning enough, but there was no link on there to the website and the other films. Then he thought about the two brothers and how they would surely be able to handle Bludd a second time round. He could help. A bit. They could take Bludd down, perhaps get rid of him as well, in the same way that they got rid of all their evidence.

"I'll help you. Wer-what do you want?"

"I want to get in the yard. Let's play it by ear after that. I need the code to get through the barrier."

"Okay, ner-no problem." Durie agreed too easily for Bludd's liking.

They slid down the slope that led from the rail track that led to the front gate of the industrial estate and Durie collapsed at the bottom, his knee giving way as he went to stand upright and Bludd caught him by his overall's hood and snatched him back to his feet.

"The code," Bludd demanded. Durie did not answer, he put his claw-like left hand to the steel box and keyed in the numbers with his thumb, the keypad hidden from Bludd's view by his mangled fingers. If he had given the number to Bludd it would have provided him with an easy route out of there, and he was counting on that not happening in any case.

Bludd shoved Durie in the small of his back and they headed towards the incinerator building. The long gate that ran across the front of the separate yard was unlocked and ajar. "Don't you say a word. And don't think about doing anything silly either," Bludd whispered in Durie's ear as he grabbed his left arm and thrust it up his back.

They arrived at the concertina door and Bludd leant over Durie's shoulder and heaved the door to his right. A beam of light shone into the dingy building and the door screeched as the rollers in the top ran along the runner. The Romanians were loading a pile of dog corpses into the left-hand incinerator. Bludd guessed that Carl was probably already in there, shoved to the back with any evidence of his ever being there thrown in with him. One of the brothers held a long steel tool in his hand that looked like a hoe, but the end had a long flat steel bar running from the end of the handle. He had just used it to nudge a dog as far into the incinerator as it would go. The brothers stopped loading and turned round. They were back in their normal clothes and looked as though they had showered, their hair slicked back and tidy, all evidence of the video nasty they had just made, gone.

Durie tried to make a break from Bludd's hold, attempting to slam his free right hand into Bludd's groin, but Bludd was prepared for the strike, as it was the only option that Durie could take to try and free himself. He twisted Durie's arm further up his back, lifting him onto his tiptoes. He pulled back on the weak wrist of Durie's left hand and snapped it backwards with his right hand, at the same time as his left hand slammed into Durie's elbow. A quick push with his left and a snap back with his right meant that Bludd broke Durie's wrist and elbow in two quick moves. Durie let out a cry of pain and went to sink to his knees, but Bludd snatched at his right hand and spun him around. Durie bent over in agony as Bludd intertwined his fingers into Durie's and pushed his wrist back. He grabbed Durie's right elbow with his left hand and held it firmly as he squeezed the fingers and snapped the wrist backwards, breaking it across the radius bone and rendering Durie useless. He leant the broken bone backwards and Durie sank to his knees, knowing what was coming next. He wanted to beg for mercy, but the words would not come out and he cursed his stammer, but he knew he would have been wasting his breath anyway. A toe connected with his chin and his head rocked backwards as the instep of Bludd's other foot swiftly arched around and dealt him a crushing blow just behind his ear.

Bludd let go of Durie's hand as he slumped to the floor. The two Romanians were on the move, lumbering over in tandem, side by side. The one to Bludd's right had the steel bar held in both hands and he carried it diagonally across his chest. Bludd would have to deal with him first. He reached down into his jacket pocket, carefully feeling for the toothed wheel that he had picked up from next to the video camera.

The brothers stopped. Bludd stopped. There were a few yards between them. Bludd needed it to be closer, he could not risk the armed man being able to actuate a full swing with the bar, and he needed to be close and narrow down the opportunity for full purchase.

"Now then, guys, let's keep things simple. Remember what happened this afternoon? We don't need to have a repeat do we? It didn't turn out well for you two last time, did it?" Bludd inched forward as he threw the questions at the brothers, without giving them time to answer, keeping their minds occupied. "Why don't you be a good lad and put the bar down, that way nobody gets hurt?" Bludd continued to ease forward. He held out his left hand knowing that the Romanian was unlikely to give the weapon over, but making him think, whilst Bludd considered what was really going to happen.

The Romanian pushed the bar above his head and Bludd drew his right hand out of his pocket, and as the brother lurched forward and swung, the bar in his right hand, Bludd jolted sideways to his right and his arm curled round and slashed the wheel across the forehead of the oncoming brother. The skin peeled upwards as his head moved forward and blood gushed from the wound. Bludd's speed had interrupted the momentum of the bar as the pain shot across Marius Lupescu's head and his swing curtailed as he released the bar an inch from Bludd. The bar struck Bludd on the left shoulder, but without momentum, it hurt, but caused no damage.

Marius squealed with the pain of his ripped open forehead and the blood spewed from the wound and cascaded into his eyes. He held both hands to his face, trying to pinch the torn skin together and rub away the blood at the same time.

Andrei Lupescu had not begun to move when his brother had launched his attack and had seen the damage done to Marius' face and backed off. Bludd had been given an unexpected moment to finish Marius off and he took it without a second thought. What would have been an uppercut punch to the chin became a throat-splicing slash of carbon steel wheel, rotating teeth ripping through the skin, slicing the Adam's apple, ripping the jugular and trachea.

Marius' bloody hands grabbed at the new wound to his throat, the blood from his forehead blinding him and his fingers slipped in the new river that had burst from his neck. He grasped at the flaps of open skin and tried to hold them together, his lungs no longer able to take in any new air. He sucked at the oxygen around him, but his chest did not inflate as nothing could reach his windpipe. He sank to his knees and collapsed at Bludd's feet as Bludd dodged to the left to avoid the flailing man. A dull metallic sound rang for an instant as the Romanian fell on top of the steel bar he had dropped a few moments earlier.

Bludd looked at the other brother. Andrei Lupescu looked in disbelief at the scene around him. Durie was unconscious ten yards away, near the door. His brother, Marius, his best friend, lay stricken before him, a pool of blood encompassing his head as his neck spat out small spurts of blood, his heart still beating slower and slower as he passed away. Andrei saw that his brother still had a look of bewilderment and shock on his blood-soaked face as he lay there surrounded by, and covered in, the red liquid.

Bludd had anticipated an instant attack from the other man. What he got was a man stepping backwards, his hand stretched out in front of him, fingers spread wide, surrendering.

"What's up, big man?" Bludd teased. "Only a big man when your brother is around?"

The big Romanian stepped back another yard.

"You worried about getting the same fate as your brother here?" Bludd prompted. "Well don't worry, that was just self-defence. I don't want to have to kill you." *Yet*, he thought, still brandishing the blood-stained wheel.

Andrei dropped his arms to his side. He stood fixed to the spot, trying to consider his options. He didn't know who this stranger was. He didn't know how much the stranger knew. Did he know about the camp? Did he know about the films and the website? Could he be reasoned with? Andrei thought that the man could not be reasoned with. He looked at his lifeless brother. He looked left and right, trying to see where he might be able to gain some advantage over an armed and angry man. A man who had already beaten him and his brother that day. Now he had killed his brother and left Durie in a heap as well. The man had skill and speed that he could not contend with. He looked over his shoulder. There were no weapons he could grab; Marius was lying on top of the only one in there. There was a pile of dog's bodies a couple of yards away. Nothing was of any use to him. Maybe he could bargain with the stranger. Maybe he could bargain with him and make him take his guard down and maybe he could pounce and get the weapon off him. Maybe he could then avenge his brother.

"What is your name?" the Romanian asked Bludd.

"Sebastian Bludd. What's yours?"

"My name is Andrei Lupescu. I am director of company."
He tried to give himself some credibility.

"Good for you," Bludd said ironically. His mind flashed
back to the company profile and the list of directors' names.
"So if you're Andrei, I guess this is Marius, then?" Bludd
nudged the prone body at the shoulder, trying to rile the living
brother. It worked.

"Please don't touch him again. He is dead. You killed him.
Please leave him." Andrei pleaded.

"What's up? Worried about his dignity?" Bludd shoved
the heel of his right foot under the dead man's shoulder and
pushed him over. Marius' head flopped to the side and his hair,
matted with sticky blood stuck to his face. "What about young
Carl's dignity?" Bludd pointed to the incinerator. "What about
the rest of them? I take it Carl was not the first. Susan tells me a
number of people have 'won their freedom'. How many? How
many won an hour or so of freedom before you and your sick
bastard brother here …" Bludd paused a second and kicked the
side of Marius' head, "… and your filthy, dirty, bastard friend
over there …" he pointed at Durie; his tone was getting angry
as he spoke. "You fucking dirty piece of Romanian shit." Bludd
gripped the handle of the pizza wheel tighter as he spoke, his
anger rising. He raised his hand above his head threateningly.
His feet were apart, in a ready stance.

"Please, Mr Bludd. Please. It was Durie's idea. He made
films, he made ideas, and he made decisions. We just carried
out orders." His hands were raised again in a mock apologetic
gesture and he moved towards Bludd. His outstretched fingers
curled round and became a fist and he swung his left foot
wildly at Bludd, trying to catch him in the ribs under his raised
right arm.

Bludd's left arm shot across and pushed the leg away, a simple manoeuvre when your body is positioned correctly. His right hand slashed down across the left cheek of the Romanian and scored the skin to the corner of his mouth. Andrei kicked out again and Bludd swivelled around and caught the shoe of the swinging foot and twisted it round, forcing Andrei to turn away from him and he swung his hand around and sank the serrated wheel into the Romanian's Achilles tendon, pushing and pulling, backwards and forward, pressure hard down. Bludd felt that he almost heard the twang of the tendon as it snapped and pinged up the back of the Romanian's calf, under the skin.

Andrei Lupescu let out an enormous cry of agony and he fell to the floor, clutching at the back of his leg, pinching at the calf muscle that was now home to a muscle that should have been stretched down to his heel. He watched as Bludd picked up his other leg and pushed the hem of his trousers up and stuck the wheel into his other Achilles. He screamed again, shouting in his own language and crying out in pain.

Bludd dropped the leg as he felt the muscle snap and the Romanian howled, shouting foreign expletives through gritted teeth. He knelt down by Andrei's head. "Stop bleating, you fucking coward." He seized a handful of the hair on Andrei's head and lifted it off the floor a few inches. "This is for Carl." He whispered as he slammed the head onto the concrete floor. "And this is for the rest of them." Andrei's eyes looked up, but they were swirling and out of focus. His head smashed onto the hard surface again. And again. And again. His eyes rolled back, and as he lost consciousness, he couldn't help but think that they were all getting what they deserved.

Bludd dragged the limp body of Andrei Lupescu to the door of the first incinerator. The Romanian was a big, heavy man and Bludd struggled as he lifted him up, first to a sitting position and then to his feet as he bundled him into the incinerator. He had not killed Andrei, but he would be unconscious for some time, and he would wake up to a pitch black, airless tomb, lying next to a, hopefully, panicking Durie and a dead brother. Bludd was going to stretch it out and make it as painful as possible for all of them.

The kiln was large enough to hold a good number of dogs. Bludd looked at the pile that had not been incinerated the night before. There were still at least a dozen bodies of various sizes, and he tried to equate it to the two big Romanians and Durie. He had only just noticed the stench that lingered in the air. Maybe he could put a couple of stinking corpses in with them to make the scenario even worse.

He put Durie in next. He was a much smaller man and much easier to manoeuvre. He laid him on the floor in front of the kiln and retrieved the steel bar from underneath Marius' body. He pushed Andrei in as far as he would go, as he came to a halt against Carl's corpse and the dog that lay in front of it. Then he put Durie in and he heard a murmur come from his mouth, "Jeremy," Bludd thought he said. He pushed Durie in with the steel rod as far as he could get him and the murmuring became louder. "Sgoin on?" Durie mumbled.

Bludd rushed to get the final body into the cremator and was surprised how much room there was after he had bumped Marius along to be pushed tightly against the grumbling Durie. He pulled a dog's body from the top of the pile. "Sweet dreams!" he shouted in, as he threw it in, closed the heavy steel door and clunked the iron rod bolt across to lock it.

Susan Kerby had not been able to keep Bludd's appearance to herself. She was excited. Apart from the new inmates, who came in irregular intervals, she had not seen anybody from the outside for five years. He had brought her news, which was by lucky coincidence. She knew that, but she could not wait to tell somebody that her mum really did care and that her stepfather had gone. She had gathered the others in the television hut.

The others were sceptical. They were pleased for her that she had received good news. But that didn't mean that they were all going to get out and be able to go back to an improved situation. None of them had ever planned to come to the camp. Some of them liked it there. They liked the camaraderie and the community they had created and become part of. They had a new family; people they could trust. Some of them did not want to leave.

Susan urged them to trust her. She didn't know the man who had appeared, yet her instinct and her judgement were to trust him. She promised them that they would all leave together and would still be able to keep in touch with each other. Perhaps they would not have to go back to where they came from. Perhaps they could stick together, live together even. Perhaps there was a job on the day shift waiting for them all and they could stay around here, but in real, proper houses. And still look out for each other. She didn't know if she had convinced them. Maybe when he returned, the man would be able to.

24

Escape

Bludd closed the concertina door and contemplated a decision he had made earlier. He would not tell Susan Kerby, or any of the other camp members, about Carl. He had purposely left his body at the back of the incinerator. The boy's body and face were so badly mutilated that he thought it best for Susan to think that he had won his freedom and was out there, reunited with his loved ones and enjoying his life. Bludd thought about Carl's family as well. It would not do them any good to see his body in such a state either. He decided it was better for them to think that he was still around somewhere, living life to the max. They could hope that he would get in touch. It would be a hope that would never materialise, but Bludd thought better that than knowing the truth. He checked his watch. It was just after seven and the light was all but gone. He would go and destroy the cameras and whatever else there was to show any evidence of the killing of Carl. Maybe there would be dozens of similar films on disc in there, maybe hundreds. He would have to destroy them all. Nobody would be watching them again, not on disc anyway. He wondered about shutting down the website that Andrei Lupescu had mentioned when he was blaming Durie for all their misdemeanours. His computer skills were OK, but he had no idea where to start when it came to this kind of thing. Maybe he could trust Max to help.

As he retrieved his motorbike, his phone trembled in his pocket. It was a text from Annabelle Judge. It read, 'Go to

St. Simon's. Follow the river. Shortest way. Bus sorted. See you at seven.'

Bludd was pleased. Pleased to have a reception on his mobile phone, and pleased that Annabelle Judge had come through. He texted her back, 'Good, well done. Just one other thing, can you bring a crash helmet with you?'

He had an inkling that he had not set her another difficult task. They lived on what was effectively a farm, although now it was just a house, with a huge amount of land attached to it. They also had two kids, who were spoiled rotten. Bludd was guessing that the kids would have some kind of quad bike, even at their age. Spoiled kids usually got things before they were supposed to, whether they were legally old enough to, or even if they were capable of handling such things. Even so, if they didn't have such a thing, he trusted Annabelle to come through again anyway.

* * *

Susan Kerby washed the dinner pots with a lad called Toby. He was one of the people she had been unable to convince. He questioned her as she passed him a dripping plate.

"So who is this guy again?"

"He says he is a private detective and he had been kind of employed to help look for me when I ran away from home."

"Can't be a very good one. It's taken him five years to find you. That was more by luck than judgement as well," he said, sardonically.

"Aw, come on. You wouldn't expect anybody to find us here, would you?"

"Suppose not. Anyway, why do you believe what he told you? You don't know him. What makes you think you can trust him?"

"I don't know, Toby. I just do. I need you to as well. We have to all go, or none of us go."

"Well, I don't want to. I think I should stay here, even if it's on my own. They will bring new people in, I should think. It will be fine, I'm sure. You go. Take the others. I'll stay. I think John will stay with me."

"But what if it's dangerous to stay? The man said that there was something bad going on here. What if it's only safe in numbers? I need to go and see my mum. Maybe you can come and stay with me until you work out what you want to do?"

"That's kind of you, Sue, but honestly, your mum won't want me there when she just got you back. I'll be fine, whatever happens."

He was putting the, now dry, plate on the side when a head appeared around the door frame and a breathless Bludd said, "Susan. Found you." Toby dropped the plate, smashing it on the wooden floor below.

"Fuck me, man. You nearly gave me a heart attack."

"Sorry," Bludd replied as he walked in the room. "I'm Sebastian Bludd. I'm a …"

"I know who you are man," Toby interrupted. "Susan has told us all about you."

Bludd looked at Susan Kerby. "Sorry," she whispered, before he could tell her off.

"No matter now. Things have changed. Mr Durie and the Romanian brothers are gone. You will be free to go. All we have to do is get you out of here."

"Some of them don't want to go," Susan Kerby said, gesturing a thumb towards Toby. "And what do you mean they're 'gone'?"

"You have to go, no arguments," Bludd replied. "There will be nothing to stay for. The company has been sold. Mr Judge has done a deal. He is abroad as we speak tying up the loose ends. It's unlikely that you will see any of them again. It's a done deal."

"What about us?" Toby interjected. "They wouldn't just leave us here, man."

"I think they were just planning to dump you all somewhere, all of you together. Believe me, these people are not the kind of people who care too much about other people. But listen, I think it's important that you all stick together. I have arranged for you to be picked up in the morning. You can all stay together, in the short term anyway. Long term, it's up to you."

"It's up to me what I do short term, long term and now term, mister," a terse Toby responded.

"I know, mate. But look, I am not trying to force anybody to do anything they don't want to. I'm just asking you to trust me." Bludd shuffled his hands in his jacket pocket, digging them deeper in, aware that if the lad saw the blood that still stained them, that trust would be the last thing he was likely to be given.

"I'm not your mate, either," Toby replied. Terse again. "But if you can get the rest of them to go, I'll go with you."

"Great. How many are there and how many don't want to come?"

Susan Kerby responded before Toby could. "There are nine of us now that Carl and the new boy have left for the night. There is only Toby that really doesn't want to leave, and John is on the fence, but that's because he generally does what Toby does."

"Well, that's pretty much settled then. Susan, please will you go and get John. Toby, you can help me figure a way out of here."

Susan Kerby left the hut and headed off to find John.

"OK. So let's say John can't be turned and you and him stay. You going to help me get the others out?"

"No problem, man. They wanna go, they can go."

"Good man. Thanks. Only thing is figuring out how. We can get into the yard, but there is no easy way of getting out of there, not without a code for the front gate. I have a way out, but it's very dangerous."

"How did you get in? Can't you go out the same way?"

"I got in by some trees that are round the back end of the forest and had a tricky jump down off the fence. Can't really do the same thing the other way, and it's not like we have a ladder or anything."

"That's what you think."

"What? You have a ladder?" Bludd asked incredulously.

"Course, man. We repaint the roofs of the huts every year." Toby stepped outside the hut and leant down on one knee, pulling an aluminium ladder out from underneath the hut.

"But ..." Bludd said, bewildered.

"I told you man, nobody is that keen to get out of here. They know that and they trust us."

"Unbelievable," Bludd said, shaking his head.

Susan Kerby returned. "John's coming with us; he says there is no point in staying if it's just the two of them."

"Excellent. Why didn't you mention the ladder?" Bludd said, still looking at Toby. Toby just shrugged his shoulders and rolled his eyes. He exited the hut and was greeted by a group of eight young people. Susan was at the front, another girl next to her, the rest, all young men, stood in a huddle behind them. Toby jumped down off the steps of the hut and stood next to the one that Bludd guessed was John. "OK people, this is what we are going to do. You know this place better than me, so

I need you to lead the way to the perimeter fence, the quickest way possible, please. Any volunteer to lead the way?" The girl next to Susan put a tentative hand up. "Great," Bludd said. "Toby, you and John can bring the ladder, if you don't mind, at the rear with me."

Toby looked at the boy to his left, who, as Bludd thought, was John. "OK man, no problem," he said.

"One last thing. Any of you got anything you need to take with you, go get yourselves organised. Back here in five," Bludd demanded. But nobody moved. Apart from the clothes that they stood in and a change of the same, as well as some normal clothes, they had nothing to speak of. No trinkets or photographs, or anything else of any sentiment. They just stood still and looked at Bludd for his next command. "Let's go then," he said.

They twisted and turned through the trees, Teri at the front, leading the way at a pace between a walk and a jog, the others in single file behind, Toby and John at the rear, Bludd behind. Toby started whistling and Bludd smiled at him. He had a funny kind of attitude thing going on, but Bludd liked him, and when he piped up with the 'hi-ho, hi-ho, it's off to work we go' from the film *Snow White*, he laughed. Toby turned around, winked at him and smiled.

They walked for about five minutes and then Teri stopped; Susan next to her, and the rest gathered around in a crowd. Toby and John propped the ladder against the fence, and Toby extended it out so that it was higher than the fence top. "How we gonna do this, man?" Toby asked Bludd.

"OK, Toby, I want you to go first. It's quite a drop to the floor from the top of the ladder, so I want you to ease yourself down as far as you can and hang from the last rung of the ladder. If you can, I want you to grab the fence and kind of shin down the uprights. When you get down, perhaps you can give the others a lift and make sure they get down OK. That all right?"

"Yeah, man, no worries." Toby was suddenly eager to please and was revelling in the extra responsibility that Bludd had purposely bestowed on him. "You hold the ladder, man," he commanded Bludd. Bludd just smiled back at him.

Toby stepped up the ladder and as he got to the top, he confidently swung around and lowered himself onto the top rung, so that his stomach rested on the aluminium step. He swung backwards and his legs kicked forward and crashed against the fence, he let go with his left arm and clutched at the green metal fence, then repeated it with his right hand, hanging there with his fingers gripping the steel and his feet flat against the fence. He shinned down one foot and hand at a time and then jumped the last few feet, landing cleanly on both feet.

"You should be in the army, man," Bludd shouted through the fence to Toby, smiling. "Susan, you go next and then you." He pointed to the other girl, Teri.

Susan followed and copied exactly what Toby had done and landed on the other side a minute later. Then Teri followed. She swung, but missed her grip on the fence with her fingers and dropped to the floor. Toby was alert and caught her at the hips, breaking most of her fall, but making the girl lose balance as she hit the floor. Her foot went from under her and her ankle cracked as it bent over awkwardly and she let out a squeal of pain.

"Don't worry," Bludd shouted through, "We'll deal with it when everybody is over. Just move her out of the way for now."

Susan dragged Teri away from Toby as he stood waiting underneath the ladder again, determined not to drop anybody else. The others followed until Bludd was the only one left on the camp side of the fence. He stepped up each rung, wary that when he went to the other side and jumped over to hang down, that the ladder might flip up and follow him over. He ushered the others out of the way from the top of the ladder and jumped over, spinning as he caught the top rung from the other side. His weight made the ladder leave the ground and the base of it flipped out and up into the air, following Bludd's downwards movement until the second rung from the top caught on the fence and jerked them to a stop. Bludd looked down and calculated the drop below him and let go, crashing to the floor and rolling backwards as his feet took the impact of the fall.

He lay on his back, winded, until Toby stood over him and offered a hand to pull Bludd up, which he gladly accepted. Bludd looked at Teri's ankle, it was already swollen and clearly she had broken it, or at best badly sprained it. "OK. There is a really steep slope here that leads down to the river. I think the best way to go down it is to sit on your bums and slide down. Just be careful of tree roots, you don't want to finish up going head first down here. Go in the same order, but Teri, you will have to go with me."

Toby led the way, expertly sliding down, but not in the sitting position that Bludd had suggested, instead he chose to stand and he looked like a surfer riding the breakers. He whooped as he went and the others began to giggle at his confidence. He was clearly the practical joker of the camp. Susan followed and did so in the way that Bludd had advised. The others followed in that way as well, John getting laughed at by Toby as he went down nervously by comparison to his friend.

Bludd crouched down and Teri hopped up onto his shoulders. There was no way he could slide down with her on his back, so he chose to scamper down and catch hold of each tree that he could make on his descent. They reached the bottom a lot slower than the others, but Bludd was pleased to be able to place Teri on the ground and get his breath back and heave a sigh of relief that he hadn't caused her any more injury.

The row of canoes was still tied in place, spanning the river. Bludd was concerned that the darkness and moisture in the air may make the passage across more treacherous than he had anticipated.

"Toby, you go first again. But I want you to go together, keep hold of each other's hands, it may be slippery, so go careful, take your time. The boats will move around when you stand on them, so take them one at a time. Teri, you're with me again."

Toby led the way, testing each canoe's movement as he stood on it. He worked out that standing in the middle of the hull of the boat meant that there was little chance for the boat to move. He also worked out that if they all stepped at the same time, so that there was always at least one foot on the hull, then they would stay almost in place. He began to bark orders to the others and they began a slow and deliberate march across the river. Teri jumped onto Bludd and he swivelled her around so that she was sat astride his left hip so he could take large sideways steps instead of clumsy strides that were not properly balanced.

They all made it across and now it was just a matter of negotiating a path around the river, which would be difficult in the darkness, but with all night they could take their time and get there safely. Bludd led them to the end of the jetty and told them to wait there for him. He held his hand in the air, fingers spanned out and held it aloft. Five minutes was the instruction to Susan and the group.

He jogged to the railway track and retrieved his Yamaha.

He turned the ignition and switched on the lights, the beam of the headlight picking out the steep drop down the embankment, bringing him close to the entrance to the industrial estate. He free-wheeled close to the end of the slope. There was a short drop to the road below. He twisted the throttle and the front wheel kicked out to allow the bike to drop down on both wheels simultaneously. He sped along the aqueduct and swiftly took the left turn onto the path and sped down the stepped path, turning right and accelerating through the bushes and stinging nettles towards the canoe club. He skidded to a halt in front of the group.

"Get on, Teri!" Bludd shouted over the noise of the engine. The girl hobbled over and sat astride the bike and Bludd got back on behind her. "Follow the light. Stay close to each other. We are going to take it slow and safe. Toby, this time you bring up the rear, OK?" Toby gave him the thumbs up and then a salute, as if to say 'Yes sir'.

The journey seemed to take forever, with no clear path and ground that went from dry to soggy to muddy depending on the distance from the river bank and the slope of the ground. The group moved slowly, hardly speaking, as if there was something in the darkness to hide from. Bludd knew that there was really nothing to fear, all the bad guys were taken care of for now, just one more to deal with and then they could all move on. He asked Teri about the group. He was surprised that a bunch of English kids were all happy to stay and not get out and get back to a normal life. He also wondered why they were all English. He had half expected at least some of them to be foreign, probably Romanian. Teri had told him that to begin with, the camp was mainly full of people of Eastern European origin, definitely some Romanian people. The brothers used to disappear for a week at a time and come back with new people as and when they needed them. Then suddenly that stopped and they just seemed to replace people with English kids.

It was, by now, just after six in the morning and only Toby was voicing an opinion, even if the others were thinking it, they were either too tired or too scared, maybe, probably, too polite, to say. "Hey, man!" the voice from the rear shouted. "Are we nearly there yet?" He sounded like a five-year-old that was on the way to a holiday, but had only just set off.

"I don't know, just keep going. It can't be much further," Bludd shouted, his voice drowned out by the motorbike's engine and the fact that he was facing forward and had a crash helmet on.

Then he saw it and he stopped. A sudden bend in the river, and a proper path that almost touched the river bank, but then darted away in the opposite direction. Bludd closed his eyes and focused hard. He could see the aerial view again and he tried to pinpoint the church that he had suggested to Annabelle Judge as a meeting point. Instead, as his mind swirled around, he found the image of where they stood now. He made his mind focus harder and used his own mind power to zoom down to the spot and comprehend how far they had to go. The path was fairly short, maybe 30 yards and then there was a gate and a stile. On the other side was a tarmac road that led, along about half a mile of twists and turns, directly to St Simon's.

Bludd took his helmet off and hung it over his wrist. "Not far at all," he shouted. He crept forward on the bike. The others following behind, starting to mumble amongst themselves.

The gate was locked. Bludd tapped Teri on the shoulder. "Looks like it's a piggy-back from here." The group bunched up and filed over the stile, Bludd left his bike propped up against the fence next to the stile then went first and helped

Teri over. Toby brought up the rear.

The group walked a few yards and then found the black asphalt of the road and made a right turn and headed for the church. Susan Kerby joined Bludd at the front of the huddle and gave Teri a reassuring pat on the leg. "Not far now is it Mr Bludd?" It was as much a question as a statement to Teri.

Bludd stopped a moment. In the distance he could see faint lights, rising up and away into the distance. It looked like the beginnings of a small village, probably, hopefully, where the church would be. "Look!" he replied, nodding in the direction of the lights. "About 400 yards, I reckon. Come on."

The group seemed to get a second wind and they all marched a little faster. As they approached the lights, Bludd could see that the church was the first building of a cluster, a street light out front lit up the area around and he could make out a cross at the apex of the roof. Outside was a mini-bus. Annabelle Judge was already there.

Toby let out a whistle from the back of the group and the others began to chatter as they saw that the journey was nearly over.

They walked along a cobbled stone path that was flanked by flat gravestones whose markings were faded and dull, 100 years of people walking off path and over them. Bludd dropped Teri down gently and turned the old fashioned black steel ring door handle and pushed the door. It was a heavy, solid oak entrance and behind it stood a heavy table; a line of candles in tall stands lit the doorway and the back of the church. A restless Annabelle Judge stood in the middle of the floor between the table and the rear pews. She skipped towards Bludd and threw her arms around him, as unexpected an action to her as it was to him. She kissed him, holding it a little longer than either of them expected. "Get a room!" Toby shouted from the doorway. The group laughed loudly.

"Seems like a happy bunch you've got here?" Annabelle asked, making no apology for the lingering kiss.

The group had started to file past Bludd and Annabelle and were taking seats on the rows of church pews. "They're not a bad bunch; even the gobby one isn't a bad lad." He thumbed in the direction of Toby, who smiled at Annabelle Judge. Bludd held his shoulder as he passed them. "Well done, mate."

"Glad to be of assistance. *Mate.* Nice piece," Toby replied, winking at Bludd and cocking his head towards Annabelle.

"Nicely put," Bludd said as he gave an apologetic smile to Annabelle, who was blushing, but quite charmed.

"Is this everyone?" she inquired. "I thought there would be more."

Bludd grabbed her by the elbow and led her down the short aisle to the front of the small church. They stopped at the altar. "There were two more. One, I must admit, I had forgotten about, but I'm pretty sure he is safe, possibly even very comfortable. The other …" He paused and looked back at the youngsters at the rear of the church. "The other is dead." His voice had turned to a whisper.

Annabelle Judge looked shocked and Bludd put a finger to her lips before she could reply. "You don't need to know the ins and outs, not yet anyway. Did you bring the helmet?"

She nodded, but her look was confused and alarmed at the same time.

"What about the help?"

"Due at seven o'clock. There will be at least two of them. I asked them to bring a team, you know like you said about bringing a psychoanalyst, or something. They said it was a bit short notice and that they might organise that if needed once they had got everybody settled." She looked down the church.

"They all seem in pretty good spirits to me."

"They are. But they don't know how lucky they are. By the way, one has a suspected broken ankle; she will need to go to hospital at some point. Anyway, I was thinking as I was walking, if the guys from Shelter are here for seven, that's perfect, we can get away as soon as we can and head for the factory."

"But what about the mini-bus? Aren't I supposed to be driving that?"

"I know, it's only a problem if only two of them turn up. We will need to borrow their car. One of them can drive the bus; you can drive the car to the factory and take the girl there, at the end of the first row, the blonde one, with you. I'll follow you on my bike. I'm supposed to be meeting somebody there at eight-thirty, but plans have changed. You need to be there to meet the employees. Tell them that the factory is closed until further notice. You know some of them, I presume?"

"Yes, I think some of them have been there for years, it just depends on whether they are still there. But what about insurance?"

"Insurance?"

"Yes, on the mini-bus and their car. I won't be insured to drive it."

"Bloody hell, you sound like my brother. Don't worry about any of that, there are more important things to worry about. Like getting rid of the factory workers, who might not take kindly to you laying them off, especially as there is no real reason that you can tell them. Probably not wise to tell them that their bosses are part of a network of paedophiles and murderers. Speaking of which, we are going to fetch your husband from the airport together, with the girl. She's called Susan by the way."

313

"OK. I'm sure I'll work out why at some point. You fill me in when you feel I need to know." She looked at her watch. "They'll be here any time."

Bludd was already walking back down the aisle. He clapped his hands. "Listen up, people." His arms were stretched out and aloft, and he realised, that in his black outfit and in this stance, he looked like a vicar about to deliver a sermon.

"Let us pray!" Toby shouted from the back row. The others chuckled.

The joker's quip was not lost on Bludd and he responded with "God bless you child." And they all laughed again. "Seriously though, I need you to listen up. Here's what's going to happen. In a few minutes, there will be some people here who will take you somewhere warm and dry and where you will get something to eat. They will put a roof over your heads and more than likely give you a medical check over and see that you are all OK. Teri, of course you will need to go to the hospital. Ask them if one of this lot can come with you. It can't be Susan; she needs to come with me. These people will give you support and help you, whether you decide to go home to your families, or if you need a fresh start, they will help you find housing. Maybe even work."

Toby replied for the group, his new officer-like status promoting him to spokesperson. "Listen, man, we appreciate that you have put yourself out here. But we were pretty happy with our lives and you just turned it all upside down. We all like working in the factory. We're pretty good at what we do now you know. Plus, we all want to stick together, man. You know where I'm coming from?"

Bludd thought for a second. "Look, it's not for me to say. But let's just run with the plan for now." He turned to Annabelle. "This lady is Annabelle Judge, her husband owns the factory, or at least for a short time he does. In the long term, maybe Mrs Judge will need some more staff. Hey, she might even need some tenants for some apartments she is going to own."

Annabelle Judge looked at Bludd with shock and annoyance. She turned to the group. "No pressure then?" she started with. "Look, I am in no position to make any promises, but I have to see how today works out and then we can see about who owns what and go from there."

The group didn't quite let out a cheer, but their chatter was upbeat at the thought of staying together. Annabelle looked at Bludd; she gave him a stern but quirky glance and then slapped his arm with the back of her hand.

The hinge of the door creaked and a man peered round and asked "Annabelle Judge?"

Annabelle and Bludd exited the chapel and explained to the two men and one woman what they needed them to do. They gave their details to the woman and asked her, more like told her, to keep them in touch with where the group was at every step of the way, including Teri's injury and their location, so that Susan could be put back into contact with them. The group boarded the mini-bus and Susan stood by the door hugging each one as they got in, squeezing Teri especially tightly as she was last to board. One of the men agreed to take Annabelle and Susan and she could collect her car from the hire company that she had got the mini-bus from. She was perplexed as to how she would explain the lack of mini-bus, but Bludd assured her that money would no doubt talk and an extension of hire would be easily agreed.

They waved as the bus left. Bludd and Susan got in the back of the car and Annabelle the front passenger seat. He got out moments later, retrieved his bike and struggled to get it over the stile and then followed the car and thought about how he was going to deal with his nemesis, Jeremy Judge. His plans were changing on the hoof. Taking Susan back home on the back of his bike would have to wait. He put the spare helmet over his arm and rummaged inside his jacket, fingered the dial on his iPod without seeing it and pressed play. A random song played, 'Get your motor running', he was told.

25

Judgement Day

They had arrived at the factory just in time to intercept the first of the workers. Annabelle Judge had recognised the first arrival as the supervisor from when she had worked at the factory. He had been confused at her showing up for the first time in years and her explanation of why they were to go home had not eased his mind. She had made promises that things would be sorted out and back to normal within the week. Promises she had no idea if she could keep, but she wanted the staff to stay onside. She had promised them all full pay and they had left quicker than a greyhound out of the traps, the supervisor promising to wait at the top of the road and turn the other lads away, assuring Annabelle of their return the following week. Bludd had waited at the top of the road for the arrival of the van from Preston Die Supplies, which had arrived earlier than the mid-morning promised by John Preston, and had promptly advised the driver of the factory closure. He had recognised him as the man that he had filmed stealing stock a few days earlier and asked him to pass a message on to his boss, that he would be sending the information they had discussed later that week. The driver had asked what the information was and Bludd had winked and tapped the end of his nose with his index finger in a 'never you mind' gesture.

Bludd watched from a distance across the car park of the airport, inwardly groaning as he saw Judge hand some of his baggage to Annabelle to carry. He sat in the rear of the black Range Rover, its dark tinted windows would keep him from sight until he was ready. Susan Kerby sat nervously across from him on the back seat, not completely sure why she was there, and nervous that it was all about to go horribly wrong.

She had explained to Bludd how the incinerator worked: the sequence of buttons to ignite the burners running along each long side, and the timer and control panel that was housed in the centre of the steel door at the front. She had told him that the burners took a few minutes to get to full temperature, and that the temperature was set on the control panel. And that depending on what you were burning and how much fat content there was, and therefore how much assistance the corpses gave to the burning process, much like pricked sausages on a barbecue, determined how long you set them to burn for. She had not questioned him as to why he needed to know these things. She thought that the less she knew, the less she would have to worry about and the less trouble she could get into.

Bludd had chuckled to himself when the girl had mentioned fat content. He was thinking of how fat Jeremy Judge was, and even at this distance, he could see that his obesity issues had only become worse. He was sure he would be a great help to any burning process. He had told the girl that she would only be there for part of the journey, while he got Mr Judge to give her something, although he had not said what. Then he had given her instructions to lie down on the floor well behind the driver's seat until he told her to get up.

The girl had done as she was told and she could hear the voice of the lady, Annabelle, and her husband, Mr Judge, as they approached the car. Bludd dropped down onto the floor well beside her, behind the front passenger seat and he held his finger to his lips to instruct her to be quiet. The boot had opened and they heard the thud of the bags being thrown into the space behind them and the boot slammed closed again. The two front doors opened simultaneously and they heard the leather seats squeak as the two people got in and got comfortable. Bludd and Susan lay there, Bludd with controlled and slow, quiet breathing, Susan, holding her breath for fear of giving herself away. The engine burst into life with a heavy growl as it moved away. Bludd lay still, holding Susan Kerby's head down as they gathered speed and then he nudged her on the shoulder and motioned her upwards.

The girl sprang up and sat back in her chair. Judge, who was facing his wife and about to continue his tale of the trip to Thailand, almost jumped out of his skin. "Jesus Christ!" he shouted. "Who the hell …?" He stopped his sentence short, a vague recognition of the face behind him.

"This is Susan Kerby," his wife interjected. "She works for you in the factory." A pause. "You know? On the night shift?" She said it with an emphasis on night shift that told her husband that she knew about the night shift.

"What is all this, Annabelle?" he asked as the car gathered speed, having left the car park and found the exit of the airport joining the dual lane carriageway.

Bludd jumped up from his hidden position. He threw his right arm around the headrest of the front seat and clamped his hand around Judge's throat. "This, Jeremy, this is your worst nightmare." And he slammed Judge's head back into his seat and put his left arm over the shoulder of the front chair and held it back at the throat with his forearm.

"Is that you Bludd?" he shouted, knowing full well that it was. "Good to see you old boy. Not sure there's any need

319

for all this rough stuff though." Judge was calm. Bludd was expecting a struggle and then he could increase the pressure on Judge's throat and make him squirm. But Judge stayed calm and his voice was serene.

"Do you know why we are here, Judge?" Bludd didn't give time for a response. "I wanted to bring Susan here to meet you, to get to know who you are and what her boss is really like. But while I was sat waiting for you, I changed my mind. I just want her to have an apology from you. That's all."

Judge remembered where he knew the girl's face from. "An apology? What for? I think you will find that this young lady was out on the streets, homeless, cold and hungry. You want me to apologise for putting her into a warm and clean environment and keeping her fed and healthy? Annabelle, darling, you must see how preposterous this is?"

Annabelle Judge took a deep breath and pulled the car over. They were on a bridge that spanned the motorway and she stopped on the hard shoulder. "Preposterous? I can think of a word that begins with 'P' that better describes you than the situation."

Judge looked perplexed. "What are you talking about, dear?" he asked, still calmness personified.

Bludd interrupted. "We saw your email to Durie and the Romanians. I think you called it 'enjoy'. Well let me tell you, I am going to enjoy seeing you squirm like that poor little girl. You filthy son of a bitch." He jerked back his arm and pinned Judge's throat tightly against the seat.

Judge's calmness suddenly drained out of him. He had no response to what he had just been told. His wife knew about the camp. She knew about the little Thai girl. Maybe she had watched enough to see the little girl's brother as well. Maybe she knew about Durie and the Lupescus' website. He turned his neck slowly to face his wife, trying to find words of defence, of justification. Before he could manage any, Annabelle Judge threw a clenched hand into his face and caught him square across the bridge of his nose. She didn't utter a word, just shifted the automatic gear lever into drive and pulled back onto the main carriageway.

Bludd pulled back harder with his left arm, forcing Judge's head back into the headrest. "Now let's get back to this apology. You see Susan here, Judge?" Judge nodded, his head stifled by Bludd's forearm, his eyes watering from the blow to the nose. "Well, I want you to apologise to her and then I want you to apologise to her again, so that she can pass it on to her family. You see, this girl has been deprived of a loving family for the last five years. Perhaps the most important five years of her life. She missed school. She has missed exams. But most of all, she has missed her family. A family that I know for a fact has been distraught over her. Worried for her every day, every hour, every single minute. To the point of nervous breakdown. Self-blame, almost self-harm. And all because you wanted some cheap labour to make your boxes, and give Durie and his mates a few playthings. Do you have any idea what you have put them through, never mind what you have deprived this girl of?"

"I don't know. I never gave it much thought. I mean, we gave these people a roof over their heads didn't we? Some of them were like starving little tramps when we took them in. Scavengers they were, some of them. They have a trade. They have their safety. They get fed. As for Jonathon, I don't know what he does with them. Honestly, I don't. I just know that it was beginning to get out of hand. I have just been in Thailand trying to sort out something to get him away from the Lupescu brothers. They have twisted his mind. Taken it too far. I want to stop them. I want to save Jonathon from them and himself."

"'Safety'? What about the little girl. You didn't bother to save her. That was completely in your hands."

Judge looked down with his eyes, his head stuck fast against the seat. "You know I have a weakness. I can't excuse it. It's always been there. It's an illness."

"Don't start trying to justify yourself. You can get treatment for illness. You behave like an addict. You haven't gone looking for treatment. For a cure. You just get your fix and then go on to the next thing. Only like a drug user, who goes from cannabis to amphetamines, to coke, to crack and whatever, you've gone from looking, to touching, to God knows what and then what we saw in your email." Bludd was conscious not to be too specific, not wanting to upset Susan, or give her any clues as to what might have happened to Carl and the others. "Now what about that apology?"

Judge stayed silent. Annabelle had not uttered a word since she had punched her husband in the face. "Have you made a will?" she asked. There was no emotion in her voice or look, which was straight ahead. They were ten minutes from the factory, and she knew what Bludd had planned. She knew that one way or another she would be taking over the factory, legally, or not.

"A will? Of course I have, dear. You can't have a multi-million pound business and shares, investments, property and so on, without having made a will." Bludd felt Judge gulp and his Adam's apple bulged a moment longer than a swallow.

"Good. I hope you are leaving me well looked after. The kids as well?"

Bludd's arm pulled tighter against Judge's throat and a realisation of why Annabelle would ask this question swept over Judge.

"Listen, Bludd, old boy. I don't know what you think I am. I don't know what you think you have seen. OK, I know you have something on Jonathon. But honestly, that has nothing to do with me, nothing at all. I admit, I have a problem. But, come on, where are you going with this?"

Bludd looked across at Susan Kerby. She looked shocked and confused. Judge had almost repeated her words when he had said what they had given her and her friends: a roof over their heads; food and warmth; a trade; dignity. "OK, so let's just say that Durie and the Romanians are not your fault. They are still your problem. You own the buildings they live in, the rooms they use. You employ all of them. I don't believe for a minute that you know nothing about them."

"I swear to God, I know nothing." Judge swallowed hard again and Bludd felt the bulge push into his forearm. He felt like his vice grip had stopped the blood from rushing to Judge's cheeks and letting his blush prove his embarrassing lie.

"You can swear to God. You can pray to God. One thing is for sure, God is not somebody you will be seeing in any kind of future." He turned his eyes to Annabelle. "I want you to drop me and my old friend here at the factory. We have got some unfinished business to take care of. I think he also wants to address the issue of the ownership of the factory. I want you to take Susan to your house. I think that you might have some clothes that will fit her? Maybe you can do her hair and make-up? I think it's time Susan's mum got to know her daughter again. What do you think Susan?"

Susan suddenly blinked and snapped out of her confused state of mind. "Go home? Honestly? I can't wait." A smile spread across her face as she spoke.

Annabelle indicated a right turn as they drove too quickly over the canal bridge. A little too quickly and their stomachs all hung for a moment. And then dropped.

"What do you want me to do with him?" Bludd asked her.

She looked across at her husband. His neck was held firm against the seat head restraint, his hands clamped onto the arm rests. He looked forward, clearly aware of his probable fate, eyes staring ahead, plump cheek flushed with too much wine and more than a little fear. "You decide. I think you have more information than me to be able to decide what is appropriate."

"You trust me to do the right thing?" Bludd inquired.

"Seb," she deliberately used his shortened name, a sign to her husband that they had become close. "I trust you more than any man I have met. When it comes to the right decision, I trust you a million times more than I do this weasel."

The car bumped along the dim potholed road and nobody spoke another word. Annabelle pulled the car to a halt at the junction of the canal bridge at the end of the aqueduct and the road outside Durie's cottage. The railway bridge ran overhead. Bludd got out and opened the front passenger door, closing his at the same time. Annabelle Judge got out of the driver's door as her husband slipped out opposite her. Susan Kerby stayed in her seat.

Annabelle Judge spoke first. "I wish I could tell you that it has been a pleasure. I can't tell you how disgusted I am with you. I know it sounds a bad thing to say, but I am so glad that your parents aren't here to see what you have become." She stepped up to Jeremy Judge's face and she spat in his eye. Judge did not respond, he jolted back and closed his eyes, wiping the liquid from his face with the back of his arm.

Annabelle turned to Bludd, clasping both sides of his face with her outstretched hands as she kissed him intensely, sliding her tongue underneath his top lip and gliding it from side to side. She darted it out again and planted a second kiss on his tingling lips, lingering, as she had before. This time it was to try and aggravate her husband, as much as to show Bludd her emotions. "See you back at mine," she said louder than necessary, for the same reason.

The word 'mine' was not lost on Jeremy Judge. He looked at the floor as he heard the door slam and the gravel crunch as the wheels slipped and gripped as the Range Rover reversed in an arc and then sped away.

Bludd shoved Judge in the back, in between his shoulder blades. "Judgement Day has arrived. Excuse the pun."

They marched across to the mechanised gate that shielded the industrial estate from unwelcome visitors. "Open it!" Bludd instructed Judge. Judge did as he was told and fingered the code into the lock. The gate cranked into action and Judge turned to Bludd.

"Where are Jonathon and the brothers?"

"All in good time. You should be more worried about yourself than them. Anyway, Durie should be pleased to see you."

Bludd led Judge across the yard in the direction of the incinerator building. He had seen a visible sigh of relief on Judge's face when he had hinted that Durie was still alive. He smiled with anticipation when he visualised the look draining from him as Judge met with Durie again. They arrived at the large wooden gate.

"Shouldn't we be going to my office? I thought you wanted me to speak to my solicitor? I am willing to sign everything over to Annabelle. Just spare me and Jonathon. I can get help for both of us. Perhaps we can put right some our wrongs."

"Put right some of your wrongs?" Bludd's voice was raised and exasperated. "You can't even find it in yourself to apologise to a young girl. A young girl, might I point out, that was lucky to be a girl. Because as far as I can see, its saved her life.

Durie's wrongs were all against boys. Boys, who thought they were going on to better things, but in truth, just died a horrible death for the gratification of a world of weird bastards. But then you wouldn't know about that, would you?"

Judge looked straight into Bludd's eyes and glared at him. "I swear on my kids' lives, I don't know what he and the Romanians get up to. All I know is that he seems to have lost himself. He was doing a great job for me, you know in the factory. But he seems preoccupied of late, like the brothers are more important to him than me."

"Aww! What's up, has Jeremy lost control of the puppet? Has his bitch found a new pimp?" Bludd mocked. "Well, tough shit. Put your dummy back in and move, it's time to finish this once and for all."

Bludd watched as the colour drained from Judge's face and he saw his eyes close. Was he resigning himself to his fate, or trying to think of another way to gain some time? A stay of execution.

"What about the paperwork? The sign over?"

"No need for it. You go missing. No evidence of you can be found here, or anywhere else. You just disappeared. Let's face it, who's going to miss you? The kids? Possibly, but I am sure Annabelle can just say you have gone abroad for a while. They are young, probably she can tell them anything and they will believe her. And who else is there? Parents? No. Friends? Not that I can think of. Not living ones anyway. I reckon that Annabelle will have to report you missing. Then she can take over the factory, save the day. Save people's jobs. The years will fly by. You don't turn up. In seven years' time, she can officially class you as dead. She can get on with life properly; you know, get herself a man. They'll be queuing round the block, let me tell you. She is one beautiful and intelligent woman."

"The police will investigate when she reports me missing. Questions will be asked. They will see us here, today. CCTV pictures from the airport, the motorway, from here." He pointed up at the camera on the corner of the office building to their left.

"As far as I can see, you were picked up and you went home. Annabelle showed you the evidence of your sick email, confronted you. You did a runner. In fact, she could use that as her line. 'Police hunt dangerous paedophile on the loose'. "You will be splashed across the newspapers, your name in lights. Then nobody will really give a shit, even your kids will understand why daddy left them. They'll probably breathe a sigh of relief. As for the CCTV, unless you linked it to the police station, which I doubt very much considering what goes on here; we can just dismantle it before she reports you missing. I guess it is linked to your home computer, so maybe we can just get rid of it at that end. You don't need to worry your sick little mind about matters of the future."

Bludd grabbed Judge at the shoulders and spun him round so he was facing the gate to the incinerator building again and pushed it open, shoving Judge through the gap as it widened. The concertina door was shut and they walked slowly up to it, Judge slowing as he approached. "Let's go find Durie," Bludd said, smiling as he opened up and ushered Judge through the sliding door.

The room was as Bludd had left it. It was dim, the light from the gap in the door the only aid to sight. Silhouettes of the two incinerators were black and daunting, like gravestones at midnight. A small pile of dogs' bodies were set out in an eerie line in front of them. The smell hit them both. Bludd had not noticed it was so bad when he had been there that morning, but his senses were busy concentrating on other things and now he was more relaxed. He held all the cards now and his senses were free to take in the whole scene. Judge retched. The dogs would have been there at least two days, more likely that they arrived on the Friday, delivered by a council vehicle that was unlikely to be used on a Saturday.

Bludd took a deep and foul tasting breath. "Come on!" he pushed Judge again.

"Does Max know you're here?" Judge asked.

Bludd sensed a tone in his voice that suggested it was a loaded question. "No. There is no need for Max to know about any of this. In fact, I should think it is for the best that he knows nothing."

Judge let out a grim smile, like he had finally found a way to buy some time. At the very least, he thought he had found Bludd's only possible weak point: his family. His smile grew wider. He could open the biggest can of worms. Maybe so big that he would be able to distract Bludd and make some kind of getaway.

"Are you sure that Max knows nothing? He knows all about this place. Diego was a director here for a while."

"Diego is dead. Max will only know what he was told over five years ago. From what I know, the Romanians came in after he died."

Judge paused before he replied, his teeth almost bursting out of his mouth through his smile. "Well, well, well. Detective Bludd isn't as clever as he thinks he is. You know nothing about Diego. He's not dead. Admittedly, he is not very well, but he lives with his partner, in Mansfield I think it is. Doesn't Max live over there?"

For once Bludd was on the back foot. He fully understood what Judge was saying, but he knew nothing about Max. He knew nothing about his home life. He certainly knew nothing about his relationship, or his sexuality for that matter. He tried to hide his lack of knowledge, and his confusion. "Whatever Max is, I know that he plays everything by the book. If he knew what was happening here, he would have been here before me, no doubt about that."

Judge let out a huge guffaw of a laugh and clapped his hands together. "Oh, Sebastian, old fellow. You don't even know about your brother and his boyfriend. Would you like me to tell you?"

Bludd didn't have time to feel the rage come up through his veins, his brain bypassed the thought process and he gave himself no time to quell the anger as it ran straight from his head to his fist and he smashed an uppercut punch straight into Judge's chin, knocking him from his feet and flat onto his back on the floor.

Judge lay on the floor, cupping his jaw with his hand, still laughing. He was sure that what he was doing was actually sealing his own fate, but he was not a fighter, he never had been. He knew that Bludd had already decided his future and he had decided to try and wreck Bludd's before he lost the chance.

Bludd stood over him. "Shut your mouth, Judge." He screamed as he pulled Judge to his feet. "You wrecked my family life once before. You aren't going to do it again." He held Judge's collar and shook him as he shouted.

Judge laughed again. He spat blood from his wounded gums. "What's up old chap, hit a nerve have I? Perhaps you enjoyed my little session with you, all those years ago, a little more than you have let yourself think. I know Max enjoyed it."

"Max wasn't there!" Bludd screeched an inch away from Judge's bloody mouth as he pulled him close. "There were only five of you."

"I never said he was there, old chap. Maybe he just enjoyed

us telling him about it. Maybe that's what made him what he is. Maybe he was jealous that you had beaten him to it."

Bludd threw Judge to the floor in his rage. He opened the bolt on the furnace door and threw it wide open. There were murmurs from inside and he heard sounds of mouths and throats gasping in air. "Thank Ger-God," said the choked voice of Jonathon Durie.

Bludd reached down at Judge's shirt collar again and dragged him to his feet, almost off the floor, slamming him onto the inside of the open door. He noticed the grotesque, twisted and mangled fingers of Durie's left hand trying to get a grip on the frame of the steel door and his right hand followed suit at the other side. Bludd kicked out at Judge's groin, all technique suddenly gone out of the window and out of his mind. Judge dropped to his knees and Bludd slammed the door shut as Durie's face appeared in the dim light, squinting against the contrast of his hours of darkness. The door thudded against his head and he was catapulted backwards, the tips of his left hand's fingers, still trying to grip the cool steel of the furnace shell, were suddenly trapped between the frame and the slamming door, crushing them, the skin and flesh over the ends of the fingers dulling the crunch of the grinding bones and nails. The scream of pain from inside the furnace still pierced through the thick layer of high temperature brick and steel and Bludd felt a pang of satisfaction. He opened the door again and heard Durie's muffled and stuttering outburst, halfway between crying and cursing him, words not coming out, fighting between the agony he was in and the panic that had triggered the onset of the worst of his speech problem. "Ber-ber-ber…" He struggled to get the word out.

"Bastard?" Bludd attempted to finish the one-word sentence of curse and blame for Durie.

Judge was still on the concrete floor, not moving, clearly in a deal of pain, but keeping his cries of pain and anger corked. Bludd almost felt a tiny amount of respect for him. But it didn't last for more than a fleeting moment. "You watching, Durie? Did you enjoy seeing the little girl on the email? She suffered an unimaginable and undignified end. You are going to get too good and too quick an ending for my liking, but times ticking on, and you lot don't deserve any more of my time, or any more of anybody else's for that matter." He picked up Judge a third time. "You enjoy watching people having the air choked out of them?" The question was for both of them.

Judge's chins were multiple and Bludd forced his thumbs underneath the lowest roll of folded skin and sank his fingers into the flesh at the back of Judge's neck. And squeezed. And squeezed some more. His thumbs dug in, fidgeting against the throat underneath the fatty tissue, placing one on the other to gain extra pressure. Judge hit out in a desperate effort to save himself, but Bludd was immune to any pain that the flailing slaps and failing punches might have offered. He held Judge against the open furnace door and felt some movement to his left as Durie's upturned hands arrived at the edge of the aperture. Bludd kicked out with a straight left leg that landed on Durie's chin and nose simultaneously and he heard a cry of pain drown out the crunch of the splintering teeth and the crack of a breaking bone. He twisted Judge around to block the incinerator doorway and pressed his thumbs harder against the faltering windpipe. Judge's arms began to flail more slowly, less anger in them as the energy began to drain from his being. His muscles were being starved of oxygen and he lost the ability to recharge what little power they possessed.

"I'm sorry," Judge murmured as he looked up at Bludd with pitiful, pleading eyes.

"What for? Raping me? Raping however many children? Killing them? Turning a blind eye to the sick fuckers you're going to share your last moments with? Which one are you sorry for? Maybe this is the apology to the girl that should have come an hour ago? Either way, it's too late." Bludd squeezed a little harder, his fingers lost in the back of Judge's fleshy neck, his thumb, invisible under the flaps of the bulbous chins.

He dropped Judge down a little, so that his back rested on the edge of the door frame. They both leant into the darkness and Bludd's face stopped in front of his old adversary. Judge's eyes began to flicker as he lost the energy to flex even the tiniest of muscles in his lids. A face lurched out of the darkness and Bludd instinctively lunged forward and a thick, heavy forehead connected with an unknown target that cracked and wretched and fell backwards, unconscious again.

Bludd's knee found the spongy top of Judge's crotch and he forced upwards with his hands and thumbs and heaved the bloated, relaxed weight of Judge into the darkness, holding him by the throat for an extra second. He loosened his grip and a sigh of wasted air expelled from Judge's lips. Bludd pushed Judge's legs at the calf muscles and twisted them at the knee to force them in through the doorway of the incinerator. His ears pricked as he thought he heard a final mumbled attempt at an apology as he slammed the blackened door closed and slid the bolt across to lock it in place.

The red digits flashed in front of him. Three zeros. The number pad and keyboard of instructions pulsed in the flashes of red light. He punched in 3.00. The digits read, '3.00'. He hoped it meant three hours and not three minutes. The instruction was keyed in. 'Enter'. Then he pressed the numbered buttons again. It flashed 800. Then he pressed the 'Enter' button again and then the one that read, 'Ignite.' Then 'Enter'.

Then the green button at the top, to the left of the red button. Both of them a row higher than all the other keys. He heard the *ssshhh* of the gas and the *whoosh* of the burner as the ignition found its target. The red numbers blinked at him and he stood gazing at the brightness of the pulsating glow as it flickered an angry beat in the darkness of the room.

Another red signal appeared and tiny blocks of light edged to the right and grew in slight increments as each moment passed. Green letters flashed up and stayed. 'TEMP', it said. The little red blocks got bigger and bigger on their eastern journey and then they flashed and stopped at the same size. 'TEMP' flashed with them and the clock ticked down to '2.59'.

Bludd turned and leant against the door of the furnace. He had never really planned to get revenge on Judge, or Durie. It had kind of fallen into his lap. That meant that he had not planned the next part. He had no idea whether to stay put and make sure the job really was done, or leave and decide his next move in more comfortable surroundings.

Then the smell started to stab at him again.

There were mounds of dead dogs still piled up and awaiting their final passage into wherever. The other incinerator stood idle and bleak, its shape blinking a dark and cold silhouette, momentarily a flash of blurry red, with a tiny hint of green.

Bludd decided that he would kill the next two hours and 58 minutes by doing the dogs a good deed and sending them to wherever their final place was. For a moment, in his mind, he saw a doggy heaven, with rolling fields and long-haired friends all scampering around in pursuit of nothing in particular. Then he gave himself a metaphorical slap in the face and opened the door to the second furnace. It was identical to the other in every way. The door gave an eerie creak as it opened and Bludd peered into the empty cavernous space that seemed to suck him in.

It took him just over 10 minutes to fill the second furnace with the bodies of the dead dogs. He realised that the lack of fat on the canines would possibly mean a longer burning time, or a higher temperature. Or both. But he also figured that even if he calculated it incorrectly, he would have at least spared them the indignity of rotting away on a cold, concrete floor for however many days it took Annabelle Judge to get things moving again. There were still a few canine bodies that had yet to be disposed of and Bludd had a plan in mind for them as well.

He also realised that the flat-ended bar that the Romanian had almost attacked him with, was actually a kind of rake. He had used it to force the dogs' bodies in, using the flat end as a sort of shovel to cram them in. It was clear that when the burn was complete, that the same tool would be used to rake out the ashes inside the tomb before the process was repeated. It crossed his mind that dog lovers sometimes kept their remains, the same as humans do with a lost relative. It also crossed his mind that they probably got a mix of the various breeds that were burnt in the one cycle, rather than just the precious remains of just their own old friend. It crossed his mind that perhaps this happened with human remains as well. Maybe humans were done individually and ethically. But maybe a tiny bit of residue found itself in the next person's ash urn. He thought, just for a moment about his ailing father.

He watched the numbers tick down on both panels. One was 12 numbers higher than the other, but flashing together in sequence. The left hand machine took an age to tick down to zero, like watching a pot that never seems to boil, and eventually a buzzer wailed loudly in the silence of the night and a green light flashed and spun to signal the end of the process.

Bludd left things for a few moments, contemplating what would now be behind the doors. He clunked the bolt back to the right and drew the door open, surprised that the heat had not transferred to the metal handle. The inside glowed red and hot and a wave of heat rushed out at him, an exaggerated version of stepping off the plane when you land in a hot destination. He covered his eyes and his face and arms seemed to take on an instant sun tan. He stepped to the side until the heat dissipated into the cool air of the building and then peered in. He felt like a magician that had made his assistant disappear, except, instead of a puff of smoke, there lay a small, insignificant layer of ash. He cast his mind back to the last time he had seen the door open. He had not been focused on the scene, just on the job in hand at the time, and so it was a surprise, even to him, how clear the picture was in his mind. A balled up, bloated, Judge before a stricken Durie, chin resting on his upper chest, eyes open but glazed over, not blinking yet still alive. A Romanian, back to Bludd, face to face with his brother, one breathing unconsciously, the other not. Both of them masking the slim-line body of the poor, tortured remains of the boy, Carl.

Bludd's bottom lip turned out and he nodded a job well done look to himself.

He put the remaining deceased dogs on top of the thin pile of ashes that lined the furnace floor and shut the door, more peacefully than he had three hours earlier, and pressed the buttons. Slim, fat-free bodies, probably 30 kilograms each. Probably about as much as Judge had weighed, probably even less. He keyed in 100, and 'Enter', 800, then 'Enter', then 'Ignite' and then the green button.

A *ssshhh* and a *whoosh*.

Job done. Case closed.

26

Reunions

Bludd had been home and showered and changed before he arrived at Annabelle Judge's house in the country. She had answered the door and looked concerned, rather than happy. They spoke on the doorstep whilst Bludd explained that her husband was no longer a concern for her or small children. And she seemed relieved. Her only worry was what to tell the children. Then Bludd had reminded her that she was now the proud owner of a factory that employed a couple of dozen people. More if she wanted them. Probably. Her face turned a little panic stricken for a moment, but then she shrugged her shoulders and told him she would 'figure something out'.

Bludd had not actually explained what had happened to her husband, or Jonathon Durie, or the two Romanians. He guessed that she had worked it out for herself. He also guessed that the girl, Susan Kerby, would have also worked it out if she had wanted to, but he hoped that she would just put it out of mind and accept that moving on was the thing to do.

They went into the house and Susan Kerby was sat at the kitchen table. The two women had eaten lunch and the empty plates sat on top of each other in the centre of the table. Two mugs of coffee, still with steam rising up out of them, sat at the top end and the far side. Susan Kerby was at the top end, hugging her hot mug, a broad smile on her face greeted Bludd.

"You want a coffee?" Annabelle asked Bludd.

"Sounds good to me. Milk, two please. You OK, Susan?

You look nice."

The girl was wearing a pink, round necked, sweatshirt. A large silver 'tick' flashed across the middle and glittery words saying 'Just Do It' sparkled underneath. Her hair was long and wavy, not curly, and it looked clean and fresh, and worked on. Her makeup was hard to notice, nothing much on her face, maybe a little toner to underline her cheekbones. But her eyes were something else. They had a light brown tone above them on the lids and a blue line underneath, on the rim of the eye, which made a reflection into the whites and made the blue of the retina even more vivid. The lashes were long and darkened with expensive mascara.

She looked stunning.

Susan Kerby smiled even wider. "I feel great, thanks to Annabelle, I actually feel feminine for the first time, probably ever."

Annabelle smiled and butted in. "It didn't take a lot. She is a naturally pretty girl. Her mum will be very proud."

They sat and talked for a few minutes. Susan was keen to get home. Bludd was keen to get her there. Bludd asked Annabelle if he could use the Range Rover and she agreed. She saw it as a reason for him to come back and collect his motorbike later. It was coming up to four in the afternoon and Bludd wanted Susan back home before dark. Susan placed the plates and the empty mugs next to the sink and Bludd eyed her up and down. She was pretty, she was tall and slim. She looked even taller in the heeled training shoes that Annabelle had given her, with a silver tick that matched the sweatshirt. The skinny-fit jeans also enhanced her height and her figure and Bludd had no doubt that she would soon be able to get back to a normal life. Her mum would be loving her, and the boys would be chasing her. Her mum would be overprotective and Susan would be understanding of why and she would put mum's wishes before her own, for a while at least, Bludd hoped.

Susan kissed Annabelle on the cheek and they hugged like they had known each other for a long time and were not going to see each other for a while at least. Bludd stood and played with his keys, two sets, and one to the Range Rover, the other his personal set. He placed his own in his pocket and held the others aloft, jangling them behind the hugging women. "Come on Susan. Let's go see your mum."

Bludd had thought about calling his old friend, Mick Dylan, who now lived with Susan's mother, but had thought to leave it as a surprise. He wasn't a lover of surprises, mainly because most of those that he delivered were not happy ones. But this one was going to be the best one he could ever remember.

The journey to Susan's family home was about 20 minutes across the low hills of Derbyshire meeting Cheshire. He flicked the radio on and found his favourite station. "What kind of music are you into?" he asked Susan.

She thought about it. "Not bothered really. I used to be into Take That, and Robbie Williams. Mum and I saw them when I was little."

Bludd didn't like to admit that he agreed with her. He liked people to think of him as a rocker really, first and foremost. But he did agree with her. Take That were good, and the song writing was excellent. So was Robbie Williams. "They are good, especially when they all got back together," he told her.

"What? Got back together? No way?"

Bludd laughed. "Way. You got a lot to catch up on."

Take That came on the radio. *Thank you, Mr Wright,* Bludd thought, *Great timing.*

'Relight my fire. Your love is my only desire'. *Quite*

appropriate. Bludd thought again as Susan Kerby joined in with the song.

Bludd had been to Susan Kerby's house on a few occasions in the past and he drove straight to it from memory. They had talked over the music about what she would do when she saw her mum. 'Cry', was all that she was sure she was going to do. Then apologise. Then play the rest of it by ear.

Bludd pulled up and put the handbrake on. He looked at Susan Kerby. Her hands were shaking. He put his hand on top of hers and gave it a reassuring squeeze. "Come on!" he said, nodding his head to the right, in the direction of the house.

Bludd got out of the car and saw Mick Dylan in the front window, stood with a cup of tea in his right hand, a saucer in his left just underneath. He seemed to be daydreaming and snapped out of it when he realised that Bludd was looking at him. Mick looked perplexed for a moment. Then Susan Kerby stepped out from the front of the car and Mick's face almost dropped to the floor. Bludd thought he could hear the clanking of cup and saucer hitting each other and then again as they hit the window sill, almost dropped from a height that would break them. Mick skipped to the right and Bludd and Susan could hear him screaming. "Janet. Janet, love. Come down. Quickly!"

The door opened and Mick stood face to face with Bludd, a tear in his eye and a giddy smile on his face. He said nothing. They heard steps on the stairs and Janet Kerby coming down slowly and tentatively. "What's up, Mick? What's all the commotion?"

Mick said nothing, he moved to the inner doorway and Bludd stood face to face with Janet Kerby. "Hi, Janet! You remember me? I tried to help find your Susan a while back."

Janet Kerby looked at him with fear in her eyes. She had waited five long years for any news of her beloved daughter. Five long, long years of waiting for bad news. "I remember. You didn't find her." Her eyes looked old and sad, and beaten. They glassed over and she looked faint.

"No, I didn't find her. Not then, anyway." Bludd shifted to his left and suddenly, standing in front of Janet Kerby, was a beautiful girl: her daughter; her Susan. Her chin dropped down, mouth wide open and then her face scrunched up and her eyes closed and then opened wide, as if in disbelief. And then she burst out a wailing cry and stepped forward and threw her arms around her daughter. She stood a short moment and her sobbing transferred to Susan, who began to sob lightly, both of their bodies shaking with the emotion running between them and through them. Janet Kerby dropped to her knees, her head resting against the stomach of her daughter and her arms clung around the back of Susan's thighs. "Thank God," she murmured.

Mick Dylan stepped towards Sebastian Bludd, arm out, hand shaking, a tear rolling down each cheek. "Thank you," he whispered as their hands met and he gripped Bludd's right hand like a vice and then clamped his left hand on top as if to amplify his gratitude. "Thanks a lot."

Bludd let go of Mick Dylan's hand and made a 'I will call you' gesture with his little finger and thumb to his face. Mick replied with a thumbs-up gesture and Bludd turned away. He glanced back at the two women. Susan Kerby had joined her mother on their knees at the front doorstep. Her head rested on her mum's shoulder and her eyes were closed tight, constant tears still running down her cheeks.

Bludd turned away quickly. He was close to the point of tears himself. He took a deep breath and composed his thoughts as he got back in the Range Rover and quietly closed the door. He drove forwards 100 yards and stopped again. He took a look at the CD collection in the centre storage box between the two front seats. He selected one that had 'NOW' in large letters in the top corner and smaller letters with 'That's what I call music' underneath. An even larger number eight, lopsided, and to the right. He slipped the CD into the slot and put the car back in gear. 'Notorious' by Duran Duran started up. *That'll do!* he thought. He pushed the 'Menu' button on the touch screen in front of him on the dashboard, closed his eyes, and remembered an address he had never been to, but had seen attached to an envelope in his parents' kitchen.

It read, 'Maxwell Bludd, 3 Orchard Grove, Ravencroft, Notts.'

Next stop was his last on this case. Next stop was his brother. And Diego Del Campo?

27

Watershed

The journey had taken the whole of the CD to play and some more. Bludd had been struck at how many of the titles were appropriate to the last few days. He wondered if any of the other in the 'NOW' series would have been as appropriate. Probably not. He listened to the radio, interjected by a calm sounding lady on the satnav, telling him to turn here and there. The radio show was labelled the 'Drive' show, as it was meant to signal most people's time for driving home from work. Bludd had not been home properly for days. He had not seen Chrissie, or her place for even longer. He had called her and told her that he was safe and that he would be home soon, meaning to her place, without realising that's what he had meant.

The soothing voice of the satnav told him that his destination was 400 yards away and that he should turn right to his 'final destination'. Bludd ignored her and drove past, needing a moment to gather his thoughts. His mind, for once, had been scrambled. What he knew, which was factually very little, had been confused even more by Judge's last gasp outburst before he had died. Questions buzzed around his head and he realised he had a whole lot more questions than he did answers. Was Diego Del Campo still alive? Was Max gay? Was he living with Del Campo? DID HE KNOW ABOUT THE RAPE? Did he know about Judge and Durie and the Romanians? Why had Del Campo come off the payroll at the packaging company?

Best way to find out was to ask. He spun the car round and

turned left into Orchard Grove. The sign said that it was a 'cul-de-sac', or dead end. It looked like a quiet road. There were only five houses in total. In fact, Bludd corrected himself, there were four houses and a bungalow. The single-storey building was at the bottom of the road, facing where he was parked. The two-storey houses flanked the bungalow equally, two to each side. All the buildings looked similar in design, clearly all made at the same time and built in such a way that they were all backed by some part of a wood, or more likely, Bludd thought as he remembered his whereabouts, some part of Sherwood Forest. Bludd scanned the road ahead. The house nearest to him, to his left was raised from the road slightly, as they all seemed to be. They all had a sloping driveway and front lawn meandering down to the path and roadside. The first one had a car in the drive and a small, pointless white fence at the front of the garden, stating that the owner clearly did not want anybody on his grass. The second house had a single car in the driveway and another on the road facing towards the bungalow. Both cars had seen better days and the grass to the front of the house had not been cut since the beginning of summer, probably a once-a-year chore for the man of the house. The two houses opposite almost had symmetry between them. Neither had any vehicle in the driveway and both were home to pristine lawns and identically built walls that ran around the green grass and up the middle of the two properties. Unlike the two to Bludd's left, both of the houses to the right had porches, of the same design and he could see that the first one had a large arched gate to the nearside entrance to the side of the house. It was like twins lived next door to each other. Bludd bet himself that if Tweedle Dum in house one had a gate, that Tweedle Dee next door would have one as well.

Bludd thought about the house numbers. On a conventional

street, houses were numbered odds on one side and evens on the other. It was something that had changed sometime after the Industrial Revolution. In the old days, houses would be numbered sequentially. Starting at one and going along in turn, one-two-three-four, and so on, so that when the street or road ended and turned back the other way, the sequence carried on. This meant that house number one was generally the one on the left of the road, and the last house on the other side, usually opposite, would have the highest number in the street or road. However, this had been changed due to the building of extra houses onto the end of rows at one end, occasionally both, of a street. The new houses could not take the sequential numbers as they had already been given to the existing houses on the opposite side. Therefore all the houses, except, usually, number one, were renumbered, becoming odds to one side and evens to the other. This meant that however long a road became during its life, that the numbers would never have to be changed again, because the sequence of increasing the numbers by two, in odds and evens, could continue infinitely.

But this was not a conventional street anyway.

Bludd moved forward so that he was sat outside the first house to his left, the small wooden fence hidden from his view in the high up driving position of the Range Rover. In the fading light he could see that the house was the proud owner of a large white number one. He could see no number attached to the second house, but that the house, now directly to his right, was number five, not number two. It said so, on a varnished wooden sign in italic letters. Number four had the same sign. The only difference between the houses was indeed the numbers. Bludd chuckled to himself as he saw the arched-shaped gate to the left of number four. Tweedle Dum and Tweedle Dee.

This all meant that number three, Max's house, was, in fact,

the bungalow. It was the single-storey property that no
him, albeit beyond the view of the rear end of a Nissan N
that was navy blue and spotted with rust. Outside the bungalo
was a new shape of Vauxhall, which Bludd thought was a
Corsa, but could not be sure as the Astra was now as small as
the old Corsa and they were very similar in shape. Beyond the
sloping grass was a ramp up to a central front door.

At that moment a car sped past him. It was a grey Audi A6
model, last year's plates. It drove straight into the driveway
to the left-hand side of the bungalow. The brake lights stayed
bright for a few seconds after the tail lights were switched
off. The driver's door opened. There was a few seconds
delay, as if the driver didn't really want to get out. Then legs
swung out of the car and the driver leant out, his elbows on
his knees, his fingers scratching against his forehead and then
running through his grey hair. Max was home. He stood up
and stretched his arms high into the air and then out to the
side. *A long journey*, Bludd thought from the car that was
60 or so yards from his brother. Maxwell Bludd wore a creased
white shirt and grey trousers. No tie and no jacket. He closed
his car door quietly and retrieved a briefcase from the back seat,
and walked up the ramp, *A disabled person's ramp.* At the front
door, he hesitated and then pulled a set of keys from his pocket
and thumbed through them, slowly, finding the right one and
opening the door, disappearing from Bludd's view. Everything
was becoming clear. The only thing that was confusing
Sebastian Bludd was the speed in which his brother had arrived.
It was very unlike him to drive so fast. The rest of his methodi-
cal, hesitant actions were quite obviously Max traits. That was
everything done with care and thought. No rushing.

Sebastian Bludd started to piece together a few facts, if he
could call them that. He had been told, by his brother, that

o had died, but then he had been told, by
͟t Del Campo was alive, but not well. The
ͱim. To his knowledge, Max had never taken
parents' house. No definitive fact here. He
...ᵤ always cited the long and unsociable hours for the reason,
and that he put his career first. Those long unsociable hours
would mean that he would be unable to care for his partner
for long periods and he would have to employ people, some
kind of nurses, to look after him while he was working. Bludd
bet himself that the next person to leave the house would be a
woman in a uniform.

He waited. He waited half an hour. It was eight o'clock
before there was any movement. The curtains closed across the
window that was to the left of the front door. A light came on
in the room to the right of the bungalow and the curtains were
drawn across the window to that room as well. The door was
now lit dimly from behind and Bludd tried to picture the layout
of the building. He guessed that there would be a hall behind
the front door and that to the first door left would be the living
room. First door right would be a bedroom, maybe used as an
office. The next door on the left would lead into the bathroom
and opposite would be the kitchen. Leading out of the kitchen
would be a back door that had a ramp easing down to a flagged
path that would lead into the garden, probably a flagged patio
area for low maintenance. Further down the hall on the left
would be two more bedrooms, the first one the master, possibly
being attached to the bathroom as a kind of en-suite, and a
further bedroom, that might now be a dining room.

Bludd had already made his mind up that his brother was,
in fact, gay and was, in fact, living with his partner, Diego Del
Campo. He laughed to himself. The straightest, by-the-book
cop in Britain, was actually a bent cop. Not in the way that bent

cops are normally stereotyped, but bent all the same.

The front door light was dimmed as it was masked by the frame of a body about to leave. Bludd reminded himself of his little personal bet and smiled as the woman left the building and put her uniformed tunic sleeves into the arms of a long overcoat that covered all of her sky blue top and most of her navy blue trousers. The woman reached up on her tip-toes and kissed Max on the cheek as he bent down and kissed her on the opposite cheek, a hand on each shoulder in a loose embrace.

The woman got into the Vauxhall and Bludd noted that it was indeed the new shape of Corsa as the woman waved a goodbye at his brother, still stood on the doorstep. Max waved back and the woman turned tightly out of the cul-de-sac and Max stood and waved a long second after she had been lost to sight. He stood a moment longer and Bludd thought that he had witnessed his shoulders drop an inch and sag, his body language exuding tiredness or depression, or both.

Bludd decided that he would wait until full darkness had completely fallen before he went for a closer look at his brother's living arrangements. So far, the tinted black windows of the Range Rover would have protected him from the view of any potential nosey neighbours. The dark would protect him from them once he left the vehicle. There was no street lighting and he was, of course, wearing black.

He wasted time by listening to a country music show on the same channel that had been playing to him and Susan Kerby on their journey earlier that day. It reminded him of his time in Nashville, when he had specifically gone there to seek out the roots of country music and had decided after three days that he had heard enough. It was a nice place, great in fact. It was clean and everything was done at a nice pace, where folk didn't seem to be rushing around. There had been an atmosphere of friendliness all over and especially in the bars, where everybody wanted to be his friend, mostly because of his slightly posh English accent, which would no doubt have helped him with the ladies if he was so inclined. But he had got sick of hearing the same music day in day out, without a break. Every bar played the same songs, or at least they sounded like the same songs. Every traffic light at every crossroads seemed to be pumping out tunes where singers sang about losing their dog, or riding their horse, or their cheating wife. Now, after 20 years of not listening to this kind of music, he still decided that he had seen enough when he was in Nashville and wished that the radio station had been playing a show about the blues of Memphis.

It was now a quarter before nine and he decided to go and take a closer look at his brother's place and perhaps reacquaint himself with Max. He got out of the car and closed the door with a click and a nudge to shut it properly. He looked around at the neighbours' houses and saw no movement. He stood up straight and walked casually and calmly down to number three, Orchard Grove. As he approached the driveway he ducked down and darted to the left of the Audi and skirted round it. He noticed that there were four windows to this elevation of the house, one for each room that he had pictured in his head earlier. The second window was the frosted kind that you get in bathrooms or toilets.

He crouched down and made a long two strides to put himself against the wall and peeked over the sill of the first window. There was a dim light in the far corner, coming from a quite ornate lamp, with a big cream shade and gold tassels hanging down. The television was in the corner that was the front left-hand corner of the building, Bludd could only make it out by the red light that signalled that it was on but off at the same time. There were two armchairs to the long wall opposite the window on the front of the building and a small nest of tables sat in between them. The room was quite sparse. Bludd had expected his brother to have portraits on the wall and decadent furnishings, not bland painted walls and a single colour carpet.

He ignored the frosted window of the bathroom. The en-suite?

Then he found his brother. In the third window, there were net curtains. A clever way of letting light in, and views out, without anybody able to see back in the other way. Not unless they were really close up, as Bludd was. He peered across the top of the window frame. The room was full of colour, with a blood red carpet, with swirly patterns running through it, the walls were a mix of a lighter red and a terracotta, rather than orange, wallpaper that gave it warmth. On the far wall were two portraits, face to face. On the right, a man with a long, grey beard and combed-back, long, grey hair, in a dark three-piece suit and tie, looking at the painter but with his body pointing to the left. Next to him was a similar picture, with a man that looked altogether more dapper than his counterpart. He was younger and clean shaven, but his hair was white and long, all at the back, receding at the top and front. Bludd knew that the pair was Johannes Brahms and Franz Liszt, but they were the wrong way round. From left to right it read Liszt and Brahms. He would pick his brother up on the mistake later.

Below the paintings was an armchair that looked like it was a recliner. There was a control handset on the right hand arm with a wire coming from it that ran spirally down to the floor.

The main feature of the room was the large, hospital-style bed that was in the middle of the back wall and pointing straight out. Bludd could see the sheets were home to a pair of very thin and wiry legs, legs that were lacking muscle through under use, knees that would have won any old-fashioned knobbly knee contest, pointed up like spears.

He could not see the rest of the man in the bed, but safely assumed that it was Diego Del Campo. He could not see him because he was masked by the back of Maxwell Bludd. His wide shoulders and back adorned by the creased white shirt and he sat with his back to the window and to his brother Sebastian as he looked in from outside. Sebastian was a little disappointed. He felt sure that had this scene been played out the other way round, that he would have sensed Max's presence by now and turned to look. Max did no such thing. Bludd moved in his crouched position to his left and looked just over Max's left shoulder. There were two drip bags hanging off a stand by the head of the bed and the tubes ran onto the bed at the pillow and out of sight behind Max's body. On the pillow lay the head of a pitiful looking man. He had little wisps of grey hair sprouting from the side of his head. He was bald on top. There was a deep furrowed scar that ran just to the right of the centre of his head and it made the shape of his head uneven. It looked like major surgery had taken place but gone badly wrong because the surgeon was an apprentice, on his first day. The man's brow was deeply lined and his eyes were sunk deep into his face and looked dark and sad and ready to close and give up. He was so thin that the skin on his cheeks had sunk as well and it stretched over his thin, beak-like nose. His skin was yellow and blotchy. Spittle ran from the corner of his mouth and Maxwell reached to his right, to a bedside table to collect a paper tissue and wipe the man's chin and lips.

Maxwell stood up and Sebastian ducked down an inch, so that he could maintain a half view of the room. Maxwell shifted round the bed and threw the tissue into a bin on the far side of the bed. Sebastian saw him wrestle with a CD and place it in a tray that he could not see, that belonged to a CD player that he could not see. He thought he saw his brother spin his wrist, as if he was turning up the volume. The music roared out and he knew that Max had indeed turned it up to the max.

He ducked back down again as Max turned back to retake his seat. He stayed low for a few seconds, listening to the music and wracking his brain to recognise the piece. He peeked over the sill again and saw his brother pick up the bottle of water at the side of the bed, next to the tissue box and he administered a gentle squeeze to the bottle to drain sufficient out of the top to offer some hydration to the sick man. He saw the man's weakness as he struggled to find the energy to swallow as his enormous looking Adam's apple pulsed too slowly and he let out a cough and the water was spat back out.

Bludd remembered the tune. It was Brahms' 'Hungarian Dance Number Five', an upbeat and lively tune for the most part. Max had sat down again and the fingers of his right hand were strumming the legs of his stricken partner, squeezing his knees at appropriate points in the tune. Both the Bludd brothers liked the music. It reminded them of their father. Sebastian watched from outside as his brother's hand tried to mimic the whole of the orchestra and the baton-swinging conductor, all played out on the legs of Diego and in the air above his head.

Then the piece finished. Then the mood changed.

A new piece came on. An altogether more sombre tune. The music breached the glass window and Sebastain Bludd sat on his haunches stretching his legs out to ease the cramp he was beginning to feel. Sergei Rachmaninov's 'Piano Concerto Number Two' blasted out. It was quite depressing in Seb's mind, but perhaps his brother liked it. *Or perhaps it was a favourite of Del Campo*, he thought. He turned again and crouched so he could view the room again. He saw his brother remove the pillow from under Diego Del Campo's head and gently, with his other arm, he lovingly rested it to almost flat against a thin bottom pillow.

Then he witnessed his brother, Max, position the top pillow over the head of his partner and he placed both his hands over the area that would cover the sick man's face. He saw him push down and the pillow plumped up at either side of his hands.

Sebastian Bludd had seen enough to know that his brother was about to commit murder and was probably about to jeopardise his career and his liberty at the same time. He jumped up and headed to the left, to the back of the house. He guessed that the front door would have been locked as soon as the nurse had left earlier, so maybe the back door was his best chance of unforced entry.

He sprinted past the last window of the side of the house and around the back. He turned right into a flagged yard and saw the back door at the top of a short, sloping ramp, with a steel frame, painted white and attached to the wall to either side. The door was painted yellow and had a white painted wooden frame. It was an old-fashioned design and Bludd was glad, as it gave him a better chance of breaking it down if need be.

He need not break it down. He pulled at the silver handle and yanked it down and pushed at the same time. It opened. He ran into the kitchen, avoiding the table to the centre and leapt through the open door that led to the hall, which ran all the way down the house from front to back. He chose the door straight ahead and swung it open wide to the right and found his brother Max, stood there in a flood of tears and holding a silenced pistol to his temple. The music seemed even louder now he was inside.

"Don't do it, Max! Please," Sebastian Bludd implored. "Nothing is ever that bad."

Max turned to him and kept the gun pointing at his head. "Isn't it? You don't know anything!" he shouted.

"Look, just put the gun down and let's talk. You'll see, it's not worth it."

Max leant back against the bed and cried out loud, the gun quivering in his hand. "It's all got too much. There's work, there's Jimmy, there's dad. And there's me. Nothing good in that lot as far as I can make out."

"You told me Diego, Jimmy, was dead."

"He is now."

"But why lie to me in the first place?"

"He was mentally dead when I told you. He has been for years. Just like dad. A cabbage. Nothing to offer life, no life left in him."

Seb edged a bit closer into the room. "What happened? To Diego, I mean?"

"The car crash happened, that's what."

"But I heard he survived."

"He did. Just like Judge and Durie did. But not really. He had massive injuries. The trauma brought on the paralysis. It's called locked-in syndrome. He hasn't functioned properly ever since. He did actually die and they brought him back. Sometimes I wished they hadn't. He was coming to see me, you see. We were all meeting up, staying at a hotel over this way. Don't you see? He was coming to see me. We were going to tell the others that we were a couple. Together. Tell them together, that we were together."

"So you are gay, then?"

Max looked at his brother with an annoyed look. It was

fairly obvious at this point. He dropped the gun away from his head. "You mustn't tell Mum and Dad."

"I don't think Mum will care, and I don't think Dad will have a clue what's going on."

"Don't disrespect Dad. He is in a mess. He's close to the end. Not that you care. You only care for yourself. What about Mum? You haven't even been to see her in months."

"Hey! Don't start beating me with the guilt stick. You're the one with the issues here. I just came to help."

"What are you doing here, at this precise moment? I didn't exactly plan and advertise what I was going to do tonight. Don't you make out your some kind of hero, who dashed across half the country on his trusty white steed to save the day. You're here by coincidence and nothing else."

"True, I can't deny that."

"So? What are you here for?"

"To find out if what Judge said about you was true. To find out what you knew about Judge and Durie. And the Romanians. To find out what you knew about me and why I ran away all those years ago. Now I'm here, I might as well stop you doing yourself in. If only for Mum's sake. She has enough to contend with. You thought about that? Why don't you give me the gun?" Seb held out his hand and took another step closer.

Max sobbed and dropped the pistol to the floor. "I am such a fucking failure. I can't even kill myself properly."

"You're no failure. Look at where you have got to. You've done so much better than me. You're top man, aren't you?"

"Top man? Don't you watch the news?"

"You know I don't. No point really, it's always bad news whenever I hear it."

"Bad news is right. Yesterday, over 150 people were killed in attacks all over Europe and I couldn't stop any of them.

We had warnings and we knew that shit was coming down, and yet I was left chasing my tail, while a bunch of terrorists run around and kill and maim hundreds of people. People that expected me to protect them. I am a fucking failure all right."

"Shit. Sorry. I didn't know."

"You know nothing."

Seb moved over and sat next to his brother. He kicked the gun from under his feet to the other side of the room, to the chair under the portraits. "I know you did your best for Diego. You didn't fail him and you did your best for Mum and Dad. You always did. Still do."

"What about you? I failed you."

"Nah. You just got in with the wrong crowd, that's all. I suppose I wished you'd seen them for what they are a lot earlier, but I wouldn't say you failed me."

"I saw them for what they are far too late. Another failure that was right under my nose."

"So you know about Judge being a paedo then?"

"What? No. I mean, I only fell out with them because they didn't stand by Jimmy like they said they would. Those Romanians came in and suddenly everything changed. Up to that point, Judge had felt some level of guilt towards Jimmy because he was driving the car when it crashed. I opened up to them about me and Jimmy and I promised to look after him, and they promised to fund it. They made him a non-executive director, with a decent salary, for basically doing nothing. Then the Romanians took over and they stopped the payments."

"That's bullshit. Judge is still majority shareholder, he could have carried on if had wanted to."

"I know. I know he just used it as an excuse to stop making the payments. So I told him to shove it. I've been picking up the tab for Jimmy's care ever since."

Seb got up and walked to the other side of the room and sat in the chair under the portraits. He stopped himself from telling his brother that they were the wrong way round. "So you didn't know Judge was a paedophile and that Durie was into some seriously sick shit?"

"I only know what you told everybody at school. You know about the shower cubicle thing."

Seb sensed a change in Max's demeanour. Like there was something he wanted to say, but couldn't bring himself to do so. The music that was playing now was Carl Orff's 'Carmina Burana'.

"What's up, Max? Is it because you know that they raped me? Judge said you knew, said he had told you. And yet you did nothing about it. Is that why you've avoided me for years? I don't blame you, you know. It's not like you were there to stop it happening. I do feel a bit pissed that you didn't dump them as friends, though. That hurts."

Max looked at his brother and then looked down at the gun. He suddenly looked very guilty and he began to sob again. "I'm so sorry, Seb. I really am."

"Why? What for? I got over you staying friends with them years ago. But don't worry, it is literally all in the past now."

"I could have stopped them."

"What, you mean that you knew that they were going to do it?"

"No." Max paused a beat. He rubbed the tears from his eyes. "I mean I could have stopped them in the act."

"But you weren't there. I would have sensed it. Judge would definitely have made something of it. He even said that he had told you about it. Past tense."

"He didn't know. Nobody knew, except Jimmy, later on. I was there. I saw the whole thing, but I froze."

Sebastian Bludd stood up and took a step forward. "You saw me get raped and you did nothing. You said nothing. You didn't try to stop it. What? Were you getting off on it or something?"

Max sobbed again. "I am so sorry."

"Sorry!" Seb shouted at him. "Sorry!" He turned away and looked up to the ceiling, his hand stretched out and he massaged his forehead with his forefinger and thumb while he thought. "Next you'll be telling me that this was the seminal moment that you realised you were a gay boy."

"No. No. I knew, I already knew. I think."

"You think. You fucking think?"

"Well, I knew I had feelings for Jimmy, that they were more than I had for the others. I heard them talking to each other, Jimmy and Richard, and I knew something was going to happen. I followed them down and I saw the others bring you in and I saw Jimmy and Richard help to hold you down. And I wished I had stopped it. Jimmy regretted it as well. He told me it was the worst thing he has ever done."

"Oh well, whoopedy fucking doo. So he regretted it, good for him. Well, I won't regret saying this. I am glad that the bastard has died a long and painful, lingering death." He bent down and picked up the pistol, twisting the silencer to make sure it was still in place. He heard it click. "As for you. You might have failed today, or yesterday, or whenever those terrorists outdid you, but at least that wasn't for the want of trying. Whereas you failed me, and boy did you fail me, through your choice? You fucking chose to watch my life change right in front of you and the only thing you could think, there and then, was that it confirmed your suspicion that you were a fucking queer." He held the gun up and pointed it at his brother. "You might as well have fucked me up the arse yourself. You deserve nothing more than what Judge got."

But Maxwell Bludd was no longer listening; he was immersed in the music and his self-pity. "I'm sorry." He pleaded again.

The music was suddenly loud again and the tension grew as the string section led the orchestra to a crescendo and the symbols crashed.

Two shots were fired. The silencer held them to a little more than a tap on a door. Maxwell Bludd fell to the floor. Another shade of red snaked across the patterned carpet.

Sebastian Bludd called the police as he went back to his vehicle. He used the phone he had stolen from Jeremy Judge. He reported a shooting and he gave them the address. He reported that he thought they required police and ambulance services.

Bludd drove calmly back to Annabelle Judge's house. He contemplated knocking on her door and taking her upstairs and he imagined not making it there and taking out on her his years of frustration, and anger, and bitterness that had just been played out in front of him again. He imagined screwing her on the stairs.

And he had decided against it. It was gone midnight and he was mentally and physically exhausted. And he had just shot his brother. It was not the night to make love. It was not the night to make love to a woman that he was attracted to, but whom he did not love. He went home to Chrissie's house and he got in bed beside her and he cuddled up to her and he told her that he was sorry for being away. He told her that he loved her. In the morning, he showed her for the first time, that he loved her and that he could love her in the way that she wanted him to.

28

Forgiveness

Ben Pickford could not believe his luck. He had stayed in the apartment for what seemed like a full day. The Romanians had not come back for him. Nor had his camp mate, Carl, ever returned. He had wedged the doors to the building open and had been to the local shopping precinct, which was about five minutes' walk away in Bromiley. He had spent time checking out the different shops and their layouts, and the cameras, or the lack of them. He made move after move and made himself a stash of food and drink and eventually returned to the apartment and stayed there. He had been there a week before the lady turned up and he thought his luck had run out.

In fact Mrs Judge, as she had introduced herself to him as, did not put him back out on the streets. She allowed him to stay in the flat. The flat which he now shared with a lad called Gary, who had also been in the camp, but they had not met in his short time there. Next door were two friends, Toby and John. They were in the camp as well, and now the four of them were best mates, working together, living together and partying together. The other apartment on his floor was where Teri lived. She lived alone and she wanted it that way. She had regular sleepovers with her friend Susan, who Ben knew from the camp.

Now it was Christmas Day and all the young people from the factory who lived in the apartments were in the Bromiley Inn public house, tucking into a Christmas dinner that Mrs Judge had laid on for them.

Life could not have been better for Ben Pickford and his friends and he cheered aloud when Toby raised a glass and made a toast, "To Mrs Judge and absent friends. Merry Christmas everybody."

* * *

Sebastian Bludd hugged his mother on the doorstep and introduced her to his girlfriend, Chrissie, and her son, Archie. They had all followed her down the hall and into the large kitchen at the back of the house. "Tea anyone?" Emily Bludd asked.

Chrissie accepted and Archie asked if she had any juice. The old lady looked at him and smiled. "Let's have a look see," she replied.

Sebastian watched her as she flittered around the kitchen, busying herself, mothering everybody. He grabbed her gently by the elbow. "I'm sorry," he whispered. "You know about Dad, and not coming round and, you know …" He didn't finish his sentence.

His mother smiled at him. "Don't be silly, dear, you have a busy life. Now you go on through. He's waiting for you. I'm going to have a good old chat with this nice young lady." She winked at Chrissie and received a smile in return.

"Won't be long," Seb whispered to Chrissie as he brushed her arm and left the kitchen opening the door to the back room. Nothing much had changed. Everything was still as he remembered it the last time he had visited. Then he looked out to the veranda. The double doors were open and he could see the forlorn figure slumped in the wheelchair, grey hair in need of a wash. He approached quietly.

"You should have killed me." It was the voice of Maxwell Bludd, full of tension, full of anger.

"Maybe. But that was too easy. You screwed my life up. You screwed your own life up. I just helped you along the way. Feels pretty even to me."

"Even? I have been in a wheelchair for near as dammit three months and will probably never walk again. Never walk properly again anyway. You call that even?"

"You thought it was OK for Diego to go through life without being able to walk or talk, or anything else for that matter. You need to get a grip and get back on your feet. Mind over matter and all that."

"Well, I can't run away like you did. Can I?"

"No, but you saying you would if you could?"

"Of course I am. I love mum, but Christ she makes a fuss." A slightest hint of a smile formed in one corner of his face.

"Always did." Seb put a hand on his younger brother's shoulder. "I am sorry, you know. It was the heat of the moment, you know." It was a statement, not a question.

"I know. I don't blame you. I was pretty despicable. It was one of the main reasons I was doing what I was doing. And you're right, it would have been too easy."

"We quits then?" Sebastian asked, hopefully.

Max looked up at the hand that hung before him. An offer of a truce. Peace between brothers who had once been the best of friends. He slowly edged towards it, grabbing it at the last moment like a snake jerks for its prey. "I suppose so," he replied with less enthusiasm than he was feeling.

"So what's it going to take to get you back in the right frame of mind?"

"Something to relieve the boredom. You know I can't work for the force again? I just can't see past these wheels at the moment."

"Well, as it happens, I might need your help. I had a call

today from a girl I met a few months back. She's called Yasmeena and she thinks her uncle might be plotting some kind of extremist recruitment campaign. She wants me to help."

A broad smile spread across Max's face as he stroked his stubbled chin. "Played me like a fiddle. Tell me more."